THE SONG OF
Jonas

THE SONG OF
Jonas

Jake Hansen

The Song of Jonas

New and Improved Version 2.0

Copyright © 2016 by Jacob Hansen

ISBN 978-0-9979034-0-9 (print)
ISBN 978-0-9979034-1-6 (ePub)

Library of Congress Control Number: 2016915986

Published by:
Higher Age Press
Seattle, WA

v. 17.1

This book is dedicated, first, to my parents, Don and Sue Hansen, whose support and encouragement was and still is invaluable. Second, I must acknowledge my friend Antoinette Spurrier and my book doctor Anne Marie Welsh, both of whose insight proved to be always helpful and inspiring. I would also like to thank the great writing teachers that I've had over the years: Marian Sugano, James Thayer, Pam Binder and a few more who never failed to guide and influence. To my loyal editors/readers: Mike Smith and Jayant Swamy. And last, but also most important, I must acknowledge that hidden Power, the Architect and Source of everything.

Contents

Necrat's Big Catch

I N THE GALAXY CALLED the Milky Way there swayed and churned a particular dual system of stars, the mother star of which many knew simply as Sol. And if on a journey through this cosmic neighborhood, one searched out the greenest, most populated planet, one would find it to be that greatest purveyor of high-strangeness; a planet called Earth, sitting third out from its life-giving star.

And on one particularly dark night, on a date which historians measured as the first day of Augustus in the year seven thousand and one of Earth's Common Era, a very unfortunate patch of lush jungle set just outside a kingdom named Heliopolis was due for a rude awakening.

The Shastra named Talley, an undercover Intergalactic Agent working as a guard in Heliopolis, dashed as fast as he could through thick jungle vines and jumped through a shallow stream, desperate to reach the village of Saqarra. Shastras were a humanoid species with the full body and limbs of humans, but with the distinctive and colorful head of a jackal, plus a canine's sensitive hearing and smell to boot.

Within his tunic Talley kept a scroll given to him by a guard from the city of Heliopolis. This scroll was a communication from a wolfman named Mamaji and a special message meant for two Shastras named Bheem and Siegfried. Talley held this scroll tightly under his tunic as the rain pelted his sweating, panting jackal face and he raced onward through the wet jungle.

He pushed his sandaled feet faster and carried his laser rifle in his other hand as he jumped over logs, and ducked beneath giant mushrooms blossoming all up the sides of wide baobab trees along his path. Soon he reached Saqarra, dashing madly between its straw huts, and causing the Shastra inhabitants to yell out in alarm or just stare at him curiously.

"What could a Shastra ever be in such a hurry about?" asked one Shastra grandmother, balancing a laundry basket on her head and on her way back from washing her clothes in the river.

Talley paid no attention to them as he avoided the fruit carts, wild dogs, and the lizard-cow genetic hybrids covered in green scales that freely roamed the village.

He swore that he heard the roar of atomic jet engines in the distance. If it was in fact an atomic jet, then he'd need to hurry. And if it was Necrat, the wolfman bounty hunter, he was in deep trouble.

He finally reached a temple carved into the side of a vertical cliff face and set beside the swiftly flowing Heliopolis River. He followed the cave openings to his left until he located his atomic chariot, hidden under palm fronds at the mouth of a small cave.

Thunder rumbled in the distance and lightning flashed bright, lighting the cave while he frantically uncovered his chariot. When he was done, he jumped in, quickly fastened on his pilot helmet, and then fired up its atomic engines. Their roar reassured him he still had a chance to reach Bheem and Siegfried in time. And in only few seconds he was flying away from the main temple in Saqarra, down the chariot road, and through the thick jungle.

"Bheem, do you read me? Do you copy, Bheem?" he called into the comm. link device on the chariot's controls. But there was no answer. "Dang it!" he yelled, punching the control panel. He desperately needed backup. There had been bounty hunters or some other type of bandits following him for days now. He'd felt their eyes on him and smelled their stench on the wind.

While punching a flurry of buttons, he primed the chariot's energy cannons just as the roar of atomic jet engines from behind reached his jackal ears. Whoever it was, they drew closer with every second.

Rain began to pummel his cockpit and the lush jungle around him. He glanced backward and saw the lights of a very long, very sleek and dangerous looking jet bike, its wings bristling with energy weapons.

"Computer, jam their guidance and communications systems!" Talley barked into his chariot's controls. But the computer wouldn't comply.

"Negative, Talley. Unable to penetrate their electromagnetic protection field. The Hiixian A.I. prevents it," the computer replied.

"Dang it! Okay, well, get me out of here, and quick!" he barked back.

He had to speed up and evade for long enough to somehow reach Shetra, or at least its closest border outpost, that is, if the dino-lizards didn't stop him before that. Maybe they'd attack Necrat instead, he wondered. But he really knew that was a long shot.

A round of lasers suddenly blasted apart his chariot's rear compartment. Then the cockpit's canopy flew off and exploded. "Holy schnikeys!" Talley yelled, holding on for dear life. His chariot's own energy cannons fired back as he held a steady course. But Necrat didn't slow down, not even a little bit.

Talley desperately fired again, swerved, and then sped up, anything to buy more time. But he was still twenty leagues from the nearest town. He worried that he might never find the Shastra Elder, Bheem, his main contact from the Ashtar Command Center.

His chariot computer beeped loudly as a deafening alarm sounded in his sensitive jackal ears. "Alert, alert, quark missile lock! Engaged, repeat, quark missile engaged!"

"Well, stop it then!" yelled Talley, punching buttons as fast as he could. "Shields up!"

"Shields are disabled," answered the computer.

"Then open a portal, anything!"

"Transdimensional drive disabled. I'm sorry, Talley...."

"What? I can't believe it!" he yelled, glancing back nervously.

Necrat's jet bike was baring down on him now. A quark missile surely wouldn't miss him.

The thick darkness suddenly turned to day as a glowing missile left the jet bike's wing. The weapon was unbelievably bright. Talley had never beheld one like it in his life.

Everything in the missile's path burned with flame and turned to ash. The whole jungle around him erupted with light, blinding Talley's jackal eyes. The rain seemed to stop for a long moment. He covered his helmet's visor and heard the wailing of twisting metal around him. Then his chariot's rear engine compartment exploded.

The chariot disintegrated around him and Talley went flying. He hit the ground hard and rolled, and when he stopped, he just lay there in the mud. The rain was soaking him now and his helmet had flown off and landed somewhere in the bushes.

He stared up at the night sky, dazed, trying to figure out how badly he was hurt. He hurt all over and was barely able to move.

He felt around his utility belt for his laser pistol, but it was gone now. He couldn't find his laser rifle either.

The sound of Necrat's jet bike grew closer and then suddenly stopped. Bright floodlights flashed on, illuminating Talley as he heard its door hiss and open. He heard two beings step out and march through the mud towards him.

He turned over on his stomach and groaned. Necrat was cruel and ruthless. He especially loved hunting Shastras, they were his favorite.

As the fireball from his chariot cooled Talley just glimpsed Tarsus's cross-shaped space vehicle hovering nearby. Tarsus was Necrat's bounty hunter partner and just as feared and deadly.

"Okay, let's see what we've got here," he heard Necrat say. "Well, my, my…. Look who we have," Necrat said, grinning wide. He planted the butt of his laser rifle in the mud and knelt over Talley's jackal head. Talley moaned as he slowly and painfully tried to crawl away. But Necrat grabbed him and turned him over, easily pinning him down with his clawed and hairy wolfman hand.

Talley froze with fear, trembling as his throat choked up. He was staring up at the most feared wolfman face in the solar system. He could be inches from death. Nobody escaped Necrat, nobody.

"You aren't having your best day, are you?" Necrat asked with an evil cackle. "Tell me, where did you think you were going? Hmmm? To find Siegfried? Maybe to tell him something important? Tell me, Talley, where is Siegfried now?"

Talley lay there silently. He couldn't speak or even think of something to say. He narrowed his jackal eyes and his fear suddenly turned into burning rage. He would never talk, no matter what Necrat did to him. He felt around in the mud and then underneath his tunic. The scroll and his laser rifle were both gone. Had the scroll flown out when he crashed? And where was his laser pistol?

"Where is Siegfried? Tell me...if you do, you just might live."

Talley refused to answer. He caught the sight of his pistol's light blinking in the mud nearby and reached for it. He touched its metal handle and removed it, all charged and blinking, ready to fire. But Necrat easily slapped the pistol from Talley's hand.

"Oh, that's a no, no," Necrat said. His pistol sailed through the air and landed in a clump of ferns. "We can't have you using that now, can we?"

Talley was trembling with rage and adrenaline now. He clenched his jackal fangs and reached for his utility belt. But as he did he realized that both his survival kit and shield generator were busted and useless.

Necrat knelt right over Talley's jackal face. "I'm going to track down your boss, Siegfried, you see…. And when I catch him, which I will, Khapre-Tum will make me the richest bounty hunter of all time."

Talley didn't answer. He just shivered with cold and glared back, too afraid to move. He wished he had his pistol or a knife, anything.

Necrat looked over the ground nearby and found a small leather case. He picked it up and flipped it open, staring right at Talley's Intergalactic Agent badge from the Ashtar Command Center. A space station set in the very center of the Milky Way Galaxy, the Ashtar Command was dedicated to protecting every civilization which belonged to the Galactic Federation.

The rains pelted Necrat as he stood and hit the comm. link device at his belt. "Tiber, bring the energy chains!" He then flipped the leather case closed and stuffed Talley's badge into his vest.

In just a few seconds the wolfman, Tiber, had fixed energy chains to Talley's arms and wrists. The chains instantly levitated him off the ground where he hung in the air, all covered with mud. They were so tight and so strong that he knew he could never break free.

Talley kicked his foot out, reaching out for the scroll which he'd just spotted lying on the ground. But it was too far away and his toe barely nudged it.

"What's that?" asked Necrat, pointing. "Do you want that?" He bent down and picked up the scroll. "Whatever it is, it's mine now," he said. "Looks important too.... Maybe I'll just throw it away." He mimed throwing it into some bushes and glanced at Talley.

Talley kicked out at Necrat with his sandaled feet, but Necrat dodged just in time. In retaliation, he struck Talley in the stomach with the butt of his laser rifle. Talley gasped and coughed, unable to breathe. Necrat laughed hysterically right in his jackal face.

Then Necrat grabbed Talley's snout, snarling and growling back through his wolfman teeth. "Try that again, please," he growled as he shoved Talley's face away. "Tiber, take this filth into the ship."

"Yes, sir," said Tiber, saluting back.

It was then that Talley noticed Tiber was a ten cubit tall wolfman covered in thick, orange hair. Tiber motioned to the energy chains which then followed his lumbering steps back towards the atomic jet, his wolfman tail swishing back and forth behind him.

They followed Necrat in through the side door and into the atomic jet's hold. Once inside, Tiber levitated Talley into a cold, metal chair set right next to a cage which held several Shastra and human prisoners. The chair instantly bound Talley in more energy chains, locking him in place. The door then shut with a loud clang.

Talley's jackal snout went into hyper drive. He smelled burnt metal, electrical discharge, wiring, the stench of the caged prisoners, special Hiixian space plastics, the hint of quark bombs and missiles held in the weapons storage area and the exhaust from the jet's atomic engines.

Then the stench of wet wolfman hair assaulted Talley's nostrils as Necrat approached his chair.

"Comfy?" asked Necrat, laughing. "Now, let's see what this scroll says, hmmm?" He unrolled the parchment, and lighting a cigar, puffed while he read. "Hmmm, very interesting. Very, very interesting."

The scroll read;

First order of the Golden Circle of Garud, Dispatch 15-42B.

> *Dear Bheem; the following directions are vital and immediate to save Earth from Khapre-Tum's invasion. Prepare yourselves and warn king Masha of Heliopolis, danger is coming. Orders are direct from Siegfried, who is the only hope for Heliopolis. Demons recently spotted just outside that city. Portals from the Underworld are opened. Find Siegfried, warn him and prepare! Help will arrive soon. The Lone Ranger has been spotted in the jungle nearby. Jonas Neferis, an Intergalactic Agent from the Ashtar Command Center, is on his way. Hurry!*
>
> *In Service to the Guardians,*
> *Mamaji Esquire*

"Hmmm, that sounds pretty important," said Necrat. "Really important, actually...."

Talley spat and yelled as he writhed in his chair, trying to free himself. But the energy chains just cinched tighter around him. With their plan revealed, he knew that the bounty hunters would further complicate things. He only hoped that Siegfried and this Intergalactic Agent could somehow avoid any traps the demons or bounty hunters would set.

Necrat held up the muddy scroll and lit its wrinkled corner with the smoldering tip of his cigar. The flames leapt upward, slowly turning the scroll into a smoldering sheet of ash.

"Call Queen Nayhexx of Hiix and tell her the good news," said Necrat.

"Affirmative," answered Tiber.

This was bad, this was really bad, thought Talley. He had to escape somehow, had to formulate a plan to get out of here and find Bheem and Siegfried. But how?

"Tiber, let's get out of here. We've got a wily old hermit to catch," Necrat said. "Plus, they're sending another agent from the Ashtar Command, probably to help out this one, here. That means Talley's more important than we or Khapre-Tum even thought. Hmmm.... What's that Agent's name?" Necrat squinted, glancing over the last tiny bit of scroll left on the floor where he'd dropped it. "Janis? Joonaaas? Janus? He's dead meat anyway, whatever his name is."

The scroll was now almost completely gone. Only scraps of ash lay on the floor now. Talley glanced down amidst the charred remains and read the broken words, 'Siegfried, Bheem,' and 'agent Jonas.'

Necrat laughed as he ground the last scraps under his heel. Then he eagerly bounced into his atomic jet's pilot seat, put his pilot helmet on, and punched in his coordinates. In an instant, they'd left the smoldering wreckage behind and shot off through the wet jungle night.

As he stood in the training arena, tense and alert, the Shastra agent named Jonas, stared up at the blinking eyes of a six-armed battle robot. He knew it had the ability to decapitate and then disembowel him, and very efficiently and easily right then and there. He glanced over at Chuck who nodded back with encouragement. Chuck was six-cubit-tall turtle-being, called a Manta, who walked upright just like Shastras and humans.

Jonas trusted that Chuck had programmed this robot not to injure him, but the number of training accidents this thing had inflicted in the last month made him cautious.

Being a Shastra, Jonas's pointed jackal ears turned just slightly and heard each whirring cog and switch within the robot's tubular casing. Attached to its cylindrical column of a body, the robot's articulating arms whipped about menacingly, displaying an array of nasty, spinning blades and electrodes, among other deadly weapons.

Jonas jumped over the first of these swinging blades and then ducked, just as a hammer swung right at his jackal head. That would have put a permanent dent in his brown-haired jackal face, even with his protective helmet on.

With three swift strokes of his training sword, Jonas parried a shower of electrified darts and then jumped back from an advancing cloud of tear gas. He ran from two swinging saw blades before he regrouped and used a spin move to plunge his blade into the first of the robot's three blinking targets.

Not pausing even for a second, the robot thrust a spear right for his face. Jonas ducked and then rolled to avoid three burning laser blasts which scoured the floor. He rolled, jumped up, and then ran to a safe distance. He noticed that the spear thrust and laser blasts had come much faster than usual.

He shot a worried look at Chuck before Jamy, another Manta, tossed a training shield to him. He caught it and quickly blocked another hammer blow that sent him flying back across the floor. He leapt up and the robot quickly advanced on him. He parried three blade-wielding arms, blocking and striking back in a quick flurry, before plunging his blade in the second blinking target with a nifty lunging maneuver. He then quickly ducked a whirring saw blade, but not without it shaving off the very top of his training helmet, nicking his left jackal ear.

The battle robot beeped and then sped up. It shot out four lasers, all from different ports, everyone-of-which Jonas's bronze training shield stopped, before the fifth one melted the shield completely. So, now useless, Jonas chucked his shield to the side.

Something seemed wrong with this robot's program, he thought. So, deciding to end this session for good, Jonas blasted the laser ports with his own laser pistol, and then leapt over another tear gas cloud that floated towards him. Or was it acid? It could have been. The cloud hurt his throat more than usual when he breathed in.

He couldn't believe it, but the robot moved even faster now, shooting darts and flinging saw blades as Jonas lunged closer, blocking the three swinging blades with this sword, until he was finally close enough to stab the robot's third target with one swift stroke.

Almost instantly, the cylindrical robot slowed to a stop and lowered all six of its arms. He then heard it power down and the training arena gate opened. Jonas stepped out, breathing hard as he removed his helmet, and wiped his jackal brow. He had to smile, though, being very pleased with his performance.

He skillfully flicked his sword onto the nearby weapons rack before he put his laser pistol back in his holster. He thought that was probably his best training session yet as he removed his training helmet and accepted a towel from Chuck and wiped himself off. He felt his left jackal ear where the buzz saw had nicked him. The hairs on its tip were much shorter than on his right ear. That was closer than he would have liked, but he understood there were always risks in training.

"Did that thing malfunction, or what? That was like Legendary mode, or something," said Jonas.

"I know, it actually was on Legendary mode. But that's because I had orders from Ashtar himself," Chuck said as he checked his control panel. "Ashtar called and asked me to give you a real test. He says it's for something important. But he didn't say what."

"He said that, eh?" Jonas asked, growing excited. "I wonder what it means. What else did he say? Maybe I've received my next mission...." Ashtar was a celestial being in charge of the Command Center.

"I don't know, man. He didn't say much else," added Chuck, shrugging his turtle shoulders. "Just one of those agent mysteries, I guess." Mar-Mar, Chuck's crocohound (a genetic combination of a dog and a crocodile), waddled right up to Jonas, panting with excitement. He knelt and gave Mar-Mar a rough and friendly pat down.

"Hmmm, that's very interesting," said Jonas. "I wonder what Ashtar meant."

"Yeah, who knows? Oh, well, I gotta go, Jonas. See ya," Chuck said. He waved goodbye before walking over to another computer screen where a first year Shastra agent waited for instructions.

"Good boy, Mar-Mar! Who's a good boy? Who's a good boy? You are! Yes, you are!" Jonas said, as he slapped Mar-Mar's side. The crocohound jumped about, panting and wagging its tail excitedly.

Just then Chantar, another green Manta turtle-being, walked up and recalibrated the battle robot Jonas had just finished fighting.

"You did great, Jonas. Legendary setting wasn't too much for you. You didn't even get injured," said Chantar.

"Thanks. You're right, I could handle that," said Jonas happily, still slapping Mar-Mar. "Although, I've never seen it move that fast or shoot that many lasers before. How high do the settings go?"

"Ten levels above Legendary, so says the manual. But the highest I've seen is just two above Legendary. That's called Ludicrous mode, and that was only once. I programmed that for Phaistos the Great, and he nearly broke the danged machine!"

"Phaistos, man...there's no one better," said Jonas, shaking his jackal head.

Phaistos was also a Shastra and the most famous of all Intergalactic Agents. Jonas had once seen Phaistos traveling down the same hallway as him and gotten Phaistos's autograph. That signature was now one of the most cherished items in his whole apartment.

"Yup, had to buy a second backup machine after that. The first one was out of commission for a whole month!" said Chantar. "Oh, well.... Hey, Zeemmer's here for his training session. Catch you later, Jonas."

"Later," Jonas said as he patted Mar-Mar one last time, bowed to Chantar, and then tossed his sweaty towel in the hamper. "Thanks for the session, guys!" he waved to Chantar and Chuck who both waved back.

"Sure thing, Jonas," they said.

As Jonas walked off, his jackal ears turned backward to hear Chantar talking with another agent that had just showed up for training, a human named Zeemmer.

"Okay, Zeemmer, I'm gonna turn on the fire and sound jets for this session. No, it's not set on Legendary mode. Yes, I swear it isn't, that was just for Jonas and because of a special request. Yes, I swear I'm telling you the truth. Zeemer, listen here...."

Jonas was soon out of earshot and in the agent locker room, where he showered and then got dressed in the standard Junior Intergalactic Agent uniform: a blue, form-fitting body-suit with his name and rank proudly pinned to his left chest, plus comfortable space slippers.

Hungry and eager for lunch, like all young Shastras basically all the time, he jumped onto a conveyor belt and was soon standing in the chow line of the closest mess hall.

Jonas slid his tray along the counter, sandwiched between a hulking gorilla-being in green armor on his left and a gryphon on his right that glared back any time Jonas accidentally bumped into him. The gryphon was huge so this was hard to avoid. It hissed back and its eagle wings flapped aggressively, slapping Jonas in the face multiple times. He knew from extensive experience that gryphons could get really aggressive and jumpy. So Jonas just smiled back and didn't say anything.

The lunch lady, an octopus-armed being with a squid head named Nanda, served Jonas plenty of space meat cubes, three scoops of concentrated protein and hormone jello (to grow strong bones and bigger muscles), and then gave him his daily brain enhancement pills, which every agent received.

He eagerly watched her scoop approach the best and most advanced brain enhancement formula, but sighed dejectedly when she skipped them over for the lower grade. Only senior Intergalactic agents received the good stuff. His life goal was to one day achieve such a high rank.

Jonas weaved through a crowd of youngsters in the mess hall, all playing Warrior Space Ball while instructors chased after them, yelling for them to stop. He sat down at his favorite table and his two best friends plopped down right next to him; they were a male wolf-being named Digger and a female Shastra named Zarry.

They ate while they discussed the recent events on the Ashtar Command, such as new missions their mutual friends were taking, new species visiting the station, and what any of them knew about future classes required to be eligible for promotion to Intermediate Agent.

"You ready for atomic chariot fighter weapons school, Jonas?" asked Digger, leaning in closer.

"Yeah, our orientation starts tomorrow. I can't wait," he said. After being denied entry into fighter weapons school twice, he'd finally gained acceptance, which was a crucial step in his agent career.

"Can I have some of your meat cubes, Jonas?" asked Digger. "They gave me tofu lizard bacon, again...." He shook his wolf-being head and snorted with disgust.

"How does tofu taste?" asked Zarry. "I've never tried it."

"Oh, this is Arcturian Tofu. It's much, much worse than regular tofu. I can't believe people eat this stuff. You aren't missing anything at all." Digger spit the tofu strip out onto his plate.

"Wow, yeah, I wouldn't touch that if I were you," said Jonas, leaning away and grimacing. He definitely felt Digger's pain. Arcturian Tofu was awful, it really was much worse than regular tofu, which he hated with a passion. "Who wouldn't eat meat, and why? Here, take my meat cubes. It sounds like you need them more than I do." He shoveled some of his meat cubes onto Digger's plate.

"Thanks, man," Digger said, letting out a huge sigh of relief now that his torture was over.

"I heard that the courses in fighter weapons school are really hard," said Zarry. "Like, barely anyone passes the first time. That's what Zan-Zan told me."

"Dude, Zan-Zan can't even fly a basic chariot," Digger said, his mouth full of meat cubes.

"His cousin told him that it was really hard. But he passed last year after his fourth attempt," added Zarry.

"It can't be THAT hard. It's not like time travel school or anything," said Jonas. "But you have to pass fighter weapons school in order to get into the basic time travel courses."

He already knew that fighter weapons school was hard. His counselors told him all about how many training failures and deaths there'd been in the past. Then there was the intense final test of fixing a broken chariot in a methane blizzard while being chased by a wild Yeti beast that was twelve cubits tall. Supposedly, that was the final exam. But Jonas also knew that these rumors were prone to exaggeration.

Jonas soon got up and returned to the buffet line. When he'd gotten a full plate of space squid nuggets and Mandarian Chicken Tenders he returned to their table and dished them out. "Here you guys go, if you're still hungry."

"Thanks, man," they both said.

"Do you think any of your past chariot accidents will come up?" Zarry asked with her jackal mouth full of space squid nuggets.

"I don't think so, even though they were both kinda bad," said Jonas. "They accepted my application anyway, but we'll see. If they make me take extra safety courses, then that's fine with me."

"You'll do okay, I've heard of way worse training crashes, and those agents all got into fighter weapons school, even though some took like five tries, I think..." said Digger. He chased his chicken tenders with his Tralorian chocolate milkshake.

"Yeah, no one died, so it didn't qualify as a 'true accident' in the tribunal's eyes. So, I had that going for me, which was nice," said Jonas.

Finished with his chicken tenders, space squid nuggets, and protein jello, Jonas washed it all down with a spicy space beer and then excused himself. "I'm gonna go brush up on some technical reading and get a good night's sleep. I'll catch you guys later."

"Good luck at your orientation, Jonas," said Zarry and Digger, both beaming with pride.

"We're going to galactic studies class, next," said Zarry.

"Okay, have fun. What are you guys studying?" Jonas asked.

"The Guardians, I think," said Digger.

"No, that's done. That was last week," added Zarry. "We're covering the intergalactic wormhole network and then we'll start on desert planets, like Monubia, actually."

"Hey cool, that's my home planet," said Jonas brightly. "I bet you'll learn tons, even stuff that I don't know."

"Probably...do they have sand worms on Monubia?" asked Digger.

"Yeah, huge ones. They're the coolest things too," said Jonas.

"Wow, sounds interesting," said Digger. "Okay, well, have fun at orientation, Jonas. Tell us how it goes."

"Oh, yeah, I'll tell you what happens, for sure," he said. He'd gone through almost every one of his agent training classes and missions with those two and was closer to them than anyone on the Command Center, except for his mentors and three favorite instructors.

"Hey, let's play Warrior Space Ball tomorrow, after my lectures are over. Sound good?" he asked.

"Yeah, sounds great!" they both replied.

Besides archery, Warrior Space Ball was Jonas's favorite sport. It was a violent sport that evolved from an ancient game called Lacrosse. Players passed an ion-charged ball with a net on the end of a stick and had to wear lots of protective gear because someone was always trying to hit you, push you over, and steal the ball from you.

When Jonas was younger he'd desperately wanted to be a professional Warrior Space Ball player, but found that he wasn't good enough to make a Monubian semi-pro roster let alone the professional circuit. This led to him exploring the option of becoming an Intergalactic Special Agent.

Jonas stood, cleaned off his tray, and then dodged the always rambunctious table of senior agents as he exited the mess hall. He felt anxious and nervous, but also excited, and with the sense that some important adventure was about to begin.

He entered his apartment, immediately dodging his practice droid that flew about the room eager to start sword and laser pistol training. He turned the droid off and then patted his flying Dog-odo Dragon named Ranchy, a genetic combination of dog and komodo dragon. Being a Shastra, Jonas was a huge fan of all the many canine species in the galaxy.

"Ranchy, you're such a good boy!" he said. He lifted Ranchy up, hugged him tight, and then scratched him behind his floppy, scaly ears. Ranchy aggressively licked Jonas's jackal face with his forked tongue. He then fed Ranchy a dead rat and kicked his shoes off and into the corner.

He decided to relax for a bit before he read, so he flicked on his hologram viewer and sank into his favorite anti-gravity leather recliner. He propped his feet up, and while holding Ranchy in his lap, watched two full episodes of his favorite show, *The Kung Fu Werewolves of Mars*.

One of the most popular shows on the Ashtar Command, *The Kung Fu Werewolves of Mars* portrayed the life and adventures of the Paddington family. They were an extended family of Werewolves who lived in the ancient pyramid city of Cydonia on a planet called Mars. The patriarch, Patton Paddington, along with his wife, Sheera Paddington, were both high-ranking masters who taught kung fu classes in the largest, oldest, and best defended Were-Buddhist temple on the planet. The show was fictional, but Jonas had heard that the planet was real and located in a solar system pretty far from their Command Center.

Jonas absolutely loved this show. It was hilarious, had lots of danger and suspense, and he thought that the kung fun styles that the werewolves used looked awesome. They were always fighting lizard ninjas or Jupiter robot spies that were trying to infiltrate their temple and steal its ancient relics.

His cleaning droid, Vanessa, rolled around the room and cleaned while he watched. She had just finished cleaning when the second episode ended. "Jonas, don't forget you have dinner reservations with your mentors, Drox and Joonai. Oh, and Jenny will be there too. Also, tomorrow you start atomic chariot fighter weapons school."

"Thanks, Nessa." Jenny was a Shastra female he'd dated for two stints back in agent school. She was still a good friend and they shared the same agent mentors. He looked from Jenny's picture to a picture of his grandfather, Paw-Paw Neferis, sitting on his altar right next to his golden statue of the Guardian, Garud. Paw-Paw's picture gazed back with dark jackal eyes framed by gray jackal hair and a beard. In the picture he sat cross-legged and held a hookah tip up to his jackal mouth. He'd loved his grandfather and missed him more than anyone back on Monubia.

"Great, it'll be good to see Jenny again," he replied while he neatly combed his jackal hair and straightened his uniform in the mirror. Still having some spare time before dinner, he sat down and reviewed his textbooks on atomic chariots.

He sat in his recliner with Ranchy on his lap and read about ion and proton thrusters, wormhole science, aetheric dampeners, inertia shields, torsion steering, different types of prana fuel, and the basics of anti-gravity technology and its long history. Then he briefly covered some chapters on the differences between physical ships, plasma chariots, and chariots constructed from thought energy. The latter he frankly never thought he would ever see, they were just too advanced. Only one such chariot was rumored to exist on the Command Center. But he'd heard that Ashtar was the only being skilled enough to even start it let alone drive it.

After dinner which included a long and pleasant conversation with Drox, Joonai, and Jenny about many things, including chariot training and a senior agent's typical first time travel mission away from the Command Center, Jonas headed back to his apartment and immediately fell asleep.

The next morning he woke up early, worked out in the agent's gym, ate, dressed in his finest agent uniform, grabbed his things, and headed to the lecture hall where chariot fighter weapons school was set to begin.

Jonas stood in the long registration line, holding his hologram books under his arm and his hologram registration chip in his sweaty hand. He was about to give his chip to a wolfman named Jabu, when the comm. link device beeped on his utility belt.

He touched it and the hologram turtle face of Chantar immediately appeared. "Jonas, I've been ordered to tell you to be in Ashtar's office in ten cycles. And make sure to bring your hologram records folder. He just called me and asked to see it. It sounds important."

"But why?" he asked confused. "I'm only a junior agent."

"I don't know. But I'd get going if I were you."

"I'm already at the training center. Chariot fighter weapons school starts like right now!"

"Those are my orders, Jonas," added Chantar, shrugging his turtle shoulders.

"Can't I go later? I've got three lectures today. This is important," said Jonas, growing more irritated. He couldn't believe it. This was one of the most important days of his young Shastra life. The other students stared as they stepped around him and descended the auditorium stairs. "This is just really bad timing…. I gotta go. I'll call you back, okay?" he said and then quickly shut off his comm. link.

Just as he did so, two Command Center security guards marched up to him and bowed. Both were Wolfmen with dark fur, were clad in green space armor, and carried rather large laser rifles.

"Jonas Neferis, junior Intergalactic Special Agent, I presume?" asked the first guard.

"Yeahhhh…. What can I do for you boys?" he asked, alarmed that such decorated guards were talking to him at all. The whole auditorium was staring at him now, even the instructors down on the stage below.

"We have direct orders to personally escort you to Ashtar's office. It's very important."

"Ummm, what's this about?" he asked, reluctantly. He just wanted to get past them and to his seat before the lecture started.

"We can't tell you here. Ashtar is formally excusing you from chariot fighter weapons school. Please, follow us."

"It's not a good idea to keep the leader of the Command Center waiting," added the second guard.

Jonas had to admit the guard was right, so, putting his hologram registration chip away and sighing with resignation, he turned and followed the guards out of the lecture hall and past the students, all still staring at him dumbly, wondering what was going on and if something was wrong. He avoided all their curious gazes as they left the lecture hall.

"Ashtar wants to see your hologram records folder as well. We must stop by your apartment, first, to retrieve it," said the first guard.

"Sure thing. This way," he said, just going with the flow now and wondering what they were up to. So Jonas returned to his apartment and dropped off his books while he retrieved his agent records folder.

He exited his apartment's sliding door and, along with the two guards, boarded the nearest conveyor belt for Ashtar's office. The guard's cryptic words had him thinking. What could be the reason behind Ashtar's wanting to see him? Could he have been demoted? Would Ashtar discipline him for his many atomic chariot accidents? He sure hoped not. He was an experienced driver, and he thought that all those accidents were behind him.

The conveyor belt took them on a long and winding path, through parts of the Command Center he'd never even seen before. The hallway décor grew fancier as they traveled farther towards the very center of the station. Finally, the conveyor stopped before a glowing door radiating with bright light. He'd never been inside Ashtar's office before, and he was almost scared to approach it.

Standing before Ashtar's office door now, Jonas thought back on the four years of training he needed to graduate and reach the rank of junior agent. At times the training had been intense, his curriculum challenging, his practice missions almost deadly. And only with intense study and focus had he passed the count-less physical and psychological examinations, the full range of written exams, and lastly, a series of dangerous test missions before graduating.

After four long and challenging years he'd grown to know the Command Center's vast hallways, numerous training centers, armories, and star chariot hangars just like his home village back on Monubia, a simple desert planet not far from the station. He was now potentially about to have the most important meeting in his short Shastra life. Beyond this door was a celestial so powerful and wise that Jonas was like a bug to him, in every way possible. Jonas felt in total awe of his situation.

"Okay, Jonas, this can't be too bad. Heck, it might even be a good thing. So, let's find out," he said to himself, psyching himself up as he stepped off the conveyor belt. Then taking a deep breath, he sighed, and finally approached Ashtar's glowing doorway.

First Days on Earth-1

J ONAS'S VOICE BROKE NERVOUSLY as he spoke into the wall screen set right next to the fanciest door on the Command Center. "Name: Jonas Neferis. Race: Shastra. Rank: First year Intergalactic Special Agent. Open, please," Jonas said as he leaned in closer.

The office door was completely engraved all over with hieroglyphics, symbols, and pictures of celestials that formed an overview of the history of the station.

The screen beeped back and he waited while it calculated whether his husky Shastra voice was actually him. After performing a quick eye scan and brain scan, the door swung open, revealing the current head of the Command Center, Ashtar himself.

Sighing nervously and straightening his bright blue, form-fitting space suit, Jonas, along with the two guards, marched into the room and bowed. Ashtar was sitting at a large table before a window that looked out into the peaceful void of space right outside the station. Jonas stood there stiff at attention and waited. He was nervous to meet Ashtar in person for the first time.

Although a celestial, Ashtar was a full human, and looked very similar to pictures Jonas had seen of him around the Command

Center. Jonas had seen a human before, but they were rare beings on that particular station. Ashtar was known to be mysterious, ancient, wise beyond measure, and of anonymous origin; at least he'd never told anyone where he was from that Jonas knew. His skin was beautiful, shining with a brilliant shade of baby blue, while his long hair flowed in blond locks that also glowed bright and golden with their own separate aura. Even though they'd never met in person, Jonas held Ashtar in the highest regard. He'd lectured for Jonas's agent courses and written many instructional books. He was far wiser than any Shastra that Jonas had ever known.

Ashtar returned his bow. Clad in a white space suit, he almost blinded Jonas with its brilliance. This suit, plus Ashtar's celestial aura, was almost too much to look at at first. And it took Jonas a while to adjust his jackal eyes to its strong glow.

"You asked to see me, sir," he said, standing tall at attention and slightly averting his eyes. He held his hologram folder with all his records, qualifications, reviews, and test scores neatly tucked under his right arm. As he stood there, his heart pounded in his jackal ears.

"Yes, Jonas. Please, step forward," Ashtar said as he waved to the guards. "Guards, you're excused."

"Yes, sir!" they both said, before they bowed, turned, and left the room.

"Jonas, you're twenty two Shastra years old, is that correct?"

"Yes, sir."

"Good. And what's your career focus right now on this Command Center?"

"Passing chariot fighter weapons school and earning Intermediate Agent rank, sir," he said firmly.

"Good, those are excellent goals, son. You are known as one of our best junior agents and I know you'll soon reach those goals without question. That's why I have called you here today. See, an important mission has come to my attention and I want one of my best agents on it. You will also earn Intermediate status when you return upon its completion."

"Yes, sir!" He liked the idea already.

"However, so far I've struggled to find a suitable agent for the mission, which rarely happens. So, after much consideration, and I've discussed this with all my advisors, I'm offering you the mission."

"Thank you, sir," he replied, struggling to hide his excitement. He wanted to do a back flip right there in Ashtar's office, but he restrained himself. "That's very unexpected, sir." A wave of relief swept over him. He wasn't being punished for his atomic chariot accidents after all.

Countless more experienced agents were ahead of him at the Ashtar Command; agents like Trajan the Swift, Drome the Burly, Phaistos the Great, and Lena the Magnificent, just to name a few off the top of his jackal head. He winced at remembering how Drome the Burly had bullied young cadets during their training sessions. The time Jonas body-slammed and pinned Drome during zero-gravity wrestling practice counted as one of his proudest moments.

"Let me describe the mission's x's and o's, first. Then decide if you want in the game or not. The ball is in your court, the option will be yours. And I'll tell you up front, son, this is not the usual mission we give to our junior agents. It will be quite dangerous and might even go into overtime."

"Where is the mission to, sir?"

"A planet called Earth-1. You took Earth Studies, correct?"

"Yes, sir. I took it for two quarters," he replied.

"Ah, good, good. Now as I've already told you, Jonas, you are one of our most qualified young agents. All your advisors, especially Drox and Joonai, say wonderful things about you. You should be very proud, son. If those two say it, it must be true."

"Thank you, sir," Jonas said, still stiff at attention. "Whatever the mission is, I'm ready, fit, and eager to serve the Ashtar Command, sir." Unless it was a suicide mission, Jonas would definitely take it. He thrust out his records folder, but Ashtar declined it with a wave.

"I have seen your records already. Five star, nearly impeccable, son," said Ashtar. He looked down and read from the wide view screen on his desk. "Proficiency in marksmanship, skilled at Warrior Space Ball, accomplished survivalist in extreme climates, deep space travel qualified. You speak multiple languages, including Gryphon, Trog, and Fishish. You're hand-to-hand combat and weapons qualified. And you passed all your intelligence gathering tests with flying colors. Very impressive, son, All-Star material...."

"Yes, sir. Thank you, sir," he said proudly.

"You have had hiccups along the way, but everyone has at least one. I'm willing to look past those," said Ashtar. "Now, please, approach the large view screen over against the wall and put on the brain-synch helmet. It's quite a nifty setup, actually."

"Sir, about the time I accidentally broke an instructor's back...I...suffered an energy surge of unexpected strength. See, what happened is, I couldn't—" he began nervously to explain this as he eyed the copper brain-synch helmet meant to read his mind.

"Yes, yes, I know, I understand all that, son," interrupted Ashtar. "Our tribunals have settled all your cases already, so there's no need to worry. Why, our best and brightest agent,

Phaistos the Great, well you know…. He turned a toilet stall into a black hole and nearly destroyed the Command Center!" Ashtar said, laughing.

Jonas was relieved to hear his record was fully cleared. He wondered how Phaistos had avoided being killed by that black hole, even though it was a small one. He respected Phaistos the Great even more now.

They reached the giant view screen on the back wall and Jonas accepted the skullcap, placing the copper contraption on his jackal head. He began sweating immediately as he felt the station's main computer begin to probe his jackal brain. Tiny electrodes pricked his jackal scalp all over and he heard soft swishing noises in his pointed ears.

Instantly, a complete and detailed list of his cadet test scores, reviews, certifications earned, and records all flashed across the large view screen. It even displayed some tiny infractions that he'd forgotten about, plus, a rare test or two that he'd failed during agent school. All of this he preferred that Ashtar didn't see, but it was already too late.

Ashtar scrunched up his blue human brow as he stared at the list. "Actually…can I see your file for a minute?" he asked.

"I…umm…was engaged in a few unavoidable incidents, sir. Some of them resulted in consequences that were regrettable," stammered Jonas, while trying to contain the damage. In reality, the truth was he'd actually crashed several atomic-powered spaceships, two of which were extremely expensive. All of these were his fault, even though he felt he was a good driver.

"I understand that, son. Just let me have a timeout to look at your stats."

With his palms sweaty and knees weak, Jonas stiffly handed over his hologram folder. Meanwhile, planet Earth's statistics flashed up on the view screen. Jonas read these to distract himself from Ashtar as he perused Jonas's hologram files and mumbled softly to himself.

"Crashed a Zeta-15 model? Ouch.... Well, no one ever said that chariot driving was easy, son."

"Yes, sir," he said, still stiff at attention.

To distract himself, Jonas read from the list of Earth-1's climate statistics. The different climates it listed far exceeded those on Monubia in diversity. Where Monubia was mostly desert, Earth-1 offered tall mountains covered in fields of white snow (something he'd only seen on one planet before). Monubia didn't contain any of the deep oceans and lush jungles that he saw on the screen. He'd only experienced hologram training sessions of those environments.

"Well, son, make sure and finish fighter weapons school as soon as possible, okay? It is important and is needed to get you wormhole circuit certified. You can't be promoted to Senior Agent without those under your belt. Understand?" Then he closed Jonas's file and returned it.

Jonas nodded. "Yes, sir. I understand."

"Good. Well then, let's detail all the players involved. Here's the quick version of Earth-1 history," Ashtar continued as he turned to the view screen. "Basically, all we know is that up to five thousand years ago Earth-1 was populated by materialistic societies in a very low evolutionary state. Now this existed over almost every continent. The face of the planet also looked much different than it does today. Few individuals followed the Truth of the Supreme Being. Even fewer ever contacted or knew that

Eternal Being intimately or even wanted to. I still struggle to believe that, but our records confirm it."

"Yes, sir. Highly unusual, sir." He wondered how Earth-1 had ever survived such a dark period.

"You see, the Guardians were hidden from the masses at that time. Lesser gods, angels, and demigods all avoided the public like it was quarantined. I'm sure you skimmed all this in Earth-1 Studies. During the cleansing period the planet's poles shifted, many continents sank, and new ones rose up or just moved about, you know, like continents do sometimes. As a result the surface changed drastically. Then when everything settled and it was safe again, the celestial Designers and Introducers paid the planet a visit. Isn't that nice?"

"Yes, sir. Amazing, sir. So, what did the Designers do?" Jonas only vaguely remembered these beings from Celestial Studies.

"Well, they did many things," continued Ashtar. "They introduced new species of plants, animals, and intelligent beings to the planet. They brought Shastras, Navans, Ghandas, Praying Mantises, Trogs, and lots, lots more. Oh, and they decided to keep humans on too."

"Very interesting," said Jonas. "Why did they decide to keep humans on the planet?"

"Why not keep them? They'd had a rough time of it up until then. And they'd lived on the planet for a very long time already," said Ashtar.

"Sure, cut them some slack," said Jonas.

"Exactly. The Supreme Being decided to continue the experiment."

"Ah, I see." Fascinated, Jonas stared at the view screen as one after another it displayed the species now living on Earth-1. For example, Earth-1 Shastras looked almost exactly like Monubian Shastras, having a human body with a jackal head. Now, Navans were very different, they appeared to be like gorillas or monkeys, but also walked upright and could talk. Jonas remembered seeing a Navan once before on Monubia. Next were Ghandas, ferocious lions, tigers, and leopards that walked and talked just like Shastras did. He'd met a few to those on a training mission to the lion planet, Felina-12.

Now, Praying Mantis beings came next and those really creeped him out. They were completely alien-like, like a folded, green tangle of insect legs and arms, and with a huge body and an equally large set of wings. He didn't trust how they looked, with tiny bug heads atop their tall bodies, and two giant, beady, bug eyes bulging outward.

He was quite familiar with Trogs, though. He even spoke decent Trog. These were intelligent ant-beings; insectoids like the Mantises. But Trogs were docile and friendly, unlike most other Insectoid species.

It appeared to Jonas that the celestial Designers and Introducers had greatly increased the diversity of intelligent life on Earth-1. They had even approved unlimited alien visitation, space travel, and trade. This was almost the exact opposite of that weird stage just before the planet's cleansing. Not unexpectedly, barely any of its low-evolved civilizations survived those planetary changes.

"There are vastly more species than are shown here. This is just a sample," said Ashtar. "Now, onto plants and animals. Most of the new species the Designers introduced were just bigger, meaner, and heartier cousins of what existed before. Of course, constant crossbreeding, genetic experimentation, and alien visitors means that newer and stranger species are constantly showing up. But the Introducers mostly keep things under control. Most plants grew bigger, smarter, and deadlier in many cases. Some attack in order to protect themselves against the bigger, more aggressive animals, like dino-lizards for instance."

"It must be dangerous to live there, sir," he said. The more Jonas learned, the crazier this mission sounded. But he knew he had to accept it. A successful, high-profile mission like this would be crucial to advancing his career as an Intergalactic Special Agent. But he still felt uneasy about it. After all, Ashtar hadn't yet revealed its purpose.

"Sir, is this strictly a survival mission? What's the objective?"

"Well, my goodness, I got too wrapped up in Earth-1's statistics. It will be partially about survival, yes. But it's really a rescue mission. See, our head agent stationed on Earth-1, a Shastra named Talley, has disappeared. All efforts to locate him and his team have failed."

The view screen displayed a hologram of Talley along with his agent record. A yellow jackal-haired head stared back at Jonas with big, piercing green eyes. Handsome and only a little older than Jonas, Talley was quite accomplished, having achieved time travel certification, reached senior agent status, and become head of the Earth Defense Force. He was also the Ashtar Command's highest ranking agent currently stationed on Earth-1.

"That's terrible, sir. I know Talley. He's one of the best Agents I've ever met."

"Everyone agrees, Jonas. But it gets worse. Demons have been spotted near Heliopolis, Shetra, and other cities. In fact, that whole area around Heliopolis is thought to be swarming with pests from the Underworld. We think something big is building on that planet. If you can find Talley, you can learn everything that's been going on there. I want you to find him and learn what he's been investigating."

"Yes, sir."

"Earth-1 is an extremely important outpost for the Galactic Federation. We feel that Talley must have gotten into real trouble to just disappear like this. Talley's one of our most trusted agents and is not known to break communication for this long."

"Yes, sir."

"And more recently, countless villages and towns have been overrun, burned, and destroyed by demons and other evil beasts. The city of sages, Kalanos, was surrounded and held hostage for over three years. More recently, an entire city of two-cubit-high moon people, you know that short, the blue humanoids?"

"Yes," he did, but only faintly.

"Well, it's been wiped out completely." He shook his blue head sadly. "We think Talley was investigating these attacks and ran into something. We need you to find him and learn what he knows."

Jonas nodded. He remained stoic and silent while his mind raced. He already knew life on Earth-1 was dangerous. Possible attacks by demons and monsters from the Underworld would create a drastic situation. If Talley couldn't hack it then it must really be bad.

"Unlicensed portals have recently been opened on Earth-1 as well. Each one of these was forbidden, not receiving Command Center approval beforehand. And I'm afraid that every one of them has come from the Underworld. Our sources confirm this."

"Yes, sir, I understand."

"Also, the bounty hunters, Necrat and Tarsus Riggs, were thought to be hunting Talley and his team. We want to know why."

Chapter Two

"Necrat and Tarsus Riggs are the vilest, most evil bounty hunters alive, sir. That means—"

"Yes.... It will be the greatest challenge you've faced yet, son."

For a long moment neither of them said a word. The mission now appeared ten times more dangerous than it did just five bleebs ago. Regardless of this, Intergalactic Agents were destined to encounter bounty hunters sooner or later. Jonas knew the two groups were mortal enemies.

Jonas quickly changed the subject. "Sir, what is the overall makeup of society on Earth-1?" He was glad when Ashtar answered.

"Most kingdoms follow eternal Laws of spiritual living. After the great cleansing, Earth's planetary spirit was rejuvenated and these Laws were re-introduced by twelve celestial beings, called the Guardians," said Ashtar. "Since then, technology, spirituality, and civilization have all advanced in peaceful ways. Leaving behind the greed, ignorance, and war of the previous age."

"Sir, I've studied the Guardians extensively in Celestial Studies and Galactic History," said Jonas. "Many such celestials are also worshipped on Monubia."

"Sure, those courses are very popular. Earth's city-states each enjoy a Guardian's protection. And each city-state's royalty and priesthood cooperate with spiritual Law. It is a very simple, yet effective system. There are always renegades, however. Take Hiix, the city of the bounty hunters, for example."

Ashtar described each city-state while the view screen displayed their capital and famous landmarks. Next, images appeared that displayed each of the twelve Guardians, one after another.

To Jonas's amazement, he saw the picture of a Shastra Guardian from Monubia, named Garud, pop up on the screen. He immediately recognized the golden jackal head and the golden robes, all shining bold and bright. There were the giant sandals and the brilliant bow of energy clasped in one hand. Jonas's jackal ears instantly perked up with excitement to learn that Garud, his childhood idol, also served the beings of Earth-1.

"Hey, that's Garud!" exclaimed Jonas, nearly dropping his hologram folder. "He's worshipped and loved on Monubia, more than all other celestials."

"Why, yes he is. But, have you met the great Guardian before in person?" Ashtar asked.

"Well, no, not personally, sir. But on Monubia he's the most famous of all the celestials," said Jonas before he quickly regained his composure and snapped back to attention.

"As he should be. In my experience his wisdom and compassion are extremely unique," said Ashtar. "I have never met a celestial like him. Along with Garud, you will have other contacts on Earth; a wolfman named Mamaji, two Shastras named Bheem and Siegfried, and a time traveler named the Lone Ranger. The last three are Shastras just like you and all have my utmost trust and confidence. They will all be your teammates once on Earth-1."

"That's excellent, sir!" said Jonas excitedly. He still couldn't help but stare, all misty-eyed, at Garud's image on the view screen.

"Our knowledge is limited on the Lone Ranger. He is a regular visitor to Earth-1, however, and has personally volunteered to help you with your mission. Bheem is now working as an Elder in a village named Shetra. Siegfried is a wandering hermit who has lived on Earth for millennia. He is very wise but also mysterious."

"Excellent, sir."

"Well, that's all for now, son. I don't want to overload you with too much information. Study more about Earth-1's plants and animals, sentient population, and your Command Center contacts. All will be stored on the comm. link device you'll be issued later."

"I will, sir."

"And I want you to know that your grandfather, Paw-Paw, would be very proud of you, Jonas. You've told us so much about him. We all know how much he meant to you."

"Yes, he did, sir. I know he'd be proud," said Jonas. But Jonas's curiosity about something he'd seen in the briefing popped up in his mind. "Why is that being called the Lone Ranger, sir? That's a very strange name...."

"It has been said he adopted it from studying Earth-1's ancient records. There was once a warrior named the Lone Ranger who was a defender of the common folk and beloved by all," said Ashtar.

"Interesting, Earth history is just full of surprises," said Jonas. Just then his stomach gurgled and groaned loudly, even though he'd eaten recently.

"Ah, you are hungry," Ashtar said, smiling. "Just like every normal young Shastra should be. Do you like Toklaxian Coffee? It's fresh, and we have crisps that go nicely with it."

"Yes, sir. That happens to be my favorite brand of coffee, sir."

"Excellent." Ashtar spoke into a small cube-shaped comm. link device. "Hexago, please bring two Toklaxian Coffees, with crisps."

"Yes, sir," Hexago beeped in reply.

In just ten seconds, Hexago, who was an orb-shaped droid, flew into Ashtar's office through a side door. It held a tray which balanced two coffees and a tin of sugar crisps. The droid stopped abruptly and hovered right beside Ashtar.

Jonas's jackal mouth began watering uncontrollably. His sensitive jackal snout could smell the freshly brewed coffee and sugary crisps even before the door had fully opened. "Sir, is this regular or decaf?" asked Jonas.

"Regular. I'm civilized, not psychotic, son," exclaimed Ashtar. He then handed Jonas a cup and took one for himself.

"I agree, sir. Agents only drink regular. My combat trainer told me that it grows hair on your jackal head."

"Good man. They've trained you well, I see," Ashtar said firmly.

Jonas beamed. He felt like he'd passed an important test.

Jonas took his first sip and almost instantly his heart raced faster while beating against his chest. Next, his jackal ears stuck up straighter and the brain-synch helmet shot right off, crashing to the floor. His throat felt like it was on fire, his tongue dangled out, and his jackal eyes bulged as wide as Monubian Melons. "Ahhh, delicious..." he said. He shook his head until his tongue retracted and his eyes could focus normally again.

Ashtar smiled, and upon taking his first sip, followed the exact same ritual.

"Excellent coffee, sir," Jonas said, raising his cup. Although strange, both their reactions were the usual result of drinking Toklaxian Coffee. They were even an advertized benefit.

"It wakes your brain up and strengthens your aura," Ashtar added as sweat poured down his blue human face.

"Now, sir, how long is the mission?" Jonas asked. His head was finally clear enough to concentrate and form coherent ideas once again.

"We will put you up in an orphanage within a jungle village named Shetra." The view screen displayed a quaint town filled with mud brick huts and buildings, plus a few simple towers and temples. "Then later on you'll move to Heliopolis and pose as a Garud priest there," said Ashtar. "I suspect the mission will be three months long, minimum. But it depends on many factors. So, what do you think, Jonas? Do you want the mission?"

"Absolutely, sir. And I promise to attend fighter weapons school when I return." He felt a great surge of joy to be receiving such a high priority mission. He'd never been so excited and nervous for anything in his young Shastra life. It felt better than when he'd graduated from the Agent Academy, and that was one of the happiest days he could remember.

"Good. I'm glad, son. This will prove to be an interesting adventure for you, I think. I just have a feeling about it. You're dismissed then. You can go pack and prepare for departure."

Jonas puffed out his chest and saluted. Before turning to leave he took one last swig of coffee and emptied his cup. This time he coughed so hard he grew light-headed and had to rest for a bit. "Excuse me, sir.... When do I start?" he asked. When he'd shaken off the coffee's affects he stood up straight again.

"Why, immediately, of course," answered Ashtar. He then took a long sip and coughed so much that he had to sit down, take a quick health shot, and munch on a sugar crisp just to keep from passing out. "Ah, that's the best coffee I've had in quite a while," he said.

Jonas completely agreed.

Jonas left Ashtar's office with his head spinning in summersaults, waffling between completely freaking out and a tense level of nervous excitement. He would be heading to a strange new planet which Garud was known to frequently visit. Maybe he'd be get to actually meet the celestial Guardian? Plus, it was such a high-profile assignment he would definitely be promoted to Intermediate Agent.

His head was still ringing and his heart still pounding from the Toklaxian Coffee as he stepped out of Ashtar's office. He knew the coffee's lasting affects meant that it was high-quality stuff and that his chakras were being purified. He next found a moving walkway that carried him through five doors and then up an elevator.

He reached the Intergalactic Barter Market and pushed through the always bustling crowd. His sniffer went crazy as he sniffed out all the different types of beings; there were Shastras, humans, Insectoids, Mantas, Grays, serpent-beings, tons of other weird alien species and sentient robots, and rows and rows of booths and anti-gravity stalls, selling almost any object or trinket one could imagine.

He gasped as a pod of floating jellyfish-beings, called Nagogs, drifted past, followed by a clutch of purple gas-cloud beings heading in the opposite direction. One of these passed right over him, leaving behind a strong sulfuric stench that he had to quickly walk away from it smelled that strong.

He paused in order to let a group of winged, green-skinned humanoids fly past. Strange, these were only three cubits tall at the most. He'd never seen these on the Command Center before, He could only shake his head in disbelief as they fluttered on by.

He walked onward while countless delicious scents drew at his jackal snout, like chocolate-covered fish and mongoid ice cream (mongoids were a delicious fruit from the planet Mongo-2). He made a routine stop at his favorite booth which sold Jupiter Space Cow burgers, Jupiter Space Cow jerky, and Jupiter Space Cow milk. Now, these special flying space cows came from a planet far, far away that Jonas had never been to before. He'd heard rumors about it, but only knew that its cows could fly, similar to Monubian flying camels, but were larger and had much shorter necks. Everything about them was delicious, their steaks, their hamburgers, their beef jerky, their milk and cheese, and most amazing was the ice cream. Jonas loved every one of these possible Jupiter Space Cow confections, which were all a high delicacy on the Command Center.

He ordered a double bacon Jupiter Space Cow cheese burger with a vanilla milkshake, before maneuvering the crowd once more. Still feeling excited, he entered his apartment and enjoyed his Jupiter Space Cow burger and milkshake. He then packed in a flurry of energy, while trying to remember everything he'd need for a three-month-long mission.

At the top of his list were extra sandals and enough squeaky toys and bones to last the whole trip. Just in case Shastra squeaky toys were too hard to find. Then he tidied up his apartment and made a hologram call to his friends Zarry and Digger and gave them the good news. Next he called his neighbors, the short, gray aliens Tom and Tim, as well his Agent School advisors, the Shastras Drox and Joonai.

Tim and Tom both instantly praised his hard work and dedication as keys to him getting selected for such a special mission. Zarry and Digger were also overjoyed for him, and promised to check in on his cleaning droid, Vanessa, and to feed Ranchy twice a day.

Afterward, he replayed his meeting with Ashtar over and over again in his mind, relishing each word and image the celestial had shown him. He couldn't believe he was taking a mission all the way to the very outskirts of the galaxy. He wanted to tell the whole Command Center about it. Most senior agents would give their own atomic chariot for this type of mission.

Ranchy was sleeping on his lap when Jonas was struck by a sudden realization. The show *The Kung Fu Werewolves of Mars*... Mars was in the same solar system as Earth-1, exactly where Ashtar was sending him. Would he have time to visit Mars and see the set of the show? Or maybe even meet the actors? He'd make sure to ask his contacts, Siegfried and the Lone Ranger, when they met.

Finally, all packed and ready, and just about to close the door behind him, Vanessa beeped for him to stop. She rolled over on her rubber treads, holding out a special pair of glasses that were standard issue for an Intergalactic Agent. These particular glasses detected different types of energy, which made them a very important item.

"Ah, thanks for remembering," he said, shocked that he'd forgotten them. "These will sure come in handy. I'll see you when I get back, 'Nessa. Then I'll finally get you those new batteries and gold plating that we talked about."

"That'll be the day..." she beeped back. "Just be careful, Jonas. Don't get yourself disassembled, alright?" Then she turned and rolled back into his apartment while mumbling to herself, "good luck.... Earth-1? What a crazy place to send someone...."

Jonas just shook his jackal head, laughing at Vanessa, as he hopped onto the closest conveyor belt heading to the Agent Jump Room. It wasn't his first time there, but every time he saw the Agent Jump Room its unique combination of sights, sounds, and smells never ceased to amaze him.

The Jump Room was filled with countless beeping and flashing electronics, covering virtually every wall, panel, and station from floor-to-ceiling. Shastras and short gray aliens with large heads and eyes, called Zetas, all busily carried equipment around the room, or studied its numerous view screens and control panels. In a far corner Shastra and wolfman soldiers were materializing and dematerializing from a particular spot. Jonas reasoned they were beaming onto or returning from space ships which orbited the space station.

Jonas wandered about, studying the fascinating scene, until a Shastra guard stopped him, saluted, and asked for his records folder. Jonas handed it over and the guard delivered it to a Shastra with a red jackal-haired head and glasses who wore a brown form-fitting suit. This was Jonas's good friend, the tech specialist named Zeeg.

"Hey, Jonas, this is your first mission to such a far away solar system, right?" Zeeg asked.

"Yep, just got the briefing today."

"Hmm, Earth-1, eh?" Zeeg said, glancing down at Jonas's file. "It'll be a quick Stargate jump. Here, a guard will get you a uniform and I'll get your other gear," said Zeeg. He then walked off while perusing Jonas's file.

Then a second Shastra guard marched over, saluted Jonas, and directed him to a conveyor belt that ran behind a barrier that measured chest high. This conveyor system sported many dials, lights, and hovering robots, all of which Jonas eyed suspiciously.

"Sir, please remove your uniform and step into our cleansing conveyor. You must be prepped for Stargate travel. Don't worry, sir. It's a very simple process."

"Alright..." Jonas said reluctantly. He'd never traveled by Stargate before, only on star cruisers and never faster than warp speed factor 3. He cautiously eyed the scientists, robots, and computer screens around the room. Then, resigned to his fate, he stripped down to his special agent underwear and stepped onto the conveyor belt.

Instantly, the conveyor belt lurched forward. And almost immediately, a floating robot covered him with a sticky substance, before rinsing him off with a high-powered hose while Jonas covered his jackal eyes. Then next he heard and felt warm lights and tones blinking and playing while shining down from above and on either side.

"Just relax, Jonas. This is a necessary precaution," he heard Zeeg say over a loud speaker.

"Alright, I'm okay so far," Jonas replied.

He opened his jackal eyes again, right as a flying droid began to dry him off with a high-powered blower. Then another droid hovered over and thoroughly poked and prodded him with long calipers. It peered in his eyes and then shone a light in his pointed jackal ears. After that it drew a small vile of blood from his arm and then flew off.

A third medical droid poked at his belly, studying his liver transplant scars (he'd been shot through the liver with a laser bolt during a training mission) and then where he'd had his left arm reattached. His arm had been cut off in a fencing duel back on Monubia.

The droid checked the feeling and strength in his left arm, and then in his hand and fingers with a sharp pin on the end of an articulating arm. Next, it checked his teeth and then astral-ray scanned his abdomen, chest, neck, and head. Finished, a green light flashed on its round diode face, giving him two thumbs up with its calipers. "A-Okay, Jonas," beeped the medical droid.

The experience had gone over without a hitch, causing Jonas to sigh with relief. He knew he would pass, but you also never knew what a medical droid would find with enough poking and prodding.

"Looks good, buddy," said Zeeg, monitoring his progress from a nearby station. "No diseases, tumors, infections, fleas, ticks, worms, radiation, or any other problems. we'll give you a healing shower just to make sure, though. Hold on."

The medical droids flew away just as the conveyor belt carried him through a rainbow of healing light. Jonas immediately felt like he was floating in an ocean of peace. He felt such transcendent bliss that he swore he was one with the universe and never wanted to leave. But then suddenly, after only five minutes, it ended, which was way too soon, he thought.

When the conveyor belt finally stopped he stepped off it and then received a strange pile of brown sheets, which a Shastra guard shoved right into his arms.

"What's this?" he asked, looking at the guard curiously.

"Shastra farmers wear these on Earth-1. It's your official identity, sir," the guard said.

"Alright, thank you," he said and bowed back. He unwrapped this mess of sheets to reveal a loincloth and a tunic, both of which were very different from his Agent uniform. However, both the loincloth and tunic proved surprisingly comfortable when properly fitted and tied, which required the guard's help. And as an added bonus, his Intergalactic Agent badge, along with a hologram picture of his grandfather, Paw-Paw Neferis, fit neatly into a fold inside the tunic.

Zeeg returned and walked him over to a station where a tray hovered in mid air, carrying an array of gadgets. "Okay, you're changing firearms for this mission. Here's the new standard issue Samson-5 laser pistol. This baby's got a crystal-based power source, over five settings, and is fully water-proof. And it will never jam on you, unlike your last piece did. You almost failed that training session on Ergo Minor and spent two weeks in the medical ward because of it."

"Yeah, but I finished the course, didn't I?" he replied.

"Yes, but...." said Zeeg, staring down over his glasses.

Jonas picked the pistol off the tray and turned it over in his hands. He felt the trigger and weighed it, before studying its many buttons and dials. It was silver and black, a little longer than usual, and lighter than his older model. "Feels great," he said, "very light."

"Yep. It's also got more power than your last model. It can stop a rampaging dino-lizard with one well-placed shot to the heart. But remember, that's only a smaller dino-lizard," said Zeeg.

"Right," said Jonas as he slipped the pistol into the holster on his belt.

"Okay, moving on. Next, there's a new force-field generator and your new comm. link device, which is already hooked into Hermes. It's all loaded with information, plus a hologram map generator that will definitely come in handy." Zeeg pointed out a small black box at the end of the tray that was about the size of a pill bottle.

Fascinated, Jonas picked up the little black device. "It's a lot smaller than usual," he said as he studied it closely, wondering how so much information could fit inside such a small object.

"Yeah, that's the idea. Easier to hide. Runs on crystal cube alpha-storage technology. You'll be able to contact the Ashtar Command from anywhere with that baby. Also, the map function will plot you to anywhere on Earth-1, even to places on other planets in the solar system if you need that."

"That'll definitely come in handy." Jonas magnetically clipped this to his utility belt right next to his laser pistol.

"Oh, and it's loaded with hologram information: detailed files on every city, culture, and being you could encounter on Earth-1. So make sure you study it. And Jonas, try not to lose this one, okay?" Zeeg paused and stared down his spectacles again. "You've lost three already, buddy."

"Those were all accidents. Well, I forgot one on the Arcturian Command Center," Jonas said as Zeeg continued staring, appearing very unimpressed. "Hey, they never returned it. Besides, you never know what'll happen out in the field...."

"Right..." Zeeg said, shaking his jackal head. He pushed his glassed back up his jackal snout and continued. "Anyhoo, moving on. There's a medical and survival kit, in case you get stranded," said Zeeg. He handed Jonas a box the size of a small book.

Jonas attached it neatly to his utility belt along with the other gadgets. He then put his laser pistol and its holster inside his tunic, right next to his Agent badge and against his side.

"So, do I look like a proper Earth Shastra?" he asked.

"I don't know. I've never been there," Zeeg answered. "You look like you're wearing rags, though."

"Hey, thanks...." Jonas said sarcastically. "You guys gave me this stuff, you know."

Zeeg walked over to his station and began to program a long row of blinking controls. Almost immediately, an energy portal appeared against the far wall. It whirled wildly and sparked while it churned within a large metal ring.

"Ashtar definitely knows what he's doing," said Zeeg. "You'll probably fit right in, though. What matters most is that the earthlings believe your disguise."

"Good point," he said. "So, is the portal locked in yet? I'm ready to go."

"Yep, the coordinates are...now set," said Zeeg as he punched the last button. "Now remember, don't panic if you end up on the wrong planet. You have a survival and medical kit. If you do get lost just call me with your comm. link and I'll open another portal. You still haven't passed chariot fighter weapons school yet, have you?" he asked with a smirk, looking back down at his control screen.

"Geeze.... You never forget to remind me about that, do you?" said Jonas. He shook his head and smiled back.

"Well...it would make things easier. I'm just saying," Zeeg said, shrugging. "And you'd have easy transportation."

"I know. Thanks for reminding me," Jonas said curtly. He lifted his duffel bag and cautiously walked up to the portal's shimmering, opal-blue surface before he stopped to study it. He was just close enough now to gently poke and caress the swirling blue liquid doorway. "Hey, how often do you send someone to the wrong place with these portals?"

"Oh, only once every two jumps or so.... It's more art than science, really."

"You're kidding, that much?" he asked, turning back.

Zeeg shook his head. "No, not really," he said, laughing as he punched more buttons.

"Geeze, you really had me there, buddy...."

The portal shook and hummed like a deep drum, its sound filling the entire room. Jonas looked around in shock as the whole jump room was now shaking.

"Alright, you can go ahead! Good luck, buddy!" Zeeg yelled above the growing noise.

Still unsure if Zeeg was joking or actually being serious, but eager to get going, Jonas stepped toward the portal. His jackal snout was now mere fractions of a cubit away from its glowing blue surface. The energy doorway swirled around chaotically, but it had absolutely no smell. He took a deep breath, closed his jackal eyes, and slowly stepped through the door of light.

Jonas was instantly hurled through a glowing white tunnel. Blazing constellations whipped past him as he shot through fields of stars and between colorful nebulae. The tunnel turned and jostled him about, curving through the very fabric of space, and so fast that he couldn't identify anything if he tried. All this happened in just a few seconds before the tunnel flashed and then disappeared.

Dizzy and confused, Jonas found himself lying face-first in the dirt. He groaned and rolled over, looking up as he opened his jackal eyes. And for the first time ever, he glimpsed a bold and blue sky framed by the arcing treetops of Earth-1.

Jonas groaned and pushed himself up. Annoyed by his hard landing, and while busy working the kinks out of his now aching shoulder, he brushed himself off and spoke into his comm. link. "Zeeg, what happened? That was a pretty harsh landing there, buddy." He rubbed his face and then methodically picked the small twigs and bugs out of his jackal hair.

Instantly, a Zeeg's hologram flashed to life. But, Zeeg was all sweaty now, and for some reason smoke billowed up all around him. His left eye twitched behind his glasses, which were now broken and rested askew on his red-haired jackal face. He looked nervously down at his station and then back up at Jonas. "Ummm, sorry, Jonas.... We had a...uh...big malfunction on our end," Zeeg said, his voice shaking with panic.

"Oh, yeah? What happened?" Jonas asked, jumping back in alarm and instantly worried.

"Umm.... My readout says the wormhole spit you out early, but you're on the correct planet. The portal is a total wreck, though." Zeeg flinched and ducked as bursts of sparks and fire exploded nearby.

"Holy jackal whiskers! What did this?" Jonas asked as his heart skipped a beat. He had no idea the Command Center was vulnerable to that. Was the Command Center even safe? Did this mean he couldn't get home?

"Well, it's hard to tell." Zeeg squelched a small fire nearby with foam spray. Then he banged the controls with an atomic hammer until they stopped beeping loudly. "The sensors that still work tell me that a powerful energy force shut down the wormhole. It spit you out early and then it attacked my instrument panel. This is just insane! I can't believe it...." Zeeg threw up his hands in frustration.

"What kind of powerful force? What's going on up there?" Jonas instantly wished that he was back on the Command Center so he could help out.

Zeeg's hologram crackled and broke up before returning. At least Zeeg looked okay.

"I don't know.... The problem is it will take a while to repair the portal. And I can't send you any equipment or weapons until then.

It's a real mess up here, Jonas...." A huge explosion erupted right behind Zeeg and he ducked out of sight to avoid the flying debris.

"Holy schnikeys! Be careful. Zeeg?" But Zeeg's face didn't return. "Zeeg, are you alright?" There was no response. There was another explosion and then the hologram vanished.

Alarmed and deeply worried for his friend as well as the whole station, Jonas just stared at his comm. link, desperately hoping that Zeeg called him back. He told the device to call Zeeg again but nothing happened. So, he sighed and placed the comm. link back on his utility belt, hoping that Zeeg was okay and could somehow repair the portal.

Although feeling restless, he knew there wasn't anything he could do to help Zeeg. He was on Earth-1 for the long haul now. Jonas just thanked the Guardians that he'd landed on the correct planet in one piece.

He blankly stared around for a time, as his current surroundings couldn't be more different from his home world of Monubia. Lush jungle greenery crowded around him on all sides. The nearest plant was a green-stalked dandelion tree, rising fifty cubits in the air. He sniffed about, finding at least a hundred new smells, all of which he'd love to individually investigate and catalog.

Nearly filtering out all sunlight from a high canopy above him, a two-hundred-cubit-tall horsetail tree rose up from the jungle surface to his right. Its trunk was covered with colorful bugs, birds, and lizards, plus long, bright neon-red hairs that blew in the afternoon breeze. His jackal instincts wanted to sniff and bark at everything, but he restrained himself and concentrated on his goal. All Shastras on Monubia received training in concentration since they were pups.

Jonas gathered his duffel bag from where it landed in a colorful patch of creepers, their stalks all winding up another horsetail tree nearby, its trunk covered entirely with giant mushrooms the size of his anti-gravity recliner back in his apartment.

Jonas raised his comm. link device and asked Hermes for a map. He carefully followed the map which appeared, while Hermes thankfully alerted him to any poisonous and violent plants along his path, and all the while he couldn't help but worrying about Zeeg and the others on the Command Center.

The next day he reported for duty at his assigned farm just outside the village of Shetra and was given work right away as a Chocoberry picker and cultivator. His cover story was that of a prospective Garud priest who had just moved to Shetra from Sad Madriss, a large city-state on the far side of the world. His routine every day was simple: four hours of work with two mandatory lunch-breaks, which all Shastras required, being always hungry.

The first shock he faced was just how different life in Shetra was compared to the Command Center. For starters, the Shetran days of the week were different, having names instead of symbols like on Monubia or colored shapes like back on the Command Center. The Shetran days went like this; Moonsday, Twosday, Weedensday, Thorsday, Friendsday, Saturnsday, and Sunday. It would take time for him to get used to a seven day week instead of his customary ten, with five for work and five for relaxation.

In addition, he found out things that he hadn't learned in Earth studies class, such as that Shetrans measured temperature in degreedoes and not in space units. Even stranger, they measured time in essential tasks to be done throughout the day, instead of with the usual intervals of bleebs or gonards as used on Monubia, or in Federation Time Units like on the Command Center.

Earth money was another oddity. Monubians exchanged the droppings of giant sand worms called Shurds, while the Ashtar Command and the Galactic Federation as a whole used Galactic Credits. Instead of these, Shetrans used coins called Gold Butons. Jonas never did find out where Gold Butons came from. Even more surprising was the fact that no one he talked to had ever heard of Shurds.

After a few days of farm work in the hot sun Jonas met his first contact, a Shastra Elder named Bheem. Bheem was also an agent from the Command Center and had been stationed on Earth-1 for a while.

Together they searched to the south for portals and then headed east, really just checking anywhere it was safe to travel without armed security. But, however much they searched they didn't encounter a single demon or find any portals that led to the Underworld. They did find two small, abandoned campsites outside Shetra. Each of these showed clear signs of recent demon habitation.

Bheem found what he said was rotten demon food, but which just looked like a brown pile of mush to Jonas. It was so disgusting that Jonas plugged his snout and refused to even sniff it.

Jonas was greatly encouraged when they found that both demon camps produced a handful of scrolls and demon style weapons all covered in strange symbols of a demon language that neither of them could read. At the second site they discovered a hidden catch of ion bombs that Jonas thankfully was able to disable without incident.

Further wandering led them to a trail of clawed footprints, and following these, plus Jonas's powerful sniffer, managed to uncover a chariot wreck near the second camp. In the bushes, all burnt by laser blasts no doubt, Jonas found an atomic chariot certification license that belonged to a Navan known to be part of Talley's team of special agents. It was a lead, but not the clear proof that he needed.

Other than that, they didn't find any more evidence as to Talley's previous activity or his current whereabouts. But laser blast marks all over the ground and the trees nearby made Jonas suspicious. There was no way to prove the wrecked chariot belonged to Talley, however. And if it had, then where were Talley and the rest of his team? Jonas wondered if they were even still alive.

Jonas now had more questions than answers, and he needed much more information before he could report anything to Ashtar. So they decided to ask around Shetra and locate their second contact, the Shastra hermit named Siegfried. Ashtar had guaranteed Jonas that Siegfried would help in their search. And so Jonas was more eager than ever to find this Shastra hermit.

With almost two weeks gone by now, Jonas grew frustrated, still having no good intelligence on any portals, he hadn't seen any demons, and had found exactly zero hints as to what had really happened to Talley.

He now considered renting an atomic chariot and searching the dense jungle on his own for Siegfried and the Lone Ranger. He knew they had to be somewhere nearby. He resisted this urge, but he knew that he had to try something. His mission's success depended on it.

Fresh Evidence

EACH DAY JONAS WORKED along his assigned row, walking between towering Chocoberry plants. Chocoberries were red and juicy berries that tasted sweet and were covered in a crunchy outer shell of chocolate. His fertilized each plant with a fertilizer ray gun and then placed the berries in the harvester that hovered along the dirt path behind him.

He usually encountered lots of dirt crabs, small flying worms, and fire lizards along his row but they were never really bothered him. He also met Terry, a praying mantis-being, whose huge bug head and beady eyes really creeped him out. He liked Terry alright, but Jonas couldn't shake his sense of shock at Terry's visage, or the suspicion that he was possibly a shape-shifting demon in disguise.

On the fourth day of his third week in Shetra Jonas ate a quick third lunch before he headed to the archery fields for their afternoon practice. When he reached the practice field he found the others already warming up and shooting targets.

He sat down and quickly laced up his archery boots and opened his bow case. He hadn't brought his own bow from the Command Center, so his friend Khafre had lent him a silver

Drammo model-X, which he said was the latest and best Shetran model, but not as good as the Heliopolan brands which were way more expensive.

Soon, his Navan friend, Khafre, arrived and plopped four water bottles down in the grass, along with a case of arrows from Franky's Crazy Archery Emporium (Khafre worked there part time as well as being an atomic chariot mechanic).

Khafre was a Navan, a type of monkey-being that Jonas had rarely seen on Monubia but was very common on Earth-1. Like Shastras, Navans walked and talked like humans, but were much stronger, usually smarter, and about a hundred times harrier than either of the other two. Khafre revealed to Jonas that he once had been a bounty hunter in the Machine City of Hiix, but had escaped somehow, a story which Jonas found to be very amazing and quite dangerous sounding. Only later on did Khafre move to Shetra and start work as a chariot mechanic.

At first, Jonas didn't trust Khafre with his secret identity as an Intergalactic Agent. Only with Bheem's recommendation did Jonas finally tell Khafre about his mission to find Talley and return him to the Command Center.

"Hey…hey… Did you guys find any clues on Talley yet? Any demons, man?" Khafre quietly asked as he sat next to Jonas and laced up his cleats.

"No, not yet, Khafre," whispered Jonas. "Just those two sites we already told you about."

"Maybe you should ask the bear-beings of Hom-Sheket for help or the Danaan eagle-beings to the south," said Khafre. "There are rumors of something big going down, man, and they might know what it is."

"What have you heard?" he asked eagerly.

"Ask Gaza, he's over there, man. It's something to do with his outpost along the border. Something like that," said Khafre.

"I'd like to hear it," said Jonas. He stood and took a few practice draws with his bow and then glanced over at the Shastra named Gaza. Gaza was currently out on the practice field shooting mind-controlled arrows at a jumping kangaroo-shaped target. The target jumped around and avoided Gaza's arrow, but he just concentrated harder and the arrow swooped around for another pass. When his arrow finally struck the target in the eye it exploded into a thousand pieces.

"Please, tell me if you learn anything else, man," said Khafre.

"Sure thing. I will," said Jonas.

"Like, I wanna fight too, man. I'm a good fighter and I know lots of the bounty hunters' secrets. Plus, if demons have been seen nearby, they've already been scoping out Heliopolis," said Khafre. He jumped up and opened a case of arrows. "Our Navan sensibilities make us good mission partners and soldiers, that's for sure, man."

"Like how exactly?" Jonas asked, intrigued, but knowing very little about Navan culture.

"Well, we Navans always set our clocks a day ahead, man, so we're always preparing for tomorrow. That way, when tomorrow comes, we've already prepared for it the day before."

"Oh, that's very interesting," said Jonas. "What a great idea. Navans sound very intelligent and unique, but very different from Shastras. What else do they do differently?"

"Yeah, we are, man. We also have a special calendar."

"Oh, really? How's it different?" asked Jonas.

"Well, Navans love the summertime, so those months are the longest. For example, Augustus has ninety days in it. It makes sense, right man? Having the best weather, it's the longest month by far."

"Oh, wow. That makes perfect sense," said Jonas. "But wait... then how long are the other months?"

"Fall and winter contain the most months, but each one can last a week or sometimes even less, man. Some months in winter are just a day or two long. Decembeer, for example...just one day. So, the fall and winter months go by really fast, man. And on top of that, there's some cool festival going on nearly every other month in the wintertime. So, there's a party every other day or so. It works out really well, man."

"Hmmm, I see. That does sound interesting and also very... unique," said Jonas, half intrigued and half puzzled by the idea of such a strange calendar.

"It could also be that Navans love investigating things that other beings often find crazy or just unbelievable. For example, Mobius, our Guardian, teaches that if you use only dry reasoning all the time it will prevent you from ever believing in something truly interesting. And if you're ever feeling down, a good party will always raise your spirits. Could be that too, man."

"Umm, wow, those are all great ideas, for sure," Jonas added. He didn't expect to learn so much about Navans, but he always appreciated learning about other species and cultures.

"Hey, Jonas, will you still have time to practice with us when you're a Garud priest?" asked Terry the praying mantis-being. Terry lunged over to Jonas with his long, green legs articulating at his massive mantis knees.

Terry believed Jonas's cover story of moving to Heliopolis to join the Garud priesthood, and Jonas had no intention of revealing his true identity. "Yeah, Terry. I think if the Garud monastery doesn't have an archery team then I'll just continue to compete with you guys," he said.

"Oh, that's super duper!" Terry said, punching the air. "You're statistically our best player. And also the most athletic as measured by Shetra's sports medical complex. Without you, we would score forty nine percent less points on each round than we currently do. I did the math myself, by the way. You're one of the best archers in Shetra, according to the metrics...."

"Yeah, thanks, we already knew that, Terry..." interrupted Khafre while he rolled his eyes. "But seriously, Jonas, imagine how terrible we were before you arrived, man. Ooof!"

"Thanks, Terry," said Jonas, laughing to himself. He found Terry's mathematical mind hilarious. But Terry was right, their team was really bad. Actually, they were the worst archers Jonas had ever played with. Since he'd arrived they'd won only two out of six matches they'd entered. It had definitely helped that Jonas was a regular contributor on his Ashtar Command Archery team.

"So, like, when is practice gonna start, man?" asked Khafre. "It's that time, you know? I've got a laser music show to get to after this, man."

"Yeah, but where's Bheem?" asked Jonas.

As an Intergalactic Agent, Bheem's mission to Earth had already lasted five years. He was now an entrenched member of the community, a fully trained energy and medicinal healer, and their archery coach on top of that.

They all glanced over at an atomic chariot that hovered along, stopped, and then opened its canopy, and right on queue out jumped Bheem. His intense, black jackal eyes glared across the field and he wore a blue and white loincloth and tunic that swished with each step. He wore a bandolier fixed across his chest, and he used an old, twisted wooden cane to walk with. Atop his cane there was lashed a shiny blue crystal which he often said had magical properties.

"I hear Bheem created a whole new strategy book for us to learn," said Terry excitedly. "It should only require five and a half practices to achieve average proficiency, given our current rate of assimilation of new information."

Jonas rolled his eyes. "I'm still learning the last one," he said. That gigantic book lay on his bedside table back in the orphanage. "But when you lose three matches in a row your coach get's pretty desperate."

Jonas stood and felt his cleats beneath him while Bheem bounded across the pitch towards them. Jonas was glad to see Bheem again, and hoped that he had some new intelligence, or at least a new lead to pursue.

"Greetins, lads! Let's be loosenin those legs and launchin some arrows, shall we? I got me a new remedy for our losin streak. I wrote me a new strategy book!" said Bheem. "I promise ya it's a real banger!" He proudly shook a bound volume that looked thicker than the entire Intergalactic Agent's Manual.

"I'm also learnin tha ten stringed Heliopolan Tanbur. It's pretty complicated but a load a fun." Bheem eagerly set down the guitar-like instrument he carried and opened the playbook just as Khafre launched into a violent coughing fit that lasted for a full minute.

"Wow, you okay?" Jonas asked as he, Bheem, and Terry all stepped back a safe distance.

"Ya alright, laddie?" asked Bheem. "That don't be soundin too good."

"Yeah, man..." said Khafre. He wiped his monkey nose with a yellow handkerchief. "I just got back from my vacation in Kalkas three weeks ago, you know. It was really awesome. Had a blast, man. But then here I am, sick again and getting worse. Just like clockwork, man, every year."

"You were sick before?" asked Terry. "Then why did you go on vacation?"

"Yeah, well, no.... See, I get sick after my vacations. I don't do anything weird, man, just hang out with my uncle, Armando, and we go sailing a bunch. Just really normal stuff, you know? I don't get it, man."

"Khafre, that be five years in a row now ya've gotten sick after returnin, lad," said Bheem. "Nuthin like that be normal, not around here with tha medicine we got. After practice let me take ya back ta my office in tha orphanage. I'll give ya tha Bheem Special, a mighty swell healin remedy. Then ya'll be right as rain, lad."

"What kind of healing remedy, man?" Khafre asked, eyeing Bheem doubtfully and rubbing his puffy, red monkey eyes. Jonas thought he looked like a proper mess.

"A slug juice potion be helpin," said Bheem, rubbing his jackal chin in thought. "Ya could also smear fresh bee pollen on ya chest. Aye, it be helpin them welts." Bheem pointed to the large red splotches that Jonas noticed were nearly covering Khafre's upper chest and neck.

"What does the bee pollen do?" asked Jonas, intrigued.

"Yeah, man?" asked Khafre. He furiously scratched his welts and coughed again, this time so violently that he nearly fainted and Jonas had to prop him up.

"By Garud's beard, lad, ya sound awful..." said Bheem. "My special bee pollen attracts tha bees and they do tha stingin on ya. If tha mixture be right, ya're healed right up. If it be off, oof!

It could hurt ya even more. But we be careful. I ain't a healer for no reason."

"Fine, I'll try anything, man."

"Bheem's told me all about his medical experience," added Jonas. "It's pretty impressive." Jonas was telling the truth. Back on the Command Center Bheem had specialized in field medicine, which included both advanced and primitive remedies.

"How long have you practiced medicine?" asked Terry.

"Ah, around twenty years, laddie, give or take a few," said Bheem. "Now let's get ta practicin, ey?"

They warmed up, ran laps, and then stretched before they took warm-up shots on simple flying disc targets. Then they tried hitting vanishing and splitting eagle-shaped and smaller, bird-shaped targets.

Jonas worked on his concentration to mentally steer his arrows. He had to admit that his mental telepathy skills needed work, while Khafre and Terry were both pretty good already. Back on Monubia and the Command Center Jonas had focused more on Warrior Space Ball than archery. But these practices made him appreciate the ancient sport even more.

Even though Bheem tried to show him how, if Jonas had to mentally steer his arrow for more than two passes, and if the target was exceptionally squirrely, then he usually missed. He didn't understand it. He could usually hit those. His head started hurting from thinking too hard about it.

Then they practiced on cross-shaped targets that hovered up in the air, with a new target extending itself further each time. Jonas was much more comfortable with these. They next used arrows that could split up, their individual parts being mentally steered towards separate targets.

A human named Booble snapped his bow in two when he lost a challenge match he was having with Khafre, trying to destroy a mechanical gorilla target. Khafre hollered and yelled in victory. Then he coughed for ten bleebs straight and was forced to take a break.

Booble lowered his head amidst the screams of surprise from his teammates. He sat next to Bheem, who gave the depressed human a private pep talk to cheer him up, and then together they studied the new skills and strategy book.

Jonas kind of felt bad for Booble, so he walked over, sat down, and patted Booble on the shoulder. "Hey, don't worry about it, buddy. You're getting better. This is only your first year, right?" said Jonas.

"No, it's my seventh..." said Booble. "But, whatever.... I bet you knew that, didn't you?" Booble said as he rubbed his head, which he'd hit on the ground after he'd fell when his bow broke and sprung back, hitting him in the face. "Hey, how'd you learn archery anyway? It's not one of the mains sports in Sad Madriss!"

"What is the main sport of Sad Madriss, man?" asked Khafre.

"Really? Yes, please, tell us what recreation they practice in the highest frequency," asked Terry.

"Jonas is probably a spy or something. Eh? Eh? You're not even from Earth-1 are you, Jonas?"

Jonas didn't know why Booble was growing so angry. It didn't make sense.

"You aren't from Earth-1, Jonas?" asked Terry.

"Terry, of course he be, laddie! Don be ridiculous!" said Bheem, glaring up at the giant praying mantis.

"He said he was from Sad Madriss," Terry said, looking confused. "I, for one, believe him. Why don't you believe him, Booble?"

"You shut up, Terry!" yelled Booble.

"My goodness, manners!" Terry replied, stepping back in shock.

Jonas's heart skipped a beat while he quickly thought of what to say. He had to play it cool as he still didn't want Booble to know his true identity. But his cover story wasn't totally air-tight, either, and Jonas really had no idea what sports they played in Sad Madriss. Most likely it was Stamel Jousting (Stamels were giant camels over thirty cubits high) or sand dune lizard racing, but that was just a guess. Sand worm wrestling was another option.

"You're probably a secret agent from some Intergalactic Command Center, right? No one just moves from Sad Madriss to Shetra to become a priest...." Booble's brown eyes widened and a nasty smirk crept across his dark human face, making him look almost demonic.

Jonas didn't panic. He'd taken two three hundred level courses on diplomatic deception and disguise, so he was fully prepared. "Booble, that's just ridiculous," said Jonas. "I've got my Sad Madriss nomad I.D. card right here." Jonas pulled it out and everyone squinted at the photo. It was a fake of course, but it looked completely real. Zeeg had given it to him before he'd left for Earth-1.

"Where are your laser pistol and your agent badge? I know they're on you," Booble said, his face scrunched up angrily.

"I believe him...he said he was from Sad Madriss. You are, aren't you, Jonas?" asked Terry.

Nobody spoke. Jonas could feel both Bheem and Khafre closely watching him. He could also feel Booble growing angrier. He had to put a stop to this right then and there.

The truth was that Jonas had both those items with him, neatly tucked into a secret compartment in his archery gear bag. If he needed to, he could remove and charge his laser pistol in under three seconds.

"That's quite a story, Booble," said Jonas calmly. "But, I don't know what you're talking about. Why don't you drop it and we can get back to practice. We need it too. We've lost three matches in a row now." He met Booble's iron gaze while he took a long swig of water.

"Whatever, you're a liar, Jonas," Booble said, and then he stomped away, huffing with rage.

"Are you a liar, Jonas? I really hope you aren't," said Terry.

"He's not, lad. Forget about it," added Bheem.

"No, I'm not, Terry," he said. But now Jonas felt like there was something dark that was troubling Booble. He'd never acted like this before, and he'd been humiliated dozens of times in practice (Booble really wasn't very good). Jonas would make sure to keep an eye on him. Jonas also hoped that none of his other teammates had ever actually visited Sad Madriss. He really needed to finish reading his mission's official cover-story saved onto his comm. link device.

"Jonas, how did you learn archery, bro?" Terry asked, his bug eyes widening with intensity.

"We used to practice a lot back home," said Jonas. That was true. Archery practice was mandatory in agent training, but Jonas would much rather play Warrior Space Ball. That's why he was only passable at archery.

They took an official break to drink protein juice and munch on fried rat meat and lizard fat snacks. When Booble and the others went to the far side of the pitch, Gaza walked over to where Jonas, Khafre, and Bheem all stood. A Heliopolan border guard,

Gaza was a green jackal-headed Shastra whose entire right ear was missing.

"Hey, Jonas, Bheem. I've heard more rumors of demons spotted near a guard outpost where I work along the border," said Gaza.

"Really? That's great news," replied Jonas. "Can you tell us more?"

"Yeah, dude, there's been tons of bandits and bounty hunters spotted near there. We see 'em about once a day now."

"Really..." exclaimed Jonas. "That's fascinating."

"Yup, and no one knows what they're doing either," said Gaza. "It's super strange. And I heard for a fact that Talley and his team were investigating them before he disappeared."

"I thought there was nothing out there but wild dino-lizards," Jonas said between bites of rat meat. "It doesn't make sense. It's a dangerous no man's land out there." Jonas was sure that he'd find any demons nearer to Shetra, or the capital of the kingdom, Heliopolis, but not as far out as the border.

"We've seen 'em, dude...demons. I tell ya. I saw them walking along our fences last night, testing them for weak points. I swear on the Guardians, dude..." said Gaza. He crossed his arms and his one pointed jackal ear flapped up and down excitedly. "You gotta believe me, dude."

"What does it mean, man?" Khafre asked between loud sips of banana protein juice. "What do demons want way out there?"

"Probably a way across the border, if they haven't already found one," said Jonas, thinking hard. "Ask around for more information, will you, Gaza?"

"Sure thing. I'll keep my eyes peeled," said Gaza. "I'm on the lookout. You can trust me, my dudes."

"Great. Thanks, Gaza," said Jonas.

Jonas studied Bheem's special Heliopolan bow while they debated what these sightings meant. He was glad to get more information, but unfortunately Gaza didn't have anything more to offer.

"All I know is, man, any bounty hunters better not be from Hiix," said Khafre. He put down his banana protein juice and picked up a special set of ion propelled arrows. "That'd be bad news, man, the worst."

"Why? Hiix is so far away," said Jonas.

"Because, they're the meanest and craziest bounty hunters out there, man," said Khafre. "No one escapes them, man, no one!"

"No one?" asked Jonas. He was well versed in bounty hunter lore and already knew that Hiixians were a rare and terrible breed. But maybe he could learn something from Khafre. "What can you tell me about them? You used to be one, right?"

"Oh, yeah, man. I can tell you everything. I've met Necrat and Tarsus, many times, man," said Khafre.

"There be time for that later," interrupted Bheem. "Jonas, can I have a wee word with ya about yar bow handling skills, lad?"

Jonas nodded and Bheem led him away from the group until no one could hear them. Jonas knew this wasn't about archery. He hoped Bheem had news that complimented what Gaza had already revealed. Besides, the phrase 'a word about your bow handling skills,' was their code for discussing secret information.

"Another Elder I've met knows tha area around Shetra better than anybody. So far he be givin me great intel, lad. He gave me a paper, here. Check it out. This be big, really big. It be from this mornin," said Bheem.

"What paper?" Jonas asked.

Bheem removed a hologram newspaper from his satchel, unfolded it, and slapped the cover. Glowing holograms leapt out from beneath a header that read, *The Heliopolan Sun.*

"What's this?" Jonas asked excitedly. He'd only read the *Jungle Chronicle* hologram newspaper.

He took the paper and read out loud. "Championship of the Solar System: Tournament breakdown and predictions, Entrant Interviews and Bios Inside, hologram pages 2-92. Flying dino-lizard migration status, page 93. New Species of Poison Spitting Plant Found, page 94. Safe Passages through the Jungle to Southern Sea Still Open, page 95. Record Summer Snows on Mt. Nabi, Sledding Open, pages 96-136."

"What's this about an archery championship?" he asked. He'd read about it briefly once, and thought it sounded important. But he realized that he hadn't read much about it because the *Jungle Chronicle* almost exclusively covered politics and finance, not sports and entertainment like *The Heliopolan Sun.* He mostly preferred the *Jungle Chronicle* because it had the best comics section out of the two.

"That be the biggest tournament in the solar system, lad," said Bheem. "It's bein held in Heliopolis this year after a two hundred year absence. Both Bentu and Tanis be competin in this one."

"Are they famous archers?" he asked.

"Tanis be the most dominant athlete in history. He won twenty championships in a row!"

"Championships of Earth-1?"

"Nah, a tha solar system, laddie...." added Bheem.

"Wow. that's impressive," said Jonas. He didn't believe such a thing was possible.

"It is, lad. But Bentu be tha local hero. He be tha son a king Masha, and a Shastra himself. But still, he'll never beat Tanis. No one ever will. He be retirin first."

"Really, that sounds awesome," said Jonas. "When's it happening?"

"It be tha openin event for tha annual Garud Harvest Festival. So, in three days time."

"So, it's a pretty big deal, then?"

"Each year thousands visit Heliopolis for the festival. Even more be comin this year. There be tons a food, a-class shoppin, and nearly endless fun."

"Wonderful. Monubia's got a festival like that. Every nomad on the planet goes." Jonas vaguely remembered the Garud Harvest festival being mentioned by Ashtar during his mission briefing.

"Yes, and I feel that Siegfried be bein there too. If we can meet em there it be savin us time, lad."

"Yeah, the longer this search takes the less chance there is of finding Talley. Bounty hunters work quickly. He may already be a captive in Hiix right now," said Jonas. He thought that if there was a chance of meeting Siegfried then they had to go to the festival. It was their best option.

"Right-o, so check out tha headin on this, laddie," said Bheem as he tapped the largest hologram picture on the front page. In the picture, Bentu, the Shastra prince of Heliopolis, shook hands with his father, king Masha, an old human with a long, dark gray beard. Bentu and Masha both wore their usual royal tunics, royal robes, and golden crowns. It was the opening ceremony of the Garud Harvest Festival which took place the day before.

"Okay, yeah, it's Bentu and Masha, the king. So....?"

"Naahh, that's not really Masha, lad...."

"It's not?" Jonas didn't understand.

"Na, look a wee bit closer," said Bheem as he tapped the picture again. "That bein there be a shape-shiftin demon. His name be Balius. A real nasty sucker, that one is."

"Does he shape shift by mind power or bio-electronic implant?" asked Jonas.

"I don't know, but I be seenin that bugger shape-shift before me very eye. He also got habits that Masha never had before. I knew Masha well, lad. And that ain't him."

"That's incredible. Things are worse than we thought then. I have to tell Ashtar," Jonas said. If true, this meant that demons had an insider in the most powerful position in the kingdom. Jonas felt a rush of fear when he remembered that Talley was actively investigating something big. Maybe this was it. Did that demon have knowledge of Talley's whereabouts? Jonas would bet three hundred Shurds that he did.

"Aye, correct, lad. I've also heard reports of border guards that be seein Talley outside tha kingdom recently. They also be spottin strange portals appearin and disappearin. These might be leadin ta tha Underworld."

"We should investigate. Where was this again?" asked Jonas.

"Near Gaza's outpost. It be a major station for tha Earth Defense League."

"How far away, exactly?"

"Near tha mountains. North, very far from here."

"I say we leave immediately. That's our best lead so far."

"Deal, lad. If we be leavin tomorrow, we be makin it back in time for tha archery contest. And then we be contactin tha bear-beins in Hom-Sheket and Danaan eagles ta tha south ta find out what they be knowin."

"Agreed. And we can ask them about locating Siegfried and the Lone Ranger. I want to find them both as soon as possible," added Jonas.

"I'll try an contact Siegfried telepathically ta meet us in Heliopolis at tha festival."

"Excellent! What are the chances he'll show up?" Jonas prayed that Bheem was right.

"No way ta know, lad. I only hope he be on Talley's trail like us. Pray that he be knowin somethin that can help. Talley was tha best agent that I ever be knowin. He puts Phaistos tha Great ta shame, lad."

"Really? That's amazing." Jonas had never heard of anyone even coming close to Phaistos in skills or knowledge. That meant they had to find Talley, and soon, if he was ever going to survive.

Jonas rose extra early the next morning, eager to pursue their new lead. He cleaned himself in the river and then donned his gadget-laden utility belt that held his laser pistol, comm. link device, force-field generator, and medical kit. He then left his apartment and met Bheem at the Elder's headquarters in the very center of Shetra.

A magnificent temple, the headquarters was decorated with shining brass stupas that pointed skyward. Mythical figures and statues of the Shastra Guardian, Garud, adorned its gaping entrance, climbing over every column and archway, and along every balcony. This façade formed a visual telling of Shetra's rich history.

"We be usin one a tha Elders' chariots," said Bheem, leading Jonas to the temple's chariot shed. "I drive them babies all tha time. So, ya be havin no problem, lad."

The automatic door slid open and Bheem pointed to a silver chariot. "That one. No one be mindin if we be takin it."

"Alright, I'll drive," said Jonas.

They found a blazing bright laser-fence completely encircling the outpost when they arrived, through which appeared a collection of white plaster domes. Towers rose between the domes, some with serious laser cannons perched on their summits. Jonas drove right up to a gate in the green electric fence, which automatically opened to allow them through.

They dismounted and Bheem hailed the captain. A gray-uniformed Shastra named Conan greeted them, his red jackal face beaming with joy. After introductions, Conan led them along the compound's green laser fence to a spot where they could speak privately.

"Please, tell us about the portals you've seen, and what you've heard or know about Talley and his team's disappearance. This information is very important to our mission," said Jonas.

"Yes, I can. Where do I begin?" asked Conan.

"Just start at the beginning, proceed to the end, and then stop," said Jonas.

"Okay, right...so we'd heard about Talley fighting off demons and monsters in this area for years now, nothing unusual about that," Conan began. The green laser fence hummed loudly beside them. Conan glanced cautiously around and then continued. "On Thorsday night, four weeks ago, was the last time he went out on patrol."

"What was he looking for?" asked Jonas.

"Well, he'd heard about demon and bounty hunter sightings three leagues to the east. And earlier a small band had attacked a guard post not even five leagues south of here. Those buggers did some serious damage. We think he was looking into that, but he labeled it Top Secret Earth Defense League stuff, so we had no real business reading his reports."

"That probably be near Gaza's outpost. We passed that on tha way here, lad," added Bheem. "Their main compound be just a blackened crater in tha earth."

"Right. So what else do you know?" asked Jonas. "Tell us as much as you can. Like, where was this portal?"

"Well, Talley and his team never reported back to us, and later we found his compound totally empty. A few of our guards did see a portal in the region where Talley and his team were investigating. I searched it out completely but never found the portal. There was just burnt grass, dirt, and some really freaked out animals. We measured the electrical currents it left behind, which were significant."

"So you found nothing? No portal and no Talley?" asked Jonas.

"No, nothing. But a second guard, a private named Lumo, reported seeing a portal near this very station. Said skeleton warriors, like huge titans, were coming out of it. Bounty hunters too."

"What in the heck are skeleton warriors doing on Earth-1?" Jonas asked, scowling as he scratched his jackal chin. "Wait, were they titans or smaller scout soldiers? Titans would be really bad news."

"Who knows? Could be anything," said Conan.

"Why would skeletons and demons be working with bounty hunters?" asked Jonas.

"Don't know. Those groups are said to hate each other," said Conan.

"That's true. May we speak with Lumo?" Jonas asked.

"When he returns from his patrol I'll tell him you're here," said Conan.

"Excellent," said Bheem.

A while later while they were still talking, an orange Shastra head came into view, popping out from behind a nearby dome. The Shastra walked up to Conan, saluted, and bowed.

"Welcome, Lumo. Do you have any news for us?" asked Conan.

"Yes, sir!" said Lumo. Lumo's jackal head looked young and noble like a hardened and well-trained soldier. He had brilliant orange jackal hair that was tinged with yellow spots and all was neatly combed.

"Well, what do you have?" Conan asked.

"Who are these two, sir? Can we trust them?"

"Private, Bheem and Jonas are my guests. Show them the same respect you would show me," said Conan sternly.

"Yes, sir!" said Lumo. "What with all the strange events going on I'm just being cautious, sir."

"I understand, but they are both high-ranking agents from the Ashtar Command Center. Bheem here is an Elder in the village of Shetra."

Lumo bowed reverently and they both bowed back.

"We be interested in any information ya have on Talley and where he and his team be now, lad," Bheem added. "We appreciate anythin ya can give us."

"I understand, sir. I've heard the same rumors as everyone else about Talley's disappearance." Lumo then described all that Conan had already told them.

"Take us there as soon as possible," said Jonas. They then all boarded the chariot and Jonas drove it through the compound's laser fence, setting a course for where the portal was last spotted.

"They said it was right here?" Jonas asked as he waded through a clearing filled with tall grasses that blew in the firm breeze. As he searched he parted the grasses with the long laser rifle Conan had given him. And while he did he actively sniffed about, trying to sort out and catalog all the different smells that he detected. He recognized many different grasses, the rich dirt, the thick mud, and traces of bugs and other small animals.

"Yes, sir. Right over there," said Lumo, nodding his orange and yellow-spotted jackal head. The setting sun reflected off his brown armor and the energy-tipped spear that rested on his shoulder. "Over those burn marks, right there. Demons were marching off that way." He pointed south along a path through the trampled grasses.

"Ya saw demons actually comin out?" Bheem asked excitedly.

"Yes, sir, me and the other guards. A whole troupe of demons too. But we don't know where they went."

Intrigued, Jonas walked further into the clearing. He could see other burn marks around the area, but they were from natural fires. Demons must have made this a temporary camp.

He put on his energy detecting glasses and scanned the field, especially the burn marks that Lumo pointed to. He caught faint traces of particles known to be associated with portals. Maybe the portal was short-lived and had vanished after only day or two.

The glasses' readout screen displayed its assessment in the voice of Hermes, the Command Center's A.I. computer. "Portal, zenon-beta type, wormhole bridge generation. Underworld in origin."

"Is that it?" he asked. Portals from the Underworld came in many types. A zenon-beta type could be simple or very large. Jonas would have to analyze these particles further to know more.

The glasses' screen flickered and then directed him to a shrub twenty cubits to his left where he found a pile of neutron grenades lying near some Hiixian free-energy batteries. This was a clear sign of bounty hunter activity.

"Hiixian quantum foam batteries, neutron grenades, thermal detonator class explosives..." the glasses stated, to which Jonas agreed.

"Not good. Major bounty hunter activity..." he mumbled as he studied the batteries and then turned the grenades over carefully. They were relatively clean and all were completely covered in Hiixian hieroglyphics which he couldn't read. He shoved them into his tunic to keep for later study.

"Conan said they attacked an outpost nearby," said Jonas. "Was Talley with you when you investigated it, Lumo?"

"No, he wasn't with us then. But we all knew he'd been tracking and fighting demons for some time. He told me it was hard to tell which ones were which and when they'd arrived," Lumo added. "He did say he'd almost found their hideout."

"Do ya have any idea where that be at?" asked Bheem.

"Not really. Maybe underground, maybe in the jungle, or the mountains," said Lumo. "He'd been looking everywhere. Talley disappeared soon after that."

"Have you seen anything else suspicious?" asked Jonas.

"Well, yeah...."

"What, lad?" asked Bheem.

"You guys had better take a look."

"Alright, let's go," said Jonas, eager to investigate absolutely everything that he could.

A short chariot drive led them to a sprawling atomic chariot wreck out in a second clearing, and littered with signs of a fire-fight. Jonas disembarked and studied the blast marks on what few small patches of grass and ferns were left. Every tree around that clearing was either cut in half or charred from laser impact.

"This chariot was found wrecked almost a month ago. Most of the rubble has been removed since then," said Lumo.

They walked over twisted sections of space aluminum, some scattered bolts, wiring, and larger, twisted panels of what had to be the chariot's hull. Jonas let his nose wander, picking up the smells of burnt metal, wolfman and Shastra hair, and the strong stench of plasma cannon discharge that made his nostrils flare.

He followed this plasma smell into the nearby bushes. And rummaging among the ferns, he found a Samson-5 laser pistol just like the one he'd been issued. "Talley would have used this. It's recent issue for all Intergalactic Agents," he said, looking up excitedly.

"Then this could very well be tha wreck a Talley's chariot," added Bheem.

"It definitely could be..." said Jonas. He didn't want to proclaim it for sure, but he would make sure to inform Ashtar of what they'd found.

"My, my..." mumbled Lumo.

"Okay, that's enough. Let's get back to the outpost," Jonas said after they'd wandered around the wreckage for a while longer. His glasses' computer had analyzed the space aluminum and other metal scraps and found that they'd originated on the Ashtar Command. With these clues he now worried even more for Talley's safety. The evidence was mounting that it was an agent's atomic chariot.

"Things are much worse than I'd thought," Jonas said to Bheem as they drove back to the outpost. "I detected major bounty hunter activity. Talley could be captured, or worse dead."

"I agree, lad. But don't be a givin up on Talley yet. First, we should be contactin Siegfried."

"I agree, Siegfried will help us locate Talley, for sure," Jonas added. "Hopefully, Talley can hang on. And even if we have to break into Hiix to find him, I'll do it. But we need a plan. I'll draw up the hologram map of the area around Hiix and look for tunnels that might lead in."

"Good idea, lad. It will be hard, but that might be tha only chance," Bheem said as their chariot zoomed between the towering concrete safety barriers. They soon arrived at the outpost where they debriefed with Conan and then enjoyed fresh mango beers, fresh running black mamba jerky, and settled into comfortable hammocks strung between palm trees for a well deserved rest.

But Jonas couldn't sleep. He kept staring up at the sky from his hammock, watching the stars, and wondering if they could even break into Hiix if they needed to. If only they could locate Siegfried and the Lone Ranger, first, then their chances of Talley surviving would still be pretty high.

Jonas knew that if they had to invade Hiix, he'd do it in an instant. But it would take everything that he'd learned during all his training to accomplish.

Tanis vs. Bentu

AFTER ARRIVING BACK IN SHETRA, Jonas and Bheem quickly drew up plans to visit the kingdom's capital, the ancient city of Heliopolis, where they both hoped to meet Siegfried and the Lone Ranger. Jonas reasoned that since shape-shifting demons and skeletons had already infiltrated the city, that those portals outside the guard post weren't the first and wouldn't be the last, not by a long shot.

The next morning Jonas woke early, but it took a great effort. He never had been a morning Shastra, not even under the most perfect circumstances. But Jonas managed to stretch, eat, and then get dressed. Both he and Bheem had decided it would be best to wear their nicest dress tunics to Heliopolis; this included new loincloths and sandals, all trimmed with gold and silk thread. A local seamstress in Shetra had tailored Jonas's to his eight-cubit-tall Shastra frame (including ample, well-placed pockets), and it ended up fitting him perfectly.

Jonas tied his utility belt around his waist and slipped his agent badge, his picture of Paw-Paw Neferis, and his laser pistol into the tunic's conveniently placed pockets (these were by far Jonas's favorite feature).

Bheem and Khafre met him in the town square where they waited for their jungle taxi. Soon a sleek and fancy atomic chariot pulled up to the orphanage gate. It was driven by a Navan with green monkey fur and wearing a yellow body-suit, who said his name was Dungee.

Dungee's route took them along a stretch of newly constructed safety lanes, where their chariot was dwarfed by the high, fortified fences that sported giant, sparking electrodes. However, the very last portion before they reached Heliopolis was still under construction. So, out of all the jungle beasts they could encounter, they unfortunately crossed paths with the most dangerous of all, the dreaded Mega Honey Badger.

The beast exploded out of the jungle brush, startling them and instantly chasing their chariot. Having recently dined, its face was stained with blood. It was marked with a thick white stripe down the back of its all-black, muscle-bound frame. The lumbering beast reached an amazing speed. It soon caught up to their chariot, nearly biting a chunk out of their rear engine compartment.

Laser pistol fire only angered it while Dungee's Peeper Spray cannon just slowed it down for a moment (Jonas swore the Earth ancients called it "pepper spray"). When a second Mega Honey Badger lunged out from the thick jungle, the two beasts fought and scrapped with each other, soon both rolling away into the bush where they thankfully disappeared.

Jonas was still shaking, sweating, and whimpering when Dungee's taxi finally stopped and let them off inside the giant barricades surrounding Heliopolis. He felt greatly relieved to have survived that surprise attack, and his heart was still racing,

Jonas's pointed jackal ears had flopped down feebly and Khafre had nearly turned white with shock.

Bheem was far less affected by their encounter, having lived in Shetra as an undercover Agent for five years now. So Bheem led them along as they crossed a few more protective barriers and checkpoints, finally officially entering the city. Once inside Bheem gave them a grand tour, covering as much of the city's architecture and famous monuments as he could.

Jonas recognized most of these landmarks from Ashtar's briefing. And only after a short while of sightseeing, Jonas's jackal neck had grown stiff from staring up at the nearly endless shining towers, brilliant golden pyramids, intricately carved temples, as well as the many impressive atomic chariots that constantly flew over their heads. They soon merged with a swelling crowd of visitors who were also heading to the archery contest.

Some of the monuments along the golden main road were so tall they blocked out the blazing midday sun. Jonas's jackal eyes teared up at seeing the beautiful, ancient statues that lined that wide and golden lane. Most of these statues depicted the twelve Guardians of Earth, and all were gold plated just like the road, plus, the many shops, towers, and the open-air farmers market that they passed.

The festival crowd kept surging and growing as they went along. And Jonas couldn't help noticing that the beings of Heliopolis wore far more elaborate garments, sandals, hairdos, capes, armor, hats, helmets, and jewelry than any he'd ever seen in Shetra or even in the richest cities on Monubia. Each human, Navan, and Shastra that he saw, not to mention beings from tons of other species, all stood taller and appeared much stronger and healthier (even the young children). Jonas couldn't imagine there being a wealthier kingdom in the solar system, but Bheem assured him there were at least two.

Their sandals eagerly clopped over the golden road while Bheem offered them tidbits of the city's history, such as Heliopolis being founded by the first Shastra to arrive on Earth-1, the first Savior, named Anunakh-Ten, and right after the great earth-changing catastrophes of five thousand years ago. "Ya see those shinin pyramids and towers, lads?" Bheem asked, pointing into the distance.

"Oooh, yeah. They have rays of energy shooting out of them, man," said Khafre.

"And their auras keep changing color," added Jonas. It truly looked amazing, like the horizon was alive with dancing colors and streaks of light.

"That be because they be transmittin different energies across tha kingdom," said Bheem.

"Like what kinds, man?"

"Well, there be many types a energy in Creation," continued Bheem. "Tha first and most useful be free electrical energy ta power and run machines and appliances ta make life easier. A second type be transmittin spiritual vibrations a healin and joy far and wide." Bheem pointed at a row of three towering monoliths that pierced the horizon.

"Heliopolis be holdin a special place in Earth-1's evolution, lads," continued Bheem. "Bein constructed at a point a sacred power and geometry, she be joinin Atlantis, Lemuria, Rome, Jerusalem, and many others as a kingdom ta be remembered by historians a every age. Regularly, tha Guardians and tha Supreme Bein be gracin her with a visit. They come ta teach tha royalty and priesthood how ta serve tha kingdom."

"Wow, man," said Khafre. "That's so cool."

"Amazing," said Jonas, shaking his jackal head. "This city is just incredible." He'd never seen anything like it in all his agent travels to at least three different quadrants of the galaxy.

The surging crowd slowed as they approached a bridge spanning the crystal blue waters of a swiftly flowing river far below. Leaning out over the side rail, Jonas glimpsed its clear, lapping waves, reflecting diamond rays of sunlight. Magnificent, sleek, ocean-faring vessels bobbed along its blue swells, their hulls cutting a steady course through the waves. Nothing like this existed on a desert planet like Monubia, at least not that he'd ever seen.

The surging crowd was funneled towards a set of incredible bronze doors that reached more than ten body-lengths above Jonas's head. These doors were affronted by giant Shastra guards, each standing ten cubits tall (Jonas had never thought that Shastras could grow so tall and muscle-bound).

Even with him squinting and leaning his jackal head back, Jonas could barely spot the hieroglyphics rising halfway up these giant doors. As they approached the gate, Bheem handed their tickets to a Shastra guard, who, bowing low as they passed, motioned them all through and into the concourse of what was the largest coliseum on the planet.

Small gift shops, concession stands, twirling and dancing mascots, as well as a huge collection of different beings surrounded them as they entered the giant concourse.

Khafre and Bheem both left him to find their seats, descending the stairway into the two-million-seat amphitheater, while Jonas walked up to the back of a concessions stand line. He stood there, waiting right behind a giant ant-being, called a Trog.

Jonas's jackal snout went haywire in that new environment. He smelled frothy mango beers, Jupiter Space Cow jerky, and freshly cooked Heliopolan all-everything nachos, among the countless other delicacies. His mouth began to water uncontrollably, and it took every ounce of his willpower not to hungrily lunge at whomever he saw carrying that deliciously cheesy dish anywhere near him.

Jonas finally ordered his food from a gray-scaled lizard-being at the counter, listening politely as it spoke in Standard Intergalactic with a lizard dialect. Jonas politely nodded back, said 'thank you' in Standard Intergalactic, and then payed for and grabbed his order of three Heliopolan all-everything nachos and three mango beers, before walking off towards the coliseum stairs.

"Let's talk a minute, lad. Come on—" Bheem said, coming out of nowhere and startling Jonas so badly that he nearly spilled their mango beers.

"Geeze, be careful, Bheem! Can you not do that?" Jonas asked after he'd rebalanced their tray and staved off a total disaster. "What's up, man?"

"Here, I'll be helpin. We be needin ta talk," said Bheem as he took the mango beers and led Jonas down a flight of stairs and into blazing sunlight.

Jonas gasped in awe at the horseshoe-shaped amphitheater that opened out before them. Its far end was opened and faced the golden royal palace of Heliopolis, all glorious and gleaming in the distance.

They stepped out onto a small rounded platform and Bheem stated their seat numbers. Both he and Jonas held onto a railing as the platform began steadily rising. They flew over the spectators below, while dodging a nearly constant traffic flow of other platforms flying about every which way.

They started in on their messy nachos while platforms whizzed past, and eagle-beings, bat-beings, and all types of other beings on jet packs, all flapped, flitted, or flew by, all busy surveying the crowd below for their own seats.

"Those portals that Lumo and tha other guards saw, they were caused by dark energies bein unleashed upon tha Earth, lad," said Bheem. "I fear it be a coordinated effort by demons ta invade tha planet. This has ta be what Talley was investigatin."

"What kind of dark energies?" Jonas asked. Invasion was a bad sign, and Jonas hoped that it wouldn't materialize. However, dark energies could mean many things, so they'd have to be ready.

Their platform barely missed a collision with a giant eagle-being as it turned at the last second, its wing slapping Jonas hard right across his jackal face (but thankfully not hard enough to make him drop his nachos or anything like that). He kept hold of the railing and shook it off while Bheem yelled at the eagle and they continued on.

"Dark currents probably be comin from tha Underworlds, lad. And some dark bein up ta no good be openin them portals. Through portals spirits, demons, and other powerful influences be comin in. These all be needin ta be found and closed, lad. They bein bad news."

"What else have you found out?" Jonas asked. He casually sipped his mango beer and scanned the coliseum crowd below so as to look natural and not draw any attention to either him or Bheem. "Anything about Talley or the Hiixian bounty hunters?"

Bheem dug into his all-everything nachos while he continued. "Na, nothin unfortunately. But we'll be findin em soon, lad. We will…. Siegfried and the Lone Ranger help us ta flush em out."

"I'm sure they will...." Jonas said hopefully, wondering when they'd meet those two Shastras, mid-crunch on one particularly cheese-laden nacho. "So, anything more on these portals? Or will we just have to explore more?"

"Only that higher order entities be havin tha power ta open such portals. Portal and time travel be very rare abilities, lad. They only be practiced by high-rankin celestials, like tha twelve Guardians," Bheem added.

Jonas nodded, but he already knew this information so he just continued scanning the crowd below. Just then they bumped right into another flying platform. Its occupants, being three very large, very irate Trog beings, spilled their mango beers all over their fancy, silvery-green tunics. Then they all yelled and cursed in their Trog language before flying swiftly away.

"What did they say, lad?" asked Bheem.

"You don't want to know," Jonas answered. Although their flying platform wasn't under his control, Jonas understood Trog psychology and that fighting with them was always a terrible idea because they were so amazingly strong. So he just bowed politely in their direction. "So, do you know of any new portals opening near Heliopolis?" he asked after the Trogs had all flown off.

"Na. But it may not be safe in Shetra anymore, lad. I'll know more after a meetin with Siegfried and tha Lone Ranger. I've heard rumors too that a new Savior bein nearby."

"Wait.... What does a new Savior have to do with Talley? And how did you find all this out?" he asked greatly confused. Their platform now descended in rapid jolts. And each of them tightly grabbed the railing and waited for the ride to smooth out again.

"I be havin other contacts, lad. And I be partially telepathic, remember?" Bheem added after all the jolting had stopped.

"Oh, yeah. That's right," said Jonas. Bheem had mentioned that before, but Jonas thought it was just an ability to guess people's birthdays, because so far that's all he'd seen Bheem do with his ability.

"I be receiving many telepathic messages from Siegfried since we be arrivin in Heliopolis. This city be harnessin and focusin great power a many different types, lad."

"Let me know if you pick up anything else, okay?"

"I will. So far at tha moment tha crowd noise be makin things tough. Telepathy be tricky, lad, especially in crowded places. I do be pickin up some wolf-beins orderin nachos on tha third level a tha coliseum, though."

"Oh, I see…. Well, what else did Siegfried tell you?" Jonas asked, eager for information.

"Na specifics, other than ta meet him and tha Lone Ranger later. We be learnin more about Talley then, lad. His help be crucial when we encounter demons an skeleton soldiers."

"I know," said Jonas. "We'll talk to Siegfried next. Hopefully he's here at the tournament. And then after that I'll contact Ashtar and tell him what we've learned so far."

"Right, lad. That be a good plan."

Their platform kept descending, finally settling into their assigned section right next to Khafre who was already seated and waiting for his all-everything nachos. Jonas and Bheem sat down just as two chairs rose up from the floor. After they landed and handed out the food and drinks, Khafre pointed out the Navan band playing music in the dirt arena below. Jonas recognized them as a famous Navan band called the Smash Brothers.

"I be loving this tune, lad," said Bheem, pointing down at the band. "I be playin it on tha atomic flute, but also be dabblin on tha positronic bongos."

"Oh, yeah? That's impressive," said Jonas. He wasn't very musical, having only taken three years of lessons on the Shastra nomad guitar, which was the absolute minimum his nomad school required. Now he wished that he'd kept with it.

"I be majorin in music as well as medicine and agent studies at tha Command Center," Bheem added.

"What else do you play?" asked Jonas. Wondering how many more types of instruments they offered at a galactic melting pot like the Command Center. There could be hundreds.

"Ah, only two more," said Bheem. "Tha nomad guitar, like tha one they be playin on Monubia, and a three necked free-energy violin. Tha last one be a real toughie, lad."

"I believe it," said Jonas, very impressed by Bheem's musical skill to say the least.

Finally the band below stopped playing and then moved to the side of the arena and behind a protective barrier and at a safe distance from the action.

"Ahhhh, I be waitin over ten years for a chance ta watch this tournament in person, lads," Bheem said as he leaned back, sipping his mango beer. "I would not be missin it even if tha world be endin right now."

Jonas hungrily dug into his all-everything nachos while he eagerly perused a tournament program resting in his lap. The table of contents listed one chapter that detailed the tournament rules (it followed Standard Solar System Archery Rules). Other chapters covered the types of targets they'd be facing and the different bows and arrows each competitor utilized, as well as their social backgrounds and particular school of training. He flipped forward and tried reading a complicated article on ion-energy arrows and how they worked, but the diverse sounds and smells all around him were so distracting that it was impossible to concentrate.

His jackal instincts really didn't stand a chance, as nearly the entire festival was squeezed into the giant stadium. Jonas continued flipping through the program, trying to calmly control himself, but soon began twitching and sweating profusely. He prayed that he could prevent himself from leaping around and barking like mad, and shoving his snout in every other being's business.

Concentrating on his program helped, but it was only when the pair of wolf-beings sitting next to him left to get more nachos that his crazy canine instincts cooled down and he could finally relax. He sighed deeply, at last being able to enjoy his nachos and read his program in peace.

The first article he read was about the tournament's announcer, a famous Ghanda lion-being, named Grover, who came from a region called Andalucia. Jonas finished the article and looked up just in time to glimpse Grover's blazing orange mane blowing in the wind. Grover stood on a hovering platform, high above the arena, preparing to address the coliseum.

"Welcome, archery fans!!" Grover yelled over a free-energy loudspeaker. The crowd's immediate response was to scream so loud that Jonas was forced to plug his ears. As he did so the arena shook beneath him, swaying from side to side. It was complete insanity compared to the more reserved archery crowds back on Monubia.

"Hey, it's gonna start, man!" said Khafre, bobbing up and down in his seat with excitement.

"This be it, lads!" said Bheem, smiling like a five year old Shastra on his birthday while elbowing Jonas and Khafre playfully.

Jonas couldn't help his excitement from building. Bheem's and Khafre's joy was just too infectious, and the stadium's atmosphere was charged with the thick energy of anticipation.

When Grover spoke again the crowd's cheering died away. "Greetings, humans, Shastras, Ghandas, Navans, and beings and creatures of all types. Welcome to Heliopolis! I present to you the challengers, from which will emerge the next champion of our solar system!" yelled Grover as he raised his hands.

The crowd yelled back in absolute pandemonium. Jonas's jackal ears ached so much that he just covered them and waited for the cheering to end. But the noise continued. He found that plugging his pointed jackal ears with torn napkins was the only thing that helped.

Grover introduced the contestants one at a time, while their personal squires followed behind them. Jonas carefully studied every contestant, wondering if Siegfried or the Lone Ranger were down there in disguise. But he was so far away that it was too hard to tell.

First up were two hawk-beings from the land of Nubis, named Archbeak and Speartail, who came marching out into the arena. Next, came three fully human Athenian priestesses. All of them were tall, dark skinned, and extremely beautiful, which his program said was the norm.

Then a black-furred bearman from Hom-Sheket emerged, followed by three Navans from Kalkas (the famous city of Navans), and all three had bright yellow monkey fur. Then there came a group of humans from some place with a name that Jonas couldn't understand or even remember.

The last few competitors were a Yeti named Magma, a short gray alien from Orion named Zeta, a red colored rock-being, a black furred wolfman, and a Danaan eagle-being named Anchises. Anchises made a big impression on Jonas. She ruffled her large green feathers as she walked into the arena all tall and proud while holding a gleaming silver bow under her large wing.

When a black jackal-headed Shastra suddenly strutted into the arena the crowd erupted again, this time reaching a frightening level. Not even shoving napkins from the concessions stand into his jackal ears helped, the noise was that loud. When the noise died down and Jonas could actually see straight, he read in the program that this young, regal looking Shastra was none other than prince Bentu, the archery champion of Heliopolis. He was basically the hero of the entire kingdom.

Bentu smiled proudly and saluted the crowd while he circled the arena. As he did, his bronze armor shone brilliantly while three Shastra squires followed him, busily hauling his bow and energy arrows. Jonas squinted through his energy detecting glasses, but to Jonas's frustration, Hermes failed to identify Bentu or any of his squires as Siegfried or the Lone Ranger in disguise.

Grover directed each archer to their individual spots, all in a line facing the coliseum's horseshoe opening. The squires set all their equipment on the row of benches behind each archer. Everyone was ready to go, but still a lone spot at the very end of the line remained empty.

The crowd grew quiet as Grover's platform rose higher into the air. "Beasts and beings, ladies and gentlemen. May I have your attention, please. It is my honor to announce the Champion of the solar system for twenty years running. He is known to you as the Primordial Primate, the Mountain of Monkey, the

Champion Chimp. I give you the greatest athlete of any sport to ever live, Tanis!"

Jonas jumped in his seat when half the coliseum suddenly erupted in cheers and the other half into venomous boos. While this was happening, the largest door leading into the arena slowly opened. Out lumbered the most gigantic monkey-being Jonas had ever seen. All covered in gray-matted hair, Tanis easily measured three times the size of any other archer present.

Jonas quickly leafed through the program and found Tanis's bio. It said that Navans everywhere revered him almost as a demi-god. Most non-Navans thought he was too brash and arrogant and had dominated Earth-1 sports for way too long. The program then stated that he'd won every single archery and wrestling tournament he'd entered going on twenty years. Jonas was very impressed. Such a dominant athlete was unheard of on Monubia.

Tanis stomped about the arena, thumping his chest, which was as wide as two large boulders, with two thick arms, each easily the width of a tree. He wore a bright blue tunic and loincloth tied about his massive monkey frame, while his whip-like tail twitched about behind him. The sheer sight of it all made Jonas's jackal mouth hang open in shock for five bleebs straight while he tried to make sense of what he was seeing.

Tanis grinned, relishing the cheers. But Jonas swore that he was enjoying the boos even more. Tanis's massive shadow eclipsed his Navan squires as they led four winged horses into the arena behind him, pulling a cart carrying his giant bow. The tournament program stated as a proven fact that this was the largest weapon to be found anywhere on Earth. Jonas believed it. If his jackal eyes weren't lying to him, the bow was at least as long as Tanis was tall, which the program listed was over twelve cubits high.

"Impossible, it can't be that big..." Jonas mumbled in awe.

But his energy detecting glasses confirmed it. "Yes, Jonas, it really is that big."

"Just look a Tanis! He be a friggin giant, lads!" yelled Bheem. "He gotta be tha biggest Navan ever recorded! Maybe he be a hybrid bein, ya know? Part Navan, part Saturnian a somethin?"

"Man, whatever he is, he's the best athlete there's ever been!" said Khafre, clapping and shouting so hard he almost spilled his nachos twice.

"He's...like, a monster or a celestial, or something..." Jonas said, shaking his jackal head.

"Can you ever imagine being as good at archery as Tanis, man?" asked Khafre.

"Nah, absolutely impossible, lad," Bheem replied. "Be no point in even tryin."

Tanis walked over to his assigned spot at the very end of the lineup just as a buzzing and crackling curtain of energy began to slowly rise up until it completely encircled the arena. It reached a considerable height above the crowd and then stopped. The tournament's program told Jonas that this energy curtain was to protect the crowd, as well as the grand palace beyond the river, from any powerful energy arrows that missed their targets.

The tournament officially started with a hawk-being, named Archbeak, who faced the first target which was a flying mechanical eagle. The eagle flew around the arena before it split into three separate targets, and when Archbeak fired her arrow, she mentally split it into three pieces. Then each separate arrow piece blasted its intended target to bits.

Jonas sipped his mango beer and clapped along with the crowd, keenly enjoying this display, as the other archers all soon followed suit. During slower moments in the action he glimpsed around for any sign of skeletons or demons disguised in the crowd, or for Siegfried and the Lone Ranger. He kept his program close though, to review the occasional foul, or a judge's ruling, or an archer's disqualification which he had to look up.

Among the entire field, only the small gray alien from Orion missed the first target. Jonas understood that the gray being was very upset, also being a fierce competitor himself. So it wasn't a surprise when the gray alien snapped its metal bow in half and then was led out of the arena by four, very royal looking Shastra guards to the sound of polite applause.

Jonas marveled at how the following rounds became an intense three-way competition between Tanis, Bentu, and Archbeak, with no other archers even coming close to matching their skill level. During one memorable stretch Tanis blasted apart a bouncing and disappearing mechanical kangaroo target.

This was followed by Bentu and Archbeak executing the same shot with the exact same precision. Unfortunately, the next three competitors all missed, their arrows careening off the dirt arena and exploding against the energy curtain. This happened so loudly that Jonas spilled some of his mango beer while the whole crowd shouted out in alarm.

Jonas kept his energy detecting glasses on during halftime. He told Hermes to zoom in on the king's luxury box, stationed off to their left and under a shaded canopy. He thought it was strange that none of the four princesses were present in the luxury box, and neither were the human queen, nor the Shastra king, Masha. This was the most highly-anticipated event in over two hundred earth years. Their absence didn't make any sense, and Jonas was confused by what it could mean.

Throughout short breaks in the tournament Jonas kept glancing over the crowd, searching for Siegfried and the Lone Ranger. But no matter how much he looked, Hermes, the supercomputer running his energy detecting glasses, kept telling him to his disappointment, that neither of them were present.

Throughout the tournament, the three favorites, Bentu, Archbeak, and Tanis, continued their domination while the field continued to dwindle. Archbeak finally missed when a spinning disc target shot out lightning bolts that knocked her expertly aimed arrow right out of the air. That now left only Tanis and Bentu.

As was the custom, both Bentu and Tanis took a short break to rest and prepare for the final round. Down below, the Smash Brothers played a few festive tunes while the groundskeepers assembled the final target.

Jonas leaned forward, eager for a better look, but the target remained hidden by a giant curtain as they set it up. He wondered if Bentu actually stood a chance of winning. He was pulling for Bentu, of course, as was about eighty percent of the coliseum by now. But Tanis was still the clear favorite. And from what Jonas had seen, every one of Tanis's shots had obliterated its target flawlessly. He was just too good.

"Ladies, gentlemen, and respected creatures from across the solar system!" Grover yelled out as the groundskeepers unveiled the final target. His voice echoed throughout the coliseum and by now all of Jonas's brain cells were vibrating with excitement.

"We are now all set for the final round of the tournament. As anticipated, only the most decorated and skilled contestants, Bentu and Tanis, have survived. Both of our champions have mastered targets of the highest difficulty, created by the most skilled engineers in all of Heliopolis. And each one has withstood the best competition that our solar system has to offer.

"And now, each of our archers will face something never before attempted in the history of archery. First, they must thread an arrow through seven floating rings. Once completed, then this same, single arrow must break apart a slab of Corconite. Now, ladies and gentlemen, you all know that Corconite is the strongest stone in this quadrant of the galaxy." Grover paused as a wave of amazement rippled through the crowd. Jonas thought the target looked impossible. The golden rings were floating up and down totally at random, and he knew quite well that Corconite was unbreakable.

"It can't be done!" "This is insane!" "Bentu's finished!" the crowd protested. Jonas tried to think what would happen if they both failed.

Grover continued. "After each contestant has attempted the target our judges will decide on a champion. Archers, since Bentu is the native prince of Heliopolis, he enjoys home field advantage and the honor of going last. That means Tanis must go first. Please, Tanis, you may shoot when ready. For you archers about to make history, we salute you!" Grover and the judges bowed to the two final archers.

Tanis scowled as he stepped forward and returned Grover's bow. The crowd continued raining down cheers and boos even as Tanis raised his giant bow, held it steady, and eyed the seven golden rings, all floating up and down at random. Jonas, Bheem, and Khafre all held their breath as they watched. Jonas crumpled up the program in his hand and his whole body tensed up.

The following sequence of events easily ranked as the most exhilarating end to any sporting event Jonas had ever seen in person. Almost in slow motion, Tanis's third eye located right in the middle of his forehead opened wide, shining with bright rays of light. Jonas watched, amazed, as it then blinked and swirled vibrantly, resembling a brilliant green diamond, while a beautiful ray of green energy enveloped his arrow whole. Tanis then pulled back the bowstring and aimed, while closing one eye.

Jonas quickly flicked through the tournament program until he found the official rules section. He then read the rule regarding the use of mystical powers. It stated that some were allowed, and weren't a reason to penalize or disqualify an archer, that is unless they attacked another contestant or one of the judges. The only mystical power that it stated would cause a disqualification was in calling forth and accepting the help of rogue spirits, demi-gods, or celestials.

Jonas put the program back down right as Tanis unleashed his arrow. The entire crowd gasped. Jonas's heart raced and leapt up into his jackal throat and stayed there.

Like a blazing streak of green lightning, Tanis's arrow perfectly threaded through each of the floating golden rings. Once finished, the flaming green arrow neatly cleaved the dark Corconite block into two equal halves.

Half the coliseum cheered in ecstasy while the other half booed, hissed, and threw garbage towards the arena below. Jonas sighed and groaned as Tanis threw his giant hands into the air, taunted the crowd and egged them on, as he was obviously enjoying it.

Jonas watched, as thankfully, the protective energy curtain vaporized every cup, every half-eaten sausage, every food-stained plate, and every cheese-covered nacho before it entered the arena below and could bury Tanis in garbage. Entire sections of the crowd, irate and dejected now, all rose and made their way for the exits.

"Well, that be it. It be over, lads..." Bheem said, sighing heavily. "No way anyone ever be matchin that shot. Not even Bentu...."

"Tanis is just the best. There's no doubt about it, man," Khafre said, grinning proudly.

"I didn't think that was possible," Jonas said, his eyes wide with surprise as he shook his jackal head. "That target was insane."

"Bentu did the best anyone could hope ta do, lad," said Bheem. "Just makin it ta a final round against Tanis, that be a great feat by itself."

While the groundskeepers replaced the broken Corconite block, Tanis continued to march around the arena, glaring up at the crowd while pounding his chest. Only after Grover gave Tanis a firm command did he finally stop and sit down.

"Prince Bentu of Heliopolis, you may now try your hand at the target.... Good luck, son—" Grover said, forcing a weak smile while his platform hovered out of range.

Jonas continued to watch but didn't want to accept that it was over. The spectators that remained all paused as Bentu approached the target line.

Bentu calmly placed an arrow in his bow and pulled back the string. While he took aim his black jackal head and dark piercing eyes looked completely still with concentration. He held the arrow steady and one of his pointed jackal ears nervously twitched. Then he breathed out and released his bowstring.

Jonas scrunched up his program once again right when he saw Bentu's arrow begin to maneuver the floating golden rings. Jonas then gripped Bheem's shoulder hard and squeezed, right as Bentu's arrow threaded the final ring. His blazing arrow next struck the slab of Corconite, completely obliterating the block and creating a cloud of black dust. When the cloud finally cleared, only a mound of fine dust and small pebbles remained.

Not a single being present uttered peep, a squeak, or even a word during a period of total silence. But then an even stranger thing happened. Jonas watched as Bentu's arrow continued flying, heading straight out through the main coliseum gate. And before the judges could react, the arrow had flown back up and over the high coliseum walls, over the protective barrier, and back into Bentu's waiting quiver.

Bentu slowly turned and bowed to the judges and then to Grover.

Tense silence electrified the entire coliseum crowd. Then all at once every pair of lungs (or whatever a being used for lungs) exploded in cheers, praise, yelps of joy and disbelief, or just gasped through sheer excitement.

Waves of thunderous yells and shrieks vibrated through Jonas's very bones. His jackal head felt like it might explode any second from the deafening crowd noise. Excited hands clutched their neighbors and nervous lips trembled as Grover's platform flew lower and met with the judges.

During this commotion Jonas took his chance and scanned the king's luxury box again. Masha was present this time, but he was acting very peculiar. The king twitched and talked to himself, and wasn't even looking down at the arena. Something was definitely wrong, so Jonas looked closer.

Jonas adjusted his energy detecting glasses until he could see the king's astral energy form. Where most usually bright, healthy, divine light should be circulating, Jonas was shocked to see twisted knots that were blocking and diminishing the normal energy flow.

Then Jonas spotted his archery teammates, the human guard, Booble, and Terry, the praying mantis. They stood beside Masha, dressed like royal guards, with bronze armor, great helms, round shields, long, red flapping capes, and bronze swords, just like the job required. But something startled Jonas and made him do a quick double-take.

Where Booble's and Terry's respective human and mantis sandaled feet should normally be, there were instead long, black, and hairy demon feet, with toes sporting sharp and curled claws. It was so strange that Jonas couldn't believe what his jackal eyes were seeing.

With Grover's conference with the judges finished, his hovering platform rose above the arena again to address the crowd. "It is my pleasure to announce the judge's final score…." Grover began.

Jonas was watching Grover, but he was so mired in doubt, he just knew there was no way that Bentu could have won. Turning away from Terry and Booble's strange looking feet, he refused to believe any until he heard it straight from Grover's leonine mouth.

His mind raced wildly. Why did Booble and Terry both have demon feet? He looked again. They were still both black and hairy. They had to be shape-shifters. It was the only explanation.

Grover continued. "Tanis's shot was perfect, superbly executed. The Primordial Primate has earned full marks." Half the crowd groaned while the other half cheered.

"However…. Bentu's shot displayed such transcendent skill, such power, such grace and creativity, that he has earned a double-perfect score." The crowd remained silent, understandably confused by what this meant. No such thing had ever happened before in an official archery tournament, at least that's what the scoring rules said in Jonas's program.

"It is with the greatest honor that I announce something so rare that it hasn't occurred in over twenty years of archery in this solar system: today a new champion will be crowned. Prince Bentu of Heliopolis, congratulations. Please step forward and receive your trophy as champion of the solar system."

Wild cheers exploded above, below, and all around them, and Jonas felt like the coliseum might collapse under his feet. Humans hugged bear-beings who then hugged nearby wolf-beings. Shastras grabbed nearby humans, then crying Danaan eagle-beings, and then kissed any nearby Ghanda lion-beings they could find. Praying mantis-beings yelled out in their clicking bug language and all the spectators still present all jumped up and down with joy, making the coliseum sway back and forth.

Not a dry eye remained as Bentu accepted the winner's Golden Arrow trophy. Then a Shastra judge handed Tanis his gleaming Silver Arrow trophy. Tanis scowled down at the tiny object. With Jonas's glasses set to maximum zoom, the trophy appeared like a metal toothpick resting in Tanis's giant, hairy palm.

Following the trophy ceremony, Bentu led a victory parade from the coliseum and down the city's wide and golden streets. The coliseum crowd spilled outside, following Bentu's golden atomic chariot, as everyone chattered, shouted, and happily laughed together while they marched into the warm jungle night.

Right at that very moment, as Bheem, Jonas, Khafre, and the rest of the crowd were heading down the main street of Heliopolis, Necrat, a wolfman bounty hunter from the infamous Machine City of Hiix, leaned against a nearby banyan tree's trunk, flipping a gold coin end-over-end while he watched them from a safe distance.

Necrat hated festivals like this. He didn't like sports either, or parties, or anything that made other beings so disgustingly happy. He hated anything fun. He enjoyed earning money, fame, and power for number one, that being himself. Everything else he felt was just a giant waste of time.

But here he was, in Heliopolis on a mission for Khapre-Tum, the skeleton god of the Underworld. Right nearby, three of his demon informants were talking in the wide shade of the banyan tree. The first demon was a black-haired beast with dagger-sharp claws and fangs, named Balak. Like Necrat, Balak hid himself beneath a hooded cloak while his eyes searched the festival crowd.

Necrat didn't like Balak one bit, or any demon for that matter. He cursed under his wolfman breath that he'd been forced to cooperate with them. But, this was his most important mission yet, and hand-given to him by Queen Nayhexx of Hiix.

He was already stressed because his Shastra prisoner, Talley, still wouldn't talk. Not even under threat of being dipped in acid, atomized, or fed to a ravenous Mega Honey Badger. How amazingly strange and utterly useless, thought Necrat.

He and Tarsus had met Balak in a gryphon tavern in Heliopolis. One where shady mercenaries and foreign travelers often gathered, the ones you wouldn't give a room to after dark no matter what they offered as payment. Balak was a typical loudmouthed, foul-smelling demon from the Underworld, and definitely no friend of bounty hunters.

But Khapre-Tum's orders had bound Necrat to using Balak's help. They all sought similar prey; the Intergalactic Special Agent, Jonas Neferis, and the Shastra hermit named Siegfried. Necrat was famous for always catching his bounty. That's what made him the best. But he'd always been able to avoid cooperating with demons until now.

Under the banyan's shade, Balak rested a laser rifle on his shoulder while he talked with two other demons. Then he meandered over and interrupted Necrat's coin flip, much to his annoyance. "There, that's Jonas, the youngest male Shastra of the group, with the dark jackal hair. He's the Intergalactic Agent, the one talking with that Navan and that crazy Shastra Elder, Bheem," said Balak. "He's always talking with those two. That lot will lead you right to Siegfried, and that's a fact."

Necrat narrowed his wolfman eyes and snorted. "Alright, Balak...but if that isn't really the Jonas I'm looking for I'll incinerate you where you sleep," Necrat said. He spat on the ground and flipped his coin again, all the while glaring down at Balak.

"Don't you threaten me, Necrat!" Balak growled through long demon fangs.

"That's not a threat. It's the bounty hunter code. That had better be Jonas, and he better lead me to Siegfried, or else...."

"It is Jonas, trust me. We've been listening to their communications. Every Moonsday he talks with someone back on his Command Center," said Balak. "Don't test me further, Necrat." Balak's demon eyes were bugging out now, all huge and ugly. Balak lowered the laser rifle from his shoulder and gently caressed its barrel of silver metal while smiling devilishly.

Necrat wanted to punch Balak right in the face, but he just growled and ignored him. He found Balak to be the least threatening creature that he'd seen in years, and Necrat knew that he could squash him like a bug in a micro cycle. Necrat had won the Bounty Hunter of the Year Award five years in a row for a reason.

He'd wrestled adult dino-lizards, ridden a giant sand worm on his own, and eaten demons bigger than Balak for breakfast. He'd literally killed a demon, skinned it, carved it up, cooked it over a free-energy stove, and then eaten the entire thing with space ketchup. And it proved to be delicious.

"So that's Jonas, eh…" mumbled Necrat. It appeared like his multiple-week-long hunt would soon be over. He flipped his coin, caught it one last time, and shoved it into a pocket under his bandolier of ion grenades.

The two other demons wandered around, mumbling to Balak in their harsh demon tongue which Necrat understood. "Necrat, you had better capture them soon. That is, if you want them alive. No one will survive Khapre-Tum's invasion," Balak added.

"I serve one employer at a time. And I never make deals with demons. That's the bounty hunter code: article five, paragraph two, sentences five through ten," Necrat said harshly. Again, he fought against the urge to punch Balak in the face and instead lit a long cigar and puffed it through clenched fangs. "I work alone, or with my partner, Tarsus Riggs." Necrat stepped out from the shadows. Only the ember-tipped end of his cigar and his wet wolfman snout were visible beneath his hood.

"I'm not in this for ancient grudges, or to start a war, or for some great cosmic purpose," Necrat said. He puffed his cigar and blew smoke rings right in Balak's face.

"Your reward," Necrat said, and he flung a jingling brown bag of coins at Balak's feet. "Fifty Gold Butons. You did your job. Now just stay out of my way." He was glad to finally be rid of Balak and even happier to finally get down to work. Images of endless gold, promotions, and praise by Queen Nayhexx were already floating around in his greedy wolfman brain.

Balak glanced down at the bag of coins and snarled with disgust. "Let's get going," he said to the two other demons. "Khapre-Tum is on his way, Necrat. The invasion starts soon."

Necrat snorted. "When my job's done then I'm out of here," he said.

"Suit yourself," Balak said. He then walked off with the second demon, leaving the bag of coins behind in the grass.

But for some reason, and to Necrat's growing irritation, the third demon remained behind. And for some unbelievable reason, that black, shag carpet looking beast walked right over to Necrat and started to sniff him aggressively all over. Then it picked up the bag of gold coins, and clutching it tightly, inched even closer.

Bad idea, thought Necrat. He patiently waited, remaining outwardly calm and managing not to move a muscle until that smelly, matted-haired demon was close enough.

When the demon's horrid breath was blowing right in his wolfman face with one quick motion Necrat lowered his laser rifle and shot out the bottom of the bag. Gold Butons went cascading all over the grass. Then he aimed the rifle's smoking barrel up against the demon's hairy chin and snarled. The beast trembled with fear.

Necrat flashed his famous smirk. "Go on—get out of here, you filthy hairball, or I'll turn you into barbeque right here," he said laughing. "Go and tell that flea-bitten freak, Balak, to eat ringworms. Go on, git!"

Trembling and stumbling about, the demon quickly gathered as many Gold Butons in its arms as it could carry and ran after Balak, spilling gold coins behind him, until he finally disappeared down a dark alleyway.

Necrat tried puffing his huge cigar while he laughed hysterically, but he couldn't. He just shook his wolfman head in disbelief and shouldered his trusty laser rifle as he continued to laugh and watch the demon's hairy behind disappear into the crowd. Then turning about swiftly, Necrat whipped his long cloak around and darted through the darkened side streets toward his hideout.

Khapre-Tum's Assignment

NECRAT'S PARTNER IN BOUNTY HUNTING, Tarsus Riggs, disengaged his cloaking device just in time to appear out of thin air right beside Necrat in the dark alley.

"Is Jonas here? In Heliopolis?" beeped Tarsus. Loud wheezing escaped his ever-present helmet as the half serpent, half android bounty hunter spoke.

"You got that right, lizard brain. And he's only a Shastra, young, weak, and harmless. We'll capture both him and Siegfried, no problem. You and I will be drinking scion-pulse drinks in an ion whirlpool in three days, I guarantee it," Necrat said.

Tarsus had actually never shown his face, ever, not even to Necrat. All his speech was electronically filtered through that black pilot helmet to form its strange half robotic, half serpent voice. It conveniently also served as his life-support system. Necrat knew this because he'd helped design and build the thing.

Tarsus had once been a proud serpent-being of the Naga race, a feared marauder, and a chariot pirate. He'd been killed by the royal guards of Heliopolis on a mission attacking that capital city. Luckily, bounty hunters from Hiix found his smoldering body, and took him back to their base where they cloned and revived him. He was given advanced android augmentations, making him more machine than serpent-being. He was now a living computer, the perfect weapon to compliment Necrat's ferociousness and cunning.

Necrat puffed his cigar and smiled wide. He felt ecstatic and had never been so sure of capturing a bounty in his life. "Let's get going, Tarsus. Old skull face wants a report and we have to transfer our prisoner," he said, referring to Talley, still chained up in the hold of Necrat's atomic space jet.

They walked on until they reached an abandoned barn on the city's farthest eastern border. The old structure was all boarded up, with planks rotting and hanging crookedly. It contained a collection of ancient and well rusted free-energy equipment inside, all busy gathering cobwebs. They boarded their own space vehicles, punched in their destination's coordinates, and checked their weapons systems one last time, before soaring up and beyond the city's border.

Once they were hovering high above the wild jungle, Tarsus punched a bright red button on his ship's controls that was labeled 'Wormhole Generator.' A sudden and bright blast filled the night sky and Necrat covered his eyes. When he looked again, a swirling portal of light was hovering in the sky a hundred cubits away. Necrat curiously watched as Tarsus's cross-shaped space cruiser slowly inched towards the swirling doorway. When Tarsus reached the wormhole door his starship instantly vanished.

Necrat followed but reluctantly, having little trust in trans-dimension portals. He watched his ship's controls closely and quickly fastened his helmet and seatbelt, preparing for the worst. He grasped the flight stick tight and held his breath as his space jet entered the twirling vortex.

Before he could even blink, Necrat was shooting along down the wormhole, moving faster and faster, drawing close to ultra-insano speed, which was at the very end of the dial. But soon the twisting route smoothed out and he calmed down. He was relieved and happily surprised that this wormhole was working just as he'd hoped. He hadn't been sucked into a random side dimension that he couldn't escape from, so that was a success. So, he let himself relax and lazily munched Hiixian meat cubes while his space jet zoomed onward. Meanwhile, the ancient astral currents steered him through the subtle dimensions beyond time and space, now very far from Earth-1.

Necrat's deep distrust of wormholes stemmed from the countless times over the years that he'd been stopped, sidetracked, and blocked from entering his destination dimension, or in the worst case scenario, one time having his ship reappear inside of a huge glacier. He'd waited inside a whole week for someone to find him and agree to thaw him out. The worst experience of all was the time his space jet proceeded to land in a boiling tar pit on a planet named Platanos. Luckily, his wolfman ears were retrieved intact from that situation, which was enough genetic material for the Hiixian scientists to re-clone and re-animate him for what was the fifth time.

When the wormhole finally spit him out, he was greeted by giant, rolling banks of smoke, hot jets of fire, and streaks of lightning flashing around his ship. Far below, stone giants, warrior skeletons, and hairy beasts all danced along the banks of bubbling rivers of fire. Necrat cracked a wide smile. He loved visiting the Underworld.

"All readings are level. Dimensional travel complete. Wormhole is now closed," beeped Tarsus.

"Okay, let's get going and visit Mr. Bones. We'll be the richest bounty hunters in all of Hiix when this thing is all done and over with," said Necrat.

"Plotting course for Skull Castle," beeped Tarsus.

Then Necrat's space jet and Tarsus cross-shaped cruiser shot off on their familiar course, accelerating through that terrible dimension, its skies all choked with lightning, smoke, and thick, churning clouds of poisoned smog, heading straight for a meeting with the skeleton god of the Underworld.

Necrat's and Tarsus's ship's computers, named Midas and Veer respectively, led them over the wretched wasteland. Necrat could barely comprehend its aethereal, dreamlike existence even though he'd passed over those regions many times. As the wastes passed beneath them, Necrat's anticipation only grew for the appointment awaiting them with that terrible being, Khapre-Tum.

Before long, the high walls of an ancient stone city appeared on the horizon. Beholding this city Necrat held his breath, which he did every time he saw it, it was that unbelievable. "Balkis, the capital city of the Underworld," his ship's computer announced.

"Ah, yes," said Necrat, sighing with satisfaction. He munched Hiixian meat cubes and smiled, watching the streets and buildings of Balkis pass below. These structures and arterials crawled with evil spirits, hairy demons, growling ghouls, skeleton swordsmen, and countless other beasts and goblins. Further onward, the roads of Balkis converged at the foot of a jagged mountain, its flanks rising to a crown that spewed hot magma. Streams of orange flame gushed forth, flowing along steep crags carved into the ancient stone face.

Hewn into that proud mountain was Khapre-Tum's castle, older than Earth itself, and formed into the haunting image of a giant skull. The bounty hunters landed atop its highest tower and disembarked. Three humongous skeleton soldiers greeted them there, their pearly white bones all clad in plates of black armor. The hovering energy chains floated Talley along behind Necrat as they all entered the fortress. The skeleton guards' armor, bones, and weapons all clanged with each giant step they took down the dank hallways that were filled with cobwebs and the distant, tortured yells of prisoners.

Necrat shuddered at having the usual lingering feeling of hundreds of eyes watching his every movement along the castle corridors. "I swear. This castle is alive," he whispered.

"Affirmative, dark energy readings have spiked since our last visit," beeped Tarsus.

A chilling wind blew through the hallway, blowing the cobwebs and rattling picture frames, freezing Necrat to the bone. He thought he heard scratching and clawing noises from behind the old, wooden doors that they passed. He also swore that nervous eyeballs were watching them from behind certain paintings hanging on the walls. Suspended candles cast flickering shadows over their path, their burning purple flames weakly lighting the dank, stone floor.

Finally, the clanging skeleton guards stopped before a towering wooden door that rose five body lengths above Necrat's head. Creaking slowly inward, the door opened into an ancient chamber where there sat the skeleton god, Khapre-Tum.

They slowly approached Khapre-Tum's huge skeleton form on his high throne. Necrat could tell that he was deeply absorbed in evil thoughts. His skull's hollow eyes stared into a large stone fireplace filled with roaring flames. He cradled a golden scepter in one giant bone hand, while the other passed wine to his mouth by a golden chalice. A flowing red mantle fell behind the skeleton's massive frame, with symbols of dark and ancient magic marking every inch of bone that was visible.

With Talley in tow, Necrat and Tarsus stopped before the massive throne, which Necrat made out as in fact being a twisting, bulging mass of skulls, ribs, and the limb bones made from Khapre-Tum's enemies. Necrat gulped, seeing the god's shriveled, prune-like heart enclosed within that massive rib cage. The charcoal black organ pumped rapidly, encased within a humming red aura that Necrat sensed was an evil power keeping it alive.

"So, the bounty hunters of Hiix have returned," Khapre-Tum said, his words echoing through the chamber. "I hope that your dimensional travel went smoothly. We have much business to discuss." As he said this his red eyes flashed bright with power.

Khapre-Tum raised his chalice and the giant fireplace roared higher, its flames nearly reaching the ceiling. Necrat yelped as every shaggy hair on his wolfman body stood on end. He was sweat heavily and fidgeted with his utility belt as he quickly backed away, so as not to catch fire.

Khapre-Tum rose, and his wide, boney feet thundered across the stone floor, sending skeleton rats and skeleton dogs scurrying out of the way. The skeleton god then sat before a giant table, also made entirely of bone. He straightened a pile of scrolls, some stone tablets, a row of quills, and then lastly an inkwell filled with blood he used for writing.

After everything was straight and neat, he leaned down over the bounty hunters. But even though sitting, he still he towered above them both. "So, what's this that you have brought me?" Khapre-Tum asked, leaning closer and smiling greedily.

"Sir, this is our number three target, a Shastra agent named Talley," answered Necrat. "He was fairly easy to capture. Deep brain scans have given us vague information on Siegfried and Jonas, but nothing else. We've been able to locate them, however, and have recently spotted them in the city of Heliopolis."

"So, you've actually seen them?" Khapre-Tum asked hopefully. "You've seen Siegfried in person?"

"Well, actually just Jonas and two of his associates. Siegfried and the Lone Ranger still prove very difficult to locate."

"The prophecy is clear, Necrat. One of them will prove very difficult in my plans to take over Earth-1 and then the solar system. Those three must be taken care of, first. Understand?"

"Yes, we understand, sir. Allow us to return to Hiix and gather all the Vril and Torsion-field weapons that our ships can carry. We will capture those mongrels and deliver them to you, right here in Skull Castle," Necrat growled, clenching his furry fists.

"Be quiet, I'm thinking," said Khapre- Tum, interrupting him with a wave of his bone hand. He took a long swig of wine from his giant goblet, and Necrat wondered where the wine went because he couldn't see a stomach in there anywhere. Then with a flick of his wrist, Khapre-Tum tossed the rest into the blazing fire. The flames jumped high that Necrat and Tarsus both yelped and leapt backward again.

"Sir, we'll catch them, I promise. It won't even be hard, like shooting infant dino-lizards in a cage," said Necrat as he patted down his fur, making sure nothing had caught fire.

But the skeleton god was busy daydreaming, staring into the roaring hearth. "How could Siegfried or an Intergalactic Special Agent even dare to raise a finger against me, an immortal god? What idiocy is this? I, who was given the keys to creation and the power to rule as I wish? And I find it puzzling, for the Supreme Being knows this…. But what are these mortals, but just playthings for the primordial forces which they will never comprehend? Why should I fear them? Me, the master of fear, ever lurking in darkness just behind the veil of their world."

Then with a sudden revelation, Necrat remembered the old Hiixian secret weapon they'd been grooming. They'd put hours, days, and weeks into preparing this stop-gap solution, just in case nothing else worked to catch Siegfried, who up until now had been their highest profile bounty. Necrat had been chasing Siegfried for years with no success. He scowled at remembering some of his more embarrassing failures.

"Sir, we have a secret weapon that is already primed and ready to use. We've been grooming it for years now, it cannot fail." He looked over at Tarsus who quickly nodded back.

"Agreed, calculated odds of success hover around the ninety-ninth percentile," added Tarsus. "The secret weapon is trained, programmed, armed, fully functional, and already out in the field. Only sound activation is necessary."

"So you've planned well, good, good…. Well, I myself love to use a good secret weapon from time to time. It helps keep the game interesting," said Khapre-Tum. Then the skeleton god leered down over Talley and narrowed his skull brow. "Now, bring the prisoner forward! Let me…study him more closely."

Necrat directed the energy chains which floated Talley around the table and before the skeleton god, whose red eyes flashed brighter. Khapre-Tum leaned in even closer.

"What's his name?" Khapre-Tum asked as he sniffed the air.

"Talley, sir."

"And what was his purpose?"

"He's a high ranking Intergalactic Agent from the Ashtar Command Center," Necrat said proudly.

"Excellent…. I promised you a reward, Necrat, and you shall have it." Then Khapre-Tum turned and yelled over at two towering skeleton soldiers, guarding the far door, who quickly disappeared. When the two skeleton guards reappeared they carried two large chests which they plopped down and opened. A small mountain of gold coins and jewels spilled out at Necrat's feet.

Necrat's eyes opened wide and he rubbed his hands together with greed. "Now that's what I'm talking about!" he said, his wolfman mouth drooling while his tongue dangled out the side.

Tarsus's black pilot helmet beeped and hissed with electronic sounds of excitement.

"This one will make an excellent addition to my trophy room," said Khapre-Tum, pointing a long, boney finger at Talley. "I've been looking for just the perfect trophy to add to it for a long time now."

Talley was practically incoherent and unable to answer. His jackal head just bobbed to one side, hanging lazily while his eyes rolled into the back of his jackal head. Necrat knew he wasn't aware of what any of them were saying. The drugs they'd given him kept him barely awake.

"We'll capture Siegfried as well as the agent, Jonas, sir. They will both make a nice addition to your collection," added Necrat.

"Good, do that and I'll give you so much gold that your ships won't be able to carry it," said Khapre-Tum.

The two skeleton guards took Talley away, the energy chains carrying him from the chamber. Necrat didn't want to know what kind of horrible fate awaited a new addition to Khapre-Tum's personal trophy collection. Freezing? Being skinned alive? Mummification maybe?

"I must now make a special visit to the royal palace of Heliopolis," said Khapre-Tum.

"For what? To blow it up?" asked Necrat.

"No, not yet. I must first give Masha and his counselors and generals my terms for their surrender," said Khapre-Tum. "If they refuse, then my demon army will level their kingdom to the ground. No mortal can resist my perfect logic and the cosmic power it wields. They will most likely surrender without a fight. And remember, Necrat, if Jonas and Siegfried can't be captured, make sure to destroy them both. You may still claim a reward if you bring me their remains."

"Now you're speaking my language, bub," growled Necrat, pounding his wolfman fist. "We'll capture them, no problemo. Jonas doesn't stand a chance, sir. I'll personally bring him back to you in a test tube."

"Excellent!" roared Khapre-Tum.

Then Tarsus and Necrat joined the skeleton god in laughing with maniacal pleasure, their combined jeers and shouts all echoing through the dank bowels of Skull Castle. They then closed the chest, which now hovered in the air, and retraced their steps, back through the darkly lit hallways, still howling with winds and tortured wailings, back to their starships.

And once strapped in, they took off, heading straight for another dimensional portal. And all the while Necrat daydreamed about his plan's alternatives, calculating, forming ideas, and reviewing weapons systems in his head and with his ship's computer, contemplating any and every option short of turning the whole Earth into one big, black, orbiting chunk of coal, sadly floating through space.

A Night Escape

BENTU'S VICTORY CAUSED A ROAR of celebration throughout the kingdom, even reaching villages along its farthest southern borders. No one disagreed with the idea of proclaiming it a universal holiday either. Much later, this particular period was voted the most righteous party in the history of the entire kingdom of Heliopolis, which was intimately detailed in a list of the top ten most epic holidays ever in the *Heliopolan Sun* hologram newspaper.

Thankfully, Shetra's stout protective walls, with their electric fences and armed guard-posts, kept out the many dino-lizards, Mega Honey Badgers, and ten-cubit-tall minibats that tried to breaking. It was undoubtedly the loud noises, as well as the constant delicious smell of barbecuing, that attracted their attention. But just in case something unexpected did happen, Jonas made sure that every night he slept with his Samson-5 laser pistol tucked under his pillow.

Everyone agreed that this party was even bigger than the one following when the last Savior, the Ghanda lion-being Omtet, drove the black-scaled dragons of Teela from the Heliopolan walls using only his fists. An entry in Jonas's comm. link device said that event was a really big deal, so their current party was definitely nothing to sneeze at.

But then in hindsight, their trip to Heliopolis to meet Siegfried and the Lone Ranger had proven to be a disappointment. They'd hoped to meet at least one of them and to learn something about Talley, but they accomplished neither aim.

And in desperation, after the archery contest was over, they had tried staking out the largest sphinx bar in Heliopolis. Right as they walked in Jonas could tell the joint was shady. Bheem swore it was rumored to be a favorite place for Siegfried to visit and relax. A waiter even assured them that Siegfried often met friends there to enjoy a pint of mango beer and to play atomic darts.

The only result, sadly, was them getting into a fight with one very salty and monstrous looking, black-winged sphinx, who easily stood at twice their height. Thankfully, Jonas's knowledge of sphinx cooperation helped him diffuse the situation. He felt glad that he'd taken two semesters of sphinx culture studies, earning top marks in his class. Jonas loved studying sphinx culture, even though he'd received a long scar down his back on the final training mission of the course.

When all the celebrating, dining, music, games, and the around-the-clock socializing finally came to a close, Jonas retreated to his apartment and pulled out his Command Center issued comm. link device for the first time in over three days.

He sat on his bed under the orange light of his hovering glow-globes and placed his comm. link device on a bedside table. "Hermes, this is Agent Jonas Neferis. Dial Ashtar, please," he said.

Rays from three glow-globes lit the statue of Garud sitting on his altar, a poster of Heliopolis's champion Warrior Space Ball team, called the Boisterous Bear-Beings, tacked up on his wall, and the wooden rack in the corner holding all his farming equipment, work clothes, and many pairs of sandals.

"Right away, Jonas," Hermes beeped back in reply. Suddenly his room was lit by the hologram of Ashtar's blue human face smiling back and glowing with blue and white light.

"Ah, Jonas, I'm glad to see you. I'm very eager to hear your recent report, son. How are things progressing in Shetra?" asked Ashtar.

"Yes, sir! Just wonderful, sir!" he said as he sat up straighter and saluted. "Sir, we found what we believe to be Talley's Samson-5 laser pistol beside an atomic chariot wreckage. However, we have no proof as to his whereabouts or who is responsible, but demons are the most likely candidate."

"Excellent, that's a good step. Although, there's still much more work to be done. Have you met Siegfried and the Lone Ranger yet?" Ashtar asked.

"No, not yet, sir. We had hoped to encounter them at the archery tournament, but we failed to do so," he said. The image of their fight with the sphinx flashed through his mind and he winced. "However, we have definite proof that king Masha of Heliopolis has been replaced with a shape-shifting demon. So have at least two of his royal guards. In addition, Bheem reports that many dark energy vortexes are currently affecting the kingdom, specifically the capital. Bheem and I have researched a few of these portal sightings along the border. But they were all closed by the time we arrived, sir."

"Amazing, great work, son. Is that all that you've learned?"

Jonas then excitedly relayed to Ashtar every detail about their trip to the guard post, their findings on portal openings, and every trace of demon and bounty hunter activity they'd found on their search.

"Swell job, Jonas! I'm very proud of you, son. Your mission sounds like it is getting on well, even though you still haven't yet encountered Siegfried," said Ashtar, beaming. "Knowing all this, you can take definite steps forward."

"Thank you, sir," Jonas said as he saluted proudly. So far he was very pleased with his report and with Ashtar's feedback. "Sir, what are my orders moving forward?"

"Travel with Bheem to a Ghanda village named Telos. It lies deep within the remote jungles, so be careful. There you will meet both Siegfried and the Lone Ranger. They will help you find Talley."

"If I may ask, sir, why Telos?" he asked. He was shocked by this sudden change of plans and the suggestion of such a far away village. "Telos is a long ways from Heliopolis, and surrounded by dangerous terrain. My hologram files also say that Telos is haunted, sir."

"I received this information from a helpful celestial whom I trust," said Ashtar. "So, you must trust me on this, Jonas. Siegfried has assured me that he knows where Talley is located. And with his help you will be able to close any more unregistered portals and then return with Talley to the Command Center."

"Excellent, sir. I will advise Bheem that we leave at once."

"I have already contacted Bheem. You may find him in the Garud temple right next door. And Jonas, before you go I must warn you..." Ashtar said, pausing cryptically.

"Yes, sir, what is it?" Jonas asked.

"Those dark energies that Bheem mentioned could distort or block all future contact by comm. link. I can't guarantee further communications with you after you've left Shetra. It's possible the Command Center could no longer send you supplies or help if you need it," Ashtar said, his blue human face glaring back severely.

In the back of his jackal mind, ever since he'd arrived Jonas had feared this was a possibility. If things got too hairy the Command

Center was always able to send an agent help or even pull him out by portal if needed. But now that might be impossible.

He wiped his sweaty jackal brow and saluted back stiffly (it was over a hundred degreedos that day). "Sir, I fully accept whatever risks this mission presents." He knew there was no other choice.

"That's good to hear, son. Trust me, we'll do whatever it takes on our end to maintain communication. So make sure to keep that comm. link handy. And never stop trying if you need anything, you hear?"

"Thank you, sir. I won't let you down," he said, saluting again.

"Excellent! Now remember, Jonas, make sure to review all the files in your hologram catalog. You should especially read about Siegfried and the Lone Ranger, to be ready when you do make contact."

"Yes, sir. Thank you. I'll review those files, for sure." Jonas had always meant to review them, but leading up to the archery championship he'd spent most of his time scanning files on archery, Tanis, and the history of Heliopolis.

"Well, that's everything from my end. May the Supreme Being bless your efforts, son."

"Yes, sir. Thank you, sir!" he said.

"Jonas…. Be careful." These were Ashtar's last words before his hologram face flickered and then vanished. Jonas looked around; he was alone in his apartment once again.

He shook as chills of dread ran down his spine. What dangers would they face in a haunted region of jungle? And now he couldn't count on reinforcements. He shook his jackal head, wondering if the entire mission was a mistake. He thought that maybe he'd taken on more than he could handle and began wondering if

Talley was even alive. He had no way of knowing, and doubted that Asthar or Siegfried fully knew either.

So, with this cloud of doubt still haunting him, but also growing eager to finally meet Siegfried and the Lone Ranger, Jonas packed his agent duffel bag with extra sandals, tunics, loincloths, and two straw hats. Then he cleaned his comm. link device, his special edition Samson-5 laser pistol, his astral energy detecting glasses, and his small medical and survival kits before he organized and affixed each one to his utility belt.

He walked across the square and met Bheem and Khafre in the chariot shed of the largest Garud temple in the compound. They picked out a chariot, boarded, and then quickly drove through the temple's rear exit. They were soon flying through the city streets, over two bridges, and towards the border of Shetra.

They drove on through the jungle, flying between the protective chariot lanes with towering concrete walls all covered with warning signs and bright blinking electrodes. When the safety lanes ended their trail traversed thick masses of trees, vines, and wild ferns.

By that time everything was enveloped in darkness. The only light came from the chariot's headlights and the beeping controls shining on Jonas's black-haired jackal face poised in concentration as he drove down the darkened chariot path.

Hours passed and Jonas at last felt confident that no one was following them. So, he put the chariot on autopilot, sat back, and finally was able to relax a bit. He closed his eyes and dozed off to the sound of the night air rushing past his pointed jackal ears.

When Jonas awoke he spent the next few bleebs listening to and sniffing at the passing air (which he felt like he could do for hours). He then removed the comm. link from his utility belt and spoke: "Hermes, please open hologram catalog files on Siegfried and the Lone Ranger."

Khafre was in the back sleeping, curled up like a giant hairball. Meanwhile, Bheem's jackal snout eagerly sniffed the passing air as he stared into the darkness, deep in thought.

Jonas watched as his comm. link blinked, flashing hologram words in the air while Hermes's soft robot voice read them aloud. "My pleasure, Jonas. Siegfried: A mysterious hermit. Species: Shastra. Age: very old, undefined. Origin: unknown, no information available. First recorded appearance: four thousand years ago in the city of Kalanos, the city of sages. Has connections with many past Saviors and Guardians, including Garud. Known to have personally trained the last Savior, the Ghanda Omtet, later killed by Khapre-Tum. Siegfried is constantly pursued by two bounty hunters from the Machine City of Hiix, Necrat and Tarsus Riggs."

The striking image of a white jackal-headed Shastra appeared and rotated in the air. His long jackal ears looked extremely straight and pointy. Meanwhile a long and curly beard (yet quite thin) dangled from beneath his moist jackal snout. Large, peaceful looking jackal eyes stared back, emanating a mysterious inner power. Half frightened, half fascinated, Jonas was instantly drawn to this magnetic being. This Shastra could prove to be a valuable ally on his quest to locate and rescue Talley.

"Interesting.... Anything else you know about him?"

"No, little information is available," Hermes replied.

Hermes continued. "The Lone Ranger: even less is known about this being. Species: Shastra. Age: unknown. Origin: Earth-1, the distant future. Occupation: time traveler, rumored to be a Savior of Earth far in the future."

Jonas watched closely, shocked and fascinated at the same time, as a strange and nearly alien Shastra head appeared before him. Amazingly, half of its brown jackal face was covered with panels of shining silver metal. It formed an impressive array of wires and plates, all interspersed with blinking lights and diodes. But most jarring of all was its electronic eye. Jonas watched as this enormous eye whirred and rotated, before it stopped, and then with a penetrating stare, instantly locked eyes with Jonas. Every hair on his jackal neck shot straight up.

This alien Shastra face looked unlike any he'd ever seen on the Ashtar Command or even Monubia. The hologram catalog stated the Lone Ranger's occupation was time traveler.... Jonas had never studied time travel before, or ever tried it, obviously. Only senior Agents qualified for those courses.

He stared at this strange face for a long time, wondering what caused a being to become partially robotic, and if it ever regretted doing so.

"Hermes, why is part of his face mechanical? What happened to him?" Jonas asked.

"Again, very little is known about the Lone Ranger. There are many theories, however."

"Oh, yeah. Like what?" he asked hopefully.

"Burned by acid while visiting Jupiter. Burned by the acid of a celestial serpent-being. Burned by acid while battling with evil robots on the robot planet, Halcion Prime. Burned by acid when...."

"Okay, okay, I get it. It was probably caused by acid of some kind. Thank you for that information…. That's enough, Hermes," he said as he shook his jackal head and tried to shove those gruesome images from his mind.

"You're welcome, Jonas. Have a good night," said Hermes. Then the floating text and the Lone Ranger's half robotic jackal face promptly vanished.

Well, that sure wasn't much information to go on, thought Jonas. So he really had no information on Siegfried or the Lone Ranger's cultural backgrounds, education, or training, other than time travel. He just hoped that he didn't unintentionally insult either of them when they finally met.

Luckily, Jonas recalled the protocol for Intergalactic Agents when meeting beings of an unknown origin and culture: the agent should stand tall, avoid prolonged eye contact, and speak slowly and clearly. But most importantly, they shouldn't touch them no matter what, not even to shake their hand, appendage, tentacle, or when exchanging gifts.

Glancing up, Jonas realized it had been a while since they'd passed any type of village or settlement. They were now officially in the middle of nowhere. Khafre still lay curled up fast asleep, snoring loudly while his tail flopped about and drool trickled out from the corner of his mouth.

Jonas decided to look on his hologram map to check the directions to Telos again. But just as he raised his comm. link to speak he saw a pair of chariot lights blinking in the darkness up ahead. His stomach tightened and his heart beat faster as these lights grew nearer. He grabbed his laser pistol and flicked off the safety.

"Who do you think that is?" asked Jonas. "Who would drive down an abandoned chariot path at this time of night besides us?"

"Get ready. This not be lookin good, lad. Khafre! Wake up!" Bheem said, glancing back at the sleeping Navan.

But Khafre just snorted, turned in his sleep, and smacked his monkey lips.

Up ahead, the chariot was now on a collision course, heading straight for them. Bheem and Jonas both fired laser rounds over them as a warning. The chariot swerved and passed them by, but then turned sharply around and began to follow them.

An engine blast coming from overhead made Jonas suddenly look up. A second chariot had joined the first. This one flew right out of the darkened sky, and flying in unison now, both chariots launched blazing energy beams in their direction. Jonas and Bheem both ducked. Jonas accelerated their chariot's speed, and before those strangers fired again, he abruptly turned their chariot at a hard angle, leaving the crude path behind completely. They now found themselves bumping and jostling about as they plowed through the dense jungle brush.

"Wake up, Khafre!" Jonas yelled back. Bheem shook Khafre, but he just snored louder, rubbed his nose, and adjusted in his seat.

"Can ya believe him, lad?" asked Bheem.

"Hold on!" Jonas yelled.

Their chariot bounced around as they smashed through a solid wall of vines. This was followed by a thick grove of ferns that slapped them in the face. Jonas swerved and they just avoided crashing into a baobab tree right at the last second. They then entered a thicket filled with large horsetail trees, all sprouting giant mushrooms along their trunks. Next, they dashed between two banyans, just barely scraping through, before Jonas accelerated again. The jungle was now a frenzied blur of dense, green shadows just flying past them.

"Lose 'em, lad!" Bheem yelled. He grabbed a handrail and glanced back to get a clear shot.

"That's gonna be hard. Hold on!" said Jonas, bearing down over the controls.

They accelerated again, but the two chariots kept gaining. The shrubs and trees hadn't slowed them down in the slightest. For the first time Jonas saw the chariot's pilots. Two demons were glaring back at him with freakishly dark, bulging eyes. They fired their energy cannons again, this time mowing down every fern, horsetail tree, and vine, clearing the jungle brush completely. Metallic shrieks and scraping sounds told Jonas that several holes now existed in their chariot's engine compartment. He just hoped they hadn't breached its central power core.

They jumped over a stump and landed awkwardly. This jolt was what finally woke Khafre. "Cheese and banana sandwiches!" he yelled as he shot upward and snorted, rubbing his sleepy monkey eyes. "Whoa! What the heck is going on, man?"

"We're being chased by demons, Khafre! Now get down!" Jonas yelled.

Five fiery laser bolts grazed Bheem's, Khafre's, and Jonas's heads right as they all ducked and hit the floor. The chariot's hull provided cover as the demons' chariot caught up with them. In the intense firefight that followed Jonas hit one demon right in the forehead with a well-aimed shot. This demon immediately collapsed. Then a second demon jumped out and reached for their chariot, it thankfully missed, falling face-first into the dirt.

Jonas swerved, crashing right into the demon's chariot. It then collided with a bulky baobab tree and exploded in a roiling fireball. Jonas, Bheem, and Khafre all ducked to avoid the shockwave and flying hot shrapnel.

Next, a demon leapt out from the second chariot, managing to land right in their cockpit. The beast knocked Jonas onto his back with a massive fist to the face. Then it thrust a harpoon into the floor, striking the point right between Jonas's legs. Jonas looked up, terrified, but also relieved he was okay.

Khafre lunged forward and with the butt of his laser rifle bashed this hairy demon in the face. The demon flinched and yelled, but it quickly recovered. It then punched Khafre so hard that he nearly flew out of their chariot. He would have too if Bheem hadn't grabbed him by the tunic at the last second.

The demon then scratched Bheem in the face and pushed him over. Jonas pulled the harpoon out of the floor, but the demon kicked it right out of his hand. Then it dove and pinned Jonas to the floor with both hands around his jackal neck. Khafre recovered enough to grab the controls and prevent them from flying into a baobab tree.

Jonas wrestled with the demon's arms, one of which held a knife aimed right at his jackal throat. The knife drew closer even as Jonas pushed back as hard as he could. He could just feel its blade moving the hairs on his jackal neck. Then slowly, with all his strength, Jonas moved his pinned arm, the one still gripping his laser pistol, and managed to point it up and in until he felt the barrel touch the demon's stomach. Then with the demon's knife a mere micro cubit from his throat, Jonas pulled the trigger and a loud blast ripped through the cockpit.

Bheem and Khafre both glanced down, their eyes wide in shock. Although Khafre was still busy steering, his face looked whiter than the stripe on a Mega Honey Badger.

Jonas sighed with relief and pushed the croaking demon off him. It rolled away to reveal the smoking blast wound on its stomach.

Jonas stood and nodded at Bheem. He then took the chariot controls from an equally relieved Khafre. Just across the gap between their chariots a demon lifted something freakishly large onto its shoulder. It was an energy cannon, and Jonas knew it could scatter their electrons over the jungle floor with a single blast.

Bheem and Khafre aimed and fired their pistols. The demon ducked just as its laser cannon released a round, hollowing out a crater in the dirt.

"Haha! He missed, lad!" Bheem yelled, pumping his fist.

But Jonas knew better, so he quickly peered over the side. An entire chunk was carved out of the chariot's hull. Their chariot now lurched about and swerved uncontrollably. Jonas managed to regain partial control, but he knew that a crash was coming. "Hang on, everyone!"

As Jonas anticipated, the demon stood and aimed its shoulder cannon again. Jonas fired a quick laser round which struck the demon right in the chest. The demon crumbled to the floor, but in its death throes the demon fired the cannon. Jonas knew this, for just after it fell, the demon's entire chariot burst into flame.

Jonas, Bheem, and Khafre all watched this chariot as it swerved in slow motion and then plowed right into them in a leg-shaking impact.

They all braced themselves while their chariot shuddered and tipped wildly to one side, before they finally lost their battle with momentum and began rolling end-over-end. Bheem, Jonas, and Khafre all tried to hang on but they soon couldn't help but being tossed from the vehicle. They all went flailing chaotically, sailing through the night air. Jonas braced himself, with his hands out, ready to hit the dirt any second. But instead he plunged headfirst into cold and deep water.

He surfaced, quickly wiping the water out of his jackal eyes. He looked up and saw that he'd flown down an embankment and landed right in the middle of a swiftly flowing river, running right through the wild jungle. He thanked the Guardians that he hadn't been splattered across the jungle floor.

Khafre surfaced a few cubits away, spitting, hacking, and coughing. Jonas vigorously shook his jackal head dry before looking up through the darkness again. There, high up on the riverbank, where their chariot had rolled to a stop, their vehicle caught fire and then exploded. Jonas and Khafre both quickly submerged again to avoid the falling debris.

"What the heck man?" Khafre asked, gasping for breath as they resurfaced.

Jonas shook his jackal head dry and wiped his eyes clear again. He knew they were lucky that they hadn't plowed into a tree or landed on the exposed rocks along the riverbank. "Hide. Over there," said Jonas. He pointed to a log tangled in vines growing out of the steep bank to their left. They both swam over and flung themselves over the wet log.

Jonas still couldn't believe they had survived that crash. But he knew they weren't out of this yet. Those demons would quickly start searching, and they wouldn't stop until they'd caught him and Khafre.

"Let's get out of here...downstream," Jonas whispered breathlessly.

"Okay, man."

While keeping their snouts and eyes just barely above the lapping waters, Jonas and Khafre cut the log loose from the brambles and floated off with the current. To resist floating too quickly, they clutched at the long grasses and branches leaning out over the river.

Something touched Jonas's foot suddenly and he kicked out in a frenzy of fear and worry that it was something dangerous. Plus, he wasn't a strong swimmer, so if it dragged him under he might not come up again. But whatever it was, it didn't stick around to bother him again so he continued on.

They traveled for what seemed like a long ways, with jumping fish and croaking toads curiously watching their progress. But the fish and toads didn't say anything and just left them alone (if in fact Earth-1 toads and fish could even speak standard intergalactic like on Monubia).

Large dragonflies and fireflies swarmed about Jonas's wet and sweaty jackal face, annoying him and obviously interested in something. His usual jackal instinct was to snap at and eat all these flies. But he resisted snapping his jaws, knowing not to create more noise in their situation.

"You alright, man?" whispered Khafre, wiping his monkey face.

"Yeah, you?" Jonas asked, his heart still racing.

"Yeah. That was just gnarly, man...."

"I know. Hey, where's Bheem?" Jonas asked while he tipped the water out of his pointed jackal ears.

"I don't know. I hope the demons didn't get him, man."

It was so dark out that Jonas could barely see anything, let alone Bheem, even if he was nearby. The fires from above cast long shadows over the waters and soon he heard the anxious and raspy voices of demons back up on the bank. They were searching for Jonas, Bheem, and Khafre, loudly trampling through the thick jungle bush as they did.

He and Khafre paused in an eddy to rest. Jonas was happy with their progress, but just up river, the demons' dark shapes were slowly moving towards them along the bank. They decided to continue on and pushed off into the current again. Jonas was thinking they just might make it out of there when he suddenly stopped and froze with fear.

He didn't want to stop, but an invisible power had forced him to do it, sending his jackal instincts into high alert. Terror rippled through him and his whole body shuddered uncontrollably. The cool waters rushed past him as he grabbed at the grasses on the bank to stay in place. He felt around for the riverbed beneath him with his toes. When he finally found the bottom he stood against the swift current.

He braced himself, still grasping at the long river grasses, his jackal instincts all going haywire. Something terrible was up ahead. He wanted to bark out madly into the darkness. But he knew that if he did laser bolts would soon be raining down on their heads.

"Come on, keep going, man," Khafre said, nudging him.

But Jonas refused to move. Each and every hair on his jackal head was standing up with fear now. His jackal ears went rigid and he growled softly. Then suddenly his keen snout sniffed the foulest, most grotesque stench he thought he'd ever encountered. He trembled, wanting to run, thinking that some monster from the Underworld was just up ahead.

"What's wrong? What is it, man?"

"Stop..." he whispered, still shaking. "There's something out there...."

Khafre grabbed a thick vine and stood up. "Do you see something, man?"

"I don't know—I don't see anything.... Wait, what is that?" he asked as he pointed downriver.

Just downstream, maybe twenty cubits away, he could see two massive shapes descending the opposite bank. Jonas and Khafre remained there, frozen, and watched as these great beasts lumbered into the water and then turned towards them. Neither he nor Khafre dared move. When the beasts crossed their immediate path they suddenly stopped, only a few cubits away now.

The beasts were close enough for Jonas to clearly see the giant white stripes running down their thick, hairy, muscular backs. Their heads rose ten cubits above the water, but they had to be much taller than that. Their feet were also touching the sandy riverbed beneath them.

Jonas couldn't believe it. Two fully-grown Mega Honey Badgers were standing in the river just four cubits away from him.

He wanted to scream out in terror. He wanted to run. But he knew they could never swim away and climb the riverbank fast enough. Only three cubits away now, the Mega Honey Badgers began sniffing around, leaning down over the water. Then suddenly they both looked right in his direction.

Jonas remained frozen. He knew that any second now one of them would lunge forward and rip him to shreds. A perfectly placed laser shot could stun one of them for a second. And with that being his only option, he slowly raised his pistol and aimed for the closest beast, right between its eyes.

He was about to fire, but then a strange buzzing sensation caught his attention. It felt like thousands of tiny pins were pricking him all over. Confused, he looked down. A bright blue aura was covering both hands and arms. What was this? Was he being electrocuted by an eel? Was it a laser bolt, slowly frying him to death, coming from a demon's weapon somewhere nearby?

But it couldn't be that for he felt neither heat nor pain. Both his fear and his wild jackal instincts drastically reduced and a great peace suddenly enveloped him. He sighed and breathed easily again. His heart beat slowed to a normal rhythm.

He watched this vibrating aura and felt its power growing in both strength and brightness. Then before he knew it the glow had completely covered his upper body. Intense pressure began building behind his eyes and threatened to burst out of his jackal forehead.

Then the river's flowing sound became amplified into a roaring deluge and he clearly heard the beasts' breathing as they sniffed him out. Their breathing sounded like a loud bellows in his jackal ears. In this deepened state Jonas couldn't think. He just stood there, waiting for something to happen, anything. Were these beasts going to attack?

Jonas locked eyes with the largest of these beasts and they stared at each other for what seemed like an eternity. Both he and Khafre would be hamburger meat for sure. He could hear Khafre breathing rapidly behind him now.

But then, unbelievably, the two beasts nodded in his direction and lumbered away, waddling up the opposite bank. Before Jonas could even speak, their striped flanks had both disappeared into the thick jungle brush.

Jonas just stood there, stunned and trembling silently. For some miraculous reason those Mega Honey Badgers hadn't lunged or swiped at them, they hadn't even snarled in his general direction.

Jonas turned to Khafre, who was also shaking uncontrollably and his monkey hair had nearly turned all white. Jonas couldn't make sense of what had just happened, no matter how hard he thought about it. Then the vibrating power subsided and it suddenly vanished. But he had exactly no time to discuss it or ask Khafre what he thought it was.

Harsh demon voices and laser blasts came from high on the riverbank so they continued wading downstream. Soon the demon voices were mixed with growls, followed by piercing shrieks of agony. The Mega Honey Badgers must have run into those demons, thought Jonas. But there was no way was he turning back to find out.

They floated on until the chariot fires were only yellow dancing specks in the night. They stopped and climbed the bank, finally taking cover behind a cluster of snake-like kapok trees. Removing his comm. link from his utility belt, Jonas quietly asked Hermes to dial Bheem.

To their joy and relief, Bheem answered. "Jonas, Khafre, thank tha Guardians ya're alive! Yes, I'm okay, lads. Meet me back at tha chariot road by a large clump a Lightnin Vines. I be hidin there," he said. "Two Mega Honey Badgers just scared off all them demons. Can ya believe it, lad?"

"Are those Mega Honey Badgers still around, man?" Khafre asked as he shook water out of his thick monkey hair.

"Na, thankfully. They all ran off inta tha jungle, lad. I seen 'em go myself."

"Alright, we're on our way," said Jonas, cutting the link. "Come on."

So they broke trail again, this time heading back to the chariot path where they eventually spotted Bheem beside a thick wall of Lightning Vines, all shining brilliantly like streaks of moonlight.

They embraced each other in big bear hugs, overjoyed to see each other.

"Where are we, man?" Khafre asked. "Do you know how to get to Telos from here, Bheem?"

Bheem smiled wide, he was extremely relieved to see they were okay. "Me hologram map says that we be close ta Telos already, lad. We be hittin it if we just stick ta tha river an head south," said Bheem. "But we got ta be careful.... Dino-lizards an Mega Honey Badgers be buildin nests in these areas. If one a those even spots ya, they be eatin ya alive."

"Yeah, that's a good idea," Jonas said, as a firm lump got stuck right in his jackal throat. He looked at Khafre, who nodded back. They then told Bheem about their encounter back in the river.

"Na way.... I can't be believin it! They would surely a eaten ya, lad!" he said.

"I swear that's what happened," said Jonas, barely able to believe it himself.

"We're telling the truth, man."

"But then what was that strange aura around ya, lad?"

"I wish I knew. But I have no idea." Jonas really did want to know, but it was just as much a mystery to him as to Bheem and Khafre.

"That just be incredible, lad. Ya two be tha luckiest beins on Earth right now."

"I know, tell me about it," said Jonas, shaking his jackal head. "I still can't believe it happened."

Next they broke trail back towards the chariot road, where their concerns turned to Bheem's hologram catalog and the list of dangerous plants it said to avoid. The worst of these were said to launch poisonous thorns while two others spat deadly venom.

When a long thorn sticking out from a vine stung Khafre in the leg, his limb painfully swelled up and turned purple. He screamed in pain, but only for a moment, for Bheem's survival kit held an antidote. After the pain and swelling subsided, Khafre was much more careful where he stepped.

They skirted around strangling vines belonging to a special constricting plant and then ran smack into a giant flower that sprayed bright mist in their direction. Their gas masks in their survival kits kept them safe, so they continued. Bheem told them that the mist was of unknown chemistry, but Jonas knew the fact that it was bright yellow in color was a bad sign.

Soon they spotted hovering glow-globes in the distance, and a small village slowly emerged from the thick brush. It consisted of brown plastic domes separated by dirt paths, and all appeared completely deserted.

They searched the first path they came to and knocked on a few hut doors, but no one answered. "Where is everyone?" Jonas asked, scratching his black jackal head and glancing around in confusion. "This is Telos, right? Ashtar said we'd meet Siegfried and the Lone Ranger here."

"Me hologram map say it is, but it could be wrong, lad," said Bheem. "We could be close, or be in a neighborin village." Bheem looked down at his hologram map again and shook his white jackal head. "Yep, this be Telos, alright. Siegfried must be around here somewhere," Bheem said, as he put away his comm. link device.

"This place is haunted, man," Khafre said. He was looking around and shaking with fear.

"I be highly doubtin it, lad," said Bheem sternly.

Jonas thought Khafre didn't look too good. Their encounter with the Mega Honey Badgers, plus, arriving in a supposedly haunted village was turning out to be too much for his Navan friend to handle. Khafre rubbed his hairy arms and glanced about nervously. He kept twitching and jumped at even the slightest noise.

"I've heard stories about this place, man. A friend of mine ran into some ghosts and goblins way out here. He said he barely escaped, man."

"I wouldn't worry, Khafre. I think if Siegfried is expecting us here, then it's probably safe," said Jonas.

"Yeah, but then where is everyone? I just don't know, man.... This place is super creepy," said Khafre. "I'm telling you, man, this place is haunted."

"Khafre, just be quiet and don't touch anything, okay?" said Jonas. "I don't think Ashtar would suggest that we meet someone in a haunted village." But as they kept searching, they didn't find a single being anywhere. Jonas put his energy detecting glasses on and scanned the village, keeping one hand on his laser pistol just in case.

Jonas began wondering if perhaps Ashtar was mistaken, or that maybe Siegfried wasn't planning on meeting them there after all. That would mean they were on their own, a painful realization.

Jonas drew near to a gate in a tall bamboo fence and saw a separate, larger section of the village just beyond it. But upon reaching the gate, a giant spotlight flashed on and blinded them.

They threw up their hands. "Don't shoot! We're not demons! We're here looking for Siegfried!" Jonas yelled. He squinted into the spotlight but couldn't make anything out.

He heard gruff and wild voices shouting from beyond the bright glare. Then the bushes rustled, followed by the sounds of energy weapons clacking and charging up to fire. "Who are they? They say they seek Siegfried?!" he heard voices saying.

"Lay your weapons on the ground and put your hands in the air. Now!" yelled a voice in a rumbling growl.

Startled, they followed its orders without hesitation.

Jonas's eyes were just now beginning to adjust to the bright lights. If he squinted just right, he could see Ghanda lion-beings, all standing tall on their hind legs just like Shastras. They had stumbled into what was a vast gathering of armed Ghandas, all pointing laser rifles, spears, and energy bows at them, and primed and ready to fire.

Jonas looked at these angry lion-beings and then back to Khafre and Bheem. His two companions just stood there, both in shock, their jaws now hanging wide open upon realizing that they were all cornered, defenseless, and were soon going to be held captive.

Meeting Siegfried

JONAS CAREFULLY STEPPED TOWARDS the light, with both his hands raised and empty. Regrettably, his laser pistol now lay at his feet, a poor position for an agent to be in. Both Bheem and Khafre had done the same.

"Hello, umm, allow me to introduce myself..." Jonas said as carefully as possible. While he drawled this sentence out, he identified their escape route as the closest bamboo fence, back and to their left. If he turned and ran as fast as he could he just might make it over the barrier.

"Yes, you may speak," a gruff voice growled back.

"Thank you. My name is Jonas Neferis. I'm an Intergalactic Agent from the Ashtar Command Center that serves this galaxy. My mission here on Earth-1 is to contact Siegfried and then locate a fellow agent whom we believe is in real trouble. He is a Shastra named Talley, and also an Intergalactic Agent. Our commander, Ashtar, advised that we travel here to Telos and meet Siegfried. I am asking for your help in finding Siegfried and Talley. Have you heard of them? And if so, do you know where either of them might be?"

The growling voices chatted amongst themselves for a tense period. Jonas waited, cautiously eyeing his laser pistol on the ground and then his escape route back over the fence. He watched the hairy manes of the fur-covered lion-beings beyond the glare, growing weary of his chances of somehow getting out of there alive.

He felt around his utility belt and found his protective energy shield's generator. With one button it would energize enough to protect him from the first round of laser blasts. That would be enough time to grab his laser pistol and then jump over the gate behind him.

Getting an idea, Jonas slowly removed his Intergalactic Agent badge from his tunic and flipped it open to reveal his I.D. The crowd loudly murmured and then a lone lion-being approached through the glare. It was a grizzled female Ghanda. She stood tall and walked upright, her tense leonine face appearing alert, and her gaze revealing a deep intelligence behind it.

As this Ghanda cautiously approached, she shouldered a rather large laser rifle she was carrying. She stopped and then studied him with her good eye. A black eye patch covered a truly righteous scar over the other. Her soft, golden mane was matted and caked with dirt in large clumps, while Jonas thought her numerous bald patches gave her a mangy, spotted appearance.

He noticed that an athletic frame bulged beneath a sparse toga and bronze breast plate, revealing her stout warrior's build. Jonas reasoned that avoiding hand to hand combat with this being would be his best option. She was easily much stronger than he was, even on his best day.

He slowly held out his badge while she snarled quietly and studied it. She then motioned back to her cohorts and Jonas sighed with relief when the spotlight was finally shut off. This was followed by the chaotic clacking and clattering of weapons being lowered, sheathed, and put away. Jonas felt relieved but kept himself alert. He still had to figure out this Ghanda's true intentions.

With his jackal eyes now fully adjusted, Jonas could see the lanes of simple plastic huts, all lit by hovering glow-globes. This scene was affronted by a full company of powerful, armed Ghandas, all just as hairy and muscular as the first. Jonas didn't doubt that each one of them could easily subdue an infant dino-lizard with one hand.

On top of their bulging muscles and shining weapons, ample streaks of war paint gave them a fierce appearance. It could also be blood, but Jonas couldn't tell for sure. They'd smeared the red and brown paint all over their arms, lion faces, and chests, forming crude symbols and shapes. Even their manes were covered by it, or it was all over their neck if they lacked a mane.

But Jonas remembered that lion-beings possessed an honorable character. He desperately prayed that these Ghandas fit that pattern. He had enjoyed Ghanda history in Species Studies Class, so he understood some of their culture. But if these weren't allies, then they would prove to be dangerous enemies.

"So, you're the one who the Great Spirit sent from the Ashtar Command," said the first Ghanda, closing and handing back his agent badge. "Earth-1 is very far from that station. But you can relax here, young agent, Jonas. Siegfried is here in this village. He is expecting you."

"By the Guardians, that's wonderful," Jonas exclaimed with relief. "Siegfried is one of my main contacts here on Earth-1. I must speak with him as soon as possible." He was ecstatic that they would meet Siegfried after all.

"Let me see your piece, first…" the Ghanda demanded, extending her open palm.

Now, handing over one's weapon was a real violation of agent protocol. But wanting to earn their trust, Jonas picked up his laser pistol, brushed it off, hesitated for just a moment, and then handed it over. He kept his hands resting on his utility belt, with his fingers right over his shield generator's power button just in case.

She slowly turned his pistol over in her hairy, clawed hands while she purred in a soothing rumble. "Hmmm, Samson-5, special edition. Only certain agents use these." Grasping the barrel, she offered his pistol back, which Jonas accepted. "Who are they?" she asked, indicating Khafre and Bheem with a long, sharp claw.

"Bheem is one of my Command Center contacts here on Earth-1. He is serving as an Elder in the village of Shetra. Khafre is a mutual acquaintance, a chariot mechanic from Shetra who's pledged to help us on our quest," said Jonas. "We encountered demons on the road, but, thankfully, we escaped. However, our chariot was completely destroyed."

The Ghanda listened while maintaining an intense stare. Both Khafre and Bheem bowed to her, but she didn't bow back. She appeared to not approve of unexpected guests.

"This is Telos, isn't it?" Jonas asked.

"Yeah, this is the village of Telos," the Ghanda answered. "We only expected two. You, Jonas, and Bheem here. The other should not have come." She glared at Khafre and growled softly.

"What the heck, man?" Khafre protested.

"It's okay. He is helping us in our mission. We had no choice but to bring him," answered Jonas, hoping to not upset her further.

"May we be knowin your name, an about tha village?" asked Bheem.

"Yes, my name is Marmaduka. This is mostly a village of Ghandas. We have lived here peacefully for centuries, although, Ghanda villages to the south attempt to raid us when food becomes scarce. We use tribal warfare when settling disputes; that is our nature. You three are the first non-Ghandas to visit Telos in over ten years, except for the one called Siegfried. That Shastra is a dear friend to all Ghandas."

"Well, that's just fascinating..." said Jonas, glad to hear that these Ghandas were friendly with Shastras at least. "So, where is Siegfried now? Can we meet him?"

"He is very close. We let him come and go as he pleases. He has been a great help to our village. We call him the White Wanderer among our tribe," said Marmaduka.

"We be needin rest soon, lassie, but first we like ta be meetin Siegfried," said Bheem.

"Yes, Siegfried said that you would need rest and refreshment. He also is eager to meet you," she said.

"So, wait, just a second.... Telos is haunted, man, right?" asked Khafre. "How can you live with ghosts and ghouls everywhere, man? And where are they?"

"No, far from it," replied Marmaduka. "We spread rumors of ghosts and monsters to keep out unwanted visitors. But none of those stories are true. Real ghouls and ghosts avoid this sacred land. Here we are protected by the forest spirits and the very trees themselves. Come now, I will take you to see Siegfried, and then you can rest." She turned and walked away, while five of the grizzliest female Ghandas followed right beside her, all clad in impressive arms and armor.

"Come on, let's be goin, Khafre," said Bheem.

"Okay, man, but you haven't heard the stories that I have—" Khafre replied, still looking around anxiously.

"Just come on," Jonas said, annoyed, as they tried to keep pace with Marmaduka's long strides.

Marmaduka led them on what became a village tour. Jonas was fascinated to learn that their domed huts were made from very special plastics which possessed some fascinating properties. The dome's interiors contained walls that provided free-energy heat or cooling, while also radiating any wavelength or intensity of light one could desire. Jonas was very impressed by this to say the least.

Some buildings could even change shape if an inhabitant expressed the correct thought pattern. And the village held ample room for each hut to expand and rearrange like this as needed. They didn't see any droids or robot soldiers about anywhere, but apparently the village employed free-energy power of some kind to power all their glow-globes, domed huts, and other useful gadgets like food printers (which Marmaduka told them were only used when hunting sources grew scarce). Jonas was very impressed that such advanced technology existed so far out in the wilderness.

"Times have grown desperate for our village, as well as for our neighbors close by," Marmaduka said while leading them down the wide village lane. "For years demons and bounty hunters have tried to drive us from this jungle, but their numbers were usually meager and mostly just a nuisance. But now their presence has grown much stronger." Marmaduka stopped under the flickering light of a glow-globe. "I sincerely hope that you will help Siegfried and the Lone Ranger protect us. Among beings that I've met from the world outside, only those two have earned our trust."

"I understand," Jonas said with deep respect.

"Ah, so tha Lone Ranger be here too?" asked Bheem.

"He comes and goes, that is his way," said Marmaduka. "He is also a wanderer, a messenger of the Great Spirit. Come, let us continue."

Marmaduka led them down an alley where many Ghandas were either hunched over or leaning against the domed structures. Jonas noticed how many of these beings were wrapped in bloody gauze and bandaged, and that most just sat there, slumped over and exhausted. A small band of Ghandas ran among the wounded, handing out water, herbs, ointments, and fresh bandages.

These new sights and smells reawakened Jonas's jackal instincts anew, making him want to run around, and growl, bark, and sniff everything in sight. All these new smells were almost too much for him to handle and it took all his self control to remain calm. But his snout kept running at around a million sniffs a second.

"Are all your Ghanda warriors female, man?" Khafre asked randomly.

Jonas directed his mind from his hyper-stimulated instincts to listen for Marmaduka's answer. He'd never noticed it before, but every Ghanda warrior that he'd seen was indeed female.

"Yes. Most Ghanda females choose the warrior path, such is the female's main vocation in our village," Marmaduka said, pounding her bronze chest-plate. "It is the ancient way of things. Male Ghandas become our prophets, artists, writers, and teachers; that is their nature. They excel at writing, thinking, and speaking truth. But we females are proud to love fighting, exploring, playing, and running through the jungle. In our Ghanda culture both roles are needed for balance. It is like this also on our Ghanda home world, Arcturus, in the Leo star system."

"Whoa, man, that is so interesting! It's almost the opposite in our Navan—" began Khafre.

But Marmaduka continued. "Jonas, Siegfried has foreseen that demons will soon return to the jungle. You and your friends must fight alongside us when that happens. But know that our Ghanda ways of fighting may seem different to you."

"I understand. Agents from the Ashtar Command are trained in many types of combat. We have studied the Leo system and its cultures in Galactic Studies."

"That is a good thing. I have met a few agents from your Command Center myself," she said. Marmaduka then reached beneath her bronze chest plate and removed a necklace made of claws, (or were they curved teeth?) and all strung on a line. "I earned this in battle from one such agent not long ago. This was my trophy," she said, rattling the necklace in the air. "I killed him for it." The other Ghandas laughed out loud upon hearing this.

Jonas couldn't see the humor in it, as he stared in shock, unable to believe that she'd killed an agent herself and wondered what had been her purpose for it. "My goodness, what led to that? That is a serious offense."

"He was a double-agent, a treacherous serpent-being. We caught him passing information to demons that later attacked our village. We skinned him and then ate him. He proved to be quite delicious," she said, slapping Jonas on the arm and laughing.

"I see, well you never know," he said as he wiped his jackal brow. "Is Siegfried in one of those huts?"

"Yes, when do we be meetin Siegfried?" Bheem asked.

"Soon now. You arrived at the right moment to meet Siegfried," said Marmaduka.

"Well, I have to admit, I totally believed that Telos was haunted, man," Khafre said brightly as they continued down the dirt pathway lit by glow-globes. "I've heard way too many stories about it over the years to remember. But I just don't get it, man. Your village isn't haunted at all."

"Over the years we've set up traps and dummies throughout the jungle. These scare off trespassers and give us privacy. Those tales which you heard were all fantasy that we spread, or were stories from travelers that we scared out of their wits," Marmaduka said as she laughed.

"But now is a very dangerous time for Telos," she continued. "And if Siegfried has called you here, then you must have a special purpose. All who meet Siegfried are changed forever. There are no exceptions to this rule. But, you must see for yourself."

Jonas was gripped with anticipation. He wondered what she had meant by that as the hairs on his jackal head all stood up straight. He couldn't wait to learn more. And he desperately hoped that Siegfried could clear things up as to Talley's whereabouts.

"Yes, he be very special," said Bheem. "I be meetin him a time, long ago, lad."

"Cool, man. So what's he like?" asked Khafre.

Jonas desperately wondered the exact same thing.

"You will see just now. Siegfried's hut is this way," said Marmaduka. She led them into a large, open square, and before Jonas knew it, they were standing before the tallest hut in the village.

Looking up, Jonas paused, his nerves on high alert as the feeling of something extremely ancient inside caused him to pause and cautiously study this large, brown hut before him. Beautiful arches, rounded windows, and quaint, finger-like turrets ran along its second story, while two bright, free-energy glow-globes hovered over the arched entryway where they now stood.

Jonas questioned whether he should enter the hut at all. It seemed like a part of him might die if he crossed its threshold, and this thought terrified him. But, although strange, the thrill of adventure steadily grew within him, replacing all his fear, which soon all but vanished.

"This way," said Marmaduka, waving them inside.

Forcing his shaking legs forward, Jonas pushed himself across the threshold. A dark hallway led them around two corners and then into an inner sanctum where there sat an old, white jackal-haired Shastra. He sat cross-legged, busily writing under the dim light of a shining wall behind him. Already faintly lit, the room glowed even brighter due to a halo hovering about the being's serene jackal face.

Jonas, normally alert and cautious when meeting new beings, felt an instant attraction to this Shastra. Instantly, both his heart and mind were electrified with pure joy. His impression was that this moment had a deep purpose. This strange being radiated an inner power such as Jonas had never encountered before.

The being looked exactly like Siegfried's hologram picture in his comm. link's catalog. But what Jonas didn't expect was to see Siegfried's companion and a human female at that, sitting right beside him. Surprised, Jonas had only seen a few humans on Earth-1 so far, and barely any on the Ashtar Command Center as well as Monubia. He'd fallen asleep during almost every Human Studies lecture because it was always right after lunch and Warrior Space Ball practice, and also because he found it really boring. So, as a result, he admitted to knowing very little about humans in general.

But somehow this human looked different. She was neat and clean-kept, with deeply mysterious, yet large and beautiful eyes. She was hardly the dirty, ignorant, short, and excessively weak being that he'd found humans to be.

Entranced, he noted how her skin was the dark color of Jupiter Space Cow chocolate ice cream, and her eyes were large like giant almonds that shimmered brightly. Her black "human fur," which textbooks always labeled as being properly called "hair," flowed in long braids down her straight back.

Jonas's jackal eyes immediately widened while his pointed ears shot up excitedly like antennae. He sniffed the air for her scent and picked up hints of dry, iron-rich clay, barbeque sauce, and fresh mango, which were all on his list of the top one hundred smells of all time.

"Your guests have arrived, sir. They very much want to meet you," Marmaduka said, bowing low.

"Ah, thank you, Marmaduka. Yes, I have been eagerly awaiting you all. At last, you've made it, my boys," Siegfried said, smiling as he stood and bowed.

"It's an honor to finally meet you, sir," said Jonas as he, Khafre, and Bheem all bowed in return.

"And you as well," Siegfried said brightly. "Please, meet my assistant, Isas. As a priestess, she has worked with me for years now, ever since meeting me on her home island of Athenia."

They all bowed and she nodded back with a peaceful smile on her lips.

With his interest in this human female now aroused, Jonas regretted not paying attention in Human Studies class. He thought back, trying to remember anything about Athenia, but he couldn't remember a single fact or anecdote.

"So, you're really THE Siegfried, man?" asked Khafre.

"Yes, in fact I—" Siegfried started.

But then Khafre flew into an abrupt coughing fit, lasting over a minute. Jonas, Bheem, and Siegfried all stepped back in alarm, observing Khafre with surprise.

"Are you alright, my boy?" Siegfried asked worriedly.

"Yeah, yeah, I am, man, I am. I've just got a little cold that's all."

Jonas had long sensed there was more to it than that but he didn't say anything at that moment.

"I see.... Why, yes, I am the Siegfried that you've been seeking," he said, still eyeing Khafre curiously. "I welcome you to Telos." Siegfried then motioned them to sit on cushions around a low table. As soon as they all sat down, Siegfried clapped his hands and the sanctum's aura instantly softened, bathing them in a sea of cool blue light which Jonas found quite pleasant.

While Bheem and Marmaduka engaged Siegfried in conversation, Jonas studied him carefully. Jonas remained cautious and skeptical, despite everything Ashtar and Marmaduka had already told him. He could tell Siegfried was different and unique. If he was a celestial in disguise, Jonas would pick up on a hint or get some indication. Or maybe the opposite was true and their intelligence about him was incorrect? Was Siegfried a shape-shifting demon by chance? He sure hoped not. But Jonas knew by now that anything was possible.

He first took note of Siegfried's white jackal face. Strong and handsome, he looked only slightly aged beyond forty earth years, give or take a few. He could pass as being a little older than Bheem. Strange for a being rumored to be over four thousand years old, thought Jonas.

Pure white hair covered his entire jackal face. Meanwhile, a wispy, thin beard dangled beneath his long snout. His two jackal ears stood up extra pointy, and covering his thin frame were a red tunic and loincloth. Both were embroidered with ancient symbols in golden thread.

When their conversation turned to more serious matters, Jonas pressed Siegfried with a question. "Sir, my mission parameters require that we ask for help in locating a fellow agent. Will you help us find him?"

"You are speaking of Talley," said Siegfried.

"Yes, I am, sir."

"I know where he currently is being held."

"That's excellent, sir! Where is he now?" he asked excitedly.

"He is currently a prisoner of the skeleton god of the Underworld, Khapre-Tum. He is being held within Skull Castle in the darkest of dimensions," Siegfried answered somberly.

This was not the answer Jonas had anticipated. If this was true, then rescuing Talley would be a hundred times harder. "Sir, how can we even reach such a place? I have no interdimensional chariot capable of making that jump. I'm not even interdimensional travel certified. It's impossible...."

Jonas's thoughts suddenly turned dark and heavy. He knew enough about Khapre-Tum to realize this task would be almost impossible. That god of the Underworld was very crafty and immensely powerful. He would have to travel to the Underworld, slip into Skull Castle unnoticed, and then face that dark god in combat, alone. There was just no way he could do all that on his own.

"Yes, it is very regrettable, but it is the truth. Don't worry, Jonas, I have an advanced chariot quite capable of making the journey," said Siegfried.

"But, sir, tha Lone Ranger? Can he be helpin us, if he be nearby?" Bheem asked.

"Have patience. I too have been in contact with Ashtar and have promised him I will help with your mission. And as for the Lone Ranger...hmmm, well, there's just no telling when a character like him will drop in. But, Bheem, I have a feeling that you will meet him very soon now."

"That be great," said Bheem, slapping his knee. "The Elders a Shetra told me all about that scallywag."

"Cool, I look forward to meeting him too," added Jonas.

"Yeah, man," exclaimed Khafre. "He's supposed to be one righteous dude."

"Yes, he is quite righteous, Khafre. But, I must relay some bad news to you about Heliopolis," Siegfried said, turning serious again. "The demon army of Khapre-Tum attacks Heliopolis as we speak. It will soon be turned into the skeleton god's capital here on Earth-1."

A shocked silence fell, turning the atmosphere dark and cold. "What can we do to help them?" asked Jonas. "We aren't prepared to face an entire army." The situation was now bigger than just finding Talley. "If Khapre-Tum takes power, then maybe none of us will escape alive, let alone Talley. And that's if we can even rescue him, sir." Things were getting worse by the second, thought Jonas.

"Yes, it is a dire situation. One with much higher stakes than Ashtar has prepared you for, I'm afraid." As Siegfried spoke an awkward silence fell over the group.

"What is Khapre-Tum like, man?" Khafre asked with morbid curiosity.

"Mere words will not help you to understand," said Siegfried. He paused abruptly to run his hand over his thin, white beard. "Khafre, do you fear the darkness?" he asked.

"No...why? That's a strange question, man."

Siegfried's voice sounded strained as he spoke again. "If you meet Khapre-Tum, then you will understand. Not darkness as the absence of light, mind you, but as the realm were evil can hide and fester. He lives and moves through a cosmic blackness, a dark energy where no true joy, love, or light may ever enter. Cold and terrible fear always precedes him."

Everyone paused and shuddered, afraid to speak after hearing this.

"I have seen him myself once, deep in the Underworld," added Marmaduka. "Since the day when I first saw him, I always sleep with a light on. When the fear of beholding him first engulfed me, I wanted to die right there. I haven't been the same since that day. But soon after a cleansing strength followed as the grace and power of Shamses, the Ghanda Guardian, helped me to face that fear, giving me a stout shield of faith and truth. She is ever with me now, and will be always."

Jonas almost couldn't understand such fear. He'd studied the Underworlds in dimensional studies, but he'd never accepted half the things his instructor had told them. They just seemed too terrifying and unreal to believe. The horrible thought of traveling there was almost too much for him to handle.

"Hmmm, that sounds pretty scary, man..." added Khafre.

"Jonas, you will play an important role in all this," said Siegfried.

Jonas nodded slowly, but had no idea what Siegfried meant by that.

Siegfried put away his scrolls and the free-energy quill. "You must help me to locate a dimensional doorway and enter the Underworld. But locating such a portal won't be hard. Wherever the demon army congregates you will find one."

"Yes, sir..." he said slowly, but unable to believe if he could actually do all that. It all sounded impossible, but he knew he'd have to try as there was no other option left.

"Ahhh...I see the Lone Ranger is right on time," Siegfried said, smiling wide. "He is always on time. That is, except when he doesn't come."

Jonas, Bheem, Khafre, Isas, and Marmaduka all perked up and peered around the chamber. But no one entered. Then suddenly a group of lights appeared, flickering about the arched doorway like a cloud of dancing fireflies. This cloud soon condensed into the form of a Shastra wearing a faded brown cloak.

Curious, Jonas watched with his jackal head tilted to one side. He wondered what kind of being had the power to appear right out of the air like that. The Lone Ranger approached, sat between Bheem and Siegfried, and then drew back his hood.

Jonas drew a sharp breath in shock. Bheem shook his head like he was waking from a crazy dream. Khafre stared at this strange being, his monkey mouth hanging wide open.

Just like in the hologram catalog, metal augmentations covered over half the Lone Ranger's handsome, brown fur-covered jackal face. But most striking of all was the mechanical eye, huge and beeping and whirring as it surveyed the room. Jonas noticed that out of his two jackal ears, one was pointed, robotic, and rotated about like a satellite dish. He'd met many Shastras on Monubia, as well as in his agent studies courses and training sessions, but never one like this.

"Everyone, meet the Lone Ranger," Siegfried said proudly.

For a tense moment nobody spoke. Although shocking and strange, Jonas was glad to finally meet him. Right away he sensed something special about this mysterious being, like he had something valuable to teach them.

"Thank you, Siegfried. It is a thrill to meet you all, whom I've already heard so much about," said the Lone Ranger in a low, raspy voice. "I am forced to be brief, for my time with you is limited. You see, I must soon return to another time for an important errand."

"No trouble at all, my boy," said Siegfried.

"We understand, sir. Ashtar said that I should expect to work with you often," Jonas said excitedly.

"Yes, Ashtar told me that you would all be here. I have also seen this exact moment in the astral records library. There resides your book of life, Jonas, all of yours do in fact. See, I am a time traveler from Earth's future. I am what you would call a Savior in that distant time. This allows me to travel the dimensions and other times and to see all these things."

"What is it that Saviors do, man?" asked Khafre. "I've always wanted to know."

Jonas wanted to know this too. He leaned forward as his pointed jackal ears perked up in anticipation.

"A great question, Khafre. As a celestial warrior trained by the Guardians, a Savior must track down the dark forces whenever evil emerges to cause chaos and havoc, as they so often love to do. But that is their nature, unfortunately."

"Good point. That's very true," added Siegfried.

"That sounds like a great job, man," Khafre said brightly.

"I second that, lad," said Bheem. "This be a rare honor, sir."

Jonas thoroughly agreed, but still he couldn't take his eyes off this being's electronic eye. The blinking red orb continued to whirr, beep, and sweep the room, as if searching for something. Jonas saw it stop a few times, perhaps glimpsing someone or something through the walls of the hut, and then zoomed in to analyze it before blinking and then continuing on. All the while the Lone Ranger talked like it was all perfectly normal. But to Jonas it was too alien to ignore.

"Thank you. It is a great job, more than you know, Khafre," added the Lone Ranger. "I wish to tell you that in my time hundreds of tales and songs have been written about Siegfried's deeds and travels. Some even mention you all as contributors to his cause. You all are famous in the distant future, in my time, and for good reason. You should all be very proud of what you have the opportunity to accomplish. I have met many celestials in my travels, but none of those others can be compared to Siegfried."

Siegfried laughed and slapped his knee. "See, now isn't that wonderful? You all have an important role to play in this. Prepare yourselves, for exciting events will unfold, I guarantee it." Then Siegfried's aura grew brighter, becoming a brilliant, pulsing blue light that filled the room.

The Lone Ranger glowed as well, but mostly just his half-robotic jackal face, and with a subtler energy that still crackled with power. Jonas could feel it, making the hair on his arms all tingle and stand straight up.

"Yes, that's wonderful," said Jonas. "That all sounds amazing, Mr. Ranger. But can you please tell us a little about how time travel works?"

The Lone Ranger's dish-shaped jackal ear quickly swung around to Jonas. He jumped and held his breath, wondering what the ear-dish was analyzing. Whatever it detected, he thought it must be a very sensitive instrument.

"Ahhh, well time is a hard thing to understand on the purely mental level, Jonas," said the Lone Ranger. "I shared your same interest and enthusiasm when I first went through agent training, back in my time. As a Savior, my job is to serve the Guardians and to protect the Earth, as I and as all past Saviors have done. Time is but a tool I use to do my job more efficiently. That is all I can express to you at the moment. Being a time traveler and a Savior, I draw the unwanted attention of dark beings that would prefer it if I never existed. For my job is to foil up their plans in one way or another."

"I see," said Jonas. He was intrigued to hear more, and not really satisfied by this answer. Although, it was a deep and esoteric subject and one far beyond his ability to understand at the moment.

"If you help us out, sir, the sooner we can find this Talley and then figure out how to stop the demon army from marching over the earth," said Isas.

Jonas's jackal ears instantly perked up. A deep joy and intense interest gripped him at hearing Isas finally speak. Her soft voice and demeanor gave him a strange yet familiar sensation, similar to those from Shastra courting rituals back on the Ashtar Command.

He thought she had to be the most beautiful human female he ever remembered meeting. He shook his jackal head, trying to break her intoxicating spell over him, wanting to concentrate on his mission. "I will do whatever it takes to find Talley and fulfill my mission, sir," he said.

"That's the right attitude," said the Lone Ranger. "Spoken like a true Shastra, Jonas. And please, don't fret about the odds. The eternal Guardians are silently helping you. And I will lend a hand as well. Remember, this conflict is well documented in my future time. Well, I must leave you now, but I promise to visit you all again."

"What future year do you come from, man?" Khafre asked. That was a good question, thought Jonas.

But before the Lone Ranger could answer, dancing pins of light appeared around him. He flicked his hood back up to cover his jackal head. "Oh, Khafre...get that cold checked out, will you? It could prove to get really nasty later on," the Lone Ranger added.

His electronic eye blinked once and then Jonas watched, spellbound, as his form slowly dissolved into tiny, white dots of light. And then like fireflies they all flew out the chamber door in an instant, making everyone jump excitedly in their seat.

They all sat there in stunned silence. Jonas felt blessed to have seen the Lone Ranger in person. "Wow, what an amazing being!" he exclaimed.

"Yes, I know. He is truly unique," said Siegfried. "Now, tell me about this cold that you have, Khafre," he asked. He turned to the Navan and intently stroked his long, thin beard.

Jonas hoped Siegfried could cure him. Khafre's sickness had left him uneasy ever since they were back in Shetra. He felt that something just wasn't right about it.

"I always come down with this same sickness, man, right after I visit my uncle, Armando. He lives in the Navan city of Kalkas. I've never found the root cause of it, man. It's just a strange coincidence or it has something to do with allergies, the food in Kalkas, or the weather. But, I don't really know, man. I've been to like three mystics for it, but they didn't understand it either."

"And they be all highly regarded mystics too," added Bheem.

"Hmm, I see...that is troubling, Khafre. If it doesn't improve in the next few days then I will have to have a look at you," said Siegfried. "I prefer simpler remedies, though. I have one that just might do the trick."

"Okay, sounds great, man. But in the meantime, we don't have any chariots to fly through any portals with," said Khafre. "Ours got blown up, man."

"Khafre makes a good point," said Jonas. "And this village's defenses seem very primitive."

"I know. That is an issue. But don't worry, we can figure those things out together," said Siegfried.

"Hey, do you know the Guardians personally, man?" asked Khafre.

"Siegfried knows a lot of beings. You'd be surprised," said Isas.

"Whoa, man...are you like telepathic? Can you read minds, man?"

"Sometimes," replied Siegfried. "Only when I need to. But I never intrude into other being's minds."

That was a relief, thought Jonas. So he sighed and relaxed, letting his mental guard down at last.

"Like how, man?"

"I have grown very close to the Guardians and the Supreme Being over the years," said Siegfried. "They have blessed me with a certain power, but I must use it wisely." As he spoke, a bright and golden halo of light surrounded him. It was so bright that Jonas could hardly stand to look at it as he partially turned away.

Siegfried continued. "Let's say that I've earned their trust. And now they speak freely with me when I need their help. It's been many years since I began roaming the Earth. My aim has always been to help its civilizations to evolve and grow. I have taught many Saviors and celestial warriors in my time."

"Whoa, that's so cool, man," Khafre exclaimed as his monkey tail whipped about excitedly, slapping both Bheem and Jonas in the process.

"Thank you, Khafre. The Guardians are very proud of all of you for joining me in Telos," added Siegfried. "No doubt you had to brave the jungles filled with dangerous dino-lizards, bandits, and Mega Honey Badgers. Not many would even think of making the journey."

"Yes, we're glad we arrived here safely," said Jonas, trying not to think of the demons and Mega Honey Badgers they'd encountered.

"And so am I. Ah, here's the coffee. I hope you all like it. We also have tea if you prefer, and sugar crisps," said Siegfried happily.

Jonas's jackal mouth began watering right away, as two box-shaped droids rolled in on wheels, and carrying trays of coffee, tea, and sugar crisps. Jonas accepted a steaming cup of coffee and a handful of crisps. He tore right in on the coffee and crisps, which were both delicious.

He noticed that these server droids resembled his own cleaning droid, Vanessa, back on the Command Center, having a long neck and two big, beady, robotic eyes.

Next Siegfried told them about Earth-1's Record Storehouses. Isas quickly joined in, being an amateur historian and scholar herself. She enthusiastically described the ancient libraries in detail to Jonas's delight, having seen them many times in person. She spoke about their origins, locations, and their function as great vaults of ancient documents from the planet's distant past. Jonas listened to all this with excitement, as it sounded fascinating. It made him want to visit them some day, when his mission was finally over.

"I've spent many long hours in the Record Storehouses," continued Isas. "There are about five accessible locations on the planet, as of today. However, although numerous and quite extensive, the records are often damaged and incomplete. I feel that at best they provide a brief glimpse into beliefs and traditions of the ancients."

Jonas, Khafre, and Bheem munched their crisps as quietly as possible while they listened to the soothing sound of Isas's voice. Jonas felt relaxed and at peace, like he was in a pleasant dream. Jonas thought he could listen to her speak for hours, all day even.

"That's so interesting, man," said Khafre.

"I agree," added Jonas. "Please, tell us everything you know about them. These Record Storehouses sound fascinating."

She continued, encouraged by their keen interest. "The ancients did us a great favor by keeping many of their records on moving pictures they called 'Films.' Scholars aren't quite sure when, how, or why this tradition began. In the original Athenian, 'Film' translates into 'truth' or 'exact record of actual events.'"

"That be makin perfect sense, lassie," said Bheem.

"I agree. I have seen many of them myself," added Siegfried.

Jonas had heard of these ancient Films before, but he'd only seen short bits of one or two in his agent studies courses.

"Modern scholars have learned much from Films," she continued. "For example, once, long, long ago, great titans walked the earth, named King Kong and Godzilla. They were a towering ape and a dino-lizard, respectively. Sadly, in their time they were both misunderstood and even persecuted. But I know that if living today, they would live peacefully among us."

"I believe that as well," Siegfried said confidently. "But the ancients weren't all barbarians. They understood much about the universe. Special records have been found which scholars say were called the X-Files. Other great records were called Star Trek. These are educational documents, being real history. This also includes what is my favorite documentary ever, a Film named Star Wars. Now, remember that Isas and I have only explored a small portion of the Storehouses. I hear they are full of historical records to be discovered."

"Despite their materialism, barbaric natures, and the tragic cleansing periods they experienced, the ancients did know much about the cosmos. Although, still not as much as we know today," said Isas.

"Fascinating," said Jonas. He was eager to learn more about Earth's ancient cultures and traditions. "I'd love to visit the Storehouses with you guys some time."

"And you will, my boy. But first, everyone, meet my bodyguard, Argos," said Siegfried just as a giant, brown-furred bearman walked into the chamber. The bearman grunted and bowed, before it sat right behind Siegfried. It had to be very hot in this jungle heat, thought Jonas, being covered in a full coat of fur. It wore simple armor and carried a laser rifle on a sling. An eye patch covered its left eye, missing from a battle, no doubt. They all said hello but Argos only grunted back in reply.

"Oh, and another thing, we know for a fact that the ancient's language, called 'English,' was created by a select group of humans called Pirates," Isas said with excitement. "It's said that these Pirates sailed the seven seas searching for treasure and adventure. They were just fascinating."

"No kidding. Earth Pirates are famous back on the Ashtar Command," Jonas said as his ears perked up. "Learning about Pirates was my favorite section in Earth Culture Studies. Arrhhh!" He said, laughing as he held up two fingers and formed a hook.

"Arrhhh!" repeated Siegfried, "ahoy matey!"

They all laughed and joked about Pirate facts and mythical lore like walking the plank, sword fighting, buried treasure, peg legs and pet parrots, the meaning of the word swashbuckling, and how an X always marked the spot on a treasure map. Isas said swashbuckling meant 'embarking on an honorable adventure,' which they all agreed had to be correct.

They started in on their third round of coffee and sugar crisps, at which point Bheem began a detailed retelling of their journey through the jungle from Shetra to Telos. Jonas and Khafre joined in, adding bits here and there, while Jonas casually stole curious glances at Isas to watch her reactions. She appeared genuinely interested, listening intently and asking good questions.

"That's a great story, you guys," Isas said after Bheem had finished. "I've spent five years serving Siegfried, so I know the dangers of these jungles. But not even I have ever seen a Mega Honey Badger up close. You were very brave to make that journey."

"Isas and I have had many trials and adventures throughout our time together," added Siegfried. "She has witnessed five attempts by the Hiixian bounty hunters to capture me. It has been an unfortunate hobby of theirs."

"Which bounty hunters, man?" asked Khafre. "I might know them. See, I used to live in Hiix, but just for a while, though. I escaped later on, man."

"Necrat and Tarsus Riggs..." Siegfried said coldly. "Even now they search the jungles, looking for us. We must reinforce this position against a coming attack. My spy sloth network tells me that one is imminent."

"Oh, great— that's just great, man!" Khafre yelled spitting sugar crisps everywhere.

"That be terrible news, lad," added Bheem. "Those two be tha meanest, most skilled bounty hunters on Earth-1, throughout tha solar system even."

"Yes, that is very true, Bheem, unfortunately," said Siegfried.

Jonas shuddered at the mention of those two infamous beings. Being an agent, he'd of course heard of them, every agent had. So he knew all about their extensive record of kidnappings, harassment, and creating general crime and chaos wherever they went.

He'd learned in Bounty Hunter studies class that Necrat had personally been vaporized, killed, flayed, and then cloned and reanimated at least a dozen times. That infamous wolfman had defeated an artificial intelligence planet all by himself, destroying an entire race of beings in the process that depended on it for survival. And he'd done that just for fun. He'd also captured warriors and kings of almost every race in the galaxy, and killed over a hundred times more beings than that.

Necrat's partner, Tarsus Riggs, was a part android, part serpent-being who was kept alive by an A.I. supercomputer called 'The Brain.' This mythical bio-computer was said to run the entire civilization of Hiix, a city known for its advanced weaponry and other destructive technologies.

But Jonas always knew that as an agent an encounter with bounty hunters was inevitable. "But if they find us, sir.... I mean, we have no chariots. And our few weapons will be inadequate," said Jonas.

"Don't worry, I can take care of all that," said Siegfried. "We will also be meeting a celestial being, a Savior, who has been sent by the Supreme Being to defeat the skeleton god, Khapre-Tum, along with his demon and skeleton army. This is a prophecy that has remained unfulfilled for a long time now."

They all stared at Siegfried, dumbfounded. Jonas doubted such a prophecy would come to pass in time to help them. He'd heard too many tales like that before to even count. Such beings were very rare and also very powerful; at least his textbooks in Celestial Studies class had said so.

"Sir, we will protect Telos and whatever else you ask in order to fulfill the mission. I've pledged that much to Ashtar," Jonas said proudly. "But fighting a war, with Savior's help or not, may prove too costly. Are you sure it's necessary, sir? There must be another avenue to pursue."

"I have seen all this unfold in the astral realms during my meditations," Siegfried said calmly. "The Savior must appear. If we don't receive the Savior's help, then Talley, Heliopolis, and all the kingdoms on Earth-1 will be lost. Khapre-Tum's tyranny would then be brutal and complete. You could not even return to the Ashtar Command Center. Khapre-Tum could prevent that. That is if we even survived a battle with the demon army."

"I understand, sir," said Jonas somberly. He remained silent, feeling unsure what to say in the face of such a possible future. "I will contact Ashtar and ask for his advice," said Jonas. "In the meantime, we will do whatever we can to help out."

"Excellent, that is all I ask," Siegfried said as his aura glowed brighter.

The others talked while Jonas tried remembering what he knew about Saviors. During his first year of agent studies he'd learned about Anunakh-Ten, who was the first Savior and first Shastra to appear on Earth-1. He'd learned about other Saviors too, who had lived on many other planets, including Monubia. Their deeds and teachings had always proved illuminating to study.

Jonas couldn't wait to meet this new Savior, if it ever happened, that is. But if he could learn something about what they were like, how they thought and behaved, and especially what divine and celestial weapons they possessed, then he could write one thrilling mission report later on.

After talking for a while longer, Siegfried yawned and finally stood. "I have greatly enjoyed this first meeting! But you must all be very tired from your journey. Khafre, Bheem, Jonas, you three come with me. Isas, Marmaduka, please excuse us. Good night."

Jonas gathered himself and stood on tired legs while he adjusted his utility belt. He'd forgotten how sore he was from their crash and then the long walk through the jungle.

"Good night, everyone," said both Isas and Marmaduka. They then stood and bowed. The others bowed back and Isas and Marmaduka left the chamber.

"What's Isas's story, man?" asked Khafre.

Jonas's pointed jackal ears turned toward Siegfried and listened with keen interest.

"She was a priestess in a forest convent on the island of Athenia. I drew her to serve me and this purpose in a dream. Since then we've taken several voyages and adventures together," said Siegfried. "The most important of these missions so far was to watch Khapre-Tum's movements and then to meet you all here in Telos."

"But what is her background? You said she's a priestess from Athenia, right?" asked Jonas.

"Just be patient. Once she warms up to you, you'll learn more about her."

"That would be really nice," Jonas said, with his heart beating like butterfly wings. With the thought of spending more time with Isas, a sudden, wonderful feeling of warmth enveloped him, centering right within his heart.

They all walked outside to see that the village's glow-globes were now all dark, and its streets empty and silent. Siegfried and Argos led them down the lane and then stopped before a cottage with open walls on every side.

"These are your sleeping quarters. In the morning we will talk again and begin to plan," said Siegfried, his face glowing like a celestial's. He quickly bowed and then both he and Argos walked off.

Jonas watched them retrace their steps through the village back to Siegfried's hut. He was glad to have finally met Siegfried, especially his charming assistant, Isas. However, the depressing fact of Khapre-Tum's attack on earth had dampened his mood.

Eager to finally get some rest they quickly inspected the cottage just to be safe, then grabbed blankets and pillows and turned out all the glow-globes. Each one picked a spot, and once settled in Jonas noticed that two fierce Ghandas, and both clad in full armor, stood guard right outside the cottage entrance.

Jonas closed his eyes and tried to sleep but his mind wouldn't stop racing. He thought about meeting a Savior, about the Lone Ranger's strange electronic jackal face, and about what Isas had told them about the Record Storehouses. After a while he found that he still couldn't sleep, so he just lay there thinking. Heavy rain began to fall outside.

He laid awake and listened to the pleasant patter of rain on the cottage roof while a cool breeze wafted through its open walls. He could smell the two Ghanda guards outside, the blood caked into their fur, and the wet, fragrant earth beneath them. Pretty soon Khafre's and Bheem's snores joined the sound of falling rain.

Jonas stared up at the ceiling and remembered that the Lone Ranger was a Savior and a time traveler. So he decided to look up his hologram catalog entry. He whispered to the small, black comm. link device, "Hermes, look up all Saviors of Earth-1, during the current Age."

His comm. link beeped, flashing bright hologram text in the air, which Hermes read as Jonas listened intently; "Sure thing, Jonas. Savior of Earth-1: a rare being. Species: variable. Origin: variable. Strengths and skills: serves the Supreme Being and the Guardians, defends justice and manages out-of-control beings, especially demons, serpent-beings, bounty hunters, and evil spirits. Manipulates many types of energy weapons, has the power of flight, possesses healing powers, and may manifest any weapon when in need. List of known individuals: the first Savior, Anunakh-Ten, the first Shastra to appear on Earth, and founder of Heliopolis. The second Savior, the Wolfman, Tikriit. Next, the red-feathered Danaan Eagle named Tetra, Mobius the monkey-being, Ramses-Metah, another Shastra. And lastly, the Ghanda, Omtet, the child of a Titan Ghanda and a cosmic Serpent. The latter was killed by Khapre-Tum three hundred years ago."

Hologram images flashed above Jonas with the text alongside it. A recurring theme among all these beings was brightly glowing eyes, as well as a twinkling third eye that rotated like a diamond and was set right between their eyebrows.

The sheer power and angelic look on each face left Jonas spell-bound. His impression of these beings was that of sacred individuals. And it made him respect the Lone Ranger even more.

Hermes continued. "Most Saviors were mentored by Siegfried, and all received final training from the Guardian, Garud. Each was a master of Creation's five electricities. And through their usage, these beings manifested great wonders and miracles."

Lastly, holograms images appeared of Siegfried's and then Garud's faces. A Shastra Guardian, Garud's golden jackal head was a glorious beacon, emblazoned with gold light. Jonas could barely look at it for too long before he had to turn away.

When he looked again to study Garud's face, Jonas realized that he'd never met another celestial being besides Ashtar. Then flipping back through the hologram catalog, he noticed that the Lone Ranger wasn't on the list at all. On second thought, that made sense since being from the future, the Lone Ranger hadn't even been born yet.

Jonas read more about Earth's Saviors and their amazing accomplishments until he finally felt tired enough to finally fall asleep. So, he fluffed his pillow, rearranged his blankets, turned on his side, and closed his jackal eyes.

Forgetting all about the hologram catalog, which continued to display Siegfried and Garud's glowing faces above him, he drifted off, listening to the peaceful chirping of insects and the pattering of rain outside. Then once more he scratched behind his jackal ears before he curled up again and fell asleep at last.

A Sacred Journey

THAT NIGHT JONAS DREAMT of a wonderful scene. He'd finally passed chariot fighter weapons school and with the highest score ever recorded on the Ashtar Command Center. He was elated, ecstatic even. And during his graduation ceremony Ashtar proudly bowed and handed him his certificate. Jonas almost couldn't believe what was happening and his joy was too much to contain. Then he heard a loud crash and looked up into Ashtar's glowing blue face.

Ashtar smiled back and then Jonas suddenly bolted upright, staring into the cottage darkness. He rubbed his jackal eyes, disappointed that he hadn't actually passed atomic chariot fighter weapons school. He sighed dejectedly as he slapped his jackal forehead.

He then looked around, alert for the cause of the crash he'd swore that he heard and for the possibility of an intruder. Both Bheem and Khafre were asleep, snoring softly nearby. But Jonas couldn't make out any shapes of other beings in the darkness.

His comm. link device was still lying on the floor, displaying images of Siegfried's and Garud's faces. He turned it off. That was when he heard the crash again. Then he threw off his blanket and leapt up. He reached down and grabbed his laser pistol, before quickly putting his utility belt on.

Glancing through the cottage walls, he cursed when he noticed that the two Ghanda guards were no longer keeping watch. "Khafre, Bheem, wake up!" he yelled. He couldn't help thinking that the bounty hunters had finally located them.

But Khafre and Bheem both just turned over and continued snoring. He knelt closer and shook Khafre by the shoulder, but he didn't move. He shook harder and yelled again, "wake up!" Khafre still didn't respond. The same happened with Bheem.

Jonas was worried that a spell or mind control ray could be causing their deep sleep. But then why wasn't he affected? He started to panic.

And now all amped up and with his heart racing, his agent instincts kicked in as he unholstered his laser pistol, checked its safety, and charged it up as he felt the cold barrel and grasped its pistol grip. He definitely wasn't dreaming this. He had no idea if Siegfried, Isas, or Argos had been awakened by this crash or were still asleep also. But he knew he couldn't defend the village on his own.

He leapt backward and almost tripped over Khafre when a blinding glow streaked through the trees, bathing the village in light. He covered his jackal eyes with one arm, thinking that it was an energy device or the glow from a bounty hunter's star ship.

He threw on his tunic and quickly slipped on and fastened his sandals. In only a moment he was sloshing through the mud right outside. It was then that the comfortable drizzle decided to become a raging monsoon. Soon he was jumping over small rivers and splashing through deep puddles as he ran towards the edge of the village where the blinding light originated.

Reaching the village border he stopped to take cover behind one of the wooden support beams holding up a covered walkway.

He crouched there, breathing heavily as he wiped the water from his jackal eyes. As he did so, he gazed intensely into the bright glow coming through the dense trees.

He peered around, desperate to find the source of that bright light. Through the glare he could still see tangled vines and flowering creepers twisting around the tall banana and baobab trees. Monkey brush vines and fiery Bromeliads bloomed brightly nearby, wrapping themselves around nearly every limb and branch. Lush mangrove trees circled a still pond fifty cubits off to his right. And not much farther away a cluster of many-armed kapok trees lazily stretched their limbs over the jagged steps of a crumbling ruin.

His pointed jackal ears perked up straighter and he listened closely. But his rotating ears didn't hear a single footstep, engine roar, or laser blast beyond the village border. Other than the pouring rain and his heavy breathing all was quiet.

Just then he suddenly realized that he'd left his energy detecting glasses back in the cottage. Those would be useful, he thought, so he glanced backward, debating whether to return and retrieve them, when a powerful blast launched him off his feet.

He landed in the mud, right on his shoulder. His whole arm hurt, and when he rolled over on the wet grass and looked up he just rubbed his jackal eyes in shock at what he saw. A proud Shastra stood tall and glowing golden beneath the covered walkway. Jonas wondered if it was a jungle spirit or maybe a celestial. But if so, he hoped it was friendly.

His fear and instinct kicked in, and flooded with adrenaline now, he removed his laser pistol and gripped it, but holding it in the air and making sure that the glowing Shastra saw it. He flicked off the pistol's safety and set it to stun.

"Who are you?" he blurted. Then he carefully stood, keeping his pistol ready, his eyes always on the glowing Shastra. This being slightly resembled the Guardian, Garud, but Jonas knew there was no way it could be him.

But the golden Shastra just stood there, calm and quiet. A bright, golden aura softly hummed about it as Jonas stared, waiting for it to speak. "Don't be afraid, my boy. I am the Guardian of all Shastras. I am Garud. I have come to train you," the Shastra replied in a booming voice.

"That's highly unlikely," said Jonas. His hands were shaking now as he stood there in the pouring rain. He couldn't help but laugh at the prospect as he quickly wiped the rain from his jackal eyes.

"Listen, demons and bounty hunters could be projecting your image to distract me. By the authority of the Ashtar Command I have sworn to protect this village. I request immediate proof of your identity." This celestial had better be benevolent, he thought. If it wasn't then he probably wouldn't stand a chance if it attacked.

Jonas's hands trembled as he reached into his tunic, took out his agent license, and flipped it open for the being to see. Hopefully, it had heard of the Ashtar Command Center before.

The giant Shastra nodded and then stepped out into the rain. Jonas stepped back through the mud in total shock as the celestial immediately grew to a towering stature, rising nearly fifteen cubits high.

"Jonas, I am a Wanderer who travels between the worlds and dimensions, seeking to help those with a special mission," he said. "I currently travel this plane as the hermit you know as Siegfried." As the being spoke, its eyes twinkled with a deep blue, cosmic light.

Jonas thought about putting his pistol away. But he just lowered it and squinted to try and block out the bright aura to see better. When he squinted just right, the being did resemble the statues and pictures of Garud he'd seen back on Monubia and in Shetra's many temples. "I'm sorry, but I need solid proof if I'll accept your claim. Demons and bounty hunters are out there and I need to be sure."

The giant Shastra threw his golden head back and let out a deep, echoing laugh. While it did so, its third eye twirled like a celestial diamond set in its forehead. "Minds that require perfect proof will never receive it, Jonas. This three dimensional reality will always lack perfection. But, why should you doubt my statement? I am the one who always looks after his loyal servants, those Shastras scattered throughout the universes. I know that you are unacquainted with me in this life. But you must feel in your heart for the highest truth." Then he raised his giant right hand and the monsoon rains suddenly stopped.

"So, you...you are Garud? The great Guardian of all Shastra races?" Jonas stammered, trembling. He slowly reset the safety on his laser pistol and placed it back in his holster. Could it really be him, he wondered.

Sudden, overpowering happiness and excitement surged through him as he finally accepted the fact that it actually was Garud. Never in all his life had he expected to meet the beloved Guardian, the celestial who was almost single-handedly responsible for all of Shastra culture, science, and spiritual development throughout the known universe.

Jonas was fascinated with ancient legends of all the Shastra celestials, gods, demigods, and goddesses. He'd always dreamed of traveling to the Guardian home planet, Nabi Loka, which was located in the very center of the universe. But since moving to the Command Center, that desire had become a faint memory.

His father, Topo Neferis, and grandfather, Paw-Paw Neferis, had always read him tales of Garud's adventures. He clearly remembered that Garud had been present at the creation of the world and had also helped write the Universal Laws at its very Beginning. On top of that he'd wrestled cosmic serpents, tamed the dark Elementals of Chaos, and guided the creation and evolution of many Shastra races to a glorious and spiritual destiny.

"I've always wanted to meet you, sir. You inspired every Shastra tribe back on my home planet of Monubia," he said, shaking with excitement. "But...what do you mean by 'training?' Are you here to help us find Talley and to train him? Is he the new Savior prophesied to help us?"

"No, Jonas, you are the next Savior, the being prophesied to defeat Khapre-Tum and usher in a new Age of the world. It was I who telepathically suggested to Ashtar's mind that he send you here to Earth-1. Don't be afraid, my boy, this is all according to the Supreme Being's eternal plans."

Jonas could feel his jackal mouth hanging open and his eyes bulging wide in shock. But he only nodded robotically as his brain had seized up. Him, the next Savior? "But...how is that possible?" he stammered. "What does that all mean? I'm only a junior Agent, sir."

"Look, here is my chariot. Climb aboard and begin the path to your glorious destiny. All questions will soon be answered," said Garud.

Not sure what else to do, Jonas glanced over to his right where he saw a shining star chariot parked on the wet grass. Jonas did a quick double take as he was sure that chariot hadn't been there a minute ago.

The chariot was constructed from a yellow, vibrantly glowing power of some kind. But of course, when the reality sank in he recognized it at once. "Prajna! Garud's famous chariot of light!" he exclaimed, nearly jumping with joy. "Is that really it?"

"Yes, of course it is," Garud said happily. "You have heard of it."

"Of course I have. Every Shastra has heard bedtime stories about Prajna, the famous chariot." With this trusty vehicle, Garud had flown to the deepest pits of the Underworld and back, to the highest angelic plains, to the farthest corners of the universe and beyond even. "May...may I board it, sir?" He stared up at Garud, almost unable to contain his excitement.

"You may."

Jonas sprinted over to the chariot, almost giggling as he did, and its glowing cockpit instantly opened. The whole interior pulsated with warm, golden light, unlike any material chariot that he'd ever seen. His hungry Shastra eyes studied the dials and screens all blinking on the pilot's lone control panel. But other than these the interior appeared bare and simple. He couldn't believe it. He was peering inside the most famous chariot in all of Shastra legend. No one back on Monubia would ever believe what he was seeing.

Jonas gazed up at Garud and the Guardian's softly glowing, yet mysterious eyes gazed back. He felt deeply reassured, and his fear and confusion all but vanished, although some did remain.

"But, what about Talley, sir?" he asked, snapping back to his mission. "He's a very important Senior Agent. I still have to rescue him."

"I realize that. But he is now imprisoned within Skull Castle. You must face and defeat Khapre-Tum in order to free him," said Guard. "I am here to help you achieve this."

Jonas was pondering the near impossibility of such an act when suddenly the Guardian's eyes shifted and revealed a terrifying abyss. Within their oval voids, as Jonas helplessly stared there appeared vast fields of stars, galaxies, and nebulae, all of them set between massive, swirling solar and stellar systems. This cosmic vision embraced him, as if his insignificant self had now become part of the universe.

The intensity and glory of this vision increased until his jackal hair all stood up, as if electrified, and his jackal head felt like it might explode. Then suddenly his consciousness snapped back into his mortal frame. Garud's eyes were still gazing at him, but they had resumed their normal look.

Jonas reverently bowed before Garud's golden sandals, touching their leather straps and the Guardian's glowing skin. Some type of cosmic dynamo-like power was now surging through every part of him and with a soft humming tone.

Jonas then rose and boarded the celestial chariot. He ran a hand over its warm, glowing rails, a solitary chair in the rear, and then the cockpit's control panel. Even though glowing and aethereal, all these objects were solid to the touch. It was all completely real, as far as Jonas could tell.

Garud then shrank down to a mere one cubit taller than Jonas. Garud then boarded the chariot just as its canopy closed over them. Garud then touched the controls and the chariot's engine awoke with a bright flash.

"With this chariot you fought Har-ma-kruti, the cosmic demon thief!" Jonas exclaimed in awe. "You escaped a supernova at the center of our galaxy and beat the god of light, Sura, in a race to win the rights to marry the Shastra nymph, Thetis. You also stole the nectar of immortality from the demon gods Kama and Draga just for fun!"

"You are a regular historian, my boy!" Garud said, laughing at Jonas's boyish enthusiasm. "I am very impressed!"

"Both my father and grandfather read your legends to me every night."

"You should see your reaction!" said Garud.

"I still can't believe it...I'm riding in Prajna, the cosmic chariot.... Okay...I'm sorry I doubted you, sir," Jonas said. He was elated, giddy, and lightheaded even.

"It's quite alright," Garud replied.

"Where are we going?" he asked. He wondered exactly how one became a Savior. He'd never studied that process before. He felt that he could definitely be too young and inexperienced for such an endeavor, but then again, here he was. He quickly relaxed and just decided to trust Garud and see what happened. He just kept shaking his jackal head, though, still unable to believe he was now standing in Prajna's famous cockpit.

"We are going somewhere very few have been," said Garud. Then the Guardian's third eye in his forehead suddenly flashed brightly and rotated with shining triangles and tetrahedrons, all blinking furiously in blue, green, and purple flashing symbols.

Jonas wondered just what celestial powers Garud and his twirling energy center possibly possessed. He'd only heard stories about them. He'd never seen such things in action or in person. As Garud's third eye spun continuously the controls beeped and flashed in response. Then before Jonas knew it, their chariot slowly began rising through the air.

He glanced upward and saw a frightening whirlpool of angry green flame right above them. Jonas gulped and grabbed the chariot's railing to brace himself. As they slowly rose towards the swirling portal of light, Jonas grew more apprehensive. He quickly looked over at Garud. The Guardian just stared at the ship's controls, stony-faced and silent.

Right when their cockpit was about to touch the swirling green door, Jonas quickly ducked and covered his jackal face. He waited for a moment, but nothing happened. Then suddenly Garud tapped him on the shoulder. Jonas carefully opened his jackal eyes and looked up.

"Come along, I want to introduce you to someone," said Garud.

Jonas found that he was looking out at a strange, metallic-silver landscape, stretching towards a distant horizon. They definitely weren't in Telos anymore that was for sure. Wherever they were it was definitely night time as countless stars dotted the sky above. Three tall spires dotted the smooth horizon. "Where are we?" he asked. "The jungle, the huts, the village...where are they?"

"We are far away from Telos. This is Earth's second moon. Its ancient name is Medea," said Garud. "The twelve Guardians use it as a meeting place."

Jonas simply nodded. But then he turned, and looking up, he nearly fell over. The giant orb of Earth-1 was directly behind him, dwarfing Medea's silvery horizon.

He started sweating and shaking with anxiety. The Earth looked gigantic and he felt like he might fall back into its atmosphere at any moment. "How...how is that possible?" he asked. He rested his hands on his knees as he breathed deeply, trying to compose himself as he quickly grew light headed.

"Be calm," said Garud. Then the Guardian waved a hand over Jonas's furry jackal head and he immediately stopped shaking and sweating. He stood and was able to shake his jackal head until he could see straight once more.

After that intense moment of sheer panic he felt relaxed again. He then realized that it was silly to even fear the chances of falling into the planet's atmosphere. Medea was a decent size, so its gravity would easily prevent him from that. Plus, there wasn't the usual risk of him puking in his space suite from space sickness, because he wasn't even wearing one. Besides, Garud was right there with him anyway, so he obviously wouldn't let that happen.

"Thank you, sir," he said, relieved to have his help.

"Come, we have an important meeting to attend," Garud said, motioning him forward.

So they walked along the smooth and silver plane, and as they did, Jonas noticed that a golden glow had engulfed them both. He reasoned that it had to be what was helping him breathe without a space suit.

"How long has Earth had a second moon?" he asked. He knew that such a thing wasn't abnormal, but didn't remember it from Ashtar's briefing.

"It was brought into orbit around the planet four thousand years ago or so. That makes it still quite new in cosmic time."

Thinking back on his studies, Jonas remembered that Earth's first moon was a space station created by divine beings and put into orbit over a billion years ago. Their Earth Studies instructor, Mr. Shinns, a pink, floating jellyfish-being who was a terrific teacher, had taught them that the ancient Earthlings had once been so confused and so precocious that they had for a time, and thankfully only for a very sad yet brief period, actually believed their moon to be just a piece of dead rock floating in space. Jonas hadn't believed it at the time. Most of the class hadn't either. It was too ludicrous. But then later his girlfriend at the time, Jenny, had confirmed it for him.

Mr. Shinns had even gone on to say how the ancient humans still believed this, even after landing multiple crude ships on its surface and walking around for a good bit. Although, Jonas suspected that those astronauts who did the actual walking knew better. Just the thought of this was hilarious to him. It made him want to study Earth history again, but more for its comedic value than anything else.

"Come, we're scheduled to meet the Supreme Being," said Garud.

Jonas did a double take upon hearing this. The prospect of meeting the Supreme Being was amazing, terrifying, and impossible to him, and all at the same time. "What? Ummm, sir.... Could you repeat that? I don't think I heard right."

"From today onward you will no longer be just a Shastra from Monubia or an Agent of the Ashtar Command Center," Garud said as they walked along, drawing nearer to the three towers. "As the seventh Savior of this Age you will be a celestial warrior, forever associated with the gods, the elementals of nature, the Guardians, and the Supreme Being. Your next step, should you choose to take it, is to meet these beings, who are as of now waiting to bestow their blessing upon you. Your celestial abilities and powers will be unlocked for the future progress of your divine mission. This is now about much more than just Talley and the Command Center."

"Oh, I see... That's wonderful, sir," said Jonas. But really he had no idea what that statement meant. He just straightened his tunic while his heart nervously completed two full summersaults. He trusted Garud enough to continue on, however. He would just have to wait and see what would happen.

Jonas did know one thing, though, that he was a full-blooded Shastra through and through. Like all Shastras, he wanted to pledge his life to an honorable purpose and then go all out, guns blazing until the very end. And if he found himself looking the god of the Underworld right in the face and happened to fail, then so be it. He would die trying. It was his sworn mission to do so. He just hoped he could make their encounter one that Khapre-Tum would never forget.

"Do you wish to continue?" asked Garud as he paused and waited, his jackal eyes twinkling bright.

"Lead the way," Jonas said firmly.

"Follow me," said Garud.

From then on Jonas knew there was no going back.

Drawing nearer, Jonas noticed that those three shining towers were in fact made of crystal. The middle one was the tallest with a door at its base. Garud stopped when they reached it.

On each side of the tower's door there instantly appeared a glowing sphinx. Both were ethereal and bright, and had large wings folded behind them. Their long claws dug into the planet's surface, while human faces gazed back with blazing eyes. They were both so beautiful that Jonas couldn't take his eyes off them.

He gulped, wondering what he should say to these celestial sphinxes. He had never met a celestial sphinx before. He wondered what their higher roles and functions might be.

But before he could ask them the left sphinx spoke in a soothing female voice. "Greetings, Garud, Jonas."

"The Supreme Being is expecting you," said the second sphinx.

Both Garud and Jonas bowed to these sentinels before the crystal door. Jonas sensed that they were scanning and studying him with their piercing human eyes.

"Yes, we wish to enter. I must introduce Jonas to the Supreme Being. From this day forward he is no longer a mere Intergalactic Special Agent."

"We understand," said the left sphinx, its eyes twinkling.

"We have foreseen this. We have been expecting you, Jonas. Please, enter," said the right sphinx, as it bowed its head down between its clawed for paws.

Both sphinxes suddenly vanished in a flash and the tower door disappeared, revealing an elevator. Jonas followed Garud inside and the crystal doors closed behind him.

The elevator rose, gaining speed until it stopped without even a jerk or a slight bump. When the doors opened Jonas's jackal eyes beheld a spacious chamber with a large window adorning a far wall. Through this window Earth's blue, brightly glowing orb could be seen stretching across the horizon, dwarfing Medea entirely.

Stepping out, Jonas couldn't help but admire the crystalline faceted angles and all the twinkling lights that reflected off of every surface in that giant chamber. He inspected some of these more closely, running his hands over a nearby wall and the elevator's closed doors.

Soon his eyes settled on a single column of golden light. It shone down from the ceiling and onto a three cubit circle in the very center of the chamber. His sensitive jackal ears flitted about nervously as he swore he heard heavenly music coming from somewhere nearby.

"The Supreme Being's chamber..." said Garud softly. "The eternal Being will now choose a form which you find familiar." Garud then urged Jonas toward the column of light.

Jonas took a deep breath and his entire body vibrated with anticipation. It was most likely a reality that no other agent, Shastra, or mortal being, if any, had been inside this sacred chamber. And if one had then not for a very long time. As he drew nearer to the column it began vibrating, twitching, and flickering quickly. Jonas watched it as he cautiously inched closer. Then almost instantly, the column transformed.

An old looking Shastra now sat before him, with a long, gray beard, and wearing thick eyeglasses. Its long and gray jackal hair was tied up into a bun, while blue and red desert robes draped its shoulders, just like those worn by the Shastra nomads of Jonas's tribe back home.

Jonas's grandfather, Paw-Paw Neferis, was now staring right at him and with a friendly smile slightly creasing his wrinkled jackal face. All this caused Jonas's mouth to hang open in shock. But, Jonas knew well that Paw-Paw Neferis had been dead for over six Monubian years. Jonas's jackal eyes began watering and his throat felt tighter. He sniffed as powerful emotions came flooding up within him.

Obviously it wasn't really Paw-Paw, but still, the resemblance was uncanny. Jonas deeply missed his beloved grandfather, and ever since his death he'd thought about him often, more than any other member of his family. He began to question his sanity. First Garud, then Prajna, then Medea and the crystal tower, and now Paw-Paw had come back from the dead. Jonas was torn, he wanted to believe that it was Paw-Paw but he couldn't.

Jonas just stood there, staring at Paw-Paw through tears of happiness, mesmerized by the being's strange, kaleidoscopic jackal eyes. Jonas almost couldn't handle the rush of love and joy exploding within as that familiar gray jackal-haired face smiled back.

Paw-Paw had been a respected Stamel herder and water trader back on Monubia(Stamels were six-legged camel hybrids with curved tusks, long tails, and the ability to run extremely fast over long distances). Paw-Paw had passed away at the ripe old age of two hundred and thirty Shastra years after contracting a serious case of flying serpent rabies. He'd received the deadly bite from a fire lizard while out trading diamonds and emeralds in exchange for a million gallon tank of water and a cart-full of ice. As Paw-Paw clung to life, dangling lifelessly from his saddle, his trusty Stamel had towed him, plus their load, all the way back to camp while also avoiding several bandits and bubbling tar pits along the way.

He stared, enraptured, and wiped the tears from his jackal eyes while trying to think of what to say.

But Paw-Paw spoke first, and telepathically, sending his thoughts, along with images, right into Jonas's quivering jackal brain. "You have finally come. I patiently watched and waited, following you throughout the cosmos, and always waiting for this special moment."

"Paw-Paw, is it really you, or—?" Jonas replied mentally, his jackal upper lip quivering.

"Jonas, as the Supreme Being I can take any form. I chose this image because I knew it would comfort you. I know how much you loved Paw-Paw and that you miss him greatly."

"But... but how? I don't understand..." he stammered as he sniffled. He blew his nose on his embroidered Command Center issued handkerchief. Sadness of Paw-Paw's death grew within him. His mind knew that it wasn't really Paw-Paw, but his heart was completely fooled. He could barely speak. He just listened intently, loving and relishing every word Paw-Paw said.

"The nature of this layered reality is deeper than your eyes could ever believe," Paw-Paw continued. "I always had my eye on you, watching and waiting." Paw-Paw stroked his gray beard as he raised a hookah tip to his jackal snout. The hookah had instantly materialized out of nothing.

Then Paw-Paw sat cross-legged on his favorite cushion and smoked his Monubian hookah, just like he had always done. And just like the old days, Jonas smelled the sweet scent of mango flavored tobacco filling the air around him.

Jonas's mind hummed softly with pleasant memories of countless hours spent with Paw-Paw, digging wells, studying sword fighting, or riding Stamels through the desert. Quite often they'd just talk and play flying fish chess late into the night. They knew it was time to stop when the crying cactuses began their wailing which signaled the rise of Monubia's second sun.

When that happened Paw-Paw would always smoke his Monubian bubbling hookah and make them chocolate-flavored coffee. He'd then read to Jonas and his brothers from a great tome tales of the Guardian, Garud, and the traditions of Monubia's many famous swords Shastras, starting with Thorius the Brave hearted. After a while (three stories at the bare minimum) Jonas would always fall asleep curled up on the floor of Paw-Paw's tent, while his grandfather faced the horizon to meditate.

"Jonas, meet my loyal generals, the twelve Guardians!" said Paw-Paw, stirring him from his reverie.

Paw-Paw gestured around the chamber as twelve celestials appeared with bright bursts of light. Jonas glanced with awe at each one. They were all giants with glowing eyes that sparkled with an inner fire.

Jonas recognized most of them from his Celestial Studies class. There was Mobius, a Navan wrapped in colorful scarves who held his trusty mace, Gandhar; Shamses, a Ghanda and creator of music and literature, holding a two-necked sitar known to vaporize demons; the Danaan Guardian, Wishu, with fiery red plumage, along with her rider, the human Guardian, Neftum, whose skin was as black as Corconite. Neftum held up his famous silver bow of Joppa.

Jonas was in a daze, trying to take this all in as Paw-Paw told him the names of the seven remaining Guardians. But those whom he wasn't familiar with he instantly forgot, their names and titles going in one pointed jackal ear and right out the other.

But all of them made a great impression on him, regardless. The last few were three human women, one praying mantis being, another Shastra, and lastly, a gryphon and a sphinx, all who appeared divinely endowed with powers that he wished to understand. Jonas knew that his comm. link catalog could fill him in on the rest of their names later.

"Jonas, my celestial brothers and sisters were all overjoyed to hear Ashtar had chosen you for this mission to Earth-1," Garud said as he stood next to Paw-Paw. "Throughout the ages we have helped uplift Monubia and Earth-1 in both peace and wisdom. All those efforts led up to this glorious moment."

Jonas listened closely while he carefully noted each being's celestial dress, magical weapons, their glowing auras, and the mystical intent blazing behind all their eyes. These details would help him make a more accurate report for Ashtar later on.

"Jonas, you must now receive the Golden Bow, as well as the mental powers that every Savior has used," continued Paw-Paw. "Wherever Evil arises in the cosmos, attempting to subdue my forces of Truth, I always send out a celestial agent to drive it back into the cold abyss."

"Do you understand, Jonas?" Garud asked.

"In a way I do, sir. But mostly I trust you, and I pledge that I will learn as much as I can in the days to come." Such lofty concepts seemed hard to grasp at first. But they always contained great depths which he longed to explore.

Up until that moment his depth of knowledge regarding the Supreme Being had come from the mouths of desert shamans, wandering holy men, or witch doctors he'd encountered while living on Monubia. He understood the concept of a web of light holding all life and creation together, but he'd never seen its structure for himself. He'd heard of the angelic realms, the afterlife, and even the darker astral dimensions. But to him these were just mental concepts, not actual experiences.

The friendly Monubian shamans had taught him about power animals, drumming trances, and visiting the Underworld to ask help from the nature elementals, spirits, and of course the great ancestors of the Shastra race, especially its saints and prophets. In this way Monubian shamans performed magic, could turn into their power animals, could heal themselves and others, and could even heal the heart of the planet itself, having an ancient and living spirit of its own.

"One must possess great bravery and humility to accept such responsibility, Jonas," continued Garud. "Those who desire power and position are unworthy to carry the divine scepter. Such beings never rise to the tallest heights of reality. Now, I hereby gift you with my Golden Bow. This weapon has defeated more demons than I could ever count."

He glanced upward at a large bow and quiver that were descending from the ceiling. He recognized it at once. Every young Shastra had heard stories of the Golden Bow of Garud and how it had defeated countless cosmic serpents and evil demons. This bow here appeared just as it did on the temple frescoes of Monubia. It stopped descending right as Jonas reached for it. The bow felt light in his hand. The silver bowstring hummed as he carefully pulled it back and he noticed that its surface was covered in rows of golden hieroglyphics.

"Jonas, this Golden Bow has been used by every Savior since Anunakh-Ten..." Garud said proudly.

"Anunakh-Ten...the first Shastra to appear on Earth-1 after the great cleansing...." Jonas murmured this with deep reverence, his eyes still glued to the celestial bow. "Wow...." He stared at the bow closely now and noticed that it weighed almost nothing. "Every Shastra back on Monubia idolized Anunakh-Ten."

"As they should. He was one of the greatest and most powerful Saviors I've ever trained," said Garud.

"Wowww..." said Jonas, staring back up at Garud.

Paw-Paw spoke next. "Along with this Golden Bow, a Savior possesses celestial powers. These include clairvoyance, bodily control, flying, healing, and psycho kinesis. But you will develop those later on. Now you have to always remember, Jonas, to never use any of these divine powers out of anger, for revenge, or to gain fame or control over others. If you did then they would all be swiftly removed. Trust me, it has happened before."

"Yes, sir, I understand," he said solemnly. "I promise to never even think of doing that."

"Good, for these divine tools can bring destruction if used selfishly," said Paw-Paw. "However, if you use the powers and weapons in service to others, the Guardians, and to me, then you will never fail. They were made just for this purpose."

Jonas nodded in agreement. A lump got stuck in his throat as he imagined what might happen if he misused them. Maybe he'd be fried by lightning or some other celestial punishment. It was probably terrible, whatever it was.

"Now, out of these powers the most useful will be the power of flight, to heal one's self and others, to manifest weapons and items from the astral realms, and to converse telepathically with all life, from the largest animals down to the smallest forms," said Paw-Paw.

As Paw-Paw spoke, Jonas intuitively understood how to use all these powers. He felt like each ability had lain dormant within him for ages and were now just being rediscovered.

"Jonas, each power relies on the fundamental Force," continued Paw-Paw. "Through this power entire universes are animated by my eternal Spirit. As a Savior you will learn how to wield this energy to accomplish great things."

The knowledge of these powers was a thrill that filled him, making his body vibrate all over like a tuning fork. The Supreme Being was now just sending images right into his squishy and quivering jackal brain. He would try hard to use them sparingly and only to serve others. To him the consequences of their misuse were clear.

"Our time together is now drawing to a close," said Paw-Paw. "Never forget, Jonas, to meditate on me and the Guardians. If you do your mind will open up to ever deepening spheres of knowledge."

"Yes, sir, I will try to." As he said this tears formed at the edges of his jackal eyes and he began to sniffle slightly. He didn't want to have to leave Paw-Paw. "Will I ever see you again, sir?"

"Yes. I can appear to you again in this form if you wish. I know that you and Paw-Paw shared many precious moments together. He loved you very much, Jonas."

"Yes, he was my favorite relative, sir. I was crushed when his soul left to join the ancestors. He supported my plan to enter the Ashtar Command's Intergalactic Agent Academy. He said that it was an honorable goal. I owe so much to his wisdom and encouragement." Jonas wiped his wet jackal eyes on the sleeve of his tunic.

"Yes, I know that, Jonas. We all believe that you have the ability to become a great Savior, a leader to Shastras and Earthlings in the future," Paw-Paw said and his voice started trailing off.

Jonas watched through salty tears as Paw-Paw's gray-bearded face slowly faded back into a column of golden light. Each Guardian then bowed and vanished in turn, leaving just Garud and Jonas left in the crystal chamber. Jonas finished wiping his eyes dry and turned to Garud, now ready to leave.

Once back on Medea's surface, Jonas glanced back up at the blue orb of Earth. He felt light and giddy, like he could just float up and off into space, he was filled with that much joy. The vision of Paw-Paw had opened a long wounded chamber in his heart but had also given it much needed healing. A lingering sadness was now lifted from him. Like a dark cloud before blazing sunlight, it had suddenly vanished.

"We will meet another time and continue your training, Jonas. Now you must return to Telos. You have seen quite a lot tonight already," said Garud as he smiled proudly.

But before Jonas could ask him when and where that would happen, Garud touched him on his jackal forehead. He was blinded by a quick flash and when he recovered he was back in the cottage, tightly wrapped in his blanket, and lying right where he'd been sleeping before all this had started. Outside the cottage the jungle was peaceful and calm. Bheem and Khafre lay fast asleep where he'd left them but Garud was nowhere to be found.

A faint glimmer of sunlight was just sneaking through the lush trees, bushes, and vines outside. Jonas laid down and pulled his blanket up beneath his jackal chin. He sighed with satisfaction as he turned on his side and closed his jackal eyes. He wanted to sleep but he just couldn't stop smiling.

He still felt a lingering thrill from his experience that night. He tried to remember every image and every word that host of divine beings had shown or said to him. He swore that it could fill a whole volume of philosophy if he could remember it all.

He remembered Paw-Paw's natural scent of dry mongoids and hearing his soft jackal voice. When finally he felt fatigue set in it only took a slight mental command for him to quickly cast himself into the peaceful realm of sleep. That night he enjoyed a vivid dream. The Monubia desert landscape was passing by. He was with Paw-Paw once again, and they were busy riding the fastest running Stamel in the entire tribe.

Fuming with anger, irritated, and all soaking wet and completely covered in mud, Necrat stomped through the side door and into his space jet, dragging a captive Ghanda behind him by her thick lion mane.

"Tarsus, warm up the chair!" he barked, violently shaking the mud and water from his thick wolfman fur. Then he slammed his laser rifle into a weapons rack where it magnetically locked into place.

Furious at the Ghanda guards for attacking at him (one had even bit him on the leg), Necrat growled as shoved his captive into a metal chair. Its energy chains instantly bound and immobilized her athletic lion frame. And standing right beside her chair was none other than Tarsus Riggs and the hologram of Khapre-Tum, glowing green with menace.

"Plug her in! Show me what she's seen!" Khapre-Tum hissed and shook his boney fist. His hollow eyes flared bright red and his skeleton form quivered with excitement.

Necrat closed the space jet door behind him. The Ghanda captive then roared so loud the force shook the entire space jet's compartment. Her snapping jaws bit the air, but Necrat just sneered back while the chair immobilized her further. It even shocked her with current until she stopped growling. Soon, she could only move her leonine eyes, as her warrior muscles were now frozen stiff.

Necrat smiled wide at beholding the terror and helplessness on her lion face. But then he noticed she was different. Where fear and panic had just been, a boiling rage began to fill her dark eyes.

"Tarsus, put the mental cap on her, now!" Necrat yelled, snarling with drool. "Get that thing on her mangy head, already." He hoped that this guard's mind held the vital information he wanted.

The skill to it was in extracting just enough information without damaging the captive's brain. He didn't yet have the technology to put his captive's consciousness into a cube storage system. But he would have it soon, which would make things much safer and cleaner.

Tarsus fastened a silver cap to the guard's wet Ghanda head, and soon her memories were flashing up on the screen floating beside her.

Khapre-Tum's skeleton hologram stepped closer. His long cape whipped about behind him while the hologram's high-pitched buzz filled Necrat's wolfman ears. "Has she seen Jonas and Siegfried?" Khapre-Tum asked. He tried tapping the screen with a long boney finger. But his glowing green digit just passed through it and he hissed angrily.

"Run it faster, Tarsus," barked Necrat. His greed and desire drove him wild now, to the point of hysteria even. And he loved every second of it. He knew that soon now, both Siegfried and Jonas would inhabit chairs right beside this Ghanda.

Tarsus beeped and the images went by faster. The Ghanda twitched and moaned painfully, until Tarsus finally paused the images. Up on the screen Necrat saw Marmaduka (another ugly Ghanda, he thought) leading Bheem, Khafre, and Jonas up to a brown, two-story temple within the central square of Telos.

"That's them...but where's Siegfried? Keep going, lizard brain," yelled Necrat.

Tarsus beeped and the images kept playing forward. As they watched, Ghanda soldiers walked up to the guard, talked with her for a while, and then walked off down the lane. Necrat pumped his fist in triumph as he finally saw Siegfried, Argos, Khafre, Bheem, and Jonas all emerge from the temple together.

Next, the Ghanda guard heard a noise and marched off into the jungle where she lifted her laser rifle and crept through the tall ferns. She then proceeded to shoot at Necrat and the demons approaching from the south. The screen's images showed Necrat fighting her, knocking her down, chaining her up, and then another Ghanda biting him on the leg before he then dragged this one back through the hold of his space jet.

"That was them!" Khapre-Tum yelled, shaking with rage. "Capture them. Kill them if you have to! I don't care what you do. Just don't let them leave that village alive. That's an order, Necrat!"

"Yes, your Excellency," Necrat said, greedily smacking his wolfman jaws. "They have very little in the way of firepower to defend themselves with. We will capture Telos easily. And if need be, I'll activate our secret weapon. That puppy will finish them off for sure."

"Your secret weapon had better work. I'm not paying you to test out equipment. You know the consequences for failure, Necrat...."

"No, more input required..." Tarsus beeped.

Necrat slapped his forehead and rolled his eyes in contempt. "Tarsus!" he started to yell, but Khapre-Tum interrupted him.

"I will proceed to turn you both inside out over a painfully slow period of time," growled Khapre-Tum, his terrible eyes fixed on Tarsus.

"Sir, the secret weapon is one hundred percent tried and tested," Tarsus beeped in reply. "It is perfect and guaranteed to work, based on my calculations. We can activate it at any time. And Siegfried can't stop it once activated."

"See, it's a little insurance policy me and the boys cooked up back in Hiix. We've been working on it for a while now," Necrat added. He lit a huge cigar and puffed eagerly. "None of them suspect a thing, not even Siegfried. Trust me."

"Fine.... Just do your job or consider yourselves both on a short list for disintegration!" yelled Khapre-Tum. Then in a flash his giant green hologram vanished.

"Why that fricking, skull-faced, bone-brained, moron..." Necrat mumbled angrily through his fangs. "Turn that thing off, Tarsus. I'm putting this one on ice with the others."

Tarsus fumbled with the wires to try and remove her mind cap while he also punched the controls on a panel beside her metal chair.

But Necrat had grown so angry by now that his last brain cell of patience was completely fried. So he lunged at the supply table and grabbed a six-inch-long needle. Then he plugged a cable attached to its loose end into the control panel, and with one swift motion shoved the needle's long tip right into her furry Ghanda neck.

He stopped when he heard a loud crunch and then waited until her cries of agony finally ceased. She shuddered and convulsed, before screaming once more as her lion head flopped limply to the side. Then Necrat smirked with satisfaction as the view screen hovering right beside her went dark.

The Athenian Marriage Form

WARM SUNLIGHT HITTING HIS JACKAL face woke Jonas from a deep slumber. Gazing out through the cottage, he noticed a sharp new freshness filling the air. Breathing invigorated him as he sat up. He methodically rubbed the sleep from his jackal eyes before he threw off his blanket, put on his tunic, and bounded out the door. He noticed strangely how he had surprising energy for it being so early in the morning.

Running past his sleeping comrades, he noticed that a beautiful glow was hovering around Khafre and Bheem, their blankets, the furniture, the cottage's support beams, and even the wet jungle path right outside their door. He walked briskly, his sandals sloshing through puddles from the heavy rains the night before.

He reached the covered walkway on the village edge, where he'd been blasted off his feet and Garud had appeared to him. He carefully inspected the planks, the roof, and the patch of grass nearby. Then a sudden burst of joy electrified him as memories from the night before came flooding back.

He quietly strolled along the walkway, deep in thought, entranced by these thrills of joy while gazing out at the jungle's brush. While he did, his mind was raised up to a lofty state as every object and every thought was cloaked with this new aura of beauty.

He even heard heavenly music flowing over from the bushes, the trees, and up from the blades of grass beneath him as he left the walkway. He felt that every leaf and beam of sunlight was whispering to him in a new language of peace. Everything which he once thought was only inert matter was in fact acutely alive with intelligence and its own intense feelings.

Beautiful dancing orbs of light passed over his jackal head and he turned and watched them fly off and over the village. He could feel the very earth beneath his sandaled feet throbbing and beating with a deep and sacred rhythm that was also in sync with his own heartbeat. The entire planet was revealing its innate and sacred sense of life to him, and to whomever else could hear.

All during this incredible experience, while he walked through the entire village, he had absolutely no concept of time. But soon his feet magnetically returned him towards the cottage where he found everyone now awake.

Siegfried sat on the floor, busy frying delicious smelling jungle-fish sausage and river-shark eggs on a portable free-energy stove. Khafre was brewing fresh coffee (although not Toklaxian brand, unfortunately). Isas sat nearby baking a golden batch of soft and fluffy biscuits to perfection. His sensitive jackal sniffer became suddenly enchanted and he eagerly investigated every smell present while he sat and waited patiently.

His jackal brain was still buzzing as Isas passed him a plate piled high with fresh eggs and sausage. He added salt and ketchup and immediately dug in. He often remembered later on how he had enjoyed that meal more than any breakfast he'd had in a long time.

While he ate he noticed everyone shooting him inquisitive glances while trying not to get caught looking. When he finally grew uncomfortable he broke the silence, the words nearly launching out of him. "Garud appeared to me last night, right over there," he said. Just saying these words thrilled him to his very core.

Everyone there froze mid-bite.

"He manifested his chariot, Prajna, and then flew us both to Earth's second moon, Medea. I met the Supreme Being there, as well as the eleven other Guardians. The Supreme Being appeared in the form of my grandfather, Paw-Paw Neferis. It was amazing. I wish you guys could have been there."

Bheem choked on his biscuit then spat it out as he knocked his coffee over. Isas dropped the river-shark eggs from her fork and then dropped both her fork and her knife with a loud clang. Khafre coughed, spitting coffee right in Argos's face.

"What, man?" yelled Khafre, dripping coffee all over himself.

"No way..." mumbled Isas. "Siegfried, does that mean?"

Siegfried slowly nodded in agreement.

"What?" asked Bheem. "Mean what, lassie?"

Argos shook himself and grunted violently, flashing his sharp bear teeth. Hot coffee covered his furry bearman face. Jonas watched, curious as to how Argos would further react as Khafre nervously tried to clean the coffee out of Argos's thick fur while apologizing profusely.

"Don't worry, Khafre. He's harmless actually," said Siegfried. "He only attacks when I tell him."

"Then tell him I didn't mean to do it, man," Khafre said in panic.

"Argos, it's alright, settle down, boy. Easy...." Siegfried said, raising a hand.

Argos stopped growling instantly. But Jonas noticed that Argos didn't take his stern bearman gaze off of Khafre for a very long time after that.

"This is very important, everyone. Jonas is telling the truth," said Siegfried. "I know, for I was there as well. Last night Garud anointed him as the next Savior to serve and protect Earth. Garud lent him use of the Golden Bow, the ancient weapon once used by Anunakh-Ten himself. Jonas will be trained to face Khapre-Tum to try and save the Earth from catastrophe. Only then may he rescue Talley and return him to the Command Center."

"Man...Khapre-Tum? No way, man.... That's just gnarly. Wait, did you really meet Garud, Jonas?" asked Khafre in disbelief. "And you're a Savior, man?"

"Well, I'll be darned, laddie," said Bheem. He leaned back with a huge smile spread across his white jackal-haired face. "It be happenin. It really be happenin.... A new Savior be comin ta earth. And I actually be alive ta see it happen, up close and in person even!"

"Yes, it all really happened just like Siegfried said," Jonas said happily. He understood their disbelief. He could barely believe it had happened himself.

"Now that I think about it, Jonas, there's this subtle blue light all around you. And your jackal eyes dance beautifully, like a celestial's," Isas said as she studied him with her large, black eyes narrowing with concentration. "This is such a rare event, Jonas, that it deserves its very own entry in the Record Storehouses."

"Agreed, that's a great point," added Siegfried.

"We should make a journey to the Record Storehouses sometime soon, Siegfried, to record all this. Jonas should come too, to get the story as close to right as possible," she said.

Jonas would love to see the Record Storehouses with her and Siegfried. In fact he had the strong desire to accompany her anywhere, it didn't even matter where. "That sounds like a lot of fun," he said. "Garud told me he'd return and that I needed more training later. So maybe we can go after all that's done."

"So, so, so, wait a frickin micro-cycle here, man.... What exactly happened to you?" Khafre asked, scrunching his monkey face. "I mean like, I wanna hear details, man!"

Jonas laughed and then he told them everything. He spared no detail, however small, and when he'd finished the others launched into a staggering barrage of questions all at once. Most of these he couldn't answer, everything about the experience still being so strange and new even to him. Siegfried answered a few questions, although to Jonas's amusement, he made sure to not reveal himself as being the Guardian, Garud. Jonas wondered who else knew. Did Isas even know?

"But what does it all really mean, man?" asked Khafre.

"Why it means that a great change will soon sweep over the whole planet," said Siegfried as his jackal eyes twinkled bright. "Earth-1 has suffered while the forces of darkness have built up influence and power, reaching a new and terrible stage. The Supreme Being has finally said 'enough is enough.' It is now answering the planet's fervent prayers for peace."

"Oh, excellent, I can finally finish my book then," said Isas, clapping her hands happily.

"Cool, what's your book about?" Jonas asked, intrigued to meet an actual writer. He really admired creative beings, as the most creative he ever got was inventing a new fencing exercise, learning about new laser rifle models, or in researching an exotic planet to visit on his vacation. But after hearing the concept for her book he instantly regretted asking.

"I've visited many different Record Storehouses, searching for psychological profiles of the past six Saviors, with a special emphasis on the young males of nonhuman species," she said. "I've already written chapters on Anunakh-Ten, Tikriit, and Omtet. Since you're the next one, Jonas, I can write your story, and then add my book to the records. All I have to do is interview you, write it up, and edit it. It won't take that long."

"Interview me? About what?" he asked cautiously.

"Oh, about lots of things...about your past, your schooling, your family, and agent training courses. And then of course I'll have to record the details and outcomes of all your future battles. Isn't that nice?" she asked with a cute smile.

"Suuurrreeee...." said Jonas just as his throat clenched up tightly and his jackal ears perked up straighter in alarm. She was going to interview him about everything and write it all down. He stole a sideways glance at Siegfried, but the hermit just winked back with a playful smile, ignoring his obvious distress. Well, there was no use protesting now if Siegfried didn't say anything against the idea. But then to his horror she and Siegfried kept discussing it.

"Being a Savior carries a heavy responsibility," added Siegfried. "You will have to fight demons, skeletons, titans, and even the Dark Ones if need be. Your struggles and victory will inspire beings across the galaxy."

"Isn't that wonderful?" asked Isas.

"Yeah..." he replied, but he really didn't know. He did think that facing all those different types of enemies sounded daunting to say the least.

"The Record Storehouses will definitely need the full account of all the seventh Savior's struggles, failures, and victories," said Siegfried. "All future generations of Earth-1 will want to study this tale some day. Maybe you could call it...oh, I don't know, something like, The Song of Jonas?"

Jonas thought the idea sounded horrible, but he couldn't say that to her. She seemed very excited and he was a typical Shastra, private, stoic, and somewhat shy. But really, none of that appealed to him at all. But he had no choice but to just roll with it. Who knew if her project would ever actually materialize or not? He sure hoped that it didn't.

"That be it. That be the perfect title, lassie!" Bheem exclaimed, slapping his knee.

"That does sound lovely," said Isas. She quickly jotted it down on a napkin so as not to forget and then slipped it into her robe.

"Yeah, it is, isn't it? That just came to me, right off the top of my head," Siegfried said brightly.

"Cool, man! I can't wait to read it," said Khafre.

"Will it be available on comm. link audio file?" asked Bheem. "I listen ta them on me chariot rides."

"Sure, why not?" she said. "I'll get to work on Jonas's chapters right away." She smiled broadly and continued to scribble on a second napkin with her free-energy pen. "Jonas, we can start with an interview about your childhood and home planet."

"Yeaaaah...okay then...." he replied, nervously tapping his knees with his hands while trying to think of a way out of this. "That...sounds realllly interesting.... Umm...I didn't know that you were a writer." Was she going to ask him about everything? About his youth, his family, his friends Digger and Zarry, and why he hadn't passed fighter weapons school yet? His stomach started to churn in summersaults.

"I've written for a long time now," she said. "I write mostly about the history of Athenia. And also the sacredness and power of the individual's path through Earth-1's different spiritual traditions. I've done most of my research in the Athenian Record Storehouse, but I've visited at least three others with Siegfried. We should all take a trip to visit at least one of them. Some of Earth-1's older cultures were very strange. But some were also incredibly interesting."

"So, what were they like, man? I only know about Navan history," said Khafre.

"Well, for example, did you know that they greatly prized a black goo called oil? And that the most important thing to them in the world were these funny little green pieces of paper that they used for currency? That's so bizarre, isn't it? Paper!"

"I've heard of money before, man. They were brainwashed into worshiping it, right?"

"Right!" said Isas, throwing her hands up. "Just incredible!"

"What is oil?" asked Jonas. "I've never heard of oil before." He'd already heard about those strange green pieces of paper, and that ancient peoples valued them more than almost anything else. Of course he found the whole idea to be absurd. But he was just glad to talk about something other than her interviewing him for her book.

"Yes, they had many diverse uses for oil, we believe," she said. "Scholars agree that this age dominated by green pieces of paper and oil was the height of some type of unfortunate, collective insanity experienced by that particular civilization. Although, come to think of it, Earth has experienced many different crazy periods filled with equally crazy ideas. Back then society was in a state of constant war, not too different from the demon and bounty hunter raids on the major cities of today. There also was a strange, subliminal programming device called a television, which I find truly amazing. So much craziness went on back then that it's hard for me to believe it all."

Jonas just stared at her, unable to believe what his jackal ears were hearing. "So, so, wait...did humans drink this 'oil' or use it as medicine? I still don't understand," he said. He wondered what it would be like to talk with an ancient human. But then he realized that they probably wouldn't understand a thing each other said.

"Unfortunately, the records on this and other topics are sparse and incomplete," she added. "But from what I've studied, there was no nutritious value in drinking this oil. Some scholars believe that oil was used as 'fuel' to run metal chariots. The ancients called these chariots 'cars.' But, it's just a working theory."

"I've heard a cars!" Bheem said enthusiastically. "I be hearin rumors that they couldn't go inta space or even fly through tha air. Is that true? If so then why did they use em at all? I don't be gettin it."

"Yeah, that doesn't make sense," added Jonas. This concept of ancient chariots called cars was a new one to Jonas. He'd only heard of roller-skates, airplanes, and horses.

"Believe it, boys. As far as we can tell it's all true," said Isas. "These cars drove on roads made of stone with rubber wheels. Whole forests and jungles were cleared to make roads for these cars to drive on."

"That's just so weird..." said Khafre. "What a waste of good jungle, man. Why not just make the cars able to fly over it?"

"I know...it was a very weird period. Their civilization didn't have free-energy either," she added. "A select minority did contain such knowledge but they kept it secret from the public for some reason."

"For their own gain, maybe?" asked Jonas.

"Or to protect it," added Siegfried.

"No wayyyy, man! That's just too crazy.... How did they get anything done without free-energy?" asked Khafre. "That's just nuts, man!"

"It sounds like that was a very strange time to be alive," said Jonas, shuddering at the thought of having to survive with such low levels of technology; like no food or matter replicators, no ion healing devices, and no wormhole travel or atomic-powered star chariots.

"Exactly. We don't really know how they survived as long as they did," she said. "Every scholar agrees that it was a very crazy time on this planet, absolutely backwards."

"Ya can say that again," said Bheem.

"They were quite a funny civilization," added Siegfried, his jackal eyes twinkling with mirth. "Mostly just humans lived on Earth-1 back then. And any Shastras, Navans, or other races that visited usually hid out in caves, underground, or in bases beneath the sea. A few beings from other stars systems did try and blend in with the main population, but they used disguises. And of course the inner Earth beings have always existed within the planet. It was a weird time to live on the surface, that's for sure."

"Sounds like it," said Jonas. He couldn't believe how different those ancients sounded from the planet's current civilization. Even his home planet of Monubia had free-energy, space tourism, and space trade, and it was just a tiny desert planet. Monubians had always appreciated their planet's nourishing spirit, had openly associated with the celestial Guardians, and had always followed spiritual Law, at least in Jonas's memory they had. But he understood that even Monubia had gone through similar growing pains in the distant past.

"I promise that we will all visit the Record Storehouses in the future after this adventure is over," said Siegfried. "That will prove an interesting education. But we will have to wait for another time. We still have much work to do."

The next three days were spent in preparation for an expected attack on Telos. Siegfried's spy sloth network had told him one was definitely coming, plus, the Ghanda guard Beeshee had gone missing, thought to be kidnapped by demons, or worse bounty hunters. Siegfried also revealed that Khapre-Tum had ordered Hiixian bounty hunters to capture both him and Jonas, and that they should anticipate an attack any day now.

Being a normal green-blooded Shastra, Jonas loved hard work and the camaraderie that came with it. So during their prep time his friendship with Bheem, Khafre, Isas, and Siegfried quickly deepened. He was surprised to learn that both he and Bheem had some of the same instructors and mentors back on the Command Center, as well as the same Warrior Space Ball coach, a ten cubit tall lizard-being named Tang who was a legend of the game.

In the meantime Khafre taught them all Navan mace fighting as well as a sport that he called 'sailing' which he enjoyed while on vacation in Kalkas, and which Jonas found fascinating. And although Jonas found Khafre to be a quirky individual, he and

Jonas soon became close friends. Khafre also loved Warrior Space Ball, but much less than archery which was one of the main sports that Navans played. He soon developed a keen interest in helping their mission succeed, which Jonas and Siegfried both appreciated.

Jonas was naturally curious and loved learning about the Navan city of Kalkas, as well as the island of Athenia. Thankfully, Isas quickly warmed to them and turned out to be quite friendly. She even joked with them freely and laughed at their cheesy humor (she found Jonas's old-timey Shastra jokes to be especially groan-inducing). She told them incredible stories of her adventures with Siegfried and when she interviewed Jonas she made sure her questions were respectful and not too probing which he was thankful for.

But because of the constant work and planning Jonas wasn't given even a free moment with which to call Ashtar. If not eating or napping in the cottage they were always slogging through the tangled brush and vines at the village's perimeter and setting booby traps, or measuring and mixing explosive potions and powders for said booby traps. They also lined all three of the roads leading into Telos with energy chains as well as trip wires that Jonas connected to electron claymores and neutron mines and which Siegfried said he had "found" in a village nearby. Lastly, they dug four foxholes and connected them with narrow trenches in which to watch and wait for an attack.

After they'd finished with everything they all collapsed from exhaustion. Jonas then washed up, returned to the cottage, and placed his comm. link on a table. "Hermes, please dial the Ashtar Command Center. Identity: Jonas Neferis, junior Intergalactic Agent."

"Sure thing, Jonas," Hermes replied. A few beeps later Ashtar's blue human face appeared. Jonas stood straight and saluted the hologram at stiff attention. He smiled, pleased to speak with Ashtar again and eager to relate all that had happened since he'd left Shetra for Telos. "Sir, Jonas Neferis, junior Intergalactic Agent, reporting on my mission's progress, sir."

"Ah, good evening, Jonas. I'm glad to hear from..., son. I hope...you are well and—fortable in Telos and have met with Siegfried...now."

"Yes, sir, I have."

"Great. I'm glad that you were able to...us. We've been trying to reach—for some time now, but the interference was just too dang—," said Ashtar.

As they spoke more Jonas could tell why that was the case. Ashtar's image and speech weren't clear for long, if at all. It faded in and out, going from identifiable to a crackling mess of static that constantly hissed and sputtered. But if Jonas squinted he made out just enough detail to see the silhouette of Ashtar's blue human face.

"I understand, sir. The transmission is also unstable on this end."

"Yes...we know, Jonas. So...(crackle, hiss). We are unable to... any supplies via wormhole."

"I'm currently not in need of supplies at the moment, sir. Siegfried will provide what we need. He is very capable. The Guardians are supporting him, sir."

"Yes, but...(hissss...warble...hiss)...—ference means dark energy....—work. Be very...careful. (garble...warble...crackle) Stick with Siegfried...all costs," said Ashtar.

Although badly garbled, Jonas understood the gist of his message: this interference was caused by a strange type of energy and to be safe he should stick close to Siegfried, which he intended to do of course.

"Yes, sir. I will, sir," he said. Then he paused to think of how to best convey what had happened to him in the past four days. There was almost too much to tell at once. Would Ashtar approve of the change in his mission's goal? "Sir, I have to report that a very interesting, errrmm...phenomenon has occurred recently. I must preface that it was highly irregular and not at all according to my mission's protocol. It wasn't covered in the Agent Manual either, sir."

"That's quite alright, son...tell—...happened," Ashtar's hologram hissed back.

Jonas felt a rush of excitement as he began the tale of meeting Garud and traveling to Medea. "Sir...did you get all that?" he asked after speaking for fifteen bleebs straight without a break.

"Yes...(garble...crackle...garble...). Quite unexpected...—very, very good news...very...proud of you.... Tell me more...return. We'll try to repair—...connection...end and...try to communicate again.... (hisss...crackle). Keep—ing, son...."

Jonas wondered if by being a Savior he could earn a faster promotion to senior agent level, and more importantly, get fast tracked through space chariot fighter weapons school and into time travel school, which was his ultimate goal. He really hoped that it did. And the sooner he passed those the sooner he'd be sent on high profile missions to undiscovered zones of the universe or be given command over a space station where he'd lead his own company of agents.

"Jonas....Be warned, son...bounty hunters are—...both...of Telos. Tell Siegfried.... Trying to capture—you...Siegfried.... Stay safe...—retry later. Over and out."

"Over and out, sir!" He saluted stiffly and then the comm. link cut out.

Jonas wondered if maybe bounty hunters were using electromagnetic weapons to disrupt their comm. links. He couldn't know, but maybe Siegfried would. Then he remembered Siegfried had requested that he devise a plan to defend the village.

Committed to drawing up the plan before he went to sleep, Jonas asked Hermes to access the Intergalactic Agent's Manual and opened the hologram catalog entry entitled *An Agent's Guide to Military Trickery and Funny Business.*

He read quickly, skipping over useless minutiae while he made furious notes and drew out crude diagrams on a scroll with his agent issued, space proof, free-energy pen. He read, wrote, and thought deep into the night and without a break. He didn't stop until his plan was fleshed-out enough that he felt it just might work.

The next evening right after the sun had set, Siegfried called a meeting in the central foxhole now in the city's main square. The foxhole faced the largest chariot path leading into Telos and was connected to three additional foxholes by narrow trenches. If Jonas stood straight up in the foxhole he could see out at ground level and survey almost the entire village.

Jonas, Bheem, Argos, Khafre, Isas, and Siegfried were joined by Marmaduka, plus, ten of the meanest looking, fully-armed Ghanda soldiers in all of Telos. In addition, two wolfmen and three Shastras joined in, who all looked very official in their beautiful uniforms. This told Jonas that they were obviously from out of town.

Siegfried addressed the assembly by introducing everyone while Argos handed out bronze shields and helmets to the attendees.

Jonas noticed that almost all these helmets were either fashioned into a lion's head or a jackal's head, and were made from a beautiful silver alloy that he couldn't easily identify. There was a sharp crest of iron or a plume of red hair decorating the crown of each of these helms. It made them resemble a style from Earth-1 history that Jonas identified as 'ancient Greek.' But he knew these were much more advanced than what those ancient soldiers had used.

"Bheem, Jonas, these are very special helmets," Siegfried said as they both curiously turned their new helmets over in their hands. "Khafre, I'm sorry but I didn't know you were coming. So I don't have any helmets that might fit a Navan, other than this one here," Siegfried motioned to Argos who handed Khafre a simple golden cap. The Navan accepted it and tightly fastened the strap under his monkey chin.

"Hey, no worries, man. This one is actually pretty cool. But let me know if you find one that fits a Navan. That would be pretty righteous, man," said Khafre. "Preferably, one that looks like Tanis or Mobius, the Guardian. You know something with style, man."

"Indeed, that would be quite righteous. I will search for one," Siegfried said.

"Jonas, have you noticed that Argos doesn't ever talk, man? Not even once since we've been here…" Khafre whispered this to him after Siegfried, Isas, and Argos had all moved to the opposite end of the foxhole where they separately addressed the all Ghanda contingent.

"Yeah, I noticed that. But it's not a big deal," Jonas said while he studied his new jackal-shaped helmet.

Khafre paused and raised a monkey eyebrow.

"What? Is it a big deal?" asked Jonas, confused.

"It's just super weird, man. You know....everyone talks at least once in a while, man," Khafre whispered back. "It just isn't normal."

"He's just getting used to being around us. I'm sure he'll open up after a few days."

"Yeah, man, but we've been working right next to him now for more than three days. I haven't heard a peep out of him, man, other than grunting and growling. It's starting to really freak me out, man."

Jonas didn't really care about any of that. In fact, he hadn't even considered it since they'd first met Argos, Isas, and Siegfried. "Oh, come on, Khafre.... You don't need to worry about that. Look, we've still got tons to do. I don't get why you even care," he said. "Maybe that's just the way he is."

"I don't know, man, but I'm just saying.... It's pretty weird, you know? Do you think that he's mad that I spit coffee in his face, man?"

"Probably not, that was three days ago."

"But, Navans say that bear-beings have great memories, man."

"Well, if it were me, I'd just forget about it," said Jonas. He was steadily growing annoyed with Khafre's obscure obsession with this, so he simply ignored Khafre's further protests as he slipped his new silver helmet over his jackal head.

It fit him perfectly, automatically forming itself to his jackal neck and face. Inside, whirring and clicking electronics instantly cooled him, providing a much needed relief from the intense jungle heat.

He was surprised at how absolutely amazing this new helmet was. It had almost every feature an agent could ever want. Its electronic readouts displayed graphs, measurements, and heat signatures for every object around him. It measured distances and temperatures (the latter in degreedoes). Plus, he could turn his head about freely, talk with absolute ease, and could hear pretty much everything happening around him perfectly. He could hear a family of dino-lizards all snoring in their sleep a ways off. One of its readout even told him that the dino-lizard's nest was forty leagues off to their right past an emerald green lake called Trumble Lake.

"This thing's amazing," Jonas exclaimed as he excitedly glanced about. He'd never worn anything like it. "Hey, Bheem, how do I look? Siegfried, where did you get these?" He looked around, testing its hearing and the display sensitivity on anything he could find.

"Very slick, lad," said Bheem. He looked out at Jonas through his own helmet and gave him two thumbs up.

"You guys look awesome, man," Khafre said as he adjusted his golden cap.

"Hey, looking slick, Khafre," Jonas said, admiring Khafre's head gear.

"Right on, lad. That thing be stoppin a laser blast from any distance," added Bheem, pointing at Khafre's golden cap.

"Cool, man!" Khafre said, feeling the cap as it sat snug on his monkey head.

"Boys, come on over," said Siegfried. "I want to speak with everyone, first. Then you can explain your plan to us, Jonas."

Jonas nodded and removed his helmet, before joining Khafre, Bheem, Isas, and everyone else now all gathered around Siegfried. They stood before a small fold-out table covered with maps that Jonas, Siegfried, and Marmaduka had drawn of Telos and the surrounding area.

"Thank you for joining us, everyone," said Siegfried. "As you all know, bounty hunters were spotted outside of Telos by three Ghanda guards and one surveillance sloth. And I am sorry to report that Beeshee has been captured."

A nervous groan traveled around the table, followed by bothered mumbling.

"Also, my sloth and bush baby spy network have informed me of a sizeable company of demons that is right now gathered near the village," continued Siegfried. "Their ultimate goal is to capture both Jonas and myself. With Jonas being the new Savior, they will stop at nothing to prevent him from facing Khapre-Tum. Is that clear, everyone?"

The crowd's grumble grew louder, becoming anxious harrumphs with a mild sprinkling of indignation. Some snarled angrily while others mumbled gruff Ghanda words that Jonas didn't understand. He definitely shared their concern, as the outlook for their engagement was appearing worse and worse all the time.

"Listen, everyone. Please, calm down," said Siegfried. Everyone was suddenly quiet. "Jonas has a plan to hold them off. As you know, he is an Intergalactic Special Agent from the Ashtar Command, so he has extensive knowledge and experience in strategy and survival. Please listen to him as you would me. Jonas, you have the Shlerpo."

Then suddenly Siegfried handed Jonas a round, bulbous mass. It was purple, about the size of a Chockoberry, and covered in long, slimy green hair. Jonas looked at this new object, surprised and mildly disgusted. It pulsated for some reason and had already covered his hand in thick slime. He looked up at Siegfried, who just smiled back. Jonas wasn't familiar with a Shlerpo but he decided he'd just roll with it anyway.

"It's the speaking Shlerpo. It gives you the authority to be listened to," said Siegfried happily. "It's a Ghanda tradition."

Jonas looked around the circle at all the Ghanda soldiers who were smiling happily back at him. "Thank you, sir," Jonas said, shrugging his shoulders but glad to be learning something new. He was eager to speak but was also growing more eager to get rid of the slimy Shlerpo with every passing moment.

So, putting his helmet down, Jonas next picked a pointer stick up with his free hand. "Good evening everyone. I have met most of you by now. And I would love to meet the rest after we're done here. Now, if you look at our first map, we've marked all the roads leading into Telos, here, and the emerald lake and its two pyramids, two hundred cubits to the east, here." Jonas pointed to the three main roads on the map. A long path connected the largest one with two pyramids along an emerald green lake, labeled Trumble Lake. "Marmaduka, have you talked with the Ghanda demigod, Trumble, who lives in the first pyramid?"

"Yes, well, we tried to. But he very quickly turned angry and kicked us out. He said that he doesn't want to get involved," said Marmaduka. "But I'm not surprised. He's always been grumpy like that."

"But, he's a demigod, right, man? Why won't help us?" Khafre asked in disbelief.

"Its fine, Khafre," said Jonas. "He is free to refuse, but it's still a shame. A demigod like him would be a big help."

"That's about what I expected from Trumble anyway," added Siegfried. "So that's not a surprise."

The crowd quickly settled down and let Jonas continue for he was still holding the speaking Shlerpo. While he spoke additional soldiers continued popping into their foxhole to join the meeting. The most outrageous of these was a purple-skinned human that Jonas had already met, named Mohab. He had a curly black moustache, was dressed in colorful scarves and robes, and carried a curved sword and knife lashed to a wide leather belt. Upon first meeting him Jonas had been instantly reminded of Earth's ancient Pirates.

"Now, a hundred yards from here there is a small bamboo hut in which we've placed life-sized mankinis of Siegfried, Bheem, Khafre, and myself," he said. With his stick he pointed out of the foxhole and towards the hut in the distance.

"Uh, Jonas, on Earth they're called manikins," said Marmaduka, correcting him.

"Really? Oh, interesting. On Monubia they're referred to as mankinis," Jonas said curiously.

"Nope, they're manikins!" someone yelled out from way in the back.

"Well, to each his own," said Jonas. "Now, where were we...oh, yes, when the bounty hunters reach the bait hut containing the... manikins...they'll trip our booby traps," said Jonas. "Then the Ghandas positioned in tree forts to our left will begin to lay down cover fire while Siegfried and I apprehend the trapped bounty hunters from the...manikin hut.... Bheem, you and Khafre fire at any demons entering the village from this entrance, here. You will both be positioned in the foxhole to our left, here."

"Got it," they both answered when Jonas indicated these positions on the map with his pointer.

"How do you know the bounty hunters will attack the bait hut at all?" asked Isas.

"There happens to be a ridiculous reward for our capture," said Siegfried.

"How much, lad?" asked Bheem.

"Oh, it's an insane amount, just ludicrous I tell you," said Siegfried, shaking his white jackal head. "That's all I really know. But it means that we can count on their greed to lead them right into our trap."

"Right. Now, all the villagers who aren't fighting have taken shelter underground," said Jonas. "Argos and Mohab, you two, plus, three Ghanda guards take the third foxhole, a hundred cubits to our right, here. Your foxhole is closest to this side road, so expect a large force to come in that way."

Argos grunted, which Jonas took to mean he understood. Mohab let out a raspy "arrrrr," and Jonas did a quick double-take. Maybe Mohab actually was descended from the ancient Pirates?

On the map Jonas pointed out the two trenches they'd dug. "Siegfried, Isas, Marmaduka, and I will be stationed in this central foxhole. If you want to get us information then use these connecting trenches, here and here. Or if you can use telepathy, then send Siegfried a telepathic message and he promises to quickly get back to you. Is everything clear?"

Everyone nodded and said, "yes, sir."

"Alright, that's everything then," he said, happy to be finished as he finally and very carefully placed the slimy speaking Shlerpo on the edge of the table. He was desperately hoping that his plan worked.

"Good. Thank you, Jonas," Siegfried said. "Now, everyone, let's get to our stations. The siren bear will signal when the demons arrive."

"The siren bear?" blurted both Jonas and Khafre. Jonas thought he'd heard wrong.

"What's that, man?" Khafre asked.

"It's a bear-being but with translucent skin," replied Siegfried. "You can see its veins and they look like wires of light. They are a very unique species, a genetic combination of a bear and a jellyfish."

"You don't say, man…. Who knew those existed?" said Khafre.

"Huh, okay then…" said Jonas, unable to picture a bear mixed with a jellyfish. It just didn't make sense. But then again, he'd seen floating jellyfish beings on the Command Center before. And by now he knew better than to question anything that Siegfried said, so it must be real.

"Their growl is just like a siren, but it's louder than any you've ever heard. Trust me," said Siegfried. "The species was just recently introduced to the region around Telos."

"I didn't believe it either until I saw me first one, lad," added Bheem. "They actually be quite friendly, but also very wet and squishy like ya'd expect em ta be."

"That makes sense," said Jonas. Although, he was quite sure he'd never try to touch one.

"Okay, enough jibber-jabber. Everyone, to your posts," said Siegfried.

They all quickly grabbed their gear and scattered along the trenches to their separate foxholes. The Ghanda soldiers all climbed out and ascended the trees, settling into forts over-looking the village.

Some stayed and congratulated Jonas, complimenting him on his plan which he greatly appreciated because he'd put lots of thought into it. "Thank you very much," he said. "It's really just the basic 'bait and snatch' maneuver I got from the Agent's Manual. Everyone learns that one in school," he said.

A wolfman named Mamaji approached Jonas and Siegfried by the map table. Jonas instantly noticed how Mamaji's brown wolfman hair was all matted and sticking out at crazy angles. His grizzly appearance, combined with the strong scent of mud, wet fur, and barbecued dino-lizard, made him an instant magnet for Jonas's sensitive jackal sniffer.

Jonas thought he was dressed rather formally for a wolfman in a suit of gray space armor and holding a space helmet under his arm. But being a canine being, he instantly inspired trust in Jonas, not to mention the desire to play chase with him and then tug-of-war while using an appropriately sized stick.

"Jonas, this is an important ally," said Siegfried. "His name is Mamaji Esquire, a Canonian (Jonas knew this was another name for a Wolfbeing), a scientist, and a war hero from a city-state named Battledore. He has fought in several conflicts against the bounty hunters from Hiix."

"It's an honor to meet you, brother," said Mamaji. He shook Jonas's hand with a hairy paw that had a firm grip along with some very sharp claws. His bushy tail wagged back and forth excitedly, almost knocking over the map table. "Siegfried is a dear friend of mine."

"Thank you for coming, Mamaji. It's an honor to meet a friend of Siegfried's," Jonas said, bowing low.

"You're the new Savior, I hear, brother," said Mamaji.

"According to the Supreme Being, yes. Although, it still seems unbelievable," he said, laughing.

"Don't worry about it, bother," Mamaji said confidently. "We Canonians have technology that can help. Plus, you've got Garud's

Golden Bow, and that thing is absolute gangbusters, I hear, brother." Mamaji playfully punched Jonas on the shoulder. "The energy readouts on that thing will tip the scale on any quark-ion pulse-ometer." He smirked and patted a blinking gadget attached to his belt.

"That makes sense," Jonas said, although totally ignorant of what a quark-ion pulse-ometer was. "Yes, it appears to be a powerful weapon. But I haven't quite used it—"

"But you will still need Siegfried's help, that's for sure, brother," Mamaji interjected, pointing sternly at Siegfried. "Because Necrat and Tarsus Riggs are the worst of all the bounty hunters. The meanest, foulest, nastiest, and slimiest out there. And. Don't. You. Forget it," he said as he tapped Jonas on the chest with each word. "Those two are out for blood, brother."

"Right. That's good to know," Jonas said, feeling slightly alarmed to be hearing this, but also believing it to be nothing new. "But I have a feeling that Siegfried is preparing us well."

"Ahh, if anyone can, it's Siegfried. But remember, Khapre-Tum is, what?" asked Mamaji, staring at Jonas like the answer was hiding right there in his tunic pocket.

"Well, uhhh, he's powerful, and he lives in the Underworld...." he said.

"He's incredibly crafty, brother, that's what! Plus, his power is nearly immeasurable. Not even a plasma detonator can scratch that skull-brained rascal," Mamaji said with an intense wolfman gaze.

Jonas gulped. Even though he knew that Mamaji was trying to help, he now felt more anxious than just a gonard ago.

"But remember, Siegfried has faith in you, brother. And so do I. Without his help the Hiixians would have wiped Battledore right off the map. And that's a fact!"

"I've studied the Hiixian-Battledorian wars. They sound like they were just awful. Battledore barely survived them," said Jonas.

"They were even more dangerous than you read about, brother," Mamaji said seriously. "But, Jonas, it is an honor to serve with the new Savior." He then bowed and marched off down the trench to their right.

"That guy was really weird, man, and super hairy..." said Khafre.

"Look who's talking," said Jonas, pointing to Khafre's thick monkey fur. "Plus, he's a Canonian. They are weird in general, and also sometimes a little lax with their hygiene and grooming. But they're usually brilliant scientists and engineers."

"Cool, man. I've only met one or two Canonians before."

"Battledore was once a sister city to Hiix," added Siegfried. "Hiix chose to use its technology to conquer and enslave other city-states, while the Battledorians broke away and used theirs to uplift and heal the planet. Because of this, Battledore has always been protected by the Guardians and other beings."

Only Siegfried, Jonas, Marmaduka, and Isas remained in the central foxhole now. They quietly watched the village outside while an anxious silence fell. The hair on Jonas's arms and on his jackal head stood up straight as he anxiously waited, afraid to even move. One hand held his laser rifle, while his other grasped the booby trap detonators. As Jonas gazed out over the village, he imagined demons creeping along just beyond the trees, poised to attack at any moment.

Jonas's jackal instincts went into a nervous state of overdrive while he waited. His pointed jackal ears perked up and twitched about as he listened closely. He sifted through an array of noisy bugs and frogs all chirping and croaking by the edge of the green lake not far away. Off to their left he heard three monkeys fighting over a pile of fruit, while five fire squirrels dashed over some roots and then up the wide trunk of a baobab tree.

Jonas wanted desperately to jump out of the foxhole and chase all those squirrels and monkeys. Then he would dive after every critter in and around the lake while sniffing out everything else along the way. And of course he would do all that while barking up a storm. But the timing was all wrong, so he made himself resist the urge. Maybe later he'd get an hour or two to explore things on his own.

"I can feel them nearby, so stay sharp," said Siegfried. His third eye twirled brightly while he glanced down at his two-thousand-year-old pocket watch.

Jonas stole a glance at this watch, but couldn't read any of the dials on its face. He knew about watches like this, that non celestials weren't able to read them at all. These special watches were known to map and measure the energies that held the universes together and that sprang from the one primordial Cause. In all, their dials were said to track and measure the intensity and fluctuations of the five cosmic energies that created and maintained gravitational waves, wormholes, portals, countless higher and lower dimensions, plus, the many celestial spheres.

"Good idea," said Marmaduka. She purred softly while she licked her paw and then stroked her mane to clean it.

They waited and waited, but nothing happened. Then the siren bear yawned loudly, sending everyone jumping and falling over each other as they gathered their weapons.

"Don't worry...hey, calm down. It's just a false alarm," said Siegfried. "It's okay. The siren bear just yawned. That wasn't the real siren."

"That was pretty loud, though," said Jonas, his jackal ears ringing.

"I know, lad. But they be gettin much louder," said Bheem.

"Geeze, alright then…" said Jonas, shaking his head and sighing with relief. Upon reflection, he thought it had sounded more like a trumpet than an actual siren anyway.

Again, they all settled down to wait, while also staying alert. Siegfried called Marmaduka to the opposite corner of the foxhole to quietly talk. Jonas couldn't believe that he was finally alone with Isas for the first time in almost three days, other than when she'd interviewed him.

He wanted to talk to her, but about what? He found everything about her interesting, her eyes, her hair, her smell, how she stood and held her laser rifle, even how she turned her head while staring out at the village. She appeared fully in control, confident that she could handle whatever they faced.

Jonas quickly tidied his jackal hair and checked his breath. Good, it wasn't a disaster. He tried to remember the Intergalactic Agent rules for interspecies relationships regarding humans. But no matter how hard he tried he couldn't recall a single one. To make matters worse, he had rarely ever paid attention in Human Studies class. He just found the subject boring. All he remembered was that humans liked being asked questions about themselves and appreciated if you were a good listener. But wait…was that true for human females or was he remembering wrong?

Now if she was an Intergalactic Agent and they were both back on the Command Center, then he knew exactly what to do. First, the potential mates each constructed a working battle robot. That step was easy enough, even though Jonas wasn't very mechanically minded, let alone an engineer. Next, their robots fought, and if the proposer's robot won, then they moved onto the Shastra specific portion of courtship, if they chose this channel (this of course was determined by what other species was involved).

The Shastra specific stages included the male offering his potential mate a dead animal, which he'd catch himself. The female would then judge this carcass by its smell and taste. And if found favorable, she would then accept his proposal of courtship. But if she rejected the carcass then the male still had two chances left. Other than carcass presentation, the potential couple could choose from a swordplay demonstration, a telepathy competition, or a Stamel race. But these were just the Shastra specific options.

Jonas personally found the first test to be the hardest. That was because for some reason every Shastra female that he'd met on the Ashtar Command was an excellent engineer. And they were all especially good at building battle robots. And even though he'd built many battle robots before, he still felt that he was a beginner (maybe they took special courses on it, but that was a guess). But despite this fact, he preferred logical, step-based systems and liked knowing the protocols beforehand.

But he decided to give the earth human method a try, just for fun. His textbooks had often called this method 'conversation.' So he quickly tried finding a topic that might arouse and engage her mentally. This was supposed to help them bond over a common interest.

So, he executed the next logical step in the process, which was approaching her and opening his jackal mouth to speak. However, he immediately regretted his decision, for what came out was this: "So, Isas, could you tell me, because I'm very curious about Athenian culture...how does a priestess from your country get married? You know if they ever wanted to.... Or maybe if you wanted to, you know, get married, to someone else, a person or a being…. Let's just say, what would you or your potential suitor, whoever they are, you know, have to do?"

He froze immediately, his jackal mouth hanging open while he tried figuring out what had just happened. He was unable to control it. The words had just gushed out like a nervous stream of word vomit. Now all he could do was pray that she, being a human female, found this an appropriate line of questioning after having just met someone four days ago. It was a long shot, but if he crashed and burned then he would ask her if she ever liked sniffing animal carcasses. He really hoped she did.

"Why, Jonas, that's a pretty forward question to ask a lady, at least where I'm from," she said. She tilted her head to the side and raised an eyebrow while she examined him.

His heart jumped and then skipped several beats. He wanted to run, but he knew he was trapped. "Oh, umm, well, yeah…. You know Shastras are known for being blunt and straightforward. See, my culture has different courting rituals than Earth-1 beings," he said, hoping that he could somehow salvage the situation. "I've heard that Athenian priestesses need to sign a special form. Like a list of tasks or something. Is that correct? It will help with my mission write-up later on," he added. Then he waited breathlessly while his ears twitched nervously and his palms sweat.

"Wow, I'm flattered that you're so interested in Athenian culture, Jonas. I'm very proud of it," she said in a calm and appreciative tone. He couldn't know for sure, but it was as if she had ignored his nervousness or hadn't even registered it at all. She smiled brightly and his heart fluttered when she playfully flipped strands of her long black hair over a shoulder.

He eagerly sniffed the air, catching definite hints of jasmine, tanned leather, and what had to be coconut oil. He wished that he could remember more to add about Athenian culture but his mind was completely blank.

"Well, let's see…Athenia has lots of different traditions, Jonas. But it's also a very small island, having just risen during the last great period of Earth changes. It's where a much older island, named Lemuria, had once existed. So now if I remember correctly, and it could be different now, I don't know, the usual way that a priestess gets married is with a signed form like you mentioned. It is said that any suitor can get one from a temple atop Mt. Nabi."

"Oh, that's interesting. So, they just climb it and then get the form, and then that's it? Wait, ummm… Mt. Nabi…. That's where Anunakh-Ten first appeared on Earth-1, right? That's pretty high up, isn't it?"

"That's correct. It's actually eighty thousand cubits high. And Anunakh-Ten was the first Shastra and Savior of this Age to arrive on Earth-1. You know your history, Jonas. I'm very impressed."

She smiled and his heart did a triple-flip. It appeared he hadn't crashed and burned after all. "Okay, so that's not too hard, right?" he asked. "Just climb up and get the form."

"Oh, no, getting the form is just the beginning. Each form contains a list of ten tasks which the suitor must accomplish. And they're usually pretty dangerous."

"Wait, how dangerous are we talking here?" He prayed it was something doable, and not an exotic thing that he wasn't trained for. But then again, he was getting way ahead of himself as he usually did.

"Well, every form is different, for one. But some tasks do get repeated. At least that's what the suitors often reveal on their death beds, when their secrecy oath expires." She began numbering out a list on her fingers. "Tasks like: wrestling a serpent demigod, visiting the dark Earth dimension, and stealing the king of Trinicon's crown. Retrieving Moltjar's hammer is one that I've heard has been on the form before."

"Who is Moltjar?" he asked.

"Oh, Moltjar is a celestial from the planet Tiberian. Other tasks are searching for relics or lost treasure, like ships of the ancient Pirate races, the Spear of Destiny, and the giant diamond at the bottom of the Atlan Ocean. That last one was part of an ancient continent called Atlantis that sank long ago. No one's found that one either."

Her scrunched up nose and eyebrows while thinking told him that she was serious about all this. "Oh, that's...very interesting.... So, that's it then?" he asked, hoping she didn't add any more to the list. The courtship rituals for Intergalactic Agents looked far easier now, by about a hundred light-years if he was honest.

"Oh, no, there are usually ten tasks on every form," she said, sighing. "That's the tradition at least. And it can't be changed... even though not one suitor has ever finished a form."

"Oh, come on now. Someone's got to have finished all ten.... right?" he asked, rubbing his jackal chin in thought. "Maybe, in the distant past some demigod did or maybe a celestial. Probably someone you've just never heard of before." But then he realized that if that was true it still wouldn't make it any easier.

"Nope, it's all been documented, Jonas. The records say that over a thousand males have tried and almost all of them died a gruesome, horrible death. Even the Savior, Omtet, tried and failed. He was in love with Sonya, the most beautiful priestess in recorded history. He's gotten the closest, so far. He got to task eight and then was subdued by a giant sea monster. After that he just disappeared and wandered the Earth as a monk for ten years. But still, stubborn beings keep trying."

"Wow, that's pretty hard core," he said. Things weren't looking good. He'd definitely have to rethink this form. At least climbing Mt. Nabi wouldn't be hard, he thought.

"It is hard core. A lot of our priestesses are very beautiful, and very talented and intelligent. I think it's something in the water or the energetic environment around Mt. Nabi. Athenia is also a very wealthy island. So...the males just keep on trying. It's a shame because most of them are really great guys," she said, sighing deeply.

"I see. So wait a second...who makes the list, and why do they make them so hard?" he asked. There had to be a loophole, some reason for hope, he thought. If not for him then to cheer her up. If he thought logically about it, if he survived a battle with Khapre-Tum then he might like to pursue a beautiful and intelligent life companion; maybe an Athenian priestess? Would one be interested in marrying a Savior? Why not? He'd never know if he didn't try. But man, those tasks sounded hard.

He found Isas to be very attractive for a human being. But more importantly, she exuded quite an interesting array of smells that he would love to investigate. Maybe Garud could help him out. Give him some clues or pointers about the hardest tasks at least. Nothing was impossible. Paw-Paw had always taught him that. And being twenty two Shastra years old meant that he was at the cusp of the marriageable age for Intergalactic Agents.

"I think Garud and Anunakh-Ten invented those rules a long time ago," she said. "Remember, Earth-1 was recovering from drastic cataclysms when the Athenian convent was established. There were constant struggles to survive the weather, the uninvited space guests, the earthquakes and tidal waves, and all the new species of plants, animals, and other intelligent beings that the Introducers brought to the planet. But if you want to know more then just ask Garud. He knows way more about it than I do."

He sensed resignation in her voice, like maybe she had given up on marriage a long time ago. "Well, there has to be a first time for everything," he said, trying to cheer her up. "Once one being cracks the list then more will follow for sure."

"Yeah, maybe. But there'll definitely be tons of publicity for whoever finishes the list first," she said, smiling again. "They'll have their pick of a ton of priestesses too. Young ladies are joining the convent all the time. It's an ancient and very honorable profession. Who knows, you might try it someday? You'll be extremely famous if you defeat Khapre-Tum." She smiled, turning her head slightly which made her appear playful and spunky. He absolutely adored her and thought that he might faint right then and there.

"Hmmm. You are right about that. There's got to be some kind of petition, though, a way to bypass that form, like for special circumstances," he said, eyeing her hopefully.

"No, I've never heard of any. You know...you're really interested in Athenians, aren't you?" she said with a devious smirk.

He smiled back. He was glad to see her happy again. And he wasn't sure, but he thought that maybe she was on to him. It wouldn't hurt if he revealed his interest in her now, would it? He thought that maybe human females would like that. It was straightforward and practical. "I am quite interested, yes. You see I'd really like to—"

But then Jonas was interrupted by the highest wailing noise he'd ever heard in his entire life. It was so loud that he bent over in pain and covered his jackal ears. "What is that?" he yelled.

Writhing on the foxhole floor, he fumbled about and finally put his helmet on. But not even that kept the noise out.

"That's the siren bear!" Siegfried yelled. Both he and Marmaduka rushed over, and as they stared out over the village, Siegfried materialized a long, blazing energy spear in his right hand. "The bounty hunters are here. Look—" he yelled and pointed.

The siren bear suddenly stopped its wailing and Jonas at last managed to stand. As he looked out from the foxhole large light-emitting beetles, some three cubits long or longer, flew up and over the jungle. Their rear ends lit up like glow-globes as they buzzed over their heads, lighting up the darkness.

Okay, that was step one, thought Jonas. The Ghandas up in tree forts had released them. Jonas breathlessly watched these beetles descend while he also heard demonic growling in the distance. Then suddenly his pointed jackal ears heard laser fire and then shouting. Then came more growling, followed by three explosions off to their left. He could see black shapes with red eyes moving through the thick jungle bush.

"That's it! I'm doing it!" Jonas yelled. He squeezed the detonators and triggered the booby traps. A long row of blazing explosions erupted along the village perimeter. Everyone in the foxhole jumped and then ducked, covering their heads.

The Ghandas in the tree forts above began firing as Jonas soon saw bright laser rounds flying over their heads towards the village border. Jonas turned on his helmet's infrared readouts. As it scanned and monitored the section of village in front of their foxhole he kept his laser pistol charged and ready to fire.

Three successive jets of fire launched up from the jungle into the air and they all ducked again. Jonas stood and his helmet's readout measured that each explosion had been exactly a hundred cubits from the foxhole. That was the mankini trap. Jonas looked to Siegfried. "That's the bait hut!" he yelled. "Come on!"

"Right, let's go!" said Siegfried and with one jump he bounded out of the foxhole.

Jonas climbed out and together they sprinted through the village, ducking laser blasts and dodging explosions along the way. A blackened patch of earth was all that remained of the bait hut. There was absolutely no sign of the mankinis anywhere. But Jonas couldn't ignore the sight of both Tarsus and Necrat hanging upside down right in the center of the trap. Levitating rings bound both of their feet while suspending them in the air.

Jonas was ecstatic, the trap had worked perfectly. He looked closer to see hundreds of creeping green bugs crawling all over the bounty hunters, while a slithering black goo coiled itself around each of them, constricting them like serpents. Siegfried never told Jonas exactly what went into making the goo and green bug part of the booby traps, but the result looked painful to say the least.

Necrat and Tarsus yelled and flailed about, trying in vain to free themselves. Of no use and well out of reach, their laser rifles, utility belts, and bandoliers filled with ion grenades and other destructive gadgets were all stuck to a magnetized crystal on the ground.

"Well, helloooo, boys," Siegfried said happily. He waved the smoke clear from his jackal face. The better to peer into Necrat's wolfman face now upside down. "It's been a while hasn't it? You two just can't stay away, can you?"

"Siegfried! Put us down! Now!" Necrat yelled.

"I'm afraid I can't do that, Necrat. As long as there's a bounty out for Jonas and myself we can't let you wander about freely, trying to collect it, can we?" said Siegfried. "You should never have accepted an offer from Khapre-Tum. This time you're way in over your head, I'm afraid."

"Siegfried, this is the last time that you escape us! I swear!" yelled Necrat. "Never! Never! Never again!" Necrat lashed out with his wolfman claws, missing Siegfried by a micro-cubit as he pulled away quickly.

Jonas trained his laser pistol right between Necrat's crazed wolfman eyes. The safety was off and he set it to kill. He would fire if Necrat tried that again.

"Affirmative, Necrat," beeped Tarsus. "By my calculations—"

"Ah, that's enough, you two—" interrupted Jonas. "There's a cold cell waiting for the both of you. Let's go." Jonas whistled at the levitating rings which floated the bounty hunters along behind him. They ducked and dodged more laser bolts, running back to their foxhole, when about halfway there Jonas stopped and froze, stiff as a board.

His pointed jackal ears turned about, listening. He heard growls from demons in the distance and then the roar of Ghandas. Listening harder, he caught a high-pitched whine that definitely wasn't the siren bear. Siegfried also stopped to listen. Jonas then noticed that the laser fire had ceased. He glimpsed about and caught demons and Ghandas all standing nearby like statues.

Something terrible was happening, thought Jonas, as a tight knot formed in his stomach. "What is that?" he asked. The whining grew louder. The hair on his jackal head all stood up straight.

Siegfried remained transfixed, silent. He finally turned to Jonas and his face looked whiter than ever. "I, I...I don't believe it...." he mumbled.

"Haha, that's right, bucko!" Necrat yelled as he laughed crazily. "Suck on that, you mangy dogs! You're done, Jonas. Hamburger meat, Shastra kebabs, burnt Shastra steak. Audios, suckers!"

Jonas looked down at Necrat. Necrat saluted him, but his other hand was holding up a small transceiver. It had to be a special plastic, for it had escaped the trap's crystal magnet. But before Jonas could ask what it was an energy shield materialized around both of the bounty hunters. Jonas instinctively looked up. Great streaks of fire leapt up and began racing over the jungle's green canopy like a tidal-wave of flames.

"What the heck?!" yelled Jonas.

"Run!" Siegfried yelled, grabbing Jonas's tunic.

But Jonas remained rooted to the ground as he watched, horrified. In that split-second hesitation the violent shockwave struck him and he went flying through the air.

He flailed and just managed to manifest his bronze shield before he crashed right through two mud huts and then painfully bounced off a third.

He finally landed and he could barely see, his head had rattled around so much in his helmet. When it finally stopped he found he was tangled in a thick mass of vines suspended high off the ground. He rested there for a bleeb, trying to make sense of what had happened.

He moved and tried feeling his limbs and examining the state of his armor and helmet. Then he checked to make sure he wasn't pierced, burned, or mutilated anywhere. He found that he pretty much hurt everywhere at the moment, but was still in one piece. He sighed with relief, feeling happy to be alive.

He got his bearings and looked for a way down. But then he heard another sound and glanced upward. An awesome, burning, roiling cloud was racing right at him with incredible speed, like a thousand bolts of lightning formed into a meteor and streaking through the jungle.

He immediately panicked. He hurried to untangle himself from the mass of woven creepers all bound with thick vines. He knew this cloud would electrocute him in a second and that would be the end of him. But his movement, plus, the weight of him and his armor, suddenly snapped all the vines and branches. He flailed wildly as he plummeted towards the jungle floor.

He bounced off branches and crashed through ferns and gigantic leaves as he fell. Then he landed on his back right on a thick pile of green moss. And as he did his helmet struck a large rock and the painful clang rattled his jackal brain. He heard a loud ringing and remembered holding the sides of his helmet in pain before his vision suddenly went dark.

An Unexpected Meeting

IT SEEMED TO JONAS that a long time had passed when he finally opened his eyes. He was lying on his back in a pile of moss, staring face up at the night sky. Leaves and ash were falling gently down and had built up a light cover on top of him. He laid there quietly, still very unsure of what was happening out in the village and if it was even safe to get up again. He listened for any signs of a shockwave or another rumbling ball of lightning. But he didn't pick up anything. All was quiet. He wondered if it was all over, and if anyone else had survived.

After a period of waiting with his mind running like crazy, he cleared off the piles of branches, leaves, and ash from himself, carefully removed his helmet, and took a long and deep breath. The night air felt cool, although he soon detected smoke that burned his snout's sensitive hairs.

He pushed himself up and even the act of standing was painful. He knew he had to find the others so he stumbled onward, hiking for a good distance through the thick brush all while wiping sweat from his furry jackal forehead. He wondered if he was actually going in the right direction when he finally reached a broad clearing. What he found there made his jackal mouth drop open in horror.

Where the village of Telos had once stood there was now a wall of black smoke and ash hovering over a severely scorched jungle floor. Jonas walked along, carefully tracing the perimeter, while his energy detecting glasses studied the barren landscape. Everything that he saw crackled with green light that looked like some strange type of energy.

The green aura was hot to the touch when he leaned down and felt a few mud bricks that lay at his sandaled feet. He couldn't believe it, but everywhere that he looked every structure had been burned, flattened, and blasted to pieces.

He prayed that someone was still alive. His heart began to race as he carefully crept into the clearing and reached one of the foxholes where he found several dead Ghandas inside. Horrified, he inspected them closely. All their limbs were contorted in the struggle to escape the fireball.

"Computer, what kind of weapon could have done this?" Jonas asked his glasses through the mounting tears. Already sore and exhausted, he was quickly growing distraught and defeated. He also wondered how he had survived that at all.

While he scanned the rubble his glasses' operating system whirred, beeped, and then answered. "Weapon; Hiixian thermal electron detonator, Alpha-class explosive, extremely powerful."

"I see...that's not good." Jonas knew that was one of the most destructive weapons available on Earth-1. "Computer, locate Necrat and Tarsus Riggs, please," he asked next.

"Affirmative, Jonas.... Their personal force fields saved them and they escaped. Both are already aboard their Hiixian star ships. Currently located two thousand leagues through the jungle to the south. Their chances of returning again are around eighty nine percent."

Thinking quickly, Jonas took out his comm. link device and dialed Ashtar. Thankfully, Ashtar's face appeared, and although broken and barely visible like before, Jonas could understand him. "Sir, we have to get out of Telos. There's been a terrible explosion—a Hiixian weapon, an Alpha-class explosive—send a Disaster Response Team—Telos is desperate for medical assistance—many Ghandas were killed—the entire village is gone."

He waited anxiously for Ashtar's reply. He knew that a Disaster Response Team could possibly arrive within one Earth day to decontaminate the fallout from Necrat's weapon, which was the priority.

Ashtar's hologram crackled with static while it sputtered periodically. But if Jonas concentrated he was able to make out his reply. "Good, you're okay...evacuate...son.... Response Team... the way...communicate soo—"

Jonas nodded back but then had a flash of inspiration. He quickly flipped through his comm. link's databank of hologram maps, looking for shelter and a good place to regroup.

Ashtar continued to speak as he flipped through the list of hologram maps. "Son, go...Kalkas. Look it...an ally with the Ashtar Com—will accept you with...arms. King...Kassam, will—help... shelter...demons from the Underworld. Tanis, the famous Navan... will help...the fight. Go—"

"I understand, sir. I've read lots about Kalkas." During the three weeks he'd spent in Shetra he'd read many hologram entries on the famous Navan city.

Kalkas was a major stronghold by the sea and protected by stone battlements rising over a hundred cubits high in places. But more importantly it was home to Tanis. He remembered Tanis from the archery tournament in Heliopolis and the program said he was the strongest, most famous Navan in the entire solar system. Jonas couldn't find a better ally in his fight against Khapre-Tum if he tried.

Kalkas suddenly looked like his best option, especially on such short notice. He knew no forts larger than Kalkas existed between Telos and the Atlan Ocean, let alone one that would willingly harbor an intergalactic agent trying to escape those bounty hunters. Jonas hoped that Kalkas hadn't already fallen to the demon army. He doubted that it had as it was thousands of leagues away from Heliopolis by atomic chariot.

He was sure that Necrat and the demon army would follow him there. In fact, it was possible someone was monitoring his communication at that very moment.

"Sir, I'll discuss this with Siegfried and then we'll make our way to Kalkas. Once there I'll communicate with you again."

"Yes...I read you...careful...Good luck, son," said Ashtar. "Over and out—"

"Over and out, sir!" he said, saluting proudly. He felt a rush of fear and intense loneliness as Ashtar's garbled hologram vanished. He started to think that if he couldn't find Siegfried, and if the bounty hunters closed in on him again, then that would be the last time he and Ashtar ever spoke.

Just as he put the comm. link back on his utility belt something strange caught his attention. He noticed that amidst all that destruction, almost every banyan tree, kapok tree, and baobab tree remained standing. All their trunks, branches, leaves, and even the vines, glowed with subtle illumination. In fact, all vegetation oscillated with incredible brightness and beauty in either a green, blue, or white light.

He bent down for a closer look. He could see right through the bark of the closest baobab tree and glimpsed its veins all vibrating with celestial light. When he removed his energy detecting glasses it appeared even clearer and brighter.

Curious, he knelt and ran a hand over the baobab's exposed roots. Its inner light hummed as he touched it, as if acknowledging his own energy. He theorized that this light had saved him when he landed in the moss pile at the base of those trees back there. Somehow this energy had shielded him from the fireball. That made sense since almost every tree remained standing, while nearly every Ghanda-made dwelling now lay in ruin. Then he looked down at his hands. This same light was flowing through them too now. It even flowed up his arms and down his legs, through his feet, and into his toes.

Amazed, he just stared at this light for a while, trying to figure out what it meant. He stopped when he heard a rustling noise off to his right. He quickly put his helmet back on and raised his laser pistol. He felt around for the force field generator on his utility belt as he crept further into the clearing, stepping over scattered rubble like he was in a space-junk yard.

Nothing emerged from the jungle so he walked towards the village center where he saw the giant baobab tree there, also invigorated by the same glowing light, had remained unharmed by the blast. Blue and red vines dangled from its branches, while mushrooms as large as satellite dishes were cemented along its wide trunk. Along almost every inch of its trunk there sprouted bright blossoming creepers.

How could all this foliage still be intact? And what on earth was this mysterious energy surrounding every tree, mushroom, vine, and creeper? He had to know.

His thought stream was interrupted by yells and blasts coming from somewhere close by. Still on high alert, he knelt, breathing rapidly while his jackal ears scanned for the source.

Then from off to his right three demons stomped out into the clearing. He took aim and fired, taking down two immediately. The third dropped its sword and dashed back into the trees. Then a sudden burst of laser fire struck the baobab's trunk right above his jackal head and he took cover behind it, lying as flat as he could against its trunk. He waited there like that for a while.

He slowly inched his head around the trunk and watched the barren landscape. When no one emerged he sighed, and completely relieved, he flopped back against the trunk where he rested, all hot and sore all over, and then removed his helmet.

At this point he just hoped and prayed that someone else had survived the blast. He didn't even move or care when a large rainbow-colored iguana crawled down the tree, onto his shoulder, down his arm, and then into a hole in the ground by his right foot.

A burning sensation beneath the bronze grieve on his left leg made him feel around underneath it. He found dark green Shastra blood on his hand so he removed the ionizator and flesh resonator from the medical kit on his utility belt. He removed his grieve and gritted his jackal fangs as he touched the wound with the ionizator and next cauterized it with the resonator. He turned away when the rancid odor of burnt flesh reached his jackal snout. He remembered the powers of a Savior included healing powers and so made a mental note to use them next time.

The loud rustle of footsteps up ahead made him jump up and drop his tools. He put his helmet back on and turned on its infrared sight, peering around the baobab trunk again. Through the thick ash and smoke the faint outline of a being could be seen approaching him. However, it didn't look like a demon or a Ghanda.

He waved and called after it, hoping that it was Siegfried, Isas, or Khafre. But the being didn't wave back. Instead, it raised a weapon and aimed right for him.

He instinctively ducked just as two bright hot laser bolts flew over his jackal head. He heard loud grunts and squeals behind him, followed by two solid thuds.

He froze, afraid to look backward. But when a familiar voice called out he slowly lowered his pistol. "Hey, Jonas, you almost got carved up like a Mastodontus roast, man." It was Khafre. He had no idea what the Navan was talking about, but at the moment Jonas was so glad to see him that he didn't care.

Jonas sighed, and gladly holstering his laser pistol, jumped with joy as he saw Khafre walking out from the cloud of billowing smoke. When he pointed behind Jonas, he turned to see two demons lying prone, only three cubits away from him, and booth clutching deadly scimitars in their hairy fists. Trembling, Jonas nudged each one with his foot. Neither of them moved.

This was his first up-close look at a demon from the Underworld. As he knelt closer his nostrils curled up as he found that they both smelled awful, like food that had been left out to rot for over a year. He then realized that without Khafre's help he'd be dead for sure.

"You saved my life, Khafre. Shastra agents always repay a life debt. You have my loyalty and protection. Thank you," he said. He bowed gratefully, and then still shaking, he glanced down again at the demon's corpses.

He embraced his Navan friend, partly to make sure that Khafre wasn't a hologram projection, an apparition, or a spirit form. But he was still his solid and hairy Navan friend that always smelled like bananas and leather.

"I'm just glad you're okay, man," Khafre said as he patted Jonas on the shoulder. "What happened to this place, man? It looks like some kind of Hiixian weapon went off."

"Yes, Necrat set off an Alpha-class explosive. It was a thermal electron detonator."

"Wow...." Khafre ran his hands through his monkey hair and brushed away ash. "Where is everyone, man? They aren't...? Are they?"

"I hoped that you would know."

"I don't, man. I got knocked out and just woke up a minute ago. My head still hurts, man."

"Mine too.... Ummm, okay, how about you check over there and I'll look through here," he said as he grabbed a charred beam atop a nearby pile and lifted.

"Siegfried! Bheem! Isas!" he yelled. But he received no response. He cleared the entire pile of debris, but only found broken pottery and small animal bones underneath. After they'd searched for a while, only to find nothing, Jonas was about to give up when a trap door opened nearby.

Jonas and Khafre both jumped and took aim, ready to fry whatever appeared, be it demon or skeleton soldier. But none other than Siegfried's hairy jackal head emerged. They lowered their laser pistols, both relieved and happy to see Siegfried again.

"Siegfried, it's you, man!" Khafre yelled. "You're alive!"

"Aye, I am. And I am also very glad to see that you boys are safe and sound," said Siegfried, smiling wide. "I was worried for a bit there." Siegfried climbed out and then dusted off his red and gold tunic and loincloth. He reached down and one by one, helped Isas, Argos, and then Bheem up and out from the trap door.

"I was beginning to believe that you'd been captured or incinerated in the blast, sir," said Jonas before he bowed at the hermit's sandaled feet. Siegfried's leather sandals and his curled toes emanated a golden warmth, reminding him again of Garud.

Siegfried grabbed Jonas by the shoulders, lifting him up and shaking him excitedly. An ancient light was gleaming behind his kind jackal eyes as tears pooled up in their almond-shaped depths. Jonas then felt a subtle current of joy pass between them and they embraced like old friends.

Additional trapdoors opened and a host of stunned lion-beings followed Siegfried as they climbed out and peered around. Others were now descending from their positions high up in the trees to join them.

"By the Guardians, Jonas! The Supreme Being is surely protecting you," Siegfried said with a sly wink. "I bet those trees back there broke your fall, eh?"

"That's correct, sir," he said, winking back. "I flew backward and then was caught in a bunch of vines. Then I fell, hit my head, and passed out for a while." He felt the tender spot still on the back of his jackal head.

Jonas and Khafre next embraced Isas, Marmaduka, Argos, and Bheem, and they all kept somberly quiet amidst the destruction, although all were glad to be reunited.

"Jonas, when that bomb exploded we saw the worst of it engulf you and carry you away like a bug in a storm. How on Earth did you ever survive that?" asked Isas. She busily brushed the dirt from her long, black curls, and somehow still looked beautiful.

"That was known as a primordial fire weapon," said Marmaduka, nodding slowly. Jonas noticed that for the first time he thought she looked shaken and scared. "Our village will need time to recover from this," she said as she looked away somberly.

"I've never seen anything like it, man," said Khafre, shaking his monkey head.

"Neither have I," said Jonas. "I think my armor saved me, plus that protective glow around every tree."

"Yeah, man, no trees were affected! But that blast was just gnarly!" said Khafre.

"Telos is a place of ancient power," said Siegfried.

"That is true. Many jungle spirits protect the trees and the land itself," added Marmaduka.

"Wow! That's amazing, man," said Khafre.

"Yes, it is," replied Marmaduka.

"Sir, I've called Ashtar and confirmed that we'll leave as soon as possible," said Jonas.

"Good. My surveillance sloth network has alerted me that the route back to Heliopolis is now blocked by the demon army," said Siegfried. "So, we can't go back that way."

"What did Ashtar say, lad?" asked Bheem.

"Not much else, the connection was very poor," said Jonas. "But he suggested that we travel to a city named Kalkas."

"Why Kalkas?" asked Isas. "That's very far away."

"Kalkas is an ally of the Ashtar Command as well as a stout fortress by the sea. Great Navan warriors live there who might lend us their help, including Tanis," said Jonas.

"Hmmm, that's a brilliant idea, man," Khafre said brightly. "I must say, man, meeting Tanis would be very cool. I've only seen him before on a hologram projection or at the archery tournament."

"Yes, that is a great idea," added Siegfried. "And Telos the Underground has a tunnel system which ultimately connects with Kalkas. So our transportation will be simple."

"But are you sure that those tunnels are safe, man?" asked Khafre.

"They are, Khafre. I have traveled them myself, many times," said Marmaduka.

"Excuse me. There are tunnels beneath Telos?" Jonas asked.

"Yes, the Telos Underground is a wide system of tunnels used for transport. They travel deep into the inner caverns of the earth as well as throughout its crust. It's the only option left to reach Kalkas quickly and safely," said Siegfried. "They are extremely safe, Khafre. Please trust me."

"Okay. I was just asking, man. But, it could still be dangerous, I'm just sayin, man," mumbled Khafre.

"Thank you, Marmaduka. We owe you so much for your help," said Siegfried. "Please, promise me that you will find Mamaji and ask him to join us in Kalkas."

"Yes, of course, Siegfried. And when all this is over we request that you grace our village with a visit. We can talk more then. But I pray that it will be in a time of peace," said Marmaduka.

Marmaduka and Siegfried then embraced while the lion-being purred loudly.

When they were done Jonas addressed her. "Marmaduka, I've already explained everything to Ashtar about what happened here. He promised to send a Disaster Recovery Team to Telos that will help your community rebuild."

"Thank you, Jonas," said Marmaduka as she bowed her lion head. "You make your ancestors proud. You've proven that you truly are one salty dog."

"You're welcome, you scallywag," Jonas said, smiling back.

"Now, everyone, the entrance to the underground is beyond the emerald lake and its pyramids, where Trumble lives," said Siegfried.

"Fair enough, let's get going," Jonas said, wondering what it would be like to meet a demigod like Trumble.

They carefully walked around the glowing piles of rubble and past a collection of twisted banyan trees set along the banks of a lake. Its waters were completely still, like a green plane of glass.

"It's beautiful," said Isas.

"What happens if you swim in it, man?" Khafre asked, peering into the shallow end. "Are there fish in there?"

"Probably nothing happens to you," said Jonas. "It just looks like a normal lake to me."

"You must first receive Trumble's approval in order to go swimming," said Marmaduka.

"So where be Trumble, exactly?" asked Bheem.

"He only appears when he wishes to," said Marmaduka. "No one can force him."

They kept walking and soon passed a set of ten stone pillars beside two towering green pyramids. They then finally reached a boulder outcropping at the base of a steep hill. "The main entrance to the Telos Underground is through that gap, there," said Marmaduka.

Although terribly dark, Jonas noticed that a faint orange light was glowing within the cave's deep recesses. But as soon as they reached the cave's threshold a green ball of light materialized before them and they all stepped back. Jonas watched with alarm as the green ball slowly churned until it became a Ghanda with brilliant green fur that stood ten cubits high. In addition to his strange green fur, an aura of green flame glowed around his tall Ghanda form.

"Who wishes to pass by my pyramids and enter my cave without first asking?" Trumble asked, his fiery eyes fixed upon them.

"We humbly ask for your permission to pass, Mr. Trumble," said Jonas, giving Trumble a half bow. "We wish to enter the Underground tunnels beneath Telos. We are on our way to visit Kalkas, sir."

"We are but poor, stranded travelers who are lost. We are also very hungry, man," said Khafre. "Please, take pity on us...."

"Khafre, that's not true," whispered Isas, elbowing him.

"Ow, it kinda is, man!" he answered.

"Dear Trumble, these are friends of my Ghanda tribe. They require safe passage to Kalkas," said Marmaduka.

But Trumble glared back with an annoyed look. "Who is it that has dared detonate a destructive device so near to my home?" Trumble asked, his aura glowing brighter. "They must be punished!"

"Yes, Mr. Trumble. It was the bounty hunters from Hiix who are pursuing us. Their weapon has destroyed the entire village of Telos," said Jonas. "We wish to enter the underground before they return."

Trumble looked back angrily. "Destroyed? But why? Who exactly?"

"Necrat and Tarsus, man!" said Khafre.

"Sir, please. The bounty hunters will be back soon. They are both shady characters of an evil sort," said Siegfried. Stepping closer to Trumble, Siegfried's third eye twirled with bright symbols as if communicating with the demigod.

"I am aware of their work," said Trumble, who growled angrily now.

"They have no honor or morals, sir. And that's putting it mildly," added Jonas.

"I am the nature spirit given charge of this lake here, these trees, and the land all about you," said Trumble. "Neither those demons nor those bounty hunters will be able to see my pyramids. And I wish to keep it that way. For I am a very private spirit who enjoys his solitude."

"Wow, I sure understand that, man," said Khafre. "Are you really a nature spirit, man?"

"Yes, I really am. And although Marmaduka's tribe has never bothered me, my sole rule is to only allow celestials to enter this cave. You must prove your worth to me or you will pay a heavy tax."

"What kind of tax are we talking about?" Jonas asked anxiously. He found Trumble to be a fascinating character, but he was also quickly growing impatient to get moving again. Necrat and more demons would soon be sweeping the area for them and they had to get out of there fast. The last thing he wanted to do was waste time arguing with a stubborn demigod.

"It's probably a really expensive tax," whispered Khafre. "Right, man?"

"It is whatever I like, monkey. For my power and protection helps to control and maintain this ecosystem," said Trumble. "I will consider the previous thousand years as to what an appropriate tax should be, be it gold, weapons, jewels, livestock, or all of these put together. Let me see now...one million Gold Butons should be enough. You've found me in a giving vein this day," he said and crossed his arms, staring back with a smug grin on his lion face. "Pay me this tribute, or I may vaporize you with a glance!"

"He can do it," said Marmaduka. "I have seen it done before."

"I believe him," said Jonas, looking to Siegfried for suggestions. "What do you think, sir?"

"Who carries that kind of money on them, man? Siegfried, you don't have that kind of coin, do you?"

"No, Khafre. I definitely don't," said Siegfried, staring away deep in thought.

"I will make a demonstration for you," said Trumble.

"We said we believe you, man!" yelled Khafre.

Jonas readied himself to manifest a bronze shield and grab his laser pistol and fight. But Trumble only stared at a rock on the ground which looked to be about the size of a thorn-covered watermelon and five cubits off to their left. Suddenly, hot green rays shot from his blazing leonine eyes and the rock exploded in a cloud of green smoke.

"Wow!" said Bheem.

"Awesome job, man!" Khafre exclaimed.

Everyone clapped and cheered for about half a bleeb while Trumble bowed in appreciation.

"Sir, I have recently been to Medea and met with the Guardians and the Supreme Being," Jonas began, hoping to avoid Trumble's eye lasers at all cost. "The Eternal being christened me as the next Savior of Earth-1 and has lent me the use of Garud's Golden Bow. If I show it to you as proof may we pass?"

"Perhaps..." mumbled Trumble. "Garud's Golden Bow, eh? I have heard of such a weapon. Allow me to see it. But if you prove to be a lair, then you will fare far worse than that stone!" said Trumble.

Jonas raised his right hand and with a firm mental command the Golden Bow materialized right there. All the others gasped and exclaimed with oooh's and ahhh's while its glowing hieroglyphs shone golden on Trumble's stern lion man face. The green-hued demigod studied the bow for a long moment, carefully reading every symbol engraved onto its surface. He even leaned in closely and appeared to speak to it.

"It looks suspicious to me. Allow me to touch it, mortal," Trumble demanded.

Jonas handed it over and the bow instantly grew in size, perfectly fitting in Trumble's green paws. But as Trumble touched the bow's golden surface, a powerful flash of energy shocked him and he quickly pulled his hand away. For a long bleeb Jonas could clearly see a deep fear sweep through Trumble's mind.

Trumble regained his aggressive stance. But he appeared softer now, as though changed somehow. He stared at the bow, dumbfounded, and then looked from Jonas to Siegfried, and then to Marmaduka, and still appearing quite serious.

"I believe you, young Shastra," Trumble said, and relaxed his tense glare. "This truly is the bow of a celestial. I am an honorable demigod, so I keep my promises. I will allow you access to my cave and I will tell all whom I meet of our encounter here today. I hope that you can heal Earth from the darkness that currently poisons Her."

"Wait, how do you know about all that, man?" asked Khafre.

"I can read the signs in the winds and in the aching song at the very heart of the planet," said Trumble. "Its songs have changed recently. The whispering trees tell me of a dark time. I wish that the sweet songs of life may return to my jungle, to the laughing streams, and the great and noble trees. Please, go and travel safely."

Trumble bowed low, and obviously relieved, and they all said thank you and returned his bow. Then Trumble disappeared in a green flash of light.

Thrilled that he didn't have to face Trumble's eye lasers, Jonas entered the cave behind Siegfried. After they'd all walked a ways, Jonas looked back just in time to see Trumble reappear and move towards where Telos had once stood. Right at that moment several flying chariots appeared above him as they scanned the spot near where the weapon had detonated.

They all reluctantly said goodbye to Marmaduka when she refused to go any further. Slipping further into the cave, Siegfried's third eye lit their way, glowing with bright and ancient symbols. Jonas counted as they descended several twisting flights of stairs, which finally ended in a dark tunnel. The air felt colder and by Jonas's count they were now hundreds of cubits beneath the jungle.

Siegfried's twirling third eye revealed a vast stone labyrinth stretching before them. In the distance, free-energy torches rested in brackets along the stone walls. The scene reminded Jonas of the catacombs running beneath Monubia. To his knowledge many Shastra tribes had lived down there for over five million Shastra years.

Siegfried grabbed a torch from along the wall and moved onward, occasionally glancing at the damp walls or down the many side corridors. Jonas watched him as each time Siegfried did he just shook his white jackal head and moved on while the others patiently followed.

After a long hike they stopped to rest. Glad for the pause Jonas leaned against the stone wall, and as he did he felt a cold, knobby object sticking right in his side. When Jonas looked down close inspection revealed the end of a humerus bone that belonged to a Ghanda skeleton laying tucked neatly into a stone niche.

The skeleton was covered in thick cobwebs while a long sword and an engraved shield rested on its dusty chest. The layer of dust was so thick that when Jonas leaned in closer he couldn't even read the shield's inscription. He then looked up and noticed that countless more niches were pocking the tunnel walls, disappearing at a sharp right turn up ahead.

By the look of the skeleton's armor and what symbols on its shield Jonas could make out, he discerned that this Ghanda warrior belonged to an ancient civilization called New Atlantis. He remembered from Earth History that this civilization had existed over three thousand years ago in Earth-1's distant past.

"Be careful, everyone. Don't touch anything," he said as he carefully backed away, not wanting to disturb the skeleton any further.

"Oh, my," Isas exclaimed. "Please, don't touch them."

"Whoa, check out that sword, man!" exclaimed Khafre excitedly.

"Khafre, don't touch it!" said Isas.

"Yeah, leave them be, please," added Jonas.

"Chill out, man. I'm not gonna touch 'em. I'm just gonna investigate." Khafre leaned closer, blowing off the dust and cobwebs, trying to read the shield's engraving.

"Come on, everyone. Let's get going," said Siegfried. "There are many ways for the bounty hunters to enter these tunnels. Necrat could be right behind us for all that we know." He handed his free-energy torch to Bheem and then manifested his own energy bow. He raised it, the glow lighting the corridor even better.

So they walked on, and Jonas noted all the countless forks and turns they took, while Siegfried kept reading the Ghanda script etched into the damp walls as if looking for something specific. But what Siegfried was searching for, Jonas didn't know.

"Which way is it to Kalkas?" Jonas finally asked.

Then all suddenly froze when terrible shrieks of metal and the sound of crashing stone shook the labyrinth walls. They all looked back, but the sounds all suddenly stopped.

"It is not a very straight shot to Kalkas from here. We will have to travel through earth's central caverns, first," said Siegfried.

"Ummm, excuse me, man...but did you say the central caverns?" asked Khafre. "No way am I going there. No way, man!"

"Why, yes. I did say that, Khafre," replied Siegfried. "Why?"

"You're crazy, man. There are things down there that are more dangerous than any bounty hunters!"

"Khafre, if you would be quiet and allow me to explain—" started Siegfried.

But a much louder bang echoed down the corridor. It was followed by an ear-piercing shriek that Jonas thought sounded like a huge mass of metal twisting in upon itself.

"Run!" yelled Siegfried, swinging his bow around.

They all took off running. After three quick turns Siegfried stopped and with his energy bow struck a square symbol carved into the wall. The floor shook beneath them and they suddenly began descending. Before Jonas knew it, they'd traveled twenty cubits down a square vertical shaft.

Amazed, Jonas had heard tales of such underground cities and even entire civilizations existing within planets throughout the galaxy. But he'd never seen one in person other than Monubia's modest system of caves and tunnels.

"Dude, it's an elevator, inside a stone tunnel.... This is just unreal, man!" said Khafre. "Hey, how far do these tunnels go, man?"

"For miles. Beneath the entire continent, basically," said Siegfried, studying the symbols that randomly dotted the walls while they continued to descend.

Fascinated, Jonas wondered just how far this shaft and its connecting systems traveled through the planet. "You mentioned hollow caverns, sir. How far do they go through the planet's crust?" he asked.

"As far as you can imagine. Some of them even connect with others on the far side of the world," said Siegfried. "This system is as old as the planet itself."

"So, exactly how many beings live down here, man?" asked Khafre.

"Countless species do. Some of these are fully animal, while the rest walk upright like Shastras. Most of them are intelligent too," said Siegfried. "And only a few are malevolent."

Jonas wanted very much to visit the planet's hollows and inner civilizations, but he knew there was no time. When the elevator finally stopped Jonas noted that the spot where their descent had begun was now just a faint glimmer above their heads.

Siegfried raised his bow and then stepped out into another tunnel. "We get off here," he said as his glowing bow lit a directional arrow stamped on the stone wall. Beneath it were words carved in Standard Intergalactic script that read, "To Kalkas."

"Now what, man?" asked Khafre.

"Observe," Siegfried said, as his jackal eyes sparkled. The third eye in his forehead flashed brightly and swirled with mystical, glowing shapes which cast out a beam of light, forming a shining energy chariot on the stone floor before them.

Jonas felt the same rush of excitement when Garud had shown him the sacred Prajna chariot before. He couldn't wait to board that legendary vehicle again.

"Hey, where have I been seein this thing before?" asked Bheem. "It be incredible!"

"Wow, cool, man!" said Khafre. "Are we riding in this?"

"It's my personal chariot, a gift from the Guardians you might say. Now, everybody, get in and hold onto your helmets," Siegfried said as they all climbed aboard.

"Wait, Jonas...would you like to drive?" Siegfried asked thoughtfully.

"Yes, sir! I love to fly chariots," he answered. He quickly put his helmet back on and oriented himself to the controls as the cockpit closed over them. A control stick instantly appeared which he grasped as the chariot rose from the floor and shot off down the tunnel. Driving Prajna proved to be easy. Its intelligent force was always communicating with him and the vehicle moved and adjusted its speed with the slightest thought.

They passed so many branching forks and passageways that Jonas swore he'd be lost down there forever if it weren't for the chariot's hologram map system that conveniently appeared on the center console.

"Hold on! We've got company!" yelled Siegfried.

Jonas feared for the worst as he turned to see a set of space jet lights shining in the distance. A sudden barrage of laser fire grazed their chariot's canopy and exploded against the stone wall.

"Necrat found a way in!" yelled Siegfried. "Jonas, get us out of here!"

"My pleasure," Jonas answered as he grasped the controls tighter and chairs sprouted up from the glowing floor. Now all buckled in, Jonas maneuvered the sharp turns at ever-increasing speeds. But every time Jonas thought he'd lost Necrat, the bounty hunter's atomic jet blasted around the corner behind them. Necrat was steadily gaining all the time no matter what Jonas did.

Jonas followed the hologram map's promptings and punched its controls. This caused a wall just up ahead to change shape and let them shoot down a side tunnel. They then accelerated through two more solid stone doors that opened at the last second to allow them through.

Jonas looked down at the controls in amazement, realizing that those stone doors had opened according to either one button or just his mental command. It had all happened so fast he wondered how it was possible.

They fired back at Necrat, but his atomic jet kept advancing. Jonas took so many turns and quick dips and rises that it was almost impossible to get a clear and steady shot. But to their benefit, almost every time Necrat got torpedo lock on them, a stone door would automatically close or a wall would instantly pop up and shield them from the blast.

But to their amazement, Necrat's weapons just blasted right through each and every barrier as they appeared. Jonas quickly reasoned that Siegfried was mentally controlling these because Jonas wasn't touching anything besides the flight stick.

Finally, Necrat's chariot launched a laser torpedo that traveled unimpeded, heading right for them. At the last second, right before it collided with their rear engines, Jonas took a sharp corner and the corridor collapsed behind them in a deafening blast.

Jonas took three more quick turns and he didn't believe that Necrat's searchlights were gone until they'd driven for a long time without any sight of them. Eventually he accepted there was no way that Necrat was still following them.

He signed and then relaxed at last. But they still had more traveling to do. So, Jonas followed the chariot's detailed hologram map as the tunnel split off, leading into a large crystal cavern. Everywhere Jonas looked twinkling points of light shone on every wall, angle, and surface. He'd never seen a subterranean chamber so large and so beautiful before.

He followed the hologram map down a second tunnel and into an even larger cavern with an artificial sun hovering in its center, lighting the entire space just like it was high noon back on Shetra. Beneath them, blue ocean waters stretched out far below, with waves reaching from one edge of the rocky cavern to the cavern wall almost too far away to see.

Robed beings walked along the beaches below, while some popped into and out of caves lining the sandy shore. Giant birds and gryphons populated the sky, while dark shapes surfaced and swam about below, jumping and making waves before disappearing in this ocean's blue depths.

They flew over the vast ocean and then entered a wide vertical crack in the cavern's far wall. On their route back up to the surface they passed through countless honeycombed caverns along a tortuous path (as marked by the hologram map), yet were always snaking upward. Their scenic route included bubbling pools of lava, a forest of towering trees, and a second ocean that was almost as large as the first but filled with orange-colored waters throughout.

They turned left at an ice pillar formation and then took a sharp right after they came to a circular mound covered with ancient stone ruins. Four additional caverns, two corridors, and three lakes later, they finally passed a stone pyramid no longer in use before the tunnel gave way to a round, golden passage.

Jonas looked at the hologram map which told him that the path they had taken through earth was finally nearing Kalkas, where it was now noon of the day following their departure. But when Jonas raised his jackal face from the controls he spotted a giant Navan that stood before a colossal doorway up ahead.

Their chariot silently touched down and the cockpit opened. They all stared in disbelief, with jaws hanging open and eyes wide with awe, at the gigantic monkey-being before them. Monstrously wide shoulders told Jonas that it definitely wasn't an ordinary normal, nor a random Navan soldier or even a royal guard. But then Jonas realized that this being was none other than the Primordial Primate, the Supreme Simian, the champion of all Navans, the most famous athlete on Earth-1, Tanis.

Tanis smiled, motioning them forward. "Welcome. Tanis glad to meet new friends," he said.

Excited and giddy to meet such a famous athlete, Jonas and the others carefully stumbled forward. But how did Tanis know they were coming, Jonas wondered. Was he telepathic? He wasn't a Guardian or a demigod, but he probably had tons of unknown talents Jonas didn't know about.

Jonas heard unintelligible mumbling and turned back toward Khafre and Bheem. Both stared at Tanis with their mouths hanging open, their eyes wide and unblinking. In response to Tanis's greeting they wheezed and mumbled nervous nonsense that Jonas couldn't make out.

The worst off was Khafre who stumbled around drunkenly and had to lean on Jonas's shoulder to stabilize himself. He also hyperventilated while his monkey tail whipped about wildly.

Siegfried, Jonas, and Isas all waved and said hello while Argos grunted.

"Jonas, it's, it's, man—" stuttered Khafre.

Jonas didn't respond. He just held Khafre up, hoping that his awkward, drunken spell ended soon.

They all bowed low as Tanis simply nodded back. "Tanis welcomes Siegfried and friends. Tanis very familiar with Siegfried and also Ashtar Command. Tanis has known many Intergalactic Agents in famous lifetime," Tanis said proudly.

Jonas could barely believe Tanis's incredible size. Every part of him was giant; his shoulders, his biceps, his tree trunk-sized legs. His neck looked more muscular than Jonas's entire body. Now Jonas was of average Shastra height, being just over eight cubits tall, but he barely reached up to Tanis's chest.

Slowly, the shock of Tanis's immense size wore off and Jonas noticed that he wore a very strange outfit. It reminded him of something familiar; a green and billowy, minstrel-like shirt that was puffy and white, that also sported frills, a large collar, and sleeves with big, poufy cuffs. On top of this interesting shirt he wore a green tunic accompanied by a green loincloth that extended into full length green tights. He wore a pointy-billed hat atop his giant monkey head with a long feather stuck in the brim that was so long it dangled out the back.

Jonas stared, dumbfounded, until he had the sudden revelation that this was the exact same outfit worn by his favorite subject from Earth-1 history class, a freedom fighter named Robin Hood.

"What is he wearing?" Isas whispered to Khafre.

"Oh, that's the standard Navan dress in Kalkas, man," said Khafre.

"Really?" she asked.

"It certainly is interesting," said Jonas. "He looks like Robin Hood, you know from Earth history."

"Who's that?" they all asked.

"What? None of you have ever heard of Robin Hood? Come on..." he said in disbelief.

"No." they all answered. "Who's that?"

"No way.... I'll tell you later," he said, unable to believe none of them had heard of Robin Hood.

"It's Tanis. man..." muttered Khafre, squeezing Jonas's arm tight. "We saw him at the coliseum. And now we're meeting him in person, man!"

"Yeah, I know, it's great. Will you let go, dude," Jonas said as he wrenched his arm out of Khafre's grasp.

"He's absolutely huuuuge," said Isas. "I can't believe it's really him...."

"I know, neither can I, man," Khafre said, nearly drooling now.

"It's nice to meet you again, big guy," said Siegfried. As Siegfried walked forward he fell in stride with Tanis and the Navan led them towards a giant doorway at the end of the golden passage.

"Tanis is very glad to see Siegfried. He is also curious to meet new Savior," he said as he turned back toward Jonas. "Tanis has met celestials and Guardians before, but never Savior. Is rare moment for him and for all of Kalkas. Whole city knows of Jonas coming. Tanis says Siegfried brought you at right time, even though you is small for Savior, Tanis think."

"Thanks, big guy. It's an honor to meet you. We're glad we made it here in one piece," Jonas added, purposely ignoring Tanis's comment that he looked small. He understood it, though, because from Tanis's point of view everyone must seem small.

Tanis put a giant hand on Jonas's back, covering his neck and entire right shoulder. He probably could lift Jonas right off the ground with just that one hand if he wanted to.

"Jonas, Tanis know how fame make stress and high expectation on you. Look at what legend Tanis must live up to! Is amazing and nearly impossible for anyone else, no?"

"Yeah, I bet it is, big guy," said Jonas, looking up into his giant Navan face.

"Yes, will be hard. Especially for Shastra which is believed to be lesser species than Navans. So, take time. Savior is big deal, yes, but Tanis is friend. No Navan respected here like Tanis. Now all Kalkas will respect you. Is good, no?" As he said this he tapped his giant chest, which Jonas noticed was as wide as the huge doorway up ahead.

"Come, everyone see Kalkas now," Tanis said as he stopped and opened the metal door.

"Of all tha beings in all tha world ta meet in a place like this..." Bheem whispered to Khafre and Jonas.

"I hear ya, man. I can't even.... He's my idol, man," Khafre said, shaking his head in disbelief.

Jonas and the others followed Tanis, but very carefully. For if they got too close, say within a three cubit radius of Tanis's huge monkey tail, it could easily whip about and knock one of them over. It was then that Jonas noticed Tanis's odor of ripe bananas and old leather.

"Jonas, you have seen Heliopolis before. Is special, no?" asked Tanis.

"Yeah, it's amazing. We traveled there for the archery tournament," he said.

"Ah, good. Well, also is Kalkas very special in similar way," Tanis said as they walked under his shadow and down a second golden corridor. "You will like Kalkas, Tanis think so. All will like."

"I can't wait to see it," said Jonas, eager to see as many famous, ancient cities on this mission as possible.

"Yeah, me too," Isas said brightly.

"You guys will love it, man," Khafre said.

Tanis led them up a smooth ramp and then grasped the wheel of a second metal door at the end of the golden hallway. This one he turned slowly as countless locks creaked and clanked within, unlatching a string of bolts before its final latch opened with a loud clang.

Jonas looked up and read a plaque just above the door written in Standard Intergalactic. It read; 'Surface: Central Square, Kalkas.'

With the giant door unlocked Tanis pushed the thick, creaking portal outward. Then he beckoned them to follow, and with legs shaking with excitement each one of them stepped out of the golden tunnel and under the bright rays of sunlight. It was then that Jonas beheld, all bathed in warmth from the noonday sun, the giant central square of the ancient city of Navans.

Minerva

JUST THEIR FIRST FEW GONARDS of sightseeing revealed many interesting differences between Kalkas and Heliopolis, in fact between Kalkas and any city on Jonas's home planet of Monubia. First off, encircling the entire city was a stone wall of towering height, rising hundreds of cubits high in places and often measuring ten cubits thick as described by Tanis. Jonas studied the edifice up close and in detail and doubted if even the bounty hunter's Alpha-Class weapons could make a dent in it. He imagined them launching scores of their energy weapons against this wall with little to no success.

Jonas noticed an impressive list of sights also accompanied this towering wall. There were buildings, towers, domes, and pyramids all made from a smooth, brightly glowing opaque material he'd never seen before on Earth.

Tanis next led them through a bustling marketplace, a second square, and then right up to the main entrance of the city's massive gate. According to Tanis, this entire gate was made from solid iron and measured exactly fifty cubits high. As they stood before it, Jonas thought that this gate had to have been forged by a titan or a celestial. It required five Navans and a special computer just to open.

A large group of Navans followed Tanis almost everywhere they went. Some of these fans asked him for autographs, while others just threw confetti, blew horns in celebration, or chanted his name in earnest. Even royal guards patrolling the entrance gate displayed a craze of excitement at seeing him approach. Then, with autograph in hand, the guards all returned to their post. They stood stiff at attention, their tails straight and not wagging even a micro cubit.

While busy admiring the giant iron gate, the disciplined Navan guards, and their beeping supercomputer nearby, Jonas felt a sudden tug on his tunic. He looked down to see a young Navan holding up a wooden bow and a free-energy writing quill. At first confused, Jonas finally figured it out, and happily inscribed the little Navan's bow with, 'Jonas Neferis, Intergalactic Agent of the Ashtar Command.'

Shaking his prize victoriously, the young Navan jumped, cheered, and skipped off into the crowd as Jonas smiled and waved after him, pleased to get at least one autograph, while noting that Tanis had already signed over fifty.

Their tour then took in a sculpture garden with statues displaying Tanis's nearly endless heroic exploits. After that they visited a floating park above the city which boasted glass floors, glistening streams, numerous tropical birds, and a collection of the most exotic, non-poisonous plants on Earth-1.

Tanis showed them around a museum with tokens and relics from his many travels, items from his personal life, and the original trophies from all his tournament victories, the latter filling an entire wing.

Everyone politely listened as Tanis explained each item in detail. At first Jonas was fascinated, but after four hours he secretly was glad when the guards kicked them out so they could close the museum for the night. Jonas knew that if not for that Tanis would have never let them leave.

Soon the royal palace came into view, with its stone turrets and towers spiraling up towards an energy shield high above the city. This reminded Jonas of the protective shield circling the arena during the archery championship. But this particular shield appeared both much bigger and much more powerful. Burly Navan guards opened the palace doors, leading them into a hallway where Navan assistants escorted each of them to their separate rooms.

While they momentarily stood in the hallway Siegfried pulled Jonas aside for a short talk. He looked about as stern as Jonas had ever seen him look, which filled Jonas with anxiety. Something was definitely bothering Siegfried, but Jonas just really wanted a nap, being so sore and tired from the explosion back in Telos and then outrunning Necrat in the underground labyrinth.

"Jonas, recently I have received an ominous vision," Siegfried began, his jackal face looking as hard as stone. "Evil forces have infiltrated Kalkas. Unfortunately, the Navans could not have detected it, let alone prevented this from happening. So, stay alert, my boy, and be sure to double-check everything, even under the sinks, pillows, and between the sheets, even the bathtub. Understand?"

"Yes, sir, I will. Intergalactic agents have a rigid search and debugging protocol."

"Good, I want you to rest and clean up, but stay alert. We'll meet out here in three hours."

"Yes, sir. I will."

Siegfried entered his apartment and a young female Navan showed Jonas to his own door. But a huge Navan guard stood there blocking the entrance. Looking extremely serious, he was also covered from head to toe in a green carpet of fur. The guard thrust out a hand and puffed out its chest, while with his other hand he pounded the butt of a long, golden spear against the marble floor, making Jonas jump with surprise.

"Halt! Show your identification!" the barked guard, glaring down at Jonas. "This VIP apartment! Only special guest can enter. Understand?!" yelled the guard as he sprayed spit in Jonas's face.

Jonas fumbled in his tunic, pulled out his Intergalactic Agent badge, flipped it open, and showed the guard his picture I.D.

The guard squinted, studying the badge carefully, when its eyes suddenly bulged as wide as dinner plates. It then grunted, bowed low, and stepped aside.

Jonas put his badge away and bowed back, thankful that the Navan had calmed down. This was no usual Navan, and the most average specimen on record was much stronger than the average Shastra. Jonas would rather not test a Navan's strength in a fight, especially not in the royal palace.

Jonas bowed back and then passed through the automatic sliding door. He quickly stepped inside and removed the laser pistol from its holster, flicking off the safety as he flattened himself against the wall and the door closed silently behind him.

If like Siegfried had said, spies had already made it into Kalkas then they could have found out which room was his. Jonas knew if that was the case then that guard outside probably wouldn't know anything about it, and so might not have searched the room completely for booby traps or recording equipment.

Thankfully, he was already an expert at sweeping and clearing rooms of booby traps, as well as disarming them. Plus, he still had his energy-detecting glasses which he carried on his utility belt.

As he stood against the wall, thinking about his next move, glow-globes suddenly illumined the apartment's entire space. Now if someone asked Jonas, he would never describe his agent quarters back on the Ashtar Command as unpleasant or even dumpy. But what he saw before him in this apartment in just the first few seconds made his old quarters look like a dank prison cell.

Everywhere that he looked bright, white walls shone with gold and contained inlaid gems the size of his hand. Bronze statues stood in niches along the wall, while murals of Kalkan history covered every remaining cubit of space. Jonas reasoned that the largest mural depicted Tanis's family history, for Tanis's portrait stood at the end of a long line of distinguished and extremely wise looking Navan warriors.

Golden glow-globes hovered beneath the vaulted ceiling, while in the room's center two great stone tables, supported by golden legs, held glass orbs that propped up a row of leather-bound books. In front of these were silver plates holding rare and out-of-season fruit.

Large, gleaming vases at each table end held neon-orange, green, and purple flowers whose scent filled the entire space. He sniffed each flower, inspecting them for thorns, poison-spitting glands, or hidden recording equipment. Consulting his hologram catalog convinced him that none of these belonged to a deadly species.

However, since every decoration, vase, table, plate, statue, and recessed niche was a potential hiding place, he carefully put his energy detecting glasses on and slid along the wall, with his jackal head on a swivel, until he reached the corner and could properly scan the whole space.

The glasses' computer voiced its analysis. "No alien energy particles or vortex readings found, Jonas. I have also failed to detect any neutron bombs or poison of any kind."

"Okay, thanks, Hermes." Just to be sure he swept and cleared the room, peering in every niche, under every table, within every vase, book, and bowl. When he was satisfied he approached the bathroom door.

He pushed the door open slightly with his foot and peered inside, but his sensitive pointed jackal ears detected no noises within. He then knelt and with one swift move rolled through the doorway, came up into a crouch, and swung his laser pistol wildly about.

As he rolled across the floor the bathroom lights flashed on and nearly blinded him. In one corner a bathtub began filling while a female voice suddenly spoke. The entire symphony of sounds so startled him that he almost shot a hole in the ceiling.

"Welcome, Jonas. Would you like a bath?" asked the soothing voice.

"Who's that?" he asked as he swung his pistol around. But there was no one there, no robots, no demons, no guards, not even a Navan housekeeper. But then who was speaking? And how did they know his name?

"My name is Minerva," said the voice.

"But, where are you?" He quickly searched around again but he saw no one.

"I am a biological supercomputer currently running the city of Kalkas. My main hub is in orbit around the planet Mars."

"Ummm, wait, Mars? The red planet?" he asked in surprise.

"Exactly. I am the latest upgrade of an ancient biological computer. I am millions of earth years old," she added. "My circuits are spread throughout space by astral connections. I am the caretaker of the entire city of Kalkas."

"What does that mean?" he asked, still sweeping the room with his laser pistol. One thing Jonas didn't trust were disembodied voices. He thought that there had to be a physical component somewhere for it to be watching him.

"I run all of Kalkas's free-energy electronic needs. The most important of these is the energy shield."

"I've heard of these types of computers. One of them runs the Ashtar Command Center," he said. He felt safe enough, so he stood and holstered his laser pistol. He thanked the Guardians he hadn't shot out the bathroom's ceiling or the giant mirror on the wall.

"Yes, a brother model. I am well aware of it," said Minerva.

"That's a relief," he replied. Next, he searched under every counter, in all the cupboards, even in the sink drains and in the toilet bowl looking for a control hub, a computer terminal, or a hologram face. But he found none of these, nor any booby traps or recording equipment.

"So, where are you, exactly…?" he asked having finally given up.

"I am everywhere. But I am currently invisible to your terrestrial sight," she said.

"I don't understand."

"My circuits are vast and exist throughout space. They store my information and transfer their data using atoms, molecules, photons, even antimatter when needed. These ancient systems were perfected long, long ago by the celestial Designers who were my creators."

"Okay, fair enough," he said, trying to understand all these details about her complexity but doing so with great difficulty. He had stopped searching for her face or robotic eyes and now just decided to talk to the air.

"Please, Jonas, enjoy your bath," said Minerva as the tub suddenly stopped filling. "I detect that your clothes and body register a high concentration of dirt and grime. They lack a necessary application of soap and clean water."

"I can't argue with that," he said, looking down at his tunic and loincloth which were both covered in dirt, mud, dust, and cobwebs. He walked over to the tub and thrust his hand through a full cubit of bubbles to test the water's temperature. It felt quite warm and relaxing and couldn't be more than one hundred and ten degreedos.

"Okay, so...I'm gonna take a bath now," he said, glancing around suspiciously, still wanting to find a robotic eye, maybe a sensor or an android head, anything to hang a towel over for privacy.

The thought of an omnipresent computer always watching him made his skin crawl. But then again, he was so tired, sore, and filthy that even if he got in the tub and a killer robot burst through the bathroom wall, he'd probably just shoot it and then continue bathing.

After he'd looked around for the last time, he shrugged his shoulders and then quickly disrobed. He hung his laser pistol and utility belt over the back of a chair which he scooched right next to the tub just in case. No respectable agent would ever be out of reach of those, even for a second.

As he slowly eased himself into the water all the tension melted from his joints, his chest, and his back. The temperature was perfect, being warm but not burning or uncomfortable. He slid the rest of the way in, resting his head against the rim of the tub. Now completely content, he didn't want to move a muscle. He adjusted just a smidge then closed his jackal eyes and sighed deeply.

"Don't worry, Jonas, I shut off my optic sensors right before you disrobed," Minerva said after he was fully submerged up to his jackal neck in bubbles.

"Ahhh, that's great," he said, although he was so relaxed that he didn't care anymore. But if she wasn't looking then how did she know he was in the tub? He gave up trying to figure it out and just closed his eyes again.

"Is the water satisfactory, Jonas?" asked Minerva.

"Ahh.... It feels wonderful. Thank you, Minerva," he answered, his eyes still closed. He no longer cared that Minerva had probably seen him undress and reasoned that a nearly omniscient bio-computer wouldn't be programmed for shame, embarrassment, or physical attraction towards other beings, either mortal, celestial, or computer and with or without clothes on.

"Jonas, may I make an observation?" she asked after a long period of silence.

"Yeah, sure, Minerva. What is it?" He wondered what might intrigue a super bio-computer, but was still too relaxed to open his jackal eyes.

"If I may say so, it appears that your jackal hair has been thoroughly caked with dirt and is in quite a messy state. May I offer a complete wash and a trim? It would be appropriate to appear as neat and clean as possible when you meet king Masha later on."

He knew it was important to look his best when he met the king, but he wasn't able to see his hair in the mirror from where he currently sat in the tub. "Yeah, that's a good point, Minerva.

But...uhhh, how will that work?" He shifted in the tub but kept his eyes closed, really hoping that he wouldn't have to get out.

"Look up, Jonas."

He cracked one jackal eye open and glanced upward. Right above him a ceiling panel opened, through which a helmet-like device lowered towards him on a cable.

"Put the Barber Helm-12,000X on your head, please," she asked.

"Okay..." he answered as he opened his other eye to better study this new contraption. "Just take a little bit off the top. Don't buzz me, alright?"

"I am programmed with over a million different head shapes and more than two thousand types of hair. I always give a perfect haircut, every time," she replied confidently.

"That's pretty impressive," he said as he reluctantly reached for the helmet. He was still wondering if this was a good idea as he grabbed the helmet and yanked it towards himself. But then he reasoned that if this supercomputer was going to kill him then it would already have done so, and probably very easily and through a much cleaner and faster method than by deadly haircut.

He carefully slipped the helmet over his jackal head and sat back and waited. He soon heard beeping, followed by what had to be tiny water jets that he could feel were wetting his jackal hair. There was another beep and then tiny brushes began massaging soap into his scalp in a circular motion. A long rinse followed, along with what could only be a trim performed by countless tiny yet precise lasers all cutting his hair at once. He gulped anxiously as the distinct odor of burning jackal hair confirmed this theory. Being a young agent, he was always very particular about how his hair looked. He knew very well how an agent could earn quick promotion just by maintaining a full and confident head of hair at all times.

"Finished, Jonas. What do you think?" asked Minerva.

The helmet lifted up off his head and then extended an articulating arm that held a mirror up to his jackal face. He turned his head from side to side while studying his reflection and running a hand through his jackal hair. He thought that he looked extremely sharp. His hair even sparkled it was so clean. This had to be one of the best haircuts he'd ever received in his life.

"Thanks, Minerva. It looks fantastic," he said. Then he dunked his jackal head in the water, shook himself off like a dog, and relaxed back against the tub wall with his eyes closed.

"Where did you learn to do that?" he asked, taking a deep breath and then a long sigh. He felt like he could stay in there for hours.

"My initial booting and programming was performed by Dr. Octavius of the celestial Designer Corps in the year Satya 7,563. This occurred approximately two billion earth years in the past. My programming began with the attunement of my alpha-waves to minor integrations, followed by vibrational pulling...."

"That sounds really interesting..." he said, adjusting himself in the tub once more. But he was just too relaxed and the topic was far too complicated for him to follow, so he quit listening entirely.

After a long time he noticed that his hands were pruned all over. That meant it was time to get out.

"Hmmm, Minerva, where can I get some new clothes? Or at least my old ones mended and washed?" he asked while sloshing his arms around and breaking up the thick layer of bubbles. He'd been in there for a while but the temperature remained warm the entire time.

"My matter replicator can construct any object, be it food, tools, or whatever item of clothing you might need," said Minerva.

"Good, then I think I'm about done in here." He stepped out and began to dry himself off, but still kept his utility belt and holster close. He was nearly finished drying off when the large mirror above the sink suddenly flashed on, transforming into a fully-functional wall screen that displayed a female Shastra face. She stared right at him and he froze, still not done drying off.

"Who? What the...?" he yelled in shock. He quickly covered himself with his towel and then reached for his laser pistol. "Excuse me! This is a private bathroom! Minerva, turn this thing off!"

"Jonas, it is me, Minerva. I display this Shastra face to communicate with you because it is familiar. But I can display any form that you wish," said the female Shastra. "Do you desire a different one?"

"Ummm...no, uhh, that's fine. Just please don't watch me dry off, okay?" His heart was still pounding as he put his laser pistol back in its holster.

"I apologize. I simply wished to inform you that there are matter replicators over to your left. Please, feel free to use them whenever you need to."

"Okay, thank you. I'm ready now." He watched the female Shastra face but she just smiled back while he tied his towel tight around his waist and then approached the white box stationed against the far wall. It reached to about his chest level. "How does it work?"

"First, it takes your measurements. Then all you have to do is choose the particular style that you want," said the female Shastra, then she vanished and the wall turned back into a mirror.

"Fair enough," he said. So, while still holding the towel around his waist because he felt he was still being watched, a green laser ran itself all over his body. After it was done, a screen on the front of the box displayed various styles of tunics, loincloths, and sandals to choose from. He scrolled past the pages of frilly Navan clothing styles until he found something not so outlandish and then he made his selections.

He watched the machine as it beeped loudly and lights flashed on its face. In less than a minute a full set of brand new and neatly folded garments, plus a nifty pair of sandals, extended out towards him on a tray. Amazed by its speed, he held these up and inspected them. They were more than satisfactory. They were actually quite fancy for coming from a matter replicator. Pleased, he quickly put them on just in case the female Shastra face reappeared.

Everything was comfortable and fit perfectly. The tunic also had ample pockets (which he always appreciated) that could hold his energy detecting glasses, his Gold Buton coin wallet, and his Intergalactic Agent I.D. and badge. Even the sandals fit great. In fact, these sandals were sturdier and even more comfortable than any that he'd ever been issued by the Ashtar Command's Clothing Department which was known to supply the best tactical sandals in the galaxy.

Staring at himself in the mirror, he thought that he looked like royalty in this brand new, bright red and yellow tunic, plus, a matching loincloth, both of which were fully embroidered with brilliant gold thread. If he were back on the Ashtar Command he'd easily be confused for an officer or maybe even a general. His own personal assessment was that he looked amazing, dashing even.

He finally donned his utility belt and holster and then got the great idea to try and contact Ashtar again, hoping the signal would come through clearer this time. He reached for his comm. link device, but then he had a brilliant idea.

He addressed Minerva. "Minerva, can you dial the Ashtar Command and put Ashtar on the mirror's view screen in here? I want to talk with him, but my comm. link has gotten poor reception lately."

"I will try. But I must inform you that, as of yesterday, a range of unexpected energy currents have been disrupting communications throughout Kalkas. I theorize these factors are similar to those which have affected your own device."

"That's very possible. But, please try."

Minerva's Shastra avatar instantly reappeared. "Calling the Ashtar Command Center, Beta-18 quadrant, Galactic Center, Milky Way. Please, stand by...."

"Sure, thing," he said. He waited there patiently, but it took less than a minute for Ashtar's blue human face to flash up on the view screen.

"Greetings, sir! I'm glad to see you," Jonas said as he saluted. "I'm glad that our connection is clear this time."

"Jonas, hello! My goodness, you sure look sharp, son. Yes, yes, the link is much better this time. Are they treating you well in Kalkas? Wait, did you get a haircut? And is that a bathtub behind you? Are you calling from a bathroom, son? This is highly irregular..." said Ashtar, scrunching his brow. Although visibly very happy to see Jonas again, he appeared to be quite confused.

"Uhhh...yes. I'm sorry about that, sir. But, yes, I am currently calling you from my apartment's bathroom," he said. "The biological computer that runs Kalkas, named Minerva, has called you for me using this particular screen in here. It was the best option available and I thought that it would get a better signal than my comm. link, sir."

"Oh, yes, we are very aware of Minerva up here," said Ashtar. "As a matter of fact, we employ her brother model to run the Command Center's systems. You are lucky, Jonas. Minerva is very close with Garud and the Lone Ranger."

"That's excellent, sir! I wasn't aware that Garud and the Lone Ranger knew her. I would very much like to meet the Lone Ranger again." he said, standing stiff at attention. "He was a very salty dog, sir."

"Yes, yes, he is. And you may see him sooner than you think. But more importantly, son, I'm glad that you've reached Kalkas safely. And I want you to know that a Disaster Recovery Team has just arrived in Telos. They are already hard at work decontaminating the jungle around the village."

"That's wonderful, sir." He was very pleased with the speed of these Disaster Recovery Teams.

"So, Jonas, what can you report about Kalkas?"

"Nothing much yet, sir. Other than Tanis greeted us here and has given us a tour. We've only just arrived, so I will report back to you again when I have more news. But I'm very encouraged that Minerva's signal could reach the Command Center so easily."

"Yes, it is a good sign. And please, son, keep me informed of your progress. Also, don't forget to be always on the lookout for spies, shape-shifting demons especially. A demon army is now setting up camp right outside Kalkas as we speak."

"Oh, my.... Really?" he asked, surprised by this unfortunate news.

"Yes, but remember, always remain faithful to Siegfried and especially to Garud. If you do this then you will be okay in the end. I'm sorry but I must go now, son. Please contact me again soon, Jonas. I look forward to hearing from you."

"Thank you, sir! I will, sir. Over and out!" he said with a stiff salute.

Ashtar's image then disappeared. But instead of going blank, the wall screen changed, displaying an image of Tanis staring back at him and holding a giant white bow.

"You bad in archery? Need new bow? Want to be great like Tanis? Then buy new Tanis Bow, Model: Clarion-250-IB. Is best bow ever, Tanis guarantee. Made of single Mastodontus tusk, Tanis brand bows bend good but break never, unless you is strong as Tanis!" Tanis said, laughing as he smiled and then held the giant bow closer. Jonas thought it looked magnificent.

"Remember, if bow make you too good then try to use less often. Or, if you is not ready for greatness like Tanis, return for full refund. Tanis promise." Tanis smiled, flashing two massive thumbs up before the view screen suddenly went blank.

"Minerva, please disable the commercials on this wall screen. I feel like I'm living in a Tanis-themed amusement park."

"Unable to execute said function, Jonas. That is forbidden in Kalkas."

"Okay, that's kind of weird, but alright."

Minerva paused and then spoke again. "Jonas, I am receiving a message from Kassam. The King asks that your party meet him in the royal dining hall in twenty minutes. Minutes and hours are the time scale of Kalkas, by the way. Not bleebs and gonards like you're used to on Monubia."

Surprised, Jonas did an immediate double-take. He'd never mentioned that he was from Monubia, but she was a nearly omniscient bio-computer, so she had probably already read his Ashtar Command file. "Oh, yeah. I've heard of minutes and hours before. They sound weird, but I know how to count them."

"Good, a grand reception awaits you. Have a nice evening, Jonas."

"Thank you."

Feeling like he was ready to get going, Jonas fastened his utility belt beneath his tunic and then slid his laser pistol right into a pocket next to the one holding his agent badge. He heard his stomach rumbling, as it always did, so he tightened his sandals down and left the apartment, nodding to the Navan guard as the automatic door closed silently behind him.

An Eagle Queen

WITH A BLINDING FLASH, Jonas suddenly found himself back in the Command Center's transport room, millions of light years from Earth-1, and with his Shastra friend Zeeg staring back at him. He'd followed Ashtar's orders and had returned to the Command Center for an important briefing.

In a terrible accident the night before, Khafre had very unexpectedly turned zombie-like, and killed five Shastras and three Navans right after Jonas had left their royal dinner with Kassam. After his capture Khafre had been brought to the Command Center for tests, to find out why he'd done it, and if his healing and recovery were at all possible.

Jonas was horrified to hear what had happened. And now he was desperate to find out why his apparently normal friend had killed so needlessly. Looking equally stunned and serious, Zeeg bowed and gave him the address of Khafre's healing chamber before Jonas walked to the nearest conveyor belt and left the Jump Room.

"Neutrino pool number four, please," he said, turning his jackal snout towards the bank of flashing lights set into the wall. "And avoid the Shastra markets, please. I'm in a hurry." He said that so the conveyor belt would steer clear of any vendors selling squeaky toys and stuffed animals, which would definitely delay his arrival.

"Identification; Jonas Neferis, junior Intergalactic Special Agent. Destination; neutrino pool four, Healing Quadrant. Affirmative," Hermes said in his calm robot voice, and then the conveyor belt started moving down the corridor.

Jonas reasoned that he'd probably passed through half of the Command Center when the conveyor finally stopped before a large silver door. "Destination; neutrino pool four, Healing Quadrant. Have a nice day, Jonas," said Hermes.

"Thanks, Hermes," Jonas said as he stepped off the belt and the door slid open.

The scene that he walked in on was unlike any he'd ever witnessed on the Command Center. Khafre lay in the middle of a circular room, submerged within a pool of gleaming, rainbow-colored liquid, which was obviously the neutrino pool. This entire scene, being so strange and alien, sent chills up Jonas's Shastra spine.

Possessed by an incessant curiosity, Jonas walked closer, albeit cautiously. A transparent plastic cocoon was covering Khafre, while tubes descended from the ceiling and attached themselves to this cover. These tubes in turn directly transported the glistening rays into the healing pool. The neutrinos gave off the full range of rainbow light waves, all dancing off the scientist's faces, Khafre's form, the floor, the ceiling, and every control panel within the chamber.

Jonas looked around, hoping to find out if both Siegfried and Isas had arrived before him. He already missed Isas's beautiful smile, her laugh, her dark and beautiful gaze. He also personally wanted to thank her for comforting him after he'd heard the news of Khafre's episode.

He walked around the glistening pool, mesmerized by its beautiful healing rays all dancing about while Shastra and human scientists busily monitored the many readout screens measuring Khafre's health, which Jonas hoped was improving. In the healing pool Khafre's face looked blank, yet peaceful. Jonas knew his friend was lucky to have survived. But no matter how much he thought about it, it just didn't make sense why such a sad and unfortunate thing had to happen to Khafre, whom he'd absolutely trusted up until that point.

Jonas heard someone call his name and he turned around. Siegfried was walking up to him, beaming with joy. Jonas was glad to see him, but he quickly glanced around and in the background, scanning the area for Isas. When he didn't see her, he vaguely remembered she was still back in Kalkas, busy greeting the soldiers that were now arriving to help defend the city.

"Ah, you've made it. Then you received my message?" Siegfried asked, returning his bow.

"Yes. I came as soon as I heard. Isas gave me the news," he said, standing at stiff attention, which was his usual habit when addressing his superiors on the Command Center.

"I'm glad that you could make it. Our friend Khafre is in dire straits, I'm afraid," Siegfried said, staring somberly into the rainbow healing pool.

"What went wrong, sir? Why would he do this and can he be healed?" Jonas asked, indicating the Shastra and human scientists around the healing chamber.

"We shall see..." said Siegfried quietly. They both somberly glanced at Khafre's calm face, covered by the beautiful neutrino rays. "Trust me, the Command Center's scientists are doing everything they can to help him. In the meantime, we have gained access to his memories."

"Oh, that's interesting. What have you learned?" he asked.

"Well, at first they were blocked by a powerful memory cap, which we were all very astonished to find," he said in response to Jonas's look of shock. "Our theory is that the bounty hunters from Hiix placed it there. I'm afraid our friend was a secret weapon for them, an assassin programmed to attack both you and myself."

Jonas could barely wrap his mind around this terrifying revelation. "How could anyone have placed a memory cap in Khafre's brain without him knowing?" Jonas asked. He shivered as he slowly comprehended the fact that their good friend had been a deadly assassin just waiting to attack him this entire time. "That's just not possible, sir. It doesn't make sense."

Jonas wondered how he could have prevented this. If only he'd stuck around when Tanis had started his Navan drinking games. But then again, if he had then Khafre might have succeeded in killing him too.

"I know this is hard to understand. But believe me, Necrat is very capable of such things and has done them before. You will understand it better once you view Khafre's recovered memories."

In agent school Jonas had extensively studied bounty hunters from different civilizations and galaxies. So he already knew about brain implants, mind control rays, and false hologram memories. He'd studied the famous mind control death rays of Atlantis, which was an ancient Earth-1 civilization. There was also the implant secretly placed under the skin of Roland the Rich, who was king of the planet Moobot. That particular implant had driven him crazy, causing him to gift his entire kingdom's wealth in gold to the Draco Serpent invaders.

Then there was the famous mind control super computer on the moon of a planet named Smars-5, which resided in the same solar system as Monubia. Through mind control implants this computer, named Afzal, had managed to gain total control and surveillance over the planet's population, keeping them in a heightened state of anxiety and conflict. Just thinking about this made Jonas shudder and his jackal hair stand on end.

Secretly Jonas had always wanted to meet someone affected by such mind control rays and methods. Although a morbid subject, his curiosity on the topic ran deep simply because learning more would give him a giant leap in his education as an Intergalactic Agent. Plus, he could write one heck of an interesting mission debrief later on.

Siegfried led him to a large control panel on the opposite end of the neutrino pool. From there they looked down on the top of Khafre's monkey head.

"It appears that every year Khafre was held captive within the Machine City of Hiix. He only thought he was visiting Kalkas," said Siegfried. "The memory cap also included implanted memories of who he believed was his uncle, Armando. When in fact no such Navan exists. But as you know, false memories can seem totally real."

"Incredible...but why did the bounty hunters choose him? And we trusted him..." Jonas said, staring down at Khafre while struggling to grasp just how this could have happened.

"We can't know why, other than he used to live in Hiix," said Siegfried. "It seems that he never really left there."

"So what about the illness he had every year when he returned from his 'vacations?' What caused them?"

"We now believe that was his body fighting off the mind control drugs, plus, whatever other brainwashing techniques they used on him, like brainwaves or proton drills. Many of these processes are known to cause fever, boils, and fatigue; the very symptoms that Khafre displayed," said Siegfried.

"I don't believe it.... Khafre could have attacked you or me at any time on our journey," said Jonas. He felt sick to his stomach and was amazed to still be alive, knowing that an assassin had worked with him and had slept nearby for many days now.

"He wasn't capable of acting out such programming on his own. And he was completely unaware of his hidden destructive impulses to kill," said Siegfried.

"What kind of weapon did he use?" Jonas's curiosity took over and he wanted to know everything about the case now.

"He used a poisoned blade. But there was no way that he brought that with him from Shetra, I'm very sure of that. It had to have been placed in his apartment ahead of time. A brainwashing queue made him conceal it and then bring it to the royal dinner. Another bounty hunter, a wolfman named Tiber, played the tone in the dining hall that activated Khafre's assassin programming. We've apprehended Tiber, and trust me, he's one nasty fellow. If I were a betting Shastra, I'd say Tiber is a close associate of Necrat."

Jonas's brain was now actively spinning in shock, and even with that he still tried to remember everything that Siegfried was saying. The sheer depth of Necrat's plan amazed him. He lamented that Navan and Shastra guards had died and silently thanked Garud and the Supreme Being for protecting Siegfried from this surprise attack.

Chapter Twelve

"Here is everything we've uncovered from Khafre's memory so far." Siegfried pushed a few buttons and the bright images of Hiixian towers and domes appeared on the wall-screen before them. Siegfried skipped forward until they saw, from Khafre's point of view of course, Khafre being bound to a giant chair that looked like a torture device. The bounty hunters then poked and prodded him with strange tools, mind control rays, and then lasers and a few other energy devices which Jonas didn't recognize.

Jonas cringed, but he didn't dare turn away from the continuing flow of images.

"I have watched all of this already. Our poor friend, Khafre, has been put through the wringer I'm afraid," said Siegfried.

Jonas thought that Khafre's brainwashing torture sessions looked horrifying, but he made himself watch every last frame in order to understand what his friend had been through.

Between each session the bounty hunters led Khafre past the City's towers, domes, and structures, usually ending their journey in an isolated armory somewhere underground. Once there, and still under mind control, Khafre was given weapons training as well as nanotech upgrades either through injections or surgery. Following this he was always drugged more and then locked in a cramped cell overnight.

Jonas was absolutely horrified to see that Khafre suffered the same routine each day: waking up, torture, drugging, brainwashing, training, and then more drugging. When the two weeks were up and Khafre was now all tired, worn out, and delirious, he was released just outside Shetra's border where he stumbled back home and then slept for three straight days.

Jonas was horrified yet fascinated, for although Khafre's torture was awful, no known Intergalactic Agent had ever seen inside the

Machine City and escaped to describe it. But Jonas still sighed with relief when Siegfried finally turned off the wall display.

"He was a programmed assassin, Jonas. And you and I were his main targets," Siegfried said, his intense eyes boring into Jonas. Siegfried then played Khafre's memories of the recent attack in Kalkas.

Jonas watched, spellbound, as Khafre slowly approached Siegfried in the royal dining hall with his dagger in hand. When he lunged at Siegfried two Navan guards rushed up to intervene. Khafre killed them both before two Shastra guards tackled him. Khafre threw these guards off, then stabbed Argos and kicked Bheem in the face before Siegfried's mental powers subdued him just as five more guards arrived.

Siegfried turned the memory playback off after the Navan guards had bound Khafre in chains and dragged him off.

"How come you never foresaw this, sir? You must have known something was wrong?"

"There were signs, yes. His illness, for one, had me on alert. But there's no way I could have predicted this," said Siegfried, motioning to the wall screen. "However, my knowledge of the Rulebook should have warned me that something like this would happen."

"Rulebook, sir? What's that?" he asked.

"Ah, the Rulebook…" Siegfried said, gazing thoughtfully into space. "You have never heard of it, I know. It is a special relic."

"Well, there's the Intergalactic Agent Manual. Is that what you mean?"

"No, no, there is a manual of much deeper knowledge. It is called the Rulebook for the Cosmic Battle of Good versus Evil. If and when Khapre-Tum addresses it, if in fact he does, then I will gladly explain it to you. But not before that."

"Fair enough, sir. Then I'm going to watch Khafre's memories again if you don't mind," he said.

"Yes, go ahead. I have something else to attend to at the moment," Siegfried said, and he walked off to another station where he spoke to a Shastra scientist working at a blinking control panel.

Suddenly Jonas heard a familiar Shastra voice coming from behind him. "Hello, Jonas, lad. So glad ya could be joining us!" That could only be Bheem.

Jonas turned just as Bheem and Mamaji (the wolfman he remembered from Telos) both bounded across the room and bowed. Bheem embraced him like they hadn't seen each other in years.

"I'm a glad that ya and Isas left that dinner early. It be a strange scene afterwards, I'll tell ya that, lad," Bheem said nodding vigorously.

"I still can't believe what happened. I've just seen all his memories. I just hope that Khafre can recover. Do you know what this thing really does?" he asked, motioning to the neutrino pool.

"Aye, I worked with these before," said Bheem. "Tha neutrinos be cosmic wavicles that help Khafre's life force strengthen and hopefully heal itself."

"That means that this healing chamber is what, Jonas?" asked Mamaji, staring intensely.

"Uhhh, amazing? Powerful? Great?" he asked, unsure what Mamaji was getting at.

"It's phenomenal, brother! That's what!" Mamaji exclaimed as he punched Jonas on the shoulder. "Gangbusters!"

"That's good to know," Jonas said, moving his sore arm away. "So then the neutrino wavicles do all the healing?" he asked. "If so, then his Shelbiv-Nexus Nerves are being re-energized also, correct?" Jonas asked, having some rudimentary medical knowledge relating to brain and memory repair.

"Na, tha wavicles just be assistin, lad. Tha patient's life force does most a tha healin," said Bheem. "Them Shelby Nerves come back but slowly, and only if tha Rooftones be recalibrated. And those only when they be animated with tha new torsion bubbles we be injectin. It be a new process, lad, but very affective."

"Yes, I've heard of torsion bubbles before. They are quite advanced," Jonas added.

"Indubitably, lad," Bheem replied.

"And the nanite bridges, they are used for tissue repair?"

"Yup, those be used, and also cellular ultrasonic drills."

"Interesting…. What about his bio-crystal matrix?"

"Workin on that too, lad. Tha prana lasers also be addin some good pep ta tha treatment."

"Excellent, those work wonders, I hear. So how long will it take for him to get back to normal then?" asked Jonas.

"Well, lad, it will be some time before his brain adjusts and all them astral nerve endins get healin. And they all been in quite a shock with all tha mind control he be put through. See, healin like this be hard, lad. He could not make it, it be possible. And not many beins be knowin how ta come back ta life. Tis too hard for Khafre ta even consider on his own, I'm afraid."

"But, Jonas, coming back to life is what?" asked Mamaji.

Oh, geeze, thought Jonas. "I don't know….uhhh."

"It is quite doable, brother, it's quite doable," said Mamaji. "I've heard of it being done. I've even seen it done once before too, out in the field."

"Wow, that's amazing," said Jonas, amazed. But still, he thought it sounded pretty impossible even although he'd heard stories in agent school about someone bringing themselves back to life once or twice. Only demigods and celestials or only one agent out of a million could ever do it.

"When he be wakin up we be givin him a shot a placebo, lad," added Bheem.

"Placebo? What's that?" Jonas asked.

"It be a special medicine. It be workin best when tha patient believes it be workin. So, mind power is tha healer, really. If tha patient believe it be enough and be healin properly, then they be healed almost every time," said Bheem.

"Amazing...." Jonas thought that was incredible, but then he didn't know nearly as much about medicine as either Bheem or Mamaji. By just being around them he was learning new things all the time. "I'd love to learn more about placebos."

"I would love ta teach ya, laddie. Tha literature on em be fascinatin and quite extensive," said Bheem. "I can give ya one now."

"That would be great, my leg is still hurting from the explosion back in Telos," he said, indicating the wound under where his armor's bronze grieve had been.

"Great, lad. I be havin one here," said Bheem. He handed Jonas a red pill which he put in his mouth and swallowed. "Now be rememberin that ya really gotta be thinkin hard that it be workin, then it work the best, and near perfectly. Is tha way these thins be, lad."

"Thanks, I'll remember that," said Jonas. He instantly imagined that the placebo was healing him and the lingering ache in his leg did begin to subside. Soon it was completely gone. "Remarkable," he said as he moved his leg easily, now pain free.

Then Bheem and Mamaji talked while they looked at Khafre's medical readout. Jonas turned back and rewound Khafre's memories of the attack. He watched as a Navan priest, identified as Drollup, walked up, talked with Khafre for a time, and then showed him a glowing purple crystal. Then a tone played out loud in the dining hall, but Jonas couldn't tell from where. In response, Khafre stood, brushed off two Navan ladies who wanted him to dance, and then began to robotically walk towards Siegfried with his poisoned knife unsheathed.

The band stopped playing suddenly and a group of Navan and Shastra guards charged at Khafre. Drollup shot beams of light from his crystal, with the beams paralyzing this first wave of guards. Soon after, more guards rushed forward and subdued the priest, followed by their deadly tussle with Khafre.

Khafre fought with a speed and lethality that Jonas never thought was possible from his Navan friend. But thankfully, he never got close enough to Siegfried to do any harm. Argos, however, got stabbed in the abdomen, but he looked okay, and didn't even yell or anything.

Jonas rewound the scene again and again, studying Khafre and Drollup. The Navan 'priest' wore disheveled robes and had dark circles under his monkey eyes, plus, hairy feet with extremely long claws. Jonas suspected that he was a shape shifting demon. He just had to be.

Jonas's energy-detecting glasses read the wavelengths that came off Drollup's purple crystal and revealed that they were the main force controlling Khafre. His aura visibly glowed brighter under the crystal's influence, while the loud tone also filled the dining hall. However, he could also detect many troubling spots and dark knot-points in Khafre's aura where the energy was blocked.

Jonas's glasses detailed these blockages and he decided he should study them further and analyze their energy signature. After that he would study Khafre's memory cap and then his augmentations and false memory implants.

He walked over to Siegfried who was talking with another group of scientists. But Siegfried suddenly stopped talking and grabbed and took him aside, speaking excitedly.

"Jonas, there is a friend of mine that I want you to meet. She is a Danaan eagle being, and the queen of her tribe in the Northern Forests of Alcion, which is back on Earth-1. Pramohana, come here and meet Jonas," Siegfried called across the room.

Jonas turned to see the figure of a giant eagle-being waddling toward them, with a golden belt around her waist that jingled as she walked. Long, green feathers covered her huge body, which appeared to be at least fifteen cubits long from the tip of her beautiful arched beak, which was much larger than Jonas's head, all the way down to her immense tail feathers.

Her searching, black eagle eyes instantly locked onto him, while with each step her large talons clacked against the chamber's metallic floor. Jonas knew that just one set of these talons were big enough to grab him and easily carry him away.

As Pramohana approached them Jonas detected a strong odor of tree bark and also what he thought had to be bird feed consisting of peanuts and sunflower seeds. He could even see a few large seeds stuck in her greenish-gray speckled breast feathers. She waddled up to them, bowed, and everyone bowed back.

"Pramohana is honored that Siegfried has called on her once again. Pramohana owes the survival of her whole tribe to Siegfried's wise counsel," she said.

"I was very honored to be able to help you and your tribe," said Siegfried.

"Pramohana has been hearing whispers that evil beings are making secret plans to take over Kalkas and to enslave the Earth. Is this true? If so, Pramohana will have none of that nonsense. She will help to prevent this in any way that she can."

While she spoke Jonas stared up at Pramohana's large eagle head in amazement. He'd never seen such a giant eagle being up close before, as they were rare on Monubia. More often the Monubian deserts swarmed with giant vultures and the many different species of Monubian flying camels, some of the latter Jonas had even flown on before.

"Thank you, old girl," said Siegfried. "I very much am in need of your help at the moment. As you know, a terrible demon army has started to surround Kalkas. As queen of the Danaan Eagle tribes of Alcion, I must ask you and your loyal soldiers to march, errr...to fly with us against the forces of Khapre-Tum."

"Pramohana knows of your need. She has already viewed the demon camp from the air. She and her counselors will discuss this matter soon and then give you a decision," she said. "But, at present Pramohana is very much interested in Siegfried's 'product,'" she said as she fixed her piercing black eyes back on Jonas. "So, Jonas, Siegfried says you are the new Savior, is this in fact correct?"

"Yes, that is what Garud and the Supreme Being have told me so far," said Jonas. "I have met with them just once."

"Hmmm, simple and clearly spoken, I see. And by your features, Pramohana can tell that you are a loyal and very determined little being. Siegfried would not have chosen you if you weren't an ideal example of your race, a true Shastra. Pramohana trusts the judgment of Siegfried and the Guardians," she said confidently.

Jonas listened but only nodded back, unsure of how to respond. He thought she must be very wise and ancient to know so much about Siegfried and the Guardians. "Thank you," he said. "I am doing my best at the moment. I have devoted all my energy as an agent to accomplishing this mission."

"Pramohana thinks this is a good sign," she continued. "Great honor will come to any Danaan tribes that serve the next Savior. You must come from a Shastra royal family then? Is it one from Heliopolis, Sad Madriss, Astrauliany? Germania? No?" she kept naming different city-states but he just kept shaking his jackal head. "Then from the land of Chin, perhaps?"

Jonas kept shaking his jackal head until she finally stopped. But now she just stared at him, appearing very discouraged and also confused. "Actually, Pramohana, I'm from none of those places," he replied respectfully. "I'm from a small desert planet called Monubia. And trust me it is very far from Earth-1."

She tilted her eagle head curiously to one side. "But then...how could you have earned the title of Savior so quickly?" While she asked him this her sharp talons tapped the floor anxiously. Then she waddled even closer, her eagle eyes growing wider. Jonas's sensitive jackal snout detected the odor of wood chips and bird seed grow much stronger. "Siegfried, this is a problem, is it not?" she asked him.

But Siegfried smiled back. "It is of no great significance, my dear. Each Savior's place of origin, their family station, and their personal preparations have all proven to be different in every instance. Jonas's illumination came just right for this Age in time."

"Hmmm, so, Siegfried, Jonas must have accomplished many great things to prove his worth," added Pramohana.

Siegfried just smiled back.

"I don't mean to disappoint you, Pramohana, but I basically was just like every other normal Shastra growing up," he said. "My family belonged to a tribe of Mega Camel herders. And I lived with them until I was accepted to the Ashtar Command for agent training."

"But...then you must have served with honors in your planet's highest ranks of the military...or you have accomplished great things as an Intergalactic Agent, no?" she asked confidently.

"Actually, I got kicked out of the Monubian Legion after only two years. And as of now I am just in my first year officially as a Junior Agent," replied Jonas. "I graduated from the academy two years ago."

"Oh, I see.... Well, then...Hmmmm," she murmured, as if stalling and thinking. "Let's see, how old were you when you realized your destiny was that of a great Savior?" Pramohana asked. "Surely, it must have been known to you at birth or shortly thereafter."

"Well, no, umm, see I actually didn't know anything until just a few days ago. That was when Garud first took me on his chariot to Medea where I meet the Supreme Being and the other Guardians. But I guess things like that only happen at their allotted time," Jonas said, shrugging his shoulders.

"Hmmm, okay...Pramohana thinks this situation is getting curiouser and curiouser."

Jonas could tell that she was now mentally struggling with this information. Her eagle face was fully contorted and she was now mumbling to herself while also numbering something on her wing tip feathers. "So wait, have you beaten a champion of the serpent races or any evil A.I. robots yet?" she asked him.

"No, not yet," he said.

"Any...demon titans?" she asked hopefully, studying him closer.

"Nope."

"A bounty hunter general or an army of their clones?"

"Not exactly. Nothing like that."

"Well, uhh...you must have trained with a Savior's weapons and already used them in battle against a celestial foe of some kind, no?" she asked, her eagle eyes bulging even wider. "So... what do you think of them, Jonas?"

Jonas gulped back a lump that was steadily forming in his jackal throat, for he'd done absolutely none of those things other than hold the Golden Bow for a bit. "Sorry, no, not yet," he said. "But, I was taught the powers of a Savior, plus, how to use the Golden Bow by telepathy."

"Oh, dear...." she said, now looking really worried. She obviously found him to be severely lacking in necessary experience. But Jonas couldn't help that, he'd only told her the truth. And he'd definitely never expected her to interrogate him like this.

Through the tense silence that followed, Jonas could see the cogs whirring and churning in her eagle head as she tried to work the situation out. An orb-shaped android suddenly floated over, breaking their silence when it offered them all freshly brewed Toklaxian Coffee, which Jonas was extremely glad to see.

Pramohana's awkward stare continued while Jonas delicately sipped his coffee, making sure not to injure himself. He had to concentrate when doing so because he'd been injured more than once before while drinking Toklaxian Coffee. He remembered how a serpent-being friend of his named Jamby had even ended up in the Command Center hospital for a week after drinking it incorrectly.

So Jonas took careful, yet eager sips, pausing often to wait for his brain to recover. And as always on the Command Center, the coffee was delicious. However, Pramohana's visible disappointment somewhat dampened his mood, and he felt like he'd let her down in a way.

"This whole situation is quite tenuous, Pramohana," said Siegfried. But then he took his first sip of coffee. In response, he vigorously shook his jackal head while his jackal eyes bulged outward and grew to the size of small Monubian cactus melons. "Wow, that's super strong! What is this stuff?"

"This is a pretty tame batch, actually," said Jonas. His pointed jackal ears were now billowing with steam, just like Siegfried's and Pramohana's at the moment. "This is about medium strength, I think, sir."

"Wow—my goodness.... Ummm," Siegfried said, pausing to stick his jackal tongue out and wag it aggressively. Then he coughed and shook his jackal head again, before wiping sweat from his brow and continuing. "Well...okay, yes, I'm okay.... Wow.... So to answer you, Pramohana, I brought Jonas along much faster than I normally would. Usually, I would have approached him after he was already married, but not before gaining promotion to the level of Senior Agent. That is the only reason for Jonas's lack of combat experience and victories against beings like celestial demons and such."

"Is that so?" asked Jonas, his jackal ears sticking up straighter with surprise. "Married? Hmmm, that's very interesting...." He wanted to ask more, but he also knew that Siegfried would never answer questions about his future, or anyone else's for that matter.

"Indeed, it is," Siegfried said, smiling back. "But, Pramohana, know that the Supreme Being has given Jonas its full blessing. Plus, Garud and the other Guardians are one hundred percent behind him." Siegfried then shot a quick wink at Jonas who nodded back.

Chapter Twelve

Pramohana ruffled her large wings and straightened herself, closely examining Jonas from head to toe. "Pramohana will observe what happens next," she said, finally addressing Siegfried. "She very much wants to help Siegfried, but the ancient Danaan customs must be followed. If Jonas proves worthy, then Pramohana will gladly pledge her forces."

She snapped her beak, standing tall and proud. "Yes... Pramohana sees certain, shall she say, 'special marks and signs' on him, yes.... See, Jonas, Pramohana is over a thousand earth years old. She has never met a Savior, but she has always trained and mentored the greatest Danaan Eagle warriors in her tribe. And know that if Siegfried has faith in you, then Pramohana believes that you must be special."

Jonas bowed and said, "thank you, Pramohana." But just as he looked up, Ashtar was walking across the chamber towards him.

Ashtar's celestial, blue human face was shining like a beacon, even among the scintillating rainbow glow of the neutrinos, swirling around the healing tank and lighting the whole chamber. "Excuse me everyone, I just want to tell Jonas what a fantastic job he is doing on his first mission," Ashtar said as he bowed to them.

Jonas snapped straight to attention. "Sir, greetings, sir!"

"Please, relax, Jonas," said Ashtar, saluting back.

"Yes, sir," said Jonas. He relaxed a bit, but still stood completely straight with his hands clasped behind his back.

"I'm afraid I have some serious news, son. Our intelligence sources have revealed to me that Khapre-Tum possesses a dangerous new weapon, capable of toppling the walls of Kalkas even with the energy shield up and working."

"My, oh, my…" Pramohana said, looking stunned. "Pramohana didn't think such a thing was possible. Things are getting curiouser and curiouser…."

But Ashtar's face Jonas could tell that he was deadly serious about this.

"Yes, I agree, Pramohana. But trust me that this new weapon is capable of shaking the very ground under the city. It does this by agitating the lower layers of the planet," said Ashtar. "Our sources have contacted Kalkan engineers who have already confirmed all the data. Several Navan spies risked their lives to gather this information and I trust that source."

"Earth beings call these agitations earthquakes," added Siegfried.

Jonas was beginning to have a bad feeling about this. If the energy shield ever came down, then the city would get barraged by a host of powerful energy weapons, one of which he'd already witnessed firsthand. And even though he knew the Kalkan walls were extremely thick, they would eventually fall if Necrat used the weapons at his disposal.

"Yes, Pramohana has felt one of these quakes. She nearly fell out of her nest when it happened."

"That must have been a powerful one, Pramohana," said Siegfried.

"Yes, it was very shocking," she replied.

"Sir, how can we stop this weapon?" asked Jonas.

"I suggest that you go on a secret mission to find and destroy it," said Ashtar.

"So we will have to infiltrate Khapre-Tum's camp, and once inside, find it, destroy it, and then escape" he said.

"Yes, Khapre-Tum is recruiting marauders and bandits from a small fishing village named Itza that is about ten leagues from Kalkas," said Ashtar. "With a proper disguise you will be able to infiltrate the demon camp from there and then locate and destroy the earth-shaking weapon."

"If that's our best option, sir, then I accept the mission," Jonas said firmly.

"Hermes has run the simulations and that has proved to be the best plan for success," said Ashtar. "Now normally I would never ask a junior agent to take such a dangerous mission. But you are our greatest hope, Jonas. We all have great faith in you, my boy."

Jonas gulped and then immediately started sweating profusely. He knew Ashtar was right. He had no choice but to take the mission, no matter how dangerous, for Siegfried, for Garud and the Guardians, for the Supreme Being and the survival of all the beings of Earth. But even if he failed, Jonas knew the ancient Shastra wisdom, that dying in the act of service to the Supreme Being was a victory in itself. Paw-Paw had always taught Jonas that and he followed and believed in it completely.

"I understand, sir. If Hermes has determined that this is the best plan then I will take it," Jonas said.

"Good, then you're next order is to report back to Kalkas. There's no time to waste, son. That machine could topple the wall at any time," said Ashtar.

"Then I'll return immediately, sir," he said. Jonas felt his heart burning with the pain of worry, for Kalkas and all those sheltered within its walls.

"It was an honor to meet you again, sir!" Jonas said as he stood up straighter and saluted. He then bowed respectfully to Pramohana. "And it was an honor to meet you, your highness."

"Pramohana is honored to meet a Savior. Such a thing is rare in the history of Earth-1. Pramohana believes that you will make a great one, Jonas."

"Thank you," he said and bowed again.

"Jonas, before you go, I must have a quick word with you," said Ashtar. "Pramohana, Siegfried, please excuse us for a moment."

"Yes, of course," said Siegfried.

Ashtar then led Jonas to the far end of the room where Zeeg stood waiting for them. "Yes, sir. What is it?" asked Jonas.

"The bounty hunters had their special weapon, unfortunately it was your Navan friend, Khafre, here," he said motioning to the neutrino pool. "But we also have a special weapon which Zeeg and I think will prove useful. I know that Garud has given you his Golden Bow. But our gift is just as ancient and powerful. And frankly, easier to use in tight spaces."

"Yes, sir."

"Please explain, Zeeg," said Ashtar.

Zeeg held out a gleaming broadsword and Jonas's jackal eyes widened with surprise. Its blade was sheathed in a golden scabbard with intricate details carved into its surface as well as the hilt. It was all absolutely beautiful and he couldn't wait to unsheathe the blade.

"Jonas, legend tells us that this sword was forged within the central sun of our galaxy," said Zeeg. "No one knows exactly who made it, when, or how. But since its creation, this blade has been passed down between the celestials. It was finally gifted to the founder of our very own Command Center, the very first of the Ashtars. It has remained in the possession of an Ashtar ever since."

Jonas gasped as he grabbed the golden hilt and removed the scabbard, exposing a shining bronze blade that glowed with a golden light. Closely inspecting this blade revealed ancient symbols that he couldn't decipher. As he held it up before his jackal face, the weapon hummed and vibrated in his hand.

"Usually only high ranking Senior Agents qualify to carry such a blade. But your mission parameters allow for us to bend this rule just a smidge," said Zeeg.

"Well, maybe more than just a smidge," Ashtar added, smiling.

"Yes, sir! Thank you, sir," said Jonas, bowing back after sheathed the glowing blade. "I will make good use of this and return it to you in one piece."

Jonas smiled as he admired the golden hilt and engraved scabbard now lashed to his utility belt. He understood well that Garud's Golden Bow was always the major weapon for a Savior. But this new tool gave him a special rush of confidence and resolve and no bow had ever done that for him. Sure, he'd fired bows before, but back on Monubia sword play had always been his favorite martial art. He'd excelled at it his whole life, more than any other activity save Warrior Space Ball.

His fencing talent was what had officially gotten him into the Ashtar Command in the first place. He'd won a cool-headed victory over an infamous six-armed Shastra named Esapañiolando, which had earned Jonas the moniker, 'the Shastra with no name,' and the title of the best swords Shastra in all of Monubia's southwestern region. Beating Esapañiolando had been the proudest moment of Jonas's young life, other than graduating from agent school of course.

Now, as Jonas stood before Ashtar with this new sword in his belt, he felt more like an ancient conqueror than an Intergalactic Agent. He smiled, knowing that if his friends and siblings on

Monubian could see him now they'd all be yelling with excitement and cheering him on.

"You definitely look the part, son. That sword really suits you," said Ashtar proudly. "We will contact you again when we have news on Khafre's recovery. But until then, may the Guardians bless your efforts to find that weapon and destroy it."

Ashtar led Jonas back to Siegfried and Pramohana who were still engaged in conversation. "It will start soon now. So think it over, old girl. With your help we stand a greater chance against that demon army," Siegfried was saying.

"Jonas, you will have to excuse Pramohana and myself. We have further matters to discuss," Siegfried said after Jonas had stopped and bowed. "Don't we, Pramohana?"

"Why, yes," she said, bowing to Siegfried. "Jonas, it was an honor to meet you. I will see you again with Siegfried, later on."

"It was an honor to meet you as well, Pramohana," he said. He returned her bow and then headed for the door. But as he turned, his sensitive jackal ears rotated backward ninety degrees so that he could still hear their conversation.

"We are expecting a full onslaught upon Kalkas if they take the energy shield down," he heard Siegfried say. "I must survey your forces and speak with your generals. What do you say, old girl?"

"We shall see..." Pramohana said, sounding absentminded. "But, Pramohana thinks it is okay if Siegfried speaks with her generals. It can't hurt any," Jonas heard her say. Then she paused to sip her Toklaxian Coffee. "Oh, my, Pramohana thinks this is quite mild. Do you have anything stronger in your cupboard?"

"That's as strong as is legally allowed, madam," Ashtar replied. "For health reasons."

"Oh, my, how quaint," she answered.

Jonas walked past Khafre one last time, all cocooned within the shining rainbow tank. The Navan looked peaceful lying there, as if he was free from all suffering and worry. But Jonas knew well that his spirit and energy body were fighting for his very life right at that moment.

Jonas paused before the pool of shimmering neutrinos while Bheem and Mamaji approached and both excitedly examined his new weapon.

"That thin'll rip a skeleton god's spine in two, that be for sure, lad," said Bheem.

"I bet it can," Jonas said proudly. He couldn't wait to use it. "The blade looks amazing."

"With this sword you will what, Jonas?" asked Mamaji.

"Uhh, I don't know?" asked Jonas.

"Why, you'll defeat Khapre-Tum for sure, brother!" Mamaji said as he slugged Jonas on the shoulder.

Soon afterward, Jonas left the healing chamber and stepped back onto the nearest conveyor belt. In only a short time he was zooming away from the Ashtar Command and twisting along the bright light of a Stargate's wormhole. He passed whole star fields and nebulae in only a second, before finally reappearing with a flash in his apartment's bathroom, once again back within the royal palace of Kalkas.

The Itza Market

FROM WHERE JONAS, THE Lone Ranger, and Isas stood atop Tanis Tower (obviously the tallest one in Kalkas) Jonas could watch the entire city, as well as the dusty plane beyond. And only a few hundred cubits from the city's impenetrable wall he could see hairy demon soldiers all busily moving about, training and aiming dark-energy M-class projectile guns and ion laser cannons smack-dab right on the main gates of Kalkas.

As he watched, these cannonade belched and spat searing rays and flame that struck the energy shield, making it crackle and sputter, and sending sparks flying in every direction. But despite all this punishment the shield held strong. Jonas had studied many types of artillery and had even fired six such energy weapon platforms on training missions. Their affects were always devastating. And now here he was, staring down these death machines all fixed on breeching the Kalkan walls.

Beyond Kalkas and out to the west, a flat and dust-covered plane stretched on until it reached a line of jagged hills on the horizon. Jonas then looked eastward, where, nestling against the blue waves of the Atlan Ocean, lay the coastal city of Itza, a sister city to Kalkas. An ancient port city, Itza had existed peacefully beside Kalkas for eons.

Jonas's eyes next traveled north from Itza, tracing the shoreline along a dry savannah until he beheld the jarring sight of the enemy's tents and pavilions. Jonas's celestially enhanced vision clearly made out many dark and brooding demonic shapes moving among these tents with sharp weapons reflecting the desert sun's blinding rays.

"Their camp is quite large," commented Jonas, breaking their silence.

"Yes, demons usually gather in large numbers when war is imminent," said the Lone Ranger, his electronic eye surveying the dusty plane. "But it has been a long time since I have seen them gathered like this."

"How long until their cannons penetrate the energy shield?" Jonas asked, glancing down at the portion of energy shield covering the tall iron gate, the exact focal point of all those searing beams and flames.

"This shield is quite powerful, so it could take days," said the Lone Ranger. "But if their earth-shaking weapon is used, perhaps only gonards remain. That's why your plan must work, Jonas."

"When can we act?" he asked. He was glad the Lone Ranger was visiting them, as the futuristic Shastra and time traveler was proving to be a fount of information.

"Within the hour," answered the Lone Ranger. "Meet me in the underground armory in fifteen Bleebs."

"Isas and I will be there," said Jonas, impressed that he knew the Monubian system of time.

"What is your plan?" Isas asked when the Lone Ranger had finally left.

"It's an old agent special taken from *An Agent's Guide to Military Trickery and Funny Business*. The plan requires disguises similar to those worn by bounty hunters from a land named Nexis. The beings from Nexis frequent the town of Itza, not being far from there. Through Itza we'll gain access to Khapre-Tum's camp. I've already told our plan to The Lone Ranger, and Mamaji is right now readying the supplies that I requested. Once we're in the demon camp we'll find the earth-shaking weapon and destroy it," he said. "Then I'll find Khapre-Tum and finish this whole thing before their army attacks. Are you ready?" he asked her.

"I'm ready for anything," she said with a smile. "What about you?"

"I became an Intergalactic Agent just for missions like this; sneaking into and out of places that I shouldn't be and breaking expensive machinery," he said. "That's the number one main goal of an agent right there, to gain a dangerous objective by the quickest, most efficient way possible."

But as soon as Jonas said this the tower began to shake and they braced themselves against the ramparts. The stone floor swayed beneath them for a long, horrifying moment. Then the shaking suddenly stopped and their shocked eyes met.

"That must be the earth-shaking weapon…" he said breathlessly. His heart raced as he glanced down at the city's wall and the energy shield. The wall still stood, while the shield's glow kept crackling, strong and bright.

"I hope that was just a test," Isas said, peeling herself from the stone battlements.

They exchanged another nod and then rushed for the door. Soon they were leaping down the corkscrew escalator as fast as they could.

They passed through a shocked throng of Navans gathered in the central square, and then found the circular entrance to the underground. Jonas and Isas both paused at the door, receiving their necessary astral brain scans, before his palm print finally made the giant handle turn. A Navan guard then pushed the computer terminal controls and the massive steel door opened.

The Kalkan underground was a wonderfully fascinating, yet completely separate world from the surface above. They navigated by hologram signs and maps on the walls as well as the random advice of Navan warriors or wolfmen and wolfwomen scientists that they often ran into.

Every being they spoke with smiled in greeting and were all eager to point them in the same general direction when they needed help. Their help, plus the hologram signs finally led them to a giant room of metallic silver from wall, to floor, to ceiling. It all appeared so pristine and so clean that an army of cleaning droids had to have recently scrubbed the entire space from top to bottom.

The room was so gigantic in scope, so large in fact, that completely shoved into a single corner of this cavernous space sat at least three squadrons of atomic-powered star chariots, and all were fully armed and ready to fly at a moment's notice. Jonas and Isas walked over to survey them, and he found that he knew most of their makes and models. With a good pilot behind the controls, these chariots could blast the demon army all over the dusty Kalkan plane.

Among the models that he recognized were Alpha-class star cruisers, Comet Spear models, and Delta wing class II fighters. These were just a few among countless others that he'd never seen before in his short agent career. The latter Delta wing fighters looked especially sleek and were loaded with deadly weapons on each side. Other ships were egg-shaped, and some even came in strange diamond shaped orientations. More than a few looked similar to a bounty hunter's atomic powered space jet.

He and Isas walked beneath their hulls and between their locked landing gear, gazing up with awe and commenting on each one. Some were double-decker chariots, some were disk-shaped, and others were long, thin and cigar-shaped star cruisers. Jonas recognized an older Zeta-R2 scout model shaped like a saucer. And one was just a hulking cube, silently hovering in the air above them.

After wandering through countless rows of towering battle chariots, some rising twenty to fifty cubits high above their heads, they finally found the Lone Ranger, waving from behind a sealed glass room in the far corner. As they drew nearer he stepped out and bowed.

"Mamaji and I have gathered all the supplies that you requested for your mission," said the Lone Ranger. "Are there any questions that you have before we get started?"

"How will we gain access to the camp?" asked Isas.

"That will be tough and very dangerous, but Jonas has a plan," said the Lone Ranger.

"What is it?" asked Isas.

"We will infiltrate Khapre-Tum's camp by volunteering at a recruiting station in Itza," said Jonas. "Once we enter the camp we destroy the earth-shaking weapon and then find a portal to the Underworld and locate Khapre-Tum."

"His plan is simple yet affective, my dear. I'm sure that it can be done," said the Lone Ranger.

"How will we blend in among the demons and escape detection?" asked Isas.

"Our disguises will match bounty hunters from the city of Nexis," said Jonas. "They include demon-fur ponchos and taking a shower in demon blood. Although gross, the latter is necessary to disguise the smell of Kalkas."

"It is the best way to enter Itza without getting caught," said the Lone Ranger. "I've done it many times," he added as Isas's expression became sour and her beautiful nose scrunched up with disgust.

Then she snorted and sneered unpleasantly. Jonas understood, but it was necessary.

"Shastra demons and bounty hunters live in Nexis and actually dress this way. Plus, demons have an excellent sense of smell. They can detect a Navan, or someone who's been near one, from many leagues away. You and I must reek like Navan by now," Jonas added.

Isas sighed, rolled her pretty eyes, and then intensely narrowed them into slits. "Okay, then let's get it over with…" she said, obviously very unhappy with their plan.

Jonas couldn't blame her, though. He decided not to mention the fact that on his training missions he'd used three disguises even more disgusting than this one.

"That's the spirit," said the Lone Ranger. Then he whistled and called over three Navans, each one hauling a cart of supplies.

"First, we'll rough up your clothes a bit," said the Lone Ranger.

Jonas and Isas stood there while the Navan assistants busily cut, ripped, and ruffled up their robes and tunics. They then smeared handfuls of dirt and charcoal into every inch of fabric. After ten bleebs of this there wasn't even a square-inch of clean skin or clothing left between the two of them. Jonas's nostrils flared up as he detected a burning, rancid smell that he could barely handle right as the Navans brought out two large buckets. These were the source of the smell, Jonas just knew it. Both were filled with demon blood.

Jonas plugged his nose and closed his eyes as the Navan assistants began to pour. The blood felt thick, slimy, and cold. Jonas relaxed when they'd finished. But he knew they were just getting started.

Next, more buckets appeared. These were filled to the brim with demon hair, and stunk even worse(if that was possible).

Jonas had experienced this many times before, but even he gagged when he almost swallowed a large clump of hair. By the time he'd spat the hair out, the assistants were all finished and he could carefully wipe every last bit of blood and hair away from his jackal mouth and eyes. They'd basically received the most repulsive shower imaginable.

He could hear Isas gasping and groaning the entire time. "Is this really necessary?" she asked, between her spitting, hacking, and scraping the demon hairballs out of her mouth.

"Absolutely, one hundred percent," the Lone Ranger said confidently. "This is the most successful disguise we've ever used to enter Itza from Kalkas. In over fifty attempts no Navan spy with this disguise has ever been caught or detected, not even once."

"Excellent," said Jonas. "That's great news."

"Now, last, are the demon-fur ponchos. It's the final touch," said the Lone Ranger. The Navan assistants then handed them each a heavy poncho. Jonas knew these once had been real, live demons, but he didn't ask how the Lone Ranger had acquired them, the blood, or the hair, but they were probably from the same donors.

Jonas slipped his head through the poncho hole while the rest of the garment fell over his shoulders and upper body. He was glad that it came with a convenient hood, which was very practical. Amazingly, when he glanced over, he saw that Isas looked as beautiful as ever, even with blood dripping from her face and the curly demon hairs all stuck to her.

"Perfect, now both of you are dead ringers for bounty hunters from Nexis," said the Lone Ranger, standing back and admiring them. "Oh, wait... hold on a sec. Those creatures always carry a laser rifle called the Jouster-3000 blaster. They're standard issue, so you guys gotta have them."

The Navan assistants disappeared and when they reappeared they were rolling carts along carrying long, rust-covered laser rifles.

"Ah, the trusty Jouster! I love these things. We used these on training missions," said Jonas. But these had to be much older models, and when Jonas accepted his own blaster, it proved far heavier than usual and he nearly dropped it. "This thing weighs a ton!" he exclaimed, feeling a twinge in his lower back. He froze for a moment and groaned softly before he straightened up. Then with one great effort he heaved the rifle back up and rested it right on his shoulder.

He looked over to see Isas already holding hers the same way, and she hadn't even complained once. "Wow, you're pretty strong," he said. "I'm impressed."

"Stronger than you think," she said, winking back. "We're sometimes known as warrior priestesses."

"You're both a complete mess," said the Lone Ranger, looking visibly pleased with his work. "You both look brilliant."

"I feel like a mess…" said Isas, still groaning and brushing blood and hair out of her eyes.

"Great, then let's get going. Oh, by the way, where's the tunnel entrance you told me about?" Jonas asked.

"Tunnel? Can't we drive there by chariot?" asked Isas.

"Not a good idea. We'll attract too much attention that way," said Jonas.

"This tunnel system is a much better route. It is big enough to comfortably stand up in and connects Kalkas directly to Itza in one straight shot," said the Lone Ranger. "Alright, you're all set now. Follow me."

They followed the Lone Ranger through a sliding door and then down a long hallway, passing many Navan soldiers before descending an elevator to a much lower level that was solely populated by furry wolfmen and wolfwomen scientists, as far as Jonas could tell.

They descended to another level filled with tall, green, bug-eyed praying mantis beings, all talking in their clicking bug language. Finally, they entered a room with three tunnels were dug into the far wall. Above each opening there hung a label of their destination. From left to right they read: 'Itza Port, Itza Market,' and 'Itza Prison.'

Jonas didn't want to know what they'd find at the end of the tunnel labeled 'Itza Prison.'

"Jonas, by now Khapre-Tum's minions have studied the previous six Saviors. So, whatever you do, don't manifest your bronze armor or the Golden Bow unless they are absolutely necessary."

"I know, that would just give us away," he said. He wiped the dripping demon blood from his hands onto his tunic. Then he gagged after getting a whiff of his own stench, being truly horrendous.

"Bingo!" said the Lone Ranger. "But the sword that Ashtar gave you, that thing's new. No one will recognize that, so it's fair game." The Lone Ranger pointed to the sword on Jonas's utility belt.

"Now, get going, you two. The tunnel is a straight shot the whole way. I'll see both of you back here after you're finished." Then the Lone Ranger motioned towards the tunnel labeled 'Itza Market.'

"Itza deal," said Jonas. He smirked and tried to hold back his laughter.

But the Lone Ranger just stared back, looking confused. "What does that mean?"

"Itza joke," he said, winking and smiling even wider.

The Lone Ranger continued to blankly stare.

"Uhhh, never mind…." he said. Jonas was confused. He thought it was funny and he didn't understand why the Lone Ranger didn't get it. By now he'd developed great respect for that time traveler and thought that they had a lot of things in common. He'd grown very close to that mysterious Shastra, so of course he wanted to make him laugh.

"Come on, let's get going," he finally said to Isas. They both bowed to the Lone Ranger, and then ducking low Isas followed Jonas into the dark passage.

They marched into the oppressive blackness. The light from the room behind them quickly shrank, until the Lone Ranger's image became a tiny pin-prick and it vanished entirely. Jonas could swear that the Lone Ranger was smiling and even laughing as he waved to them good bye.

Walking on, Jonas was relieved that at least he could stand up. But even with that he still had no idea how high the tunnel was actually, for above him was nothing but darkness.

He forced himself to focus on their objective as his hands fumbled forward, feeling along the damp and crumbling dirt wall. The heavy Jouster-3000 blaster bounced against his back as he walked.

Soon Jonas began to sense a gentle upward slope. This incline grew steeper as they climbed toward visible cracks of light up ahead. Carefully creeping forward, he finally stopped and looked up at the slivers of light now shining directly onto the floor before him.

Since this appeared to be the tunnel's end (only damp wall existed beyond this point) he blindly felt around the walls until he found a wooden ladder. So, being a practical Shastra, he climbed this ladder toward the thin rays of light above. Right when those dust-ridden beams of light were shining in his face, he reached up and pushed against the ceiling.

It slowly creaked upward, proving to be a trap door lid. He raised this just enough to be able to stick the top of his jackal head out and look around. Sniffing vigorously, he detected things like dry wood, barrels filled with mead, delicious cured meats, the hot air of the planes, and lots and lots of dust. This was all mixed with a salty breeze coming from off the coast.

He was looking around a storeroom filled with boxes, bottles, packages, and barrels stacked from floor to ceiling. There was no one around so he poked his jackal head out farther. "I'm gonna get out and look around. Stay down here until I get back, okay?" he whispered down to Isas.

"Okay, just hurry up—you're dripping demon blood right in my face—" Isas whispered back.

"Oops, sorry about that," he said, forgetting he was still all covered in demon filth. He climbed out and silently lowered the trap door. As he glanced about, his jackal eyes fell on a perfectly shaped box. He pushed the box along until it rested right over the trap door lid. "I'll be right back," he whispered down to her through the floorboards.

"Be careful" she whispered back.

He nodded to her and then tiptoed to the door and cracked it open, but only after he raised his hood so it hid his jackal face. Just outside was a chaotic and bustling, open-aired market, filled with fishermen, merchants, traders, and soldiers, all mingling, trading, and yelling beneath a patched, brown canopy that flapped overhead. An ocean breeze was blowing up dust along with countless interesting smells that he wished to explore in detail one by one.

A troupe of demon soldiers suddenly came marching towards him so he leaned back behind the door and just stood there, breathing heavily and praying they hadn't seen him. When he looked again they had all marched on through the crowd, where they were yelling and shoving Navans, Shastras, humans, and scaly lizard merchants out of the way.

Upon studying this scene he felt these beings were so busy trading weapons, packages, armor, trinkets, fishing tools, and general foodstuffs with seashell currency that no one would even notice him and Isas, and they could just walk around and gather information. All he and Isas had to do was avoid the demons and everything would go smoothly.

"We're in a storehouse in the Itza marketplace," he said, lifting the trapdoor and helping Isas up.

"What's out there?" she asked as she wiped her eyes and glanced around the storeroom.

"Mostly marauders, bandits, traders, and some fishermen. And a few demon soldiers."

"Sounds like a charming crowd. We should blend right in then," she replied, pointing at their disguises.

"Exactly. Let's go."

They opened the storeroom door and checked to make sure the coast was clear before they entered the busy marketplace. "I think we should buy something. You know, to blend in more," Isas whispered in his jackal ear as they pushed through the crowd. "Plus, I'm getting hungry."

Jonas couldn't argue with her reasoning. "Okay, good idea. There's a fish stall over there," he said. "Let's try that."

"Great, I love fish," she said excitedly. "I'm famished."

So they approached a stall with a green-scaled fish-being standing behind the counter. It was about as tall as Jonas and had the same body type, with arms and legs like a human, except everything was covered in green fish scales. Jonas tried sniffing the fish-being out, but his and Isas's stench was so foul and the blowing dust so strong and pungent that he couldn't detect anything.

Isas gasped when she got closer and saw this fish-being for the first time. The being appeared to be from Oceania by the look of his fish head, plus, the gold chains and medallion that it wore. The being's knobby fish eyes stared back curiously, studying their bounty hunter outfits while Jonas quickly read the menu.

"Hello, how are you?" said Jonas. He hoped Oceanians weren't the sworn enemies of Nexis.

The fish-being remained calm while awkwardly moaning a reply in what Jonas identified as the most common of the fishish languages. Thankfully, Jonas's Agent training had included language courses in both conversational and advanced fishish.

"Oh, thank you. That's very kind of you," Jonas replied in formal fishish while he continued studying the menu. The Oceanian nodded back and seemed to be pleased with his language skill, so Jonas continued. "We'll have one order of the mega-squid tentacles, please. Do you accept Galactic Credits?" he asked as he fiddled in the pocket of his tunic. Just then he caught Isas staring at him, her face drawn back with a look of complete shock.

"What, didn't I tell you that I spoke fishish?" he asked.

She shook her head and smiled. "No, I don't recall, Jonas. You just keep on surprising me."

"Well, I can hold a basic conversation," he said.

The stall owner slimed back a chorus of groans which Jonas took to mean, "Yes, we do, sir. Your order will be ready in five bleebs."

"Thank you. Here you go," he said, handing the fish-being a ten Galactic Credit chip.

The fish-being tossed him half a sea star, nodded fiercely, and then left the counter. Jonas pocketed the half sea star, although he really had no idea what it was worth in fish-being money. But the proprietor was calm and a fight hadn't broken out, so Jonas felt that the transaction was a success.

Two bleebs later the fish-being returned with a white bucket holding three green tentacles, all cleanly detached from their previous owner, whatever it had been. Still partially alive, they were all squirming up the brim of the bucket towards freedom.

Jonas shivered with disgust but then quickly composed himself. He knocked the friskiest tentacles back into the bucket and then handed the whole things to Isas. "Okay, here you go. Enjoy...." He grabbed her arm and maneuvered the crowd while looking for signs that might lead them to Khapre-Tum's camp.

"Okay...okay...that. Is. So. Disgusting..." she said as she poked and flicked the tentacles still trying to escape.

But then Jonas and Isas both froze as a faint rumbling traveled beneath their feet. The whole market shook and every shack and stall swayed from side-to-side. But the merchants, fishermen, and soldiers only stopped what they were doing for a moment. They all looked around and then just continued on with their business like it was nothing.

Just then Jonas turned his jackal head and managed to get a glimpse of Kalkas through a slit in the canopy. The mighty Kalkan walls were still standing and the energy shield remained a shimmering beacon across the plane.

"Come on, eat your tentacles. They're good for you. And the crowd might grow suspicious if you don't," he whispered, raising his hood a bit to scan for an exit.

"I can't…. They're just too….gross."

"Just do it. If you don't eat them, the fish-beings might be offended. Tentacles are a delicacy."

"Okay, here goes…" she said and then gave a loud sigh.

He heard a loud squish, followed by groans, grunts, and then heavy breathing. But Jonas didn't dare look. If he did, he knew that he'd laugh out loud and draw unwanted attention to himself.

"Oh, you know what? These actually aren't that bad…." she said in a muffled voice. "It has a tough outer layer. But then a hint of barbecue sauce and cinnamon once you get through that."

"They're actually quite healthy, that's what I've heard," he said out the side of his jackal mouth.

"Let's just get out of here and find the camp. I can't wait to take off this outfit," said Isas. She was constantly scratching herself and adjusting her poncho between bites of tentacle. "This thing is driving me absolutely crazy—"

"Yeah, you're right," he said, as he scratched himself where the demon hair touched his upper arms.

Next they turned down an alley and walked along its tents and shacks. It appeared simple and very run-down, but he'd seen worse markets before on his training missions, especially on the four post-apocalyptic, warlike planets he'd visited.

The worst markets usually displayed skulls and skeletons stuck to posts or dangling from buildings, and those were just the basic decorations. These markets often sold different styles of torture devices, as well as magic potions, poisons, ancient spell books, and destructive energy devices, none of which he saw in Itza. And there weren't any vendors selling slaves, body parts, or bones. So that was an encouraging sign for Earth-1.

He kept walking down the lane and then stopped. His pointed jackal ears stuck straight up at attention, on high alert as they scanned the alley.

"Volunteers needed! Khapre-Tum seeks volunteers for war against Kalkas!" Jonas tried to locate the source, his ears turning like antennae. "There will be plenty of battle, looting, and plundering, guaranteed! Don't miss out on a great opportunity!" yelled the voice.

He finally determined that these words were coming from a tall, hairy demon just up ahead and to their left, and standing before a large tent. "Come one, come all! Lawless behavior required! Previous marauding and bounty hunting experience recommended! We offer health benefits and paid vacation days after the fall of Kalkas!"

"That sounds pretty promising," said Jonas. He nudged Isas who was busy struggling with her next tentacle. "What do you think about talking to this guy?" he asked.

"Be careful, Jonas…" she said skeptically. She then caught and finally started on her second tentacle. "Here, try one. The center isn't that bad." She placed one of the slimy tentacles in his hand and he had to grasp it tight as it wiggled violently, trying to escape.

Jonas swallowed hard as they approached this tall demon, his jackal instincts silently screaming in alarm and praying for him to turn around. He started sweating harder, which caused the demon blood and hair to run down his jackal face. His heart pounded faster with each step.

"We're bounty hunters from Nexis, as you can see, obviously…" Jonas said, nervously addressing the demon.

The demon glared down with two giant, red eyes and growled through its sharp fangs. All this was framed between two long, curved tusks.

"I'm…Brain Crusher…. And this here is my partner…uhhh… Blood Sniffer," Jonas blurted. He felt near panic just for a moment when he realized that they hadn't picked fake names.

Isas grunted, chewing on her second tentacle while it wiggled in her mouth.

The demon stopped growling and then just grimaced at them. "Hmm, tentacles…. I love those," the demon finally said, pointing to the bucket Isas was holding.

"Me too," said Jonas as he waved his tentacle in the air. "By the way, each of us has five years of bounty hunting experience for the Nexis National Guard. It's a very elite group."

"Bounty hunters, eh? Come on in," said the demon. Then it parted the tent flap and they followed it inside. They found themselves at the back of a line stretching towards a demon sitting behind a table up ahead. This demon was talking while it wrote on a long scroll.

Jonas studied the lineup. It was composed of barbaric, nasty looking characters and reached entirely out through the back of the tent to a transport chariot idling in the hot sun. They waited for a long time and when they finally reached the front of the line the head demon looked up from its scroll. "Qualifications....?" asked the demon.

"Err, umm, lots of murder and mayhem...especially farmers, children...and their little pets of course. Arrrr!" said Jonas, grimacing painfully.

"Mostly pets, though. Arrrr!" snarled Isas.

"Yeah, those be our favorite, mate, especially the little dogs... and...uhhh, rabbits too. We hate them the most..." Jonas blurted out. "We take them and make a stew out a them. This stew we be sellin on the black markets...Argghhh!"

Isas nudged and glared at him.

He got the message and immediately stopped talking, not wanting to overdo the act and blow their cover. He desperately hoped that this demon was a fan of ancient pirates.

"And we're quite dirty, arrrr!" added Isas. "We never be bathin!!"

The demon, who had up until then been listening patiently, finally spoke again. "Aha! You scallywags, both speak Pirate! I am somewhat of a historian myself," the demon said, smiling back.

"Aha, arrrhhh!" they both repeated.

"Yes, yes, good, good...now, well, tell me, please, what other types of mayhem do you practice?" the demon asked, working his free-energy pen across the scroll with a flurry of excitement.

"Oh, many types of mayhem," said Jonas, trying to think. "Things like...burning crops and killing livestock, really nasty stuff."

"We're pure riff-raff, arrrr!" Isas said between bites of tentacle.

"Hmmm, yes.... Riff-raff...excellent...just wonderful," said the demon, writing even faster now. "You two are just perfect. Here, take these badges. The chariot outside leaves in five minutes." The demon handed them each a badge in the shape of skull and crossbones.

"Arrrr! Badges?! We don't need no stinkin—" Isas began to say. But Jonas quickly elbowed her, stopping her before she finished.

"Thank ya, matey! Holy shnickeys, it be the ancient Pirate emblem. That be just swashbucklin!" exclaimed Jonas. And then he pinned one of the badges to his poncho and the other on Isas. He was very glad to get official badges. In fact, Jonas collected official badges and actually had three boxes filled with them back in his apartment.

"Yep, that's the exact same logo. Pretty neat, huh? Next!" the demon yelled, waving to the beings waiting behind them.

They pushed through the exit and found the transport chariot idling outside. They took seats in the chariot's rear bed, between two frog-beings on their left and two lizard-beings on their right. The next thing Jonas knew, the chariot shook and began to pull away from Itza.

Right across from them sat two extremely ugly Shastra demons, both of whom were from Nexis, as each was covered in the same demon blood, fur, and demon ponchos. The tallest of these silently nodded to them in recognition, followed by the frog-beings and the lizard-beings all croaking and hissing in concert.

Jonas and Isas both quickly snarled back and nodded. No one actually spoke real words as the chariot bounced over the dusty plain, flying towards the ominous camp in the distance.

Clouds of dust swirled about them as everyone disembarked in Khapre-Tum's camp. Jonas's jackal senses were immediately overwhelmed all at once by the sound of barking demons and a host of new, very unique, and very rotten smells. Waving away a cloud of dust, Jonas nodded to their driver who then took off back towards Itza. Then he and Isas snuck behind a large tent to hide from the crowd.

As they trudged through the camp they were absolutely punished by the hot sun. Besides the overwhelming heat the first things they encountered were numerous extremely tall and well-armed skeleton warriors that infested the camp. Jonas had never before seen these things up close, nor had he expected them in such numbers. Now, this skeleton presence, along with the periodic rumblings beneath his feet, increased his desire to find the earth-shaking machine.

"That thing's got to be here somewhere.... If we only had a clue or a specific area to search..." he said, growing more anxious by the minute. The fact that his jackal instincts wanted to wildly sniff every demon and skeleton within ten cubits of him made it that much harder.

He was about to take his energy-detecting glasses out when Isas pointed to a demon standing before a large, dark tent that was just up ahead. The demon leaned on a very long, very massive-looking sword while his black demon eyes watched the crowd intently. "Ask that demon over there," she suggested.

Hesitant to talk to these skeletons and demons, but growing more anxious by the minute, Jonas nodded. "Okay, let's go."

"What are you gonna say?" she asked.

"I'll think of something...."

Since his pirate voice had worked before Jonas decided to try it again. "Arrrhh! Excuse me, matey... Do you be knowin where Khapre-Tum's filthy weapons be located? You know, them energy ones, and them, them barmy earth-shakers you got? Arrrhhh! We be lookin for one earth-shaker in particular. We be settin to repair the barnacle-covered contraption! Arrhhh! Then we be speakin to the boss, he be named Khapre-Tum, am I right, matey?"

The demon glared back but didn't speak or move.

"Arrrrr!" Isas yelled, while shaking her last tentacle in the demon's face.

Jonas looked at Isas and scowled. "Maybe he not be the speakin type?" Jonas asked. "Or he be a landlubber, maybe...."

Slowly, the demon reached for a blinking gadget on its belt. When it did, Isas jumped and accidentally dropped the tentacle which splattered on the demon's foot.

Well, that wasn't ideal, thought Jonas. He tried not to panic, but the demon's dark eyes had narrowed to burning slits. Flashing its long fangs, it slowly lifted its giant sword and Jonas's jackal hairs all stood on end.

"Aha! You scurvy braggart, I just remembered! Your machine be right down this lane," said Jonas, nodding furiously. "Arrrhhh!" He grasped Isas's arm and snarled. "Arrhhh! Thanks, but we'll be goin then, matey."

The demon paused, confused whether to raise its sword further or lower it back to the ground.

Jonas and Isas walked away from the demon as fast as they could and through the crowded lane. Jonas looked back to find the hairy demon was still staring at them. He had put his sword away, however, much to Jonas's relief.

"What was I thinking?" he asked, shaking his jackal head as they walked briskly along.

"I think we've lost him, or at least I can't see him any longer," she said, turning back around while holding her hood partially over her face.

Jonas lowered his own hood, put his energy detecting glasses on, and adjusted their settings. Soon he was glimpsing through tent flaps, the walls of buildings, and even inside the crates and boxes within different structures, fully determined to find the earthquake weapon.

Jonas and Isas passed a group of skeleton warriors grumbling about impressive feats they had seen Khapre-Tum accomplish lately and also what they were planning to do to Kalkas once the energy shield was breached.

"I can't believe what they're saying," Isas mumbled in shock. They next passed a group of lizard-beings and more skeleton warriors, all growling about their plans to destroy Kalkas as well.

Jonas nodded. He didn't expect anything less from that crowd. "First time around demons and lizard-beings?" he asked her.

"No, but it's been a while. I wasn't looking forward to it, I can tell you that."

Jonas's jackal instincts flashed onto high alert again, meaning that something or someone dangerous was behind them. He glanced backward. Slowly following them was the same demon he'd asked for directions earlier. It carried the giant sword on its hairy shoulder and had an evil gaze fixed on them. Jonas shuddered and turned away when it raised and then spoke into a comm. link device held in its giant, clawed hand.

Jonas's heart was pounding now. He had to think fast.

"It's the demon from earlier," said Isas.

"I know."

"What are you going to do?"

"Don't worry, I've got it handled," he said. He approached the closest tent, stopped at its entrance, and motioned for her to keep close. Isas did so, but looked visibly tense and worried. Then Jonas glanced through the flaps and into the tent behind them. Then he looked back at the demon, still drawing closer.

"What are you going to do?" Isas whispered.

"Wait here for a moment," said Jonas.

"Why?" asked Isas. "That demon is right over there," she said, punching him in the arm.

"Four demons are inside a tent three spaces behind this one here. Within it is Khapre-Tum's earth-shaking weapon. I just saw it," Jonas said excitedly. "Don't worry, the inhabitants will be leaving momentarily. Once they do we'll enter, and we'll lose this demon following us."

"What? How do you know that?" asked Isas.

Jonas smirked and tapped his energy-detecting glasses.

When he looked again, the four demons were gone. So Jonas grabbed his golden sword by the hilt and nodded to Isas. "Annnd we're clear. Let's go!" he said. Just then a group of tall skeletons crossed the lane, obstructing them from the large demon's view. Jonas grabbed Isas and passed into the tent behind them.

They burst in on three startled lizard-beings that were playing cards, bowed respectfully, and then walked out the back of that tent, down another alley, through one more tent which was empty, and then through a third flap.

They both abruptly stopped, gasping with excitement at a cylindrical metal machine suspended off the ground on four legs. It was visibly active, humming loudly, and wrapped in countless beeping, flashing buttons, wires, and blinking lights.

Jonas's jackal eyes passed over all these dials and lights, and over the cylinder's surface, until they fell on a bright, red laser, shining down through a hole in the dirt floor. Jonas's sweaty palm gripped his sword and he walked closer, his eyes following a black power cable that led from the machine's underbelly and out the corner.

"This is it," he said, wide-eyed with excitement as his energy-detecting glasses zoomed in on the machine.

"Earth-shaking machine, Hiixian construction, manipulating Earth's magnetic resonance. Charged and ready to attack Kalkas with alpha crust waves. Contains power levels possibly able to disable Kalkan energy shield," beeped Hermes.

"Thanks Hermes," he said. He focused back on Isas. "We've found it!"

"So, then what are you going to—?" Isas began.

But before she could finish her sentence Jonas unsheathed his bronze sword and cut the power cable with one quick swipe. The red laser instantly went out and the cylinder ceased all its rumblings and electronic chirpings. His second swipe cut the machine in two equal halves. Crystalline parts, chips, and wires, plus, a weird kind of gel all came spilling out onto the floor.

With deep satisfaction he walked around the machine, crunching the crystal guts and wires beneath his sandals. "Seems about right," he said, convinced he'd done his job.

Then he stepped back and wiped his sweaty jackal brow. "Okay, let's go find Khapre-Tum's tent," he said. The thought of facing Khapre-Tum made him shake with adrenaline. But he knew he was ready to finish his mission and return home.

He glimpsed out through the tent with his glasses again and saw large, dark shapes approaching. "Hold up!" he said. "Wait...."

There were at least three of them. One was a hairy demon, carrying a long broadsword over its shoulder. Jonas gulped. He knew they were in serious trouble.

"Don't worry," she said, laying a hand on his arm. "Remember what the Lone Ranger said? No spy from Kalkas has ever been caught in Itza."

"Yeah, I remember..." he said worriedly.

But then the tent flap suddenly fluttered open, revealing the large demon that had followed them earlier. He stood there blocking their exit, with an evil grin spread across its dark demon face. It glanced angrily from the Jonas to Isas. Their hoods were both drawn back and Jonas was holding his celestial sword unsheathed. The demon glanced at the machine's innards, trampled under Jonas's sandaled feet.

"I've found them, sir. Yes...it's Jonas and Isas," the demon said with a growl into his comm. link.

"Aw shnikey's..." Jonas cursed under his breath.

The demon raised its sword and rushed forward. In a flash, Jonas lunged low as the demon slashed at him with its blade, only missing him by inches. He then jumped behind the demon, reached around its black, hairy head, and put it in a firm headlock. He then tightened his arm.

The demon fought back, struggling, yelling, spitting, and growling as Jonas held on for dear life. When it finally stopped thrashing about helplessly Jonas released his hold and the demon flopped onto the floor, letting out one last disgusting gurgle.

"Is it dead?" Isas asked.

"Who knows..." he said, both horrified and relieved at the same time. Jonas kicked its giant, clawed hand just to make sure it wasn't awake. It didn't move. "That means our cover is blown. Any second now more demons will arrive and annihilate this entire tent. Let's get the heck out of here and back to Kalkas!" he yelled.

"But, what about Khapre-Tum? We aren't finished here," Isas protested. "We can prevent a war from ever happening!"

"Listen, we won't make it within fifty cubits of that tent, wherever it is!" said Jonas. "The whole camp will come down on us if we don't get out of here right now. That would be a suicide mission. I'll get another chance to fight Khapre-Tum later. Now, let's get out of here!"

Isas stared at him for a long moment. Even while covered with demon blood and demon hair, her gaze mesmerized him and her eyes sparkled with beauty.

They suddenly dashed outside, rushing chaotically through an endless row of tents. Already, he could hear demons and skeletons yelling and rushing through the camp to investigate. "Let's grab a chariot!" he yelled.

"Good idea," she said, running as fast as she could and trying to keep up.

The demon and skeleton growling grew louder and Jonas suddenly heard bells and alarms sounding as they dashed and ducked between tents and canopies and around lookout towers.

"Over there!" he shouted, pointing at a large tent off to their right. They dove in and stood, finding three atomic chariots inside, all unattended.

"Great! So...which one?" she asked.

"Doesn't matter!" said Jonas. He leapt onto the nearest chariot, helped Isas up, and then frantically punched the controls. The twin atomic engines roared to life and the tent flapped about wildly, tugging at its stakes and filling the entire space with dust.

"Hurry up and get us out of here!" Isas yelled, slapping his arm.

Five demons then suddenly burst into the tent, aiming laser blasters all charged and ready to fire.

"I'm hurrying!" Jonas yelled.

The very next instant they were thrown forward as their chariot burst out through the rear of the tent. A hail of laser fire singed their hoods and ponchos as Jonas then stopped the chariot cold, spun it around, and punched the accelerator. They were soon zooming through the camp at incredible speed.

Jonas gripped the controls as they plowed through rows of tents, sending skeleton warriors, serpent-beings, what looked like ghouls and werewolves, and of course demons, all flying out of their way. In a short time they cleared the camp perimeter and were now speeding over the dusty plane towards the massive Kalkan walls in the distance.

Jonas sighed with relief when he finally glimpsed the shimmering energy shield, meaning they were finally in the clear. But then he looked over at Isas and he saw that her face was filled with worry. Then he jolted upright, realizing that in order to enter the city they had to somehow turn off the protective energy shield, not to mention get past the energy cannons set outside its walls.

"Jonas! The energy shield—" blurted Isas.

"I know— Mamaji, shut off the energy shield and open the gates!" he barked as he punched the chariot's comm. link switch.

There was a loud crackle and then Mamaji's husky wolfman voice responded. "Who is this? Whoever you are, you're driving an unregistered chariot. Identify yourself, brother."

"Mamaji! Turn off the shield and open the gates!" yelled Isas.

"Who is this?"

"Mamaji! This is Jonas! We've disabled the earth-shaking weapon!" he yelled, as the air rushed past his jackal face now only an inch above the controls. "If you don't open the gate those canons are gonna blow us away!" Jonas glanced backward. Three chariots, filled with demons, were right behind them now.

"Jonas?! Is that Isas with you, brother?" asked Mamaji. "Where are you guys?"

"Mamaji! We. Are. Being. Chased. By. Demons!" Isas screamed, slamming her fist against the control panel. "Open the gate! Now!"

"That will take me minutes, sister…I can't just do that instantly," replied Mamaji.

"We don't have minutes!" she yelled.

"Mamaji, if you don't turn off the shield and open the gates we're both dead!" Jonas screamed.

"Geeze…okay, okay. Now, let me see…ummm…" mumbled Mamaji. "Oh, brother, how can I…?"

Their transmission suddenly broke off as energy bolts struck their chariot's rear engine compartment, shaking them violently. Jonas swerved, avoiding more energy beams, and now racing right for the energy shield and the long row of cannons pointed at the Kalkan gate.

Isas tried aiming her Jouster-3000 blaster, but with all his erratic driving she only lurched about, unable to get a clear shot. They hit a bump and she accidentally squeezed the trigger, sending four blue energy orbs into the air, sailing over the dusty plane in slow motion.

"Holy schnikeys!" Jonas yelled as the orbs exploded in plumes of blue fire, digging giant craters in the earth. The demon chariots swerved erratically and one of them crashed into a large boulder, exploding spectacularly, while the other two swerved out of the way, scraped their hulls together, and then straightened out.

"Mamaji? What's the shield's status?" yelled Jonas.

Then he glanced up. The energy shield showed no signs of change. It hadn't even dimmed a little bit. When Jonas heard screeching jet engines behind him, he turned and stared open-mouthed, unable to believe what he saw.

Necrat was flying like a streak of fire on a jet pack, heading right for them, and carrying a terrible looking laser rifle, undoubtedly aimed right at Jonas's jackal head.

"It's Necrat!" Isas yelled.

Jonas gulped and shook his jackal head in disbelief.

Necrat flashed his evil grin and winked back, drawing closer by the second.

"This is gonna be close," said Jonas. They both ducked and Jonas swerved their chariot as Necrat's laser bolts buzzed his pointed jackal ears and singed the top of Isas's ponytail.

All this commotion quickly drew the attention of the demons gathered before the energy shield and they all began frantically turning their weapons platforms around. Some even dismounted and took aim with laser rifles.

Jonas held their chariot steady just enough for Isas to blast their path clear right before they burst between the smoldering platforms. They came out in one piece with only a hundred cubits between them and the blazing energy shield, still at one hundred percent power, and with the huge iron gate still closed behind it.

"We'll never make it! Jonas, turn us around!" Isas yelled.

"Come on, Mamaji! Come on!" yelled Jonas, pounding the controls.

The demons now turned their energy cannons back around and had fixed them in their crosshairs. Only seconds remained before they would either be vaporized by the shield or blasted to pieces.

Necrat was so close that he could shoot out their chariot's controls if he wanted to and there wasn't enough room left to turn their chariot around. So Jonas grabbed Isas and braced himself to jump at the last second.

But there was a sudden, blinding flash. Jonas blinked as the energy shield completely disappeared. Then the giant gate cracked open a hair and Jonas aimed straight for this ray of light. They barely fit through as their chariot scraped against the thick iron doors and threw sparks everywhere.

Isas tightly gripped his arm as they closed their eyes. They shot through the gap, skidded out of control, and then careened off a tower before slamming into another.

Jonas glimpsed the ground, then the tower's peak, and then ground again as their chariot rolled across the square. Both he and Isas held on for dear life and they finally stopped tumbling, settling on the chariot's side with a metallic crunch.

Jonas flopped on his back, dazed, exhausted, and with everything hurting. But at least they'd made it.

He became immediately worried that Necrat and the demons could now enter the city with the gate open. With his heart pounding, he gazed up through the dust and smoke. He could barely glimpse the energy shield through the haze as it flashed back to life and the solid iron doors eased themselves closed.

Jonas rubbed his eyes. If he squinted he could just see Necrat's wolfman face scowling through the narrowing gap in the gate. His hairy visage then disappeared as the iron doors closed with a loud clang.

"Well, what do ya know, Isas? Itza done..." Jonas said as he laughed and punched the air.

She didn't answer.

He shook his head and breathed easily, resting against the chariot's hull for a bit. He couldn't believe that they had made it back to Kalkas in one piece.

Exhausted, he sighed and lifted Isas in his arms. He then parted the stunned crowd as he carried her limp body down the torturous tunnels and towards the underground healing chambers far beneath the city.

The Chair

RUSHING FURIOUSLY AND BURNING with rage, Necrat and Tarsus both returned to their tent gathered as many gadgets and weapons as they could carry. Afterward they caught up with a caravan consisting of two large dragons, both belching fire and stomping away from the camp towards Kalkas. When they finally arrived at the energy shield, Khapre-Tum pushed apart the two large cannons blocking their way, and his two pet dragons, named Tiny and Chompy, waddled right through.

Necrat and Tarsus paused in shock at first seeing these two towering beasts. Tiny was nearly forty cubits high, covered with black scales, and had huge spikes running down his long, whip like tail. When he opened them his flapping wings nearly blocked out the sun.

When Chompy's mouth opened Necrat could see that it was filled with more rows of sharp and murderous fangs than he'd ever seen. Both dragons paced back and forth before the energy shield, following their dragon wrangler, a demon named Norm. He held a beeper which controlled the behavioral modification collars fastened around both dragons' long, scaly necks.

"That's enough, Siegfried!" Khapre-Tum yelled as he stopped and faced the city's iron gate. "No more tricks! No more secret spies or shenanigans either! Come out and face me right now! If you won't, then send that rascal, Jonas, in your place! You should know that I am following the Rulebook to the letter from now on! If one of you don't come out then I will use my arrows and extensive skeleton god kung fu to destroy Kalkas! You're both dead Shastras! Do you hear me, Siegfried! You're Shastra barbeque!!"

As Khapre-Tum yelled insults and stomped about, he grew taller until he finally stood twenty five cubits high in Necrat's estimate. Khapre-Tum raised a giant bow made from what looked like solid white bone. He then laid an arrow made of blazing, pulsing light against its bowstring. Necrat guessed that this arrow alone was about the size of a small atomic powered jet bike.

"Norm, tell Tiny and Chompy they can snack on whatever creatures exit through those gates when they open," said Khapre-Tum.

"Yes, sir!" Norm hit the controls on his watch and the two dragons roared and began circling before the front gate.

"Get ready for things to get crazy.... Brace yourself!" Necrat yelled to Tarsus.

Tarsus stared back but just beeped in confusion. "More data needed to recalculate..." he said.

"Just shut up and get down!" Necrat yelled. He dove at Tarsus and pushed him behind the base of the closest energy cannon just when Khapre-Tum released his arrow.

When the arrow struck the energy shield, its blazing explosion nearly blinded Necrat before he managed to cover his eyes. Hot, burning sparks and crackling rays flew past them and out over the dusty plane. After the air had cooled, Necrat carefully peered out from around the cannon to see the shield sputtering and flashing briefly off and on. After a full minute of this it returned to humming along at full power and brightness just like before.

"Siegfried! Come out or I will use my wild card! Or did you forget that I can control the electronics within any city? All matter is my servant, even the very ground upon which Kalkas was built!" Khapre-Tum yelled while shaking his giant bow.

Necrat closely watched the iron gates, searching for any movement or maybe a messenger that might come out and speak. But nothing like that happened.

More determined and fuming with rage now, Khapre-Tum drew one arrow after another, each one brighter and more terrible than the last. Each time an arrow-missile struck the energy shield Necrat and Tarsus ducked out of the way to avoid the shockwave. With each successive blast Necrat felt that the barrier would fall at any moment.

However, these moments of the shield flashing on and off were always followed by its glimmering return to full strength. After Khapre-Tum had fired seven missiles in a row, there were still no voices or messengers offering their surrender, and definitely no space ships or atomic chariots had emerged either. The iron gates remained closed and refused to move.

"Get the energy chains ready, Tarsus," said Necrat. "That gate will open soon."

"Siegfried, give Jonas up or I will break down every brick in that wall myself!" roared Khapre-Tum. He drew another arrow, and both Necrat and Tarsus, and surely every demon there watching the scene unfold, expected that next arrow to spell the final injury that weary shield of energy could endure.

Deep beneath the Kalkan underground, at the terminal end of a trail formed by countless twisting tunnels and vast, large chambers, as well as armories and space chariot hangers, Jonas, Argos, Bheem, Isas, Mamaji, Pramohana, Tanis, and Siegfried all huddled together, tense and quiet, and staring at the same single view screen. Their anxious eyes all watched as this screen displayed the horrible scene unfolding above ground.

"How long will the energy shield hold?" asked Jonas. He and Isas had both already cleaned off all their demon blood and fur and visited the resident medical staff of wolfmen and wolfwomen doctors for a checkup. And now, standing before that view screen, Jonas dreaded Siegfried's answer, for he felt it could only be for a few moments longer. Sweat began forming on his jackal brow, and his eyes were fixed directly on the screen displaying Khapre-Tum, Necrat, Tarsus, and the two dragons, Chompy and Tiny.

Jonas chewed on his plastic bone squeaky toy while he watched Khapre-Tum string and fire one arrow after another. His usually straight, pointed jackal ears flopped sadly to the side, but at least chewing the bone in his jackal fangs helped to calm him.

Bheem asked to use his squeaky toy next, so Jonas lent him the dry end that he hadn't slobbered all over. Khafre's monkey tail laid firmly stuck between his legs in fear, while Pramohana nervously chewed her eagle wing tips. Argos stood there silent like always.

"Shield strength at fifty percent, Siegfried," announced Minerva.

"Thank you. Minerva, reroute reserve power from Phobos when needed," commanded Siegfried.

"Affirmative."

On the screen, Khapre-Tum struck the energy shield with what was now the tenth arrow. Upon its impact the shield quivered and then disappeared. But after a long and breathless moment, the gleaming barrier struggled back to life again.

"Shield strength now at thirty percent," said Minerva.

"That shield won't last long, brother, not if he keeps this up," said Mamaji.

"Sir, did you foresee this happening?" asked Isas.

"Yes....this possibility has always existed in the aether," said Siegfried. "Khapre-Tum knows the ancient ways, the inner workings of matter, and the Rulebook, and all quite well, unfortunately."

"Sir, what *exactly* is in this Rulebook that you keep mentioning?" asked Jonas. He wondered why he'd never heard of it before during any of his agent training. If he remembered correctly, this was now the fifth time Siegfried had mentioned it.

"Oh, yes..." said Siegfried. He smiled and stared off into space while fondling his pointy white beard as if distracted by something. "I had hoped that Khapre-Tum would not address the Rulebook this time."

"But why?" Jonas asked. "Please, tell us what it is."

"It contains many important rules and regulations that are all impartial and binding. They are beyond change by any being in creation, even the Guardians. If Khapre-Tum calls on one of its rules, then it must be followed, even by Garud himself."

"Yes, but what is it?" asked Isas. "You've never mentioned the Rulebook to me before!"

"Believe me, I've never even heard of it either, sister," Mamaji said.

"Tanis glimpsed it once. Was very interesting," Tanis said while he nodded.

"My dear, I never had the need to mention it before now. But, I think the time has come to explain it to you, to everyone," said Siegfried.

Jonas's pointed jackal ears adjusted themselves, turning towards Siegfried like satellite dishes to listen more closely.

"The Rulebook is a very important document," continued Siegfried. "Its rules and guidelines regulate the struggle between good and evil. It has always been followed, even when no one specifically addresses its precepts. Creation cannot allow any of its rules to be broken. Its Laws will not allow it."

"Ya mean a single book regulates all types a these situations? And has done so fa millions a years? And that Khapre-Tum follows it, and fairly?" Bheem asked, amazed. "I don believe it.... That be too much ta handle, sir."

"For billions of years," Siegfried replied seriously. "Believe it. It's all very real."

"Pramohana believes it," said Pramohana. "Ancient Danaan tales describe such a book."

"And yes, Khapre-Tum must follow it," Siegfried added. "He must no matter what he says. He has the skill of convincing others that he won't follow it or that he has a secret way around its rules by using half-truths and falsehoods to control the minds of others. He is very adept at this, for the Rulebook allows such things."

Siegfried then pulled a thick, leather-bound tome from his tunic. The book's cover was completely wrinkled all over as well as being embroidered with gold, making it look severely ancient. He blew on it and a thick layer of dust flew in everyone's faces. They all waved away the dust, all hacking and coughing, and when he cracked the cover open bright celestial lights blasted outward, followed by moths and butterflies all fluttering up and away to freedom.

"Must be quite a special book, brother," said Mamaji. Everyone agreed as they all glanced at its brightly glowing pages cradled in Siegfried's palm. But Jonas found that the glow was so bright he couldn't read even a single word.

"Few these days even know of its existence," added Siegfried. "And in this Age it is seldom called upon. However, I always keep a copy with me, just in case. Let's see now...." He continued mumbling to himself while he waved away the bugs and began thumbing through the browned and tattered pages. As he turned each page they released celestial rays of beautiful light and color.

"So, what kind of rules does this thing describe exactly?" asked Jonas. His curiosity now overwhelmed him to the point that he strained even harder to read the text over Siegfried's shoulder. But the glow made it almost impossible, and whatever script he did manage to glimpse appeared to just be scrambled hieroglyphics. So eventually he gave up trying.

"It contains every possible rule you could imagine," said Siegfried. "This book has existed since before time began, in some form or another."

"Wow, Pramohana thinks that is a very long time, indeed," she said.

"It is, Tanis knows this for a fact," he added.

"Yes it is. Now, every Guardian, god, demigod, angel, archangel, demon, and devil must follow these rules, and with absolutely no exceptions," continued Siegfried. "Good and evil, light and darkness, have struggled in opposition for untold ages. And their struggle will continue on until creation is dissolved."

"I see. But, what rules would Khapre-Tum ever willingly address?" asked Jonas.

"Any one which he feels will give him an advantage. It could be one of many, I'm afraid. We will just have to wait and see what he comes up with," said Siegfried. He shut the thick book with a loud bang and everyone jumped back.

Looking back at the view screen, they all watched as Khapre-Tum launched another round of energy arrows. After the last of three successive blasts, the energy shield fizzled and then completely faded from sight. Everyone braced themselves as the chamber shook and vibrated from the force of their impact.

"Shield power at twenty percent. Shield power at ten percent. Shield power now at five percent, Siegfried," said Minerva. Jonas detected a slight hint of fear in her usually soft, robotic voice.

Jonas dreaded the unavoidable failure of their greatest line of defense. He wondered what Siegfried had planned for when the shield finally gave out.

"If he destroys the shield, then what be happenin, sir?" asked Bheem.

"Then we defend the city," said Siegfried. "It's the only option."

Jonas stared in shock as Khapre-Tum drew back what he knew would be the final insult to the city's poor and abused energy shield. Isas turned away, unable to watch. Jonas dreaded what would happen next.

But Norm, the dragon wrangler, approached Khapre-Tum and spoke for a tense moment. To Jonas it felt like an eternity. And Jonas couldn't believe it when Khapre-Tum suddenly lowered his giant bow and put his arrow away. Then Necrat and Tarsus approached and engaged Khapre-Tum in another, even longer conversation that had Jonas scratching his jackal head.

Jonas imagined them planning on using ion detonators to blow open the city's thick iron gates once the shield finally fell. Sweating heavily and clenching his jackal jaws, Jonas prepared himself to manifest the Golden Bow and rush up to the surface to defend Kalkas along with the others.

But instead of firing this final arrow, Khapre-Tum put the bow away. He now began to walk around the energy shield, shaking his bone fist and yelling threats while the bounty hunters trailed behind him.

"Wait...what's he doing now?" asked Isas. "He didn't fire his arrow?"

"Shield power is holding stable at five percent, Siegfried," said Minerva. "Currently rerouting backup power from Phobos."

"Sir, do Kalkas be havin laser weapons that can fire back?" asked Bheem.

"Yes, these do exist," said Siegfried. "But they cannot be fired through the shield when at full strength."

"Why...?" asked Isas.

"The beams would be repelled back, sister," added Mamaji. "It's just too dangerous. But if the shield fails, then what?" he asked her.

"Umm, I don't know..." she said awkwardly, looking to Jonas for help. But Jonas could only shrug his shoulders.

"Then those cannons will be used, sister, that's what," said Mamaji confidently.

"That makes perfect sense," said Jonas. "He's right."

"I see..." she replied.

Then a terrible boom suddenly shook the control room and Jonas felt the entire underground chamber shake around them.

"What is that?" Isas yelled over the noise. Jonas wondered the same thing.

"It's Khapre-Tum stomping his feet and having a temper tantrum, that's all..." said Siegfried. "His strength is enough to accomplish this shock, but not much else. It won't knock the walls down, trust me, my dear."

Jonas hoped that he was right. But Siegfried had been wrong once before. So Jonas just kept staring at the view screen, believing that something was about to happen, but not sure what it would be.

"So, Siegfried, what is your plan?" asked Minerva.

"Please route as much power as you can from Phobos. I will send technicians to the shield generator room in Kalkas for repairs and support. But right now I must continue Jonas's training," said Siegfried.

Up on the surface, Khapre-Tum was still yelling threats and insults, and while he did, his giant, bone feet shook the ground with each step. "Siegfried! I will soon control that entire city! No one is safe within its walls! I swear that when I attack again, it will fall in a day!" he yelled.

Siegfried then turned the view screen off, letting everyone relax at last. Jonas's jackal ears regained their natural pointy state and he finally put his squeaky toy down. Pramohana stopped biting her wing tip feathers and Khafre's tail resumed its usual sway.

"That's quite enough," said Siegfried. Jonas felt that the Shastra hermit actually looked aged and gaunt, like he'd gone without sleep for several days.

"Was what he said true, sir?" asked Jonas, thinking he'd missed something. "Can he control electronics and even matter itself?" Surely, if that were true, Khapre-Tum would have shut down the energy shield by now and forced the gates open. But of course, nothing like that had happened.

"Yes, he possesses those powers," Siegfried said quietly. "But as long as the shield stands we are protected. And remember,

Khapre-Tum's power cannot penetrate this far underground. Minerva's energy reserves we keep us safe for a few more days."

"That sounds pretty serious. I mean, if he can actually do those things," said Isas, sounding scared.

"What do we do for the time being, sir?" asked Jonas. He knew they should do something productive to further prepare themselves and not dwell on these dark possible outcomes for too long.

"At present, the only thing we can do. That is to prepare and wait. You must continue your training, Jonas," said Siegfried, nodding gravely.

Jonas was always ready for more training, hopefully with the Golden Bow and its celestial missiles. But he still couldn't shake the intense and lingering fear that Khapre-Tum could destroy the energy shield any moment.

And for once, Siegfried's wise words and his saintly presence didn't instill Jonas with his usual confidence. Siegfried's jackal eyes looked darker, sunken, and hollow, totally unlike his usually wise and inspiring self. Maybe the same fear and doubt also haunted him? It sure was affecting Jonas, and by the looks on all the others' faces, everyone else as well.

Jonas eagerly continued his training there within the main armory of the Kalkan underground. His toughest test was the Higgs battle robot, created especially by Mamaji. Jonas had heard of these models before, and they were known to be extremely dangerous. It was a training model which Mamaji had "modified," making it fifty cubits tall. And even though Mamaji had assured him many times that he'd deactivated the robot's killing functions, still Jonas knew Higgs robots were known to suffer malfunctions on more than a handful of occasions.

To make matters worse, or "more interesting," as Mamaji had put it, this particular model's shoulders contained giant mounted rocket launchers. And for some morbid reason its left hand had also been replaced with a wrecking ball, of all things. By the end of his fifth training session with this robot Jonas was very tired and very sore. The main thing he'd learned was that only a well-placed sound vibration arrow from the Golden Bow could shut the robot down completely.

His favorite cure after one of these training sessions was to take a lengthy dip in one of the famed luxuries of Kalkas: a plasma-spin-whirly tank. These tanks contained hot, bubbling, ion-infused water, which, along with about fifty different types of swirling jets, all evenly massaged and perfectly relaxed his tired muscles.

He followed this routine after every training session, which also included a healthy dose of Heliopolan all-everything nachos to munch on, plus, three delicious mango beers. He then spent the night in one of the underground's larger healing chambers to recuperate further. And each morning he awoke fully refreshed and ready to do the whole thing over again.

After his fifth straight day of this routine, during which he'd gained much needed confidence using the Golden Bow, the following morning Jonas ate a quick breakfast of banana toast before he sought out Minerva's wall screen in his apartment bathroom, feeling eager to give Ashtar an update.

And so thirty Bleebs later Jonas had completed his breathless retelling of recent events, to Ashtar's wide-eyed surprise. He covered their expedition to Itza, disabling the earth-shaking weapon, their escape, and then Khapre-Tum's assault on the Kalkan energy shield before halting at just the right moment, and then lastly, his training sessions with the fifty-cubit-tall Higgs model robot.

"I'm very glad to hear that you're giving it one hundred and ten percent effort, son," said Ashtar. "That's very exciting, and I'm super pumped to hear it! It sounds like you're closing in on the fourth quarter of your mission."

"Thank you, sir," said Jonas. "It's been a real whirlwind these last few days."

"You've done very well by just taking it one day at a time, son. You shouldn't be too angry to not have found Khapre-Tum's tent. Greater beings have dropped the ball on much easier missions than what you attempted. You've destroyed their earth-shaking machine, which is most excellent. But remember that Khapre-Tum still has lots of trick plays in his evil playbook."

"Yes, I understand that, sir."

"You've been showing great toughness and execution so far. I'm also very happy to hear that the Lone Ranger has chosen to stick around for an extra period or two. It seems that he's really taken a liking to you. You won't find a better teammate than him, I guarantee that. He truly is a salty dog."

He felt a rush of joy at hearing this praise, even though he still regretted not finding Khapre-Tum's tent. "Yes, sir, thank you, sir. But, now the Lone Ranger has disappeared again. He seems to not hang around for too long. And no one can tell me where he went or where he's from," said Jonas. "Not even Siegfried knows, sir."

"Oh, yes, that rascal can never be tied down for very long. Such beings are ever free. They come and go as they please. And as to his origin, well I think that will always remain a secret. No one, not even I have been able to pry that out of him, and I've tried many times."

"I understand. That's very interesting, sir." Jonas felt a tinge of disappointment at hearing that the Lone Ranger had even kept his origin secret from Ashtar. He began to wonder if anyone knew.

"But remember, Jonas, to never press such a being too much for information. In the end we must all appreciate whatever knowledge he offers, and his eagerness to help the Command Center's agents, which he has done many, many times throughout the years that I've known him."

"Yes, sir. I very much hope to meet him again someday. He is a very strange but also very interesting being."

"I know. He truly is a unique character. You will see him again, son, if you maintain contact with Siegfried. Those two have a special bond which I haven't quite figured out yet. But I have a feeling that their friendship goes back a long ways. At least Siegfried has admitted that much to me."

"Yes, sir," Jonas replied as he saluted back. "Sir, do you have any information on Khafre's recovery?"

"That is one strong Navan there, son. When he first arrived here, I must admit that I was skeptical. It was almost curtains for him there for a moment. But he's stayed in the game like a champ and I have faith that in time he will make it to the finish line with a full recovery."

"Thank you for bringing him up to the Command Center, sir," Jonas said, relieved to hear the good news. "He probably wouldn't have survived if you hadn't done so. That's what Siegfried told me."

"It was the right move for Khafre at this stage in the game," said Ashtar.

"I totally agree, sir."

"Jonas, I have to tell you that your toughness and determination, plus, Siegfried's confidence in you, just proves to me that I was right in choosing you for this mission. I want you to know that your performance has been excellent so far. I very much look forward to your next report, son."

"Yes, sir!" he said, saluting proudly. "Thank you, sir!"

Ashtar's tone suddenly grew serious. "Jonas, I have news that the currents of energy that are currently issuing out from the Underworld and getting stronger all the time. As a result, they could block our communications even more than before. If this continues we may not succeed in transferring Khafre back to Earth-1. He would then have to remain here into overtime, that is until things clear up again."

"I understand. I trust that the Command Center team will do what's best, sir," he said, saluting stiffly.

"Well, that's everything then, son. I must be going. I'm meeting with a special delegation from Trinicon later on to discuss a difficult situation. Keep up the good work, son. Over and out. Ahoy!" said Ashtar.

"Over and out. Ahoy, sir!" he yelled back, saluting again. He hoped Ashtar could figure out the Trinicon situation. Trinicon was an alternate Earth in a darker astral realm that sometimes proved to be a handful even for a wise celestial like Ashtar.

Ashtar's image quickly vanished. But then, the view screen instantly changed to display the image of Tanis who was modeling a giant bow. He stood next to a picture of an archery coliseum that was floating amidst swirling clouds on the planet Jupiter.

"Does you love archery? Badly want to see Tanis compete in person? See him squash Bentu like bug in biggest rematch of all history? Then come to Jupiter, get tickets and watch next archery championship of solar system in person. Tanis guarantee a great victory." Tanis smiled and then flashed two thumbs up.

"View screen off, please, Minerva," he said, now very sick of that commercial, having seen it at least fifty times since he'd arrived in Kalkas.

"Turning off now," Minerva said. And just like that Tanis's grinning monkey face and the floating coliseum disappeared.

To ensure Jonas's privacy and relaxation in between training sessions, Kassam lent him use of his own personal vacation tent. Set up on the outskirts of the city, it sat directly on the opposite side from the entry gate and on the ocean facing side of Kalkas, but still sheltered within the towering stone walls. It was also situated right beside Minerva's shield generator control room as well as a royal guard outpost, but to Jonas's approval not much else was around.

This royal vacation tent was nothing short of complete luxury, including extensive carpeting, hanging tapestries, a bed with red silk sheets, as well as tables holding busts and statues of the Guardians. There was a weapons rack sitting in one corner that looked to Jonas like it could hold all of his celestial armor and weapons. And everything within the tent space was beautifully decorated with sparkling red paint and gold foil. The whole thing must have cost Kassam a fortune in Gold Tanins, which Jonas was not surprised to learn was the money of Kalkas and named after Tanis.

On the downside, there were five overzealous Shastra servants constantly hovering around him. And after only a short time he already wished that they would just leave him alone. But unfortunately, Kassam had ordered that they watch him at all times, so they wouldn't leave no matter what he said.

In between his training sessions Jonas relaxed in the tent and chatted with Bheem and Isas, or they all watched episodes of *The Kung Fu Werewolves of Mars* on a hologram projector that Kassam provided. They also drank mango beers and soaked in the royal plasma-spin whirly tank, which Jonas swore was far superior to the Command Center soak tubs (it was much larger and contained five times the number of swirling jets and nifty massage settings).

On the fifth day since Khapre-Tum attacked the energy shield, Jonas was relaxing in an antigravity recliner in the royal tent while he read a hologram book on the ancient Pirate races. The book told about how Pirates had invented Earth-1's standard language as well as its early fashion and musical tastes, among countless other things that he didn't know before. Isas busily typed on her free-energy writing pad, compiling a chapter about young male Saviors when the entire tent suddenly started shaking violently.

Jonas fell out of his antigravity recliner and his hologram book went flying. Isas yelled, tightly clasping her writing pad while the Shastra servants all screamed and ran about hysterically. The entire tent swayed and the tables, weapons racks, and statues all rattled precariously. Jonas feared that the entire structure might collapse on them. "Stay here. I'm going to go check outside! I'll be right back!" he yelled over the chaotic rattling.

But Isas just glared back. "No way! I'm coming with you!" she yelled as she rushed over to the weapons rack and grabbed a shield and her laser pistol.

More loud booms blasted Jonas's sensitive jackal ears and shook the tent. "What is that?" he asked. Had the bounty hunters already repaired the earth-shaking weapon? The idea seemed impossible, but then what was happening?

So Jonas fumbled about, frantically putting on his bronze armor before he grabbed his golden sword and both he and Isas stumbled outside. His heart was pounding now, putting his jackal instincts on high alert as they balanced themselves against the high wall and ran alongside it, always heading for the main gate. But Jonas got an intuitive hint and suddenly stopped and looked up.

Confused, it took him a long moment to realize that he wasn't seeing something that should definitely be there. The energy shield was gone. Where it had once been, always sizzling and glowing high above them, was now only an open vista of bright blue Kalkan sky.

His heart skipped several beats as he just stared upwards, open-mouthed and racked with disbelief. The city was completely defenseless. But how was that possible? Something must have happened to Minerva, but what?

He exchanged a worried look with Isas and they ran even faster. Soon his pointed jackal ears heard more loud booms and crashes, which Jonas theorized had to be the demon's laser cannonade finally striking the front gate. Each report shook the ground beneath them while loose rocks and dust rained down from the towering wall above.

They reached the central square at last and finally glimpsed the main gate of Kalkas when a powerful blast threw them ten cubits back from the wall. Jonas landed and then rolled to a stop, dazed and bruised all over. Screams pierced the air and he spit red dirt from his jackal mouth. He then tried to wave away the thick dust and smoke billowing up everywhere. Through the haze he saw a giant hole in the nearest portion of the wall that formed an open portal to the outside.

"Everyone, get away from the wall! Hurry!" Jonas yelled. He turned and yelled to Isas. "Get them out of here!"

Isas jumped up and began to guide the hysterical bystanders back from the wall and towards the underground. The scene was absolute chaos, Navans ran through the streets, screaming and dashing across the square and between its high towers. A group of Navan and Shastra soldiers emerged from the underground and helped Isas lead the civilians beneath the city.

Jonas next heard loud screeching and looked up. He was very glad to see it was Pramohana, flying towards him in close formation along with a second Danaan eagle with bright blue plumage and carrying Argos on its back. Bheem rode Pramohana on a leather saddle while balancing a deadly lance across his knee. Pramohana and the other eagle-being landed next to Jonas and bowed.

"What happened to the energy shield? The walls are getting pummeled!" he said, pointing at the gaping hole in the wall. The blue ocean waves were visible right outside, just beyond the barrels of the demon's energy cannons.

"Somethin interfered with Minerva and tha shield be malfunctionin!" Bheem replied. "We be defenseless, lad. Tha demon army be at tha main gate already. Come on, lad!"

"I'll be right there," he said as he tightened his bronze armor. Now the battle was real and he wondered just how long the walls could withstand this bombardment. He put his helmet on and then manifested a bronze shield while both Pramohana and the other eagle being flew off. Jonas followed as they both soared toward the iron gate.

But then sensing something strange, Jonas stopped and turned around. He tried finding Isas in the crowd but couldn't. Looking around more, he wondered if he shouldn't just quickly inspect that large gap left in the wall. So his Shastra curiosity took over and he walked forward, running his hands along the hole's edges. An explosion of light suddenly flung him backward, crashing him into a stall selling Tanis branded tunics, sandals, loincloths, bows and arrows. This knocked the wind out of him so he just lay on his back for a moment, struggling to breathe.

He finally stood and held his head in his hands to try and stop the loud ringing. He stumbled forward and managed to look up at the wall again, and that's when he froze. A few cubits up ahead, a glowing energy portal was crackling bright. He wondered if Zeeg had opened up a portal somehow in order to send him reinforcements.

He yelled out in shock and leapt backwards as none other than Necrat and Tarsus Riggs emerged from the swirling doorway. "What? Not you two!" he barked out, enraged. Jonas rushed towards them, and raised both his sword and shield.

"Ah, ah, ah...not today, Jonas," Necrat said, wagging a hairy claw.

Tarsus hit a button on his utility belt, and instantly Jonas's sword and shield were ripped from his grasp. They both sailed through the air and right into Tarsus's arms.

Jonas could barely believe what had happened. He looked at his empty hands and then to Necrat. But before he could manifest a second weapon, Necrat's utility belt beeped and launched four sets of energy chains which bound his wrists, arms, legs, and ankles. They were so tight that all he could do was flop in the dirt and roll onto one side.

He looked up and flashed his jackal fangs as Necrat approached. Jonas struggled in vain to break free, while also barking and growling like mad.

There was a huge crowd of soldiers nearby, but they were all gathered around the main gate, which was hundreds of cubits away. As the bombardment of the gates continued none of them paid Jonas even the slightest attention.

"You're coming with us, you little mutt," Necrat said as he knelt beside him. "You'll be my biggest payday yet. Okay, let's get out of here, Tarsus."

Jonas was so angry that he just growled back through clenched jackal fangs. He couldn't believe those bounty hunters had breached the wall. And where was Siegfried? Where were Isas and Bheem? He yelled for help, but no one could hear him through the constant clamor of battle.

Necrat whistled and the energy chains follow him, lifting Jonas off the ground. Slowly, ominously, the chains levitated Jonas towards the shimmering blue door. His jackal ears still heard the loud explosions of energy missiles in the distance. The war for Kalkas had begun.

The next thing Jonas knew, he was in a large, single roomed laboratory, surrounded by cold metal from wall to wall.

"Put him in the chair," growled Necrat.

Jonas heard the portal close right as the energy chains set him into a metal chair that instantly locked him in place. He glimpsed demons walking past outside of a large window on the opposite wall. Jonas shuddered with dread at realizing that he was now a prisoner in the demon camp.

Jonas mentally tried to manifest the Golden Bow, but nothing happened. Then he tried drawing his shield and sword back to him, but they remained tight in Tarsus's scaly serpent hands.

Then an audible buzzing sound like electricity in the air caused all his jackal hair to tingle and his sensitive jackal ears begin to ring, which made him feel dizzy and numb. And soon he was barely able to form a complete thought. He felt like he was falling asleep so he tried struggling against the sensation. His eyelids felt like they weighed a thousand Nooblars. Nooblars were a Monubian weight of such extremes there was no way even a thirty cubit high mega camel could even hope to lift it, let alone his own jackal eyelid muscles.

Several orb-like droids hovered through the air towards him. Each one held sharp instruments all ready-made for what Jonas thought had to be highly efficient torture and dissection. The hair on his jackal head all stood up in fright as he struggled against the chains.

The tools these droid's carried included cutting lasers, long needles, and tiny whirring saws, as well as bright, sparking electrodes. Jonas grunted and squirmed, trying desperately to escape while these droids approached. But his energy chains, plus, the chair's magnetism, were just too powerful.

"Feel that, Jonas? The electricity all around you? That prevents you from summoning your weapons. Its a little toy the boys from Hiix and I developed just for you and Siegfried. It stifles your concentration and dulls the brain's electrical communications, rendering all your celestial powers useless. Isn't that nice?" Necrat said with an evil smile.

"Necrat! You are aiding and helping a being so evil that it will eventually destroy this planet. You will gain nothing from this!" Jonas yelled with what felt like his last ounce of effort. "Of all the beings to align with, you chose Khapre-Tum??!!" Blind with rage now, he barked through his jackal fangs, but soon he lost the energy to continue.

Jonas recoiled as the torture droids advanced but then stopped, hovering mere cubits from his jackal face. Their sensors beeped and blinked while the crackling electrodes sparked hot, burning the air before his sensitive jackal snout.

"Oh, I disagree. I will take what I need from old Mr. Bones and then be done with him. He is just a tool to gain obscene wealth and power," Necrat said with an evil glint shining in his wolfman eyes.

"When will it be enough?" barked Jonas.

"Who knows? Maybe Queen Nayhexx of Hiix will tell us..." Necrat said while he adjusted a three-cubit-long needle on the closest droid. "She and the Hiixian scientists were the ones that decided on our mental programming. But after all this is over I'll make sure and find you in whatever prison you're rotting in, and then we can have a little chat about it. Doesn't that sound nice?" Necrat asked him and then roared with laughter.

Necrat puffed on a long cigar and blew the smoke right in Jonas's face. "I love my job..." Necrat said, cackling madly. "Who else gets to capture a Savior, torture him, and become obscenely wealthy? No one that I know! This is just too incredible to believe. What luck..." he mumbled as he walked away.

Jonas heard buttons being punched and dials being adjusted behind him. Then a much louder humming began, its vibration filling the entire room. Jonas tried turning around to see the source but he couldn't turn far enough. He suddenly felt the sensation of being drained and he suddenly grew more fatigued. But how? Was the chair doing it?

An alarm beeped on Necrat's utility belt and he stopped his incoherent rambling. "Aha! It's that time already! This just keeps getting better and better," he said gleefully. "Jonas, you'll be very interested to see what's happening now in Kalkas."

Suddenly one of the orb-shaped androids backed up and cast a glowing hologram beam onto the laboratory floor.

Jonas squinted through Necrat's cigar smoke as hologram images played out before him. In these images Tanis, Isas, Bheem, Siegfried, and Pramohana all huddle behind a fallen portion of the Kalkan wall. The chaotic sounds of laser beams, explosions, and swords clanging together came from somewhere nearby.

"Khapre-Tum has challenged Jonas to single warrior combat, is according to Rulebook, no?" Tanis was saying over the sound of explosions and laser blasts sailing over their heads. "But, Jonas gone now. Tanis must fight in Jonas place, no?"

"Yes, Khapre-Tum has addressed the Rulebook," said Siegfried wearily. "He has the right to request single warrior combat with a Kalkan champion. The ancient precepts must be followed. This would be a great sacrifice for you to make, big guy."

If Jonas was seeing correctly, Siegfried had dirt smeared all over his white jackal head, pointed ears, and wispy beard, plus his fancy red and gold tunic was all torn and bloodied. "The Rulebook says that if you succeed the demon army will retreat and this battle will end."

"You don't have to do this, Tanis," said Isas. The city's massive iron gates were visible behind her, but they were lying in the dirt, all mangled and twisted. "Khapre-Tum is just too powerful,

Tanis. Jonas is the only one foretold to be able to fight him. Right, Siegfried?"

"But, Jonas gone now," said Tanis. "Now Tanis is powerful champion of Kalkas. Best chance to end fight quickly is for him to beat Khapre-Tum. Tanis win, he guarantee!" He pounded his massive monkey chest with thunderous blows.

"If Tanis has even a slight chance of defeating Khapre-Tum, then Pramohana thinks he should at least try," she said, nodding her giant eagle head. "Pramohana thinks Tanis is right. Tanis can win. He is Tanis after all."

But at that same moment an unidentified and heavily robed being leaned in from out of the hologram's frame and whispered in Bheem's pointed jackal ear. Bheem jackal eyes flashed wide with surprise and he nodded back.

"Siegfried, I'm sorry, but I just gotta leave ya. But it be for somethin important, I promise ya, sir. Please, excuse me. This umm, 'being' here and I got an important, errr, business engagement ta attend ta," Bheem said awkwardly.

"A business engagement!?" Isas yelled back. "Right now? Like what?"

"Leave him be. He must do this," added Siegfried. "Do what you need to do, Bheem."

Now all flustered and excited, Bheem looked back at the stranger kneeling behind a fallen chunk of the Kalkan wall. It wore a long robe with a dark hood, but it didn't speak a word.

Jonas tried to identify the robed being from where he sat but he couldn't. Was it Garud, perhaps? Or another of the Guardians? He could only pray that it was.

Siegfried nodded. "Go, and don't delay, boys!" he said.

Jonas knew something was up, but he didn't dare smile, although he desperately wanted to. Bheem and the robed stranger then stood and quickly disappeared from the hologram's frame.

They all turned back towards Tanis as he stood and hoisted a giant bow over his shoulder. Immediately everyone ducked within a ten cubit radius to avoid being decapitated.

"I will accompany you, Tanis," Siegfried said, as he stood, cradling the Rulebook.

"Thank you. Tanis need gain back honor for Kalkas. He is expected to save city," said Tanis. Then he roared and pounded his hairy monkey chest with his fists (his chest was literally the size of two giant boulders). He then walked off, heading across the Kalkan plane toward the demon army, while Siegfried trailed behind him.

"Do you feel that, Jonas?" Necrat interrupted as he paused the hologram images.

Jonas just stared straight forward, refusing to answer. Hot, burning anger boiled in his throat and rose up into his jackal face. He'd never hated anyone in his whole life like he hated Necrat at that moment.

"The chair is draining your astral energy, in case you were wondering. Khapre-Tum says your energy will make him all-powerful. He may be right, I don't really know. It will prove to be a great inconvenience for you, however," said Necrat. He laughed and puffed his cigar.

"Necrat, when I break out of this chair, I swear by the Guardians I'm gonna snap your hairy neck!" yelled Jonas. "We should have killed you back in Telos when we had the chance!"

"You can try and escape," said Necrat. "But the more you struggle, the more the chair drains you and the tighter its chains become. Hiixian scientists think of everything, don't they? Oh, and by the way, Siegfried will occupy a chair next to you, very soon."

Jonas suddenly noticed he was feeling faint, like he was falling backward into his chair. But he hadn't moved and neither had the chair. He was still frozen and immobile and he couldn't turn his head or even blink an eyelid.

"Let's see how Tanis is faring now, shall we?" Necrat asked as he unpaused the hologram.

With his eyes locked on the hologram image, Jonas watched as Tanis and Siegfried boarded an atomic chariot and flew over the plane between the two armies. They then stopped before the towering skeleton god, Khapre-Tum, standing there like a nightmarish vision, and holding his gold-bladed scythe.

"Khapre-Tum, I, Tanis, challenge you to a duel!" yelled Tanis. He then pounded his massive chest and jumped down from the chariot, his giant feet shaking the ground. Although far away, Jonas felt these tremors all the way in Necrat's laboratory.

Now, even though the Mountain of Monkey was a massive presence, Khapre-Tum still dwarfed him by at least five cubits. Could Tanis beat Khapre-Tum? Jonas began to pray, hoping he stood a chance at least.

Khapre-Tum stared down at Tanis with a confused look on his skeleton face. "You are not Jonas…. Whoever you are, you are very foolish to meet with the god of Death," hissed Khapre-Tum. His white skull flashed a wide grin while red lights burned within his dark eye sockets. Bright, crackling flames leapt up from his large bone feet.

Soon a crowd of demons, skeleton warriors, and serpent-beings had gathered around them. And at the same time a group of exhausted and filthy Kalkan soldiers arrived, hoping to watch too.

Along with the Navans there were Danaan eagle beings, giant humans, and Shastras, as well as many others who all gathered around those two titans about to do battle.

Jonas had a sudden flash of impending doom, so he silently began to pray for the Guardians to help and protect Tanis.

Siegfried walked between the two titans, opened the Rulebook, and read aloud. "Do you both agree to not create any earthquakes, tidal waves, storms, or to accept physical or magical help from any celestials, spirits, witches, demigods, or any other warrior, currently living or dead?" asked Siegfried.

"Yes!" they both said.

"Do you agree to not destroy Kalkas or any other nearby cities? And to keep all combat within this dimension and on this particular planet?" asked Siegfried.

"Yes!"

"Good. Then bow to me. And bow to each other. And, fight!" Siegfried yelled. He closed the Rule Book and backed out of the makeshift ring.

Slowly, the titans circled each other. Tanis brandished a huge iron mace that gleamed in the bright sunlight. In response, Khapre-Tum unsheathed his sword made of bone and drenched in leaping fires. They stepped around the arena very carefully, adjusting their postures and planning their moves, before they finally both rushed forward.

They clashed so quickly and violently that Jonas could barely make anything out as horrible ripping, slashing, and tearing sounds echoed through the laboratory. Jonas's sensitive pointed jackal ears ached and he held his breath, fearing what might happen next.

Earth-shaking rumbles accompanied the clashing of metal, bone, and fists. Their crushing blows tossed up clouds of dust, and soon any view of them was totally obscured.

Five bleebs passed like this before an eerie calm descended, and Jonas watched as bit by bit the dust settled. Only Khapre-Tum was left standing, with one bone foot, all crackling with flame, firmly planted on Tanis's hairy monkey chest. The Primordial Primate lay there motionless with eyes closed, his face blank, lifeless.

Jonas watched Tanis for a long moment, trying to catch any signs of life, of movement, or maybe a second effort. But intuitively he knew the duel was over.

"Hmmm, about what I expected," Necrat said, puffing his cigar. "To think that Tanis even stood a chance was idiotic at best. Good thing I bet five thousand Gold Butons on Khapre-Tum," he said, laughing hysterically.

Jonas felt absolutely crushed. How could such a legendarily strong being like Tanis fail at anything? Now Jonas wondered if Tanis was even alive as he just stared at the hologram, hoping Siegfried intervened or that Tanis got up and fought on, something....

But nothing like that happened. Tanis simply lay there while Khapre-Tum trounced around the arena, hollering and celebrating his victory. Jonas didn't want to watch this, but he also found it impossible to look away.

The strange pulling sensation resumed, and Jonas was forced farther back into his chair while Tarsus and Necrat hooked even more wires to him. They added chords and electrodes, all running back to a machine humming softly behind him.

On the hologram image Navan medics emerged from Kalkas and wrapped Tanis in banana leaves and began levitating him back into the city, floating him along using a baton-shaped anti-gravity device.

Jonas couldn't move and he couldn't speak. Salty tears ran down his hairy jackal face as he watched, finally fully realizing that his Navan friend, the Champion Chimp, the Primordial Primate, the beloved and legendary hero of Kalkas, might never get up again. Then Jonas felt a pinprick in the back of his neck and everything suddenly went dark.

Jonas woke with a jolt. He'd been sleeping, but he had no idea for how long. He looked around what section he could see of the laboratory and didn't see Necrat or Tarsus. He noticed that he no longer felt as tired as before and could even move his arms and legs.

He sniffed at the air to see what he could detect, but he didn't pick up any hint of Necrat's matted wolfman fur or Tarsus's slimy scales and beeping electronics. So he wiggled himself up to the edge of the chair and was just able to stand before his medical wires and tubes suddenly yanked him backward.

"Just be quiet an hang tight for a sec. We almost got ya out a here, lad," someone said behind him as Jonas lay awkwardly in the chair where he'd fallen. He could barely see a cloaked figure crouching behind his chair, working furiously with dials and buttons on a control panel.

Jonas swung to his right, turning as far as his chains and tubes allowed. He finally looked straight on at the cloaked figure just as it pushed back its hood. Jonas breathed a sigh of relief when he saw Bheem's white jackal face smiling back.

"How'd you get in here? Who's that with you? Isas? Mamaji?" he excitedly asked as he noticed a second being kneeling at the chair's controls.

Bheem didn't answer as he walked around the chair and started untangling Jonas's tubes and wires and loosening his energy chains. "It's good ta see ya, lad. We came just at tha right time. Any longer and ya might be a goner."

"Thank the Guardians you showed up. But wait, how'd you get in here?" he asked.

"We snuck in by a secret tunnel outside a Kalkas tha Lone Ranger knew about, an very carefully, I be addin. Only because tha energy shield be down were we able ta use tha tunnel at all. Now hang on, lad. We'll have ya free in a wee bit."

"It's good to see you again, boyo," he heard a familiar voice say as the Lone Ranger popped out from behind the chair's controls. His half robotic jackal face whirred about and his huge electronic eye focused right on Jonas. "I'm just about done reversing the polarity on this gizmo. Got to give you back all your energy those varmints took."

"Yeah, where are they?" Jonas asked, still unable to believe that Bheem and the Lone Ranger had actually made it into Khapre-Tum's camp. It meant he had a good chance of escaping in one piece.

"I don't know where they went ta, lad. They must a stepped out fer somethin," said Bheem. "They used an energy field ta prevent ya from breakin out. Quite ingenious, actually. We turned that darned thin off, first."

"Wait a minute...we're almost there. Get ready...." said the Lone Ranger.

Jonas suddenly felt his body go stiff as a wooden board. He vibrated and tightly gripped the chair as a sudden current shot right through him and his jackal eyes bulged open wide. He felt like a million volts were coursing through his every muscle, bone, and nerve, finally going straight up through his spine. In one tremendous flash this trembling spark reached his brain and his third eye burst open with an explosion of light, like a window in his mind had been thrown open. His body hummed as its every cell was being tuned by this influx of astral power.

He then heard a crash and looked over at the laboratory's front door. It had flung open and was now letting a group of angry demons flood in.

"Hang tight, lad!" Bheem yelled. Both he and the Lone Ranger fired laser rounds as the demons continued to rush forward. When their rifles overheated, they set them down and charged with their swords unsheathed.

Jonas still wasn't free. And now, instead of the continued thrill of his astral energy returning, he felt it draining out once again. Somehow, the flow-switch had been reversed.

He felt himself falling backward, farther and farther behind into a dark pit. Everything went black and he couldn't move, not even a single pointed jackal ear. The bright door in his mind was instantly shut, followed by a pure darkness that enveloped him whole. Then right in the center of his field of view a black portal swirled to life and he heard Khapre-Tum's laughter echoing in his jackal ears from far away. This evil cackle was joined by weapons clashing in some distant and invisible region of space. Jonas trembled as he tumbled farther into this cold, dark abyss.

He screamed out when he felt an intensely cold crushing sensation that was almost too much to bear. But just as he felt he might die from it, at the point where his chest and jackal head felt like they were about to explode, everything paused.

The crushing feeling eased somewhat and he heard a divine voice speaking through the darkness behind him. It said, "It must be that time. May Jonas be awakened." He felt a sudden thrill of intense joy as he beheld some unseen cog of creation beginning its first movements, however slightly and silently, somewhere deep within the cosmos.

"Garud? Paw-Paw?" he asked into the dark void. Was that the Supreme Being speaking or a Guardian? He asked again, but received no answer.

He saw a second flash and turned towards it. And as this new light approached his gaze, it displayed countless expanding universes in a cosmic panorama that sucked the breath right out of him. But then he strangely no longer had the sensation of having a body. He was pure consciousness now, omniscient, a bodiless spirit-being.

But how? And why? He continued wondering this while he observed the scene objectively and it filled him with humility and awe. All the while he flew past entire galaxies and universes in an instant.

He felt himself growing more and more powerful and knew he could break free of the bounty hunter's chair if he could only return to the laboratory and open his eyes. He imagined this very outcome with total concentration, and then in a quick jolt his cosmic travels suddenly stopped.

He felt himself floating within a large tent and looking down at none other than Khapre-Tum. But the skeleton god had no clue that he was present at all. The giant skeleton just sat before his monitor, watching it track Jonas's astral energy as it was being removed. Jonas looked closer. The monitor displayed Jonas's Shastra body, still sitting immobile in the chair back in Necrat's laboratory.

Jonas quivered with fear at seeing the skeleton god so up close. But soon this fear turned to fascination at the fact that Khapre-Tum was so completely oblivious to his presence. The skeleton's large form heaved with each breath he took while a searing red aura hovered about him. Suddenly, the monitor screen beeped and flashed a warning. Jonas intuitively knew this meant his astral energy was returning.

"Necrat! Tarsus! Stop this! That's an order! It's reversing!" yelled Khapre-Tum. A swift kick with one of his bone feet sent the monitor and everything it was connected to crashing to the floor. Huffing and scowling now, he marched to the back of the tent and entered a giant black sphere resting in the corner. Once inside, the door silently closed and not a single seam remained.

Jonas opened his jackal eyes, back in the chair in Necrat's lab again. He felt like his heart was filled with warmth, so much so that a wonderful, golden light was emanating from his chest. His limbs felt much stronger now, and when he flexed them his energy chains immediately broke and fell to the ground. Then the chair behind him began shaking until finally it blew apart.

The rush of energy he felt was like a raging, chaotic storm. Blinding rays of golden light blasted out from his chest, striking every demon and skeleton soldier in the lab. When the blinding flash subsided, every enemy stood frozen in a horrific, twisted pose.

Shocked and silent, both Bheem and the Lone Ranger looked from Jonas to all these petrified soldiers. Bheem approached the closest statue and touched its arm. It fell over sideways, crashing into the next one in an unstoppable domino effect as every frozen soldier tumbled to the floor, leaving only piles of ash behind.

Bheem and the Lone Ranger all watched this sight and then turned to Jonas with both their jackal mouths wide open and their tongues hanging limply out the side.

As Jonas calmly looked down at his hands, he experienced a strange sensation while opening and closing them, and felt a strength and vitality flowing through their every bone, nerve, and tiny finger muscle. He felt the ever-deepening thrill of a sacred moment unfolding.

"Jonas, by Garud's beard! What was that, lad!?" Bheem asked, snapping him out of it.

The Lone Ranger nodded at Jonas with definite pride on his robotically augmented jackal face. "It's about time, boyo!" he said with a laugh. "I knew you had it in you."

But Jonas had no time to ask what he meant by that, for next they heard muffled coughs and groans coming from a far corner of the laboratory. They all looked over to see Tarsus and Necrat lying there, and both somehow still alive. They all then jumped up, rushed over, and quickly bound both bounty hunters in energy chains they found lying around the lab.

"Let's get out of here before more demons arrive," said Jonas, looking to the lab's main door.

"Alright, but we can't leave them two alive," said Bheem, indicating Necrat and Tarsus. "Not with what they done, lad!" His jackal eyes were bulging with rage now.

Jonas thought hard about this, sifting through his own hatred for those two and trying to find a deeper truth. A clear and calm answer soon crystallized in his mind. "No, I can't allow that. I want them both left alive," he said, firm and determined, and glaring back at Bheem. "If I face Khapre-Tum and succeed, then we'll make sure these two are tried on the Command Center and properly punished."

"What! Ya be crazy, lad!" Bheem yelled. "That's if ya can capture 'em again!" He shoved his laser rifle barrel against Necrat's hairy, wolfman temple and charged it up, ready to fire. "Jonas, they destroyed Telos, lad. They be nearly killin ya, twice!"

Jonas shook his jackal head and firmly pushed Bheem's rifle away.

Bheem looked desperately to the Lone Ranger, who wore a thoughtful yet grave countenance. "Jonas is right. We leave them alive, and that's final," the Lone Ranger said.

"I don't be likin this, lad," said Bheem, shaking his jackal head in disgust.

"That's my final word, Bheem. As the Savior, I'm telling you, that's my decision." He understood Bheem's surprise, but a peaceful and confident feeling within told him it was the right thing to do.

"Let's get out of here," the Lone Ranger said as he jumped up and ran for the door.

"Great idea," said Jonas, who followed along with a reluctant Bheem.

Bheem quickly handed Jonas a cloak which he wrapped around himself. But he made sure to manifest his bronze armor underneath just in case, now that the laboratory's electrical grid was disabled.

Together, the three of them shuffled along through a maze of black tents all bustling with demon and skeleton warriors wherever they turned. Disguised in their cloaks, the Lone Ranger led them through the camp, and soon they had passed its perimeter and were weaving between large boulders for cover, always heading towards a collection of small hills in the distance. Upon reaching the base of the closest of these hills, the Lone Ranger stopped and rested beside a break in an outcropping of boulders.

As they rested in the shade, relieved to be free of the camp, Jonas removed all the bandages and small tubes still stuck to his arms and his jackal neck. He still felt the lingering sensation of great energy flowing through him, coursing through his veins, muscles, brain, and even charging his jackal hair with small sparks.

His sensitive jackal ears then perked up as he heard panicked chaos erupting back in the demon camp. He sniffed the air intently, but detected no hints of any demons, beasts, or skeleton soldiers anywhere near their current location.

"Okay, so what be the plan now, lad?" Bheem asked, looking at Jonas and the Lone Ranger. "Let's get going, eh?"

The Lone Ranger then addressed Jonas, his electronic eye whirring and beeping. "Through this fissure here is a secret tunnel leading to a village south of Kalkas."

Jonas and Bheem both nodded and then followed the Lone Ranger, squeezing sideways through the fissure and between these large boulders. They were soon forced to crawl on all fours until the passage finally widened, forming a spacious hollow where they could stand again.

The space was empty save for a manhole cover outlined in the dirt. Bending down and brushing the dirt away, the Lone Ranger slid the cover to the side and climbed down into the dark shaft. He stopped halfway and then motioned for Bheem to follow.

"I'm staying behind, you guys," said Jonas abruptly. They both stared back in shock, but Jonas just crossed his arms and remained obstinately silent. He'd made up his mind that if he was going to face Khapre-Tum, then this was the time to do it.

"What?" Bheem yelled. "Let's get out a here, lad!"

"You two return and protect Kalkas. It's my destiny to confront Khapre-Tum," he said firmly.

The Lone Ranger nodded back that he understood. "If you wait until nightfall you might catch Khapre-Tum by surprise," said the Lone Ranger.

"I intend to do just that," he said.

"What? No, ya need ta come with us, lad," Bheem said. "Right, Mr. Ranger? Kalkas needs Jonas more than ever. Pramohana be injured, and badly, nearly half tha army.... Look, Tanis be defeated! Did ya know that! Tha gates, they be crumblin. And tha energy shield? Disabled.... Lad, without Jonas and tha divine weapons, Kalkas not be survivin tha night."

Bheem was right, Kalkas did need him badly. Jonas couldn't help thinking about the Kalkan army, Pramohana and Siegfried, and Khafre back on the Ashtar Command. He then thought about Mamaji, and how he'd helped Jonas with his training, and then he thought about all the Navans, Wolf-beings, Shastras, and human soldiers suffering from the heavy bombardment of Kalkas.

"Bheem...he's right. He must face Khapre-Tum, alone," the Lone Ranger said.

"Trust me, it's the only way to stop Kalkas from being completely destroyed," said Jonas. "Khapre-Tum won't be expecting me to return. Trust me, it has to work. Now come on...you guys need to get going."

Bheem remained stubbornly silent, his white jackal face hard and severe.

The Lone Ranger disappeared down the hole and Bheem sighed, finally coming to terms with the situation. "Good luck, lad," said

Bheem. "Ya're a good agent, one a tha best I ever met. I'll be seein ya when ya return ta Kalkas, triumphant."

"Thanks, Bheem," he said. "Take care of Isas and Pramohana while I'm gone. They need you right now."

Bheem nodded, saluted him, and then sighed before disappearing down the manhole.

Jonas sat there alone in the dim twilight, staring at the manhole, deep in thought. But as he did the Lone Ranger's partially robotic jackal head suddenly poked back out.

"Jonas, please, if you put your trust and faith in Garud and the Supreme Being you can never go wrong," said the Lone Ranger. "I have lived this path for a long time, so I know it works."

"Thank you. I understand," he said.

"I also know much more about you than you could ever guess. I can see your energy body at this moment and I can tell that you possess all the tools and traits of every past Savior, many of whom I've met in my travels through time. I'm very impressed with how much you've advanced in just a short period."

"Thank you, sir. You've been a great influence on me," said Jonas. "I'm honored that you've helped with my training."

"And you too have influenced me, more than you know. But right now, you must prepare yourself to face Khapre-Tum. He must be defeated, or this planet will suffer a horrible fate. I've visited a few of the possible timelines where Khapre-Tum's army was victorious, leading to him controlling the entire solar system. Believe me, Jonas, those are very sad, very dark realities that must be avoided."

"What? How do I, or we, fail and let Khapre-Tum take over? Tell me, so that I can—"

"I can't reveal such things to you at this time. That is an important rule of time travel. But remember, the Supreme Being and Garud will guide your thoughts and actions if you are in tune and surrender to them. Surrender is not giving up through cowardice, but is the annihilation of your mortal weaknesses and selfishness, fear and distrust, ego and obsessive thoughts. You must become nothing before the Supreme Being, then it will anoint you with the full realization of a Savior and you will experience the full flowering of your destiny as a child of that Infinite Power."

"Thank you," said Jonas as he breathed deeply. This was all overwhelming, and almost too much for him to take in at once.

He was shaking now, as tears formed in his jackal eyes and the Lone Ranger's robotic jackal face watched him closely. "I will do whatever I can to prevent Khapre-Tum's victory," said Jonas. Tears were now falling onto his tunic, imagining what kind of suffering and enslavement would result should he fail and Khapre-Tum conquer the planet. Preventing that would be the single most important goal in his young Shastra life.

"I have faith in you, Jonas," said the Lone Ranger. "Garud always chooses his Saviors well, remember that. Now, Bheem and I must return."

A peaceful stillness enveloped the grotto as Jonas wiped his jackal face, now all wet with salty tears, on the sleeve of his cloak. While they'd been talking the tall shadows had slowly continued to advance over the grotto.

With their farewell complete, the Lone Ranger solemnly nodded while his electric eye blinked, studying Jonas carefully. The Lone Ranger then raised a free-energy lantern and disappeared down the manhole for the last time.

The Underworld

JONAS COULDN'T STOP THINKING about Siegfried and Isas, and about Garud, wherever the Guardian was at the moment. But after a while his thoughts drifted towards his coming encounter with Khapre-Tum.

He thought all this while squatting beside the manhole, waiting for the sun to set. Was Tanis still alive? What about Siegfried, Isas, or Pramohana? More importantly, how much longer could Kalkas hold on? He worried about all this, including if he could even find Khapre-Tum at all.

He gazed back through a narrow fissure in the rock, but could only see the windswept tents of Khapre-Tum's camp in the distance. As he inhaled, a warm breeze wafted the pleasant odor of the plain's dry, red dirt right into his jackal snout. In the short time that he'd sat there, his tears had all dried up and become caked with dust amongst his matted jackal hair.

He felt the need for divine guidance, so he sat and began to meditate. Sitting down crossed-legged, he closed his eyes and concentrated on his third eye. In an instant, the glowing lights of an astral realm appeared before him. It enveloped him and everything else, including the rocks, the sky, the ground, and even the lone manhole.

Then amazingly, he saw Garud walking towards him. The Guardian was strolling beneath a boundless tract of glittering nebula, stretching high above the land. With each step the Guardian's golden sandals lit the dark astral grid beneath him. Through his enhanced spiritual vision, Jonas perceived that this dark grid, marked by white astral lines, stretched into a near-infinite number of dimensions beyond their own. There seemed to be no end to its awesome reach and beauty.

"Good evening, Jonas," said Garud. "I am glad that you sought my help."

Jonas fell forward, bowing low with awe and tightly grasping Garud's golden sandals. He ran both hands over the golden flesh on the Guardian's feet, and felt their astral glow warming his jackal face. "My lord, I am overjoyed to see you here. Please, give me strength and show me the way to victory."

"I have some information that will help you. I know the keys to defeating Khapre-Tum."

"Great! What is it? Is there more than one way?" he asked with excitement. A magical joy crackled in the air that surrounded Garud. Jonas sensed that several celestials and demigods were watching them at that moment from just behind a thin veil.

"Seek him out within his healing chamber of Corconite stone," said Garud.

Jonas then had the vision of a giant black boulder, polished to a perfect sphere, and located within a large tent, somewhere within the skeleton god's camp. "Ahh, I can see it now, sir."

"Good. Now, remember that he is most vulnerable in two places: his shrunken heart and his spine, right at the base of the neck. Strike either of these with your golden sword or an arrow from the Golden Bow. But be careful, my boy. Khapre-Tum is a skilled trickster, so be on your toes. Now, a portal just inside or near his quarters can be used to travel to Skull Castle. If you can locate it, take it, find Talley, and return him to Kalkas."

He saw a vision showing him Khapre-Tum's vulnerable points; his shrunken, prune-like heart, as well as his long, boney skeleton neck. "I will, sir," said Jonas, shivering from the very sight of these.

He bowed low again, and when he looked up, the astral dimension, Garud, and the astral nebula above had all vanished. He was alone now, kneeling in the dirt, while long shadows steadily crept across the enclosure.

He had no idea how long his vision had lasted; but it could have been over an hour or more. His jackal ears perked up and he listened intently, noticing that all noise from the energy cannons across the plain had stopped. He waited until the shadows chased away the last shards of daylight before he wrapped his cloak tightly around himself and squeezed back out through the rock fissure.

As he walked towards Khapre-Tum's camp he prayed that demon and skeleton warriors slept at night like regular earth beings. As he got closer he noticed that nearly every black tent he saw was illumined by flickering torchlight.

Upon reaching the camp, he crouched and darted between tents, avoiding every demon and skeleton guard that was still awake or wandering about keeping watch. These watch guards all cradled dangerous-looking laser rifles while their plate armor clattered loudly and they marched along the rows of dark tents.

Each torch bracket lit the narrow lanes between tents, but Jonas kept to the long, quivering shadows cast between these paths, better to evade the night watchers' eyes which could easily penetrate nearly every corner and avenue. More than a few times Jonas curled up and held his long, brown cloak drawn tight over his jackal head and body, making him appear to be part of a nearby tent. In only a short while he avoided detection that way at least four times.

As he crouched there underneath his cloak waiting for the shadow of one particularly formidable-looking demon to finally turn and walk away, his third eye suddenly alerted him that a group of Kalkan soldiers were being imprisoned right in the next tent over. He knew he couldn't just leave them there, so when the demon was finally gone he darted across the dirt lane and dove beneath the flap.

Once inside, he saw a long row of cages stretching out before him, and all of these were fitted with sizzling energy bars. Jonas's heart immediately sank at seeing over a hundred cages there, most of them holding between one and three prisoners each. Among these were Navans, Shastras, Danaan eagles, humans, and wolfmen, even a few praying mantis beings were seen slouching, huddled together within their cramped enclosure.

Jonas rushed over and knelt beside the first cage that he came to. By gently nudging its shoulder, he roused a Navan that was sleeping on its side. "Pssst, wake up. It's me, Jonas...."

The Navan stirred, yawned, and then slowly cracked an eyelid. Upon seeing Jonas, both its eyes shot open with excitement. He nearly grabbed the cage's bars, but then stopped himself at the last second. "Jonas—can—can you get us out of here?" he whispered.

"I'll try. But I need your help finding Khapre-Tum's tent. Do you know which one it is?"

"It's the one in the very back of the camp. It's quite large and is guarded by ten of the toughest, nastiest skeleton warriors I've ever seen."

"Hmm, I need a way to get in there...." He scratched under his jackal chin, deep in thought.

"What are you gonna do?" asked the Navan. "My name's Chevy by the way."

"Well, Chevy, I'm going to end this battle before it's too late. Wait here and I'll spring you free. I've got a plan and I need you to coordinate it with the others."

"Of course! What is it?" Chevy asked.

So Jonas explained his plan in detail. It wasn't unique or even an unusual one. In fact, it was a standard prison escape plan called the 'Bait and Snatch,' which he'd taken right from the Intergalactic Agent manual.

After freeing Chevy, Jonas, along with Chevy and his two Navan cell-mates, knocked out the four demons guarding the tent's entrance outside and locked them in Chevy's cage. Next, they found the main controls for all the other cages and disabled their energy bars (except for a cage that held two serpent-beings who Chevy said were really rotten characters). With that done Jonas and a few prisoners gathered weapons from a nearby tent while Chevy explained his plan to the rest.

When he'd finished, almost thirty armed prisoners were nervously waiting behind Jonas while he crouched at the tent's opening. Jonas watched and waited while two more demon guards marched past. When those two guards had finally gone, he signaled back. "Okay, Chevy. Go!"

Chevy and about twenty of the others crept past him, running forward and sparsely lit by the swaying torchlight. Jonas grew tense as he waited and his breathing became fast and shallow. He nervously sniffed about for more signs of demons and skeleton guards, but none came.

Chevy's group suddenly stopped beside a tent twenty cubits from Khapre-Tum's, itself being just up ahead to their right. Before Jonas knew it, laser rounds were ripping through the darkness, coming from Khapre-Tum's tent. A group of extremely tall skeleton warriors were firing at them and Chevy's group immediately fired back. Soon the camp was lit by a blur of laser beams, plus demons and skeletons all chaotically running through the camp, trying to figure out what was going on.

That was Jonas's signal. So he ducked low, snuck around to his right, and passed behind five tents. Then he turned and ran down the lane until he found himself parallel with the laser battle. When he was sure that no one had followed him he lifted the side flap and entered the rear of Khapre-Tum's tent.

He stood and quickly scanned the interior. Just up ahead, bright torches lit the walls of a sphere made from the smoothest, blackest stone. It was both colossal and perfectly round. Jonas thought that it looked like one of the cannon balls used by the ancient Pirate races he'd read so much about.

Shaking with excitement, Jonas slowly approached the smooth, black sphere. His hands trembled as he searched for a door, a handle, or a latch to open it with. But he found nothing. Then the sphere vanished and he jumped backward, rubbing his jackal eyes, shocked by what he saw.

Khapre-Tum lay there, stretched out on a flat, gray stone table. It looked like he was sleeping. Jonas couldn't believe it. His skin crawled and his stomach churned as he gazed upon the god of the Underworld, lying there, still and quiet. The tent was otherwise deserted, so Jonas crept forward and quietly unsheathed his golden blade.

Raising the sword, he aimed the point right over Khapre-Tum's armored breastplate where his shrunken heart would be. Sweat poured down his hairy jackal face while his hands trembled. If he succeeded in this one act, then his mission would be complete. And here, lying out before him, was his nemesis, alone and defenseless.

He yelled out and thrust the blade down with everything he had. The sword threw sparks out as it pierced Khapre-Tum's armor, shrieking terribly until the blade finally stopped.

Jonas winced as he leaned on the hilt with one final push, forcing the blade right through and out the stone slab beneath. Jonas stepped back and watched, breathlessly waiting for a reaction, but Khapre-Tum remained unconscious.

His heart beat faster and his mind began racing. What did this mean? Was his mission over? Just like that? He'd expected a reaction, at least something.... He started to panic, wondering if he'd somehow missed Khapre-Tum's black and shriveled heart. He pulled up on the hilt to try and remove the blade. But as he struggled he couldn't make the sword budge even a micro cubit.

He leaned on the hilt and rested. That's when Khapre-Tum's bright and burning red eyes suddenly flashed open and locked right on Jonas whose heart nearly stopped.

Khapre-Tum's mouth opened and exploded with laughter, and the sound was so haunting and chilling that its echo reverberated around inside his jackal skull. Jonas leapt backward, and the pain was so intense it nearly blinded him. He covered his jackal ears and manifested his helmet, but he just fumbled and dropped it while he stumbled about awkwardly.

Then a dark cloud came surging out from Khapre-Tum's gaping mouth, like a whirling black snake made of smoke. It hovered before him, quivering for a moment, before it lunged for him. This snaking cloud easily picked Jonas up and tossed him around violently, tearing the tent to pieces.

Suddenly the tent and all their surroundings disappeared. He was tumbling down this dark cloud, heading towards a black pit about to swallow him up. Was this an evil spell to disorient him before Khapre-Tum struck him down for good? Or had he died already?

These fearful thoughts spun out of control as he tumbled into nothingness. But the next thing he knew his feet struck firm and solid ground. He found that he was in a dark cave with a lone cliff off to his right. He looked around some more, and determining that he was alone, he walked over to the cliff and peered over its ledge. Intense heat and a sulfuric stench rushed up towards him, forcing him back.

He felt his jackal face. All his hair was still there, although the ends felt warmer and most had curled backward, especially his whiskers. His wet jackal snout was now warm and tender. He peered more carefully over the ledge this time to see a snaking trail of lava far below. It bubbled and writhed, running along the base of a deep trench.

He was sure that he was in the Underworld, but where? Did it even matter if he was trapped? And if he could defeat Khapre-Tum and rescue Talley how would he then return to Kalkas? Maybe the hologram catalog on his comm. link would tell how to find a portal. For some reason Necrat hadn't removed it as he could still feel it attached to his utility belt.

As he was thinking this, a sudden burst of laughter echoed throughout the cave. He froze, for that could only be Khapre-Tum. But where did it come from?

He slowly turned, and all the jackal hair on his head stood up. Khapre-Tum was only twenty cubits away, and still had Jonas's golden sword buried right in his chest. He glared back at Jonas and with one swipe snapped the blade in two. Its hilt went clanging across the stone floor and then over the ledge and into the lava below.

Jonas gulped and his heart immediately sank. That weapon was supposed to have been his great advantage. He could barely believe that a sacred weapon given to him by Ashtar himself could be broken so easily.

"Jonas, welcome to my ancient fortress," said Khapre-Tum in a grating, hissing voice so repulsive that it made Jonas's pointed jackal ears ache. "You are a guest in Skull Castle. You will watch as the Underworld swallows up the whole Earth. Soon, the Dark Ones will reform the face of Creation and then I will be its ruler. My ancient covenant with those Dark gods gives me this right. But don't worry. A glorious destiny awaits that small, helpless planet, Earth. The Supreme Being is powerless to stop me."

Jonas didn't answer. He couldn't even think straight. He just stared blankly while an icy terror filled him, making him shiver all over. Khapre-Tum's armor was a deep black and riddled with sharp spikes that appeared pretty much unbreakable. Nearly every visible one of his white bones was covered with tattooed magical runes that filled Jonas with dread.

Atop his massive skull was a mighty helm of iron affixed with two horns, each curving up to a deadly point, while a long, black mantle flapped behind him. But most terrifying of all were his red, hot, burning eyes.

"Jonas, I have an offer to extend to you, one which I advise that you accept. I will only ask this once." Khapre-Tum then snapped his fingers and they were suddenly transported. They reappeared in a palatial suite, gleaming with the most precious gems imaginable along its walls, pillars, and even the ceiling. The splendor that surrounded him exceeded even the royal palace of Kalkas.

As he stood there frozen in shock, a wobbly skeleton limped over to Jonas and offered him a plate of small cakes, plus, a goblet of red wine. Jonas refused these and turned his snout away. But then, against his will and forced by an unseen power, his arms reached out and took two cakes and then lifted the goblet from its tray.

Then, stiff and awkwardly, his legs forced him to sit in a cushion-backed chair right beside Khapre-Tum, who glared down from his own magnificent, golden, gem encrusted, throne that just appeared out of nowhere. Filled with fear, and realizing that even his body wasn't under his control, Jonas forgot all about the luxury surrounding him and remembered a very special piece of advice given to every Agent on the Command Center. That was to never trust something dead that acted like it wasn't. He considered his current situation the very definition of the rule. So he just focused on Khapre-Tum and prepared himself to hear the skeleton god's proposal.

"Jonas, I offer you this; the sole, overriding command of my army, which will conquer the entire planet. And after that, your great powers as a Savior will help me to easily defeat the Guardians. Then the solar system will be mine and the Ashtar Command, your old home, will fall next. But don't worry, for a much greater Command Center will take its place. And I will make you the master over its star systems. No Guardian or celestial will ever offer you this power and position." He stopped speaking to slowly sip wine, but he kept his glaring eyes fixed on Jonas.

Jonas boiled with anger even at the idea of betraying Ashtar. "That's ridiculous! I owe my whole life to Ashtar!" declared Jonas, now shaking with rage. "You're insane.... I could never accept such an offer." The thought was repulsive to him. It would mean treason against Siegfried, Garud, the Guardians, and the Supreme Being itself.

"Tell me, Jonas," Khapre-Tum began again, leaning over in his high throne. In the corner a fireplace burned hot with flames that shone brightly on the golden walls of the chamber. "When did Ashtar ever offer you such power, or position? He's only made you suffer and struggle, and caused you great pain and frustration. Hasn't he? The Command Center rejected your application to space chariot fighter weapons school three times in a row, didn't they? Tut, tut, that's so cruel.... You were the most talented student in your class, Jonas, and for some reason they held you back a year, while letting younger, less-talented cadets go ahead of you and earn Intermediate Agent rank." Khapre-Tum shook his skull in disgust. "Such mistreatment, such disrespect.... You must have been very deeply hurt by all that."

"It's only because Ashtar accepted me for training that I am an agent today," he said, growing angrier now. "If not for him and the Command Center's support, I'd still be a nomad, wandering the deserts of Monubia."

"Yes...but Ashtar also sent you straight to Earth-1, and with very insufficient training, didn't he? To this truly wretched galactic outpost that is filled with dangerous wild animals, and also very far from the Command Center. On top of all that, you have seen what my army has already done to Kalkas. It truly is a shame for you to fail so close to your goal, Jonas." Khapre-Tum's red eyes burned into him as he spoke.

Jonas remembered many such painful events from Agent School and his early career; he'd had accidents and failures, sure, as well as more than a few injuries. He'd often been late to meetings or overslept, and gotten pretty sick a few times. All this clearly stood out in his mind's eye at that moment.

But, all these bumps and setbacks had been great learning experiences, no matter how embarrassing or frustrating they had been. "Yes, many such things, and others like that, all happened. But no student ever sailed perfectly through Agent School. Even Phaistos the Great broke his toe once and also failed an art class."

"Oh, but think about that pretty little Athenian priestess, the one you're smitten with, hmmm, hmmm?" Khapre-Tum said with a repulsive grin. "Isas…that's her name, isn't it?"

"What about her?" Jonas yelled, feeling like his jackal head was about to explode with rage. "If you hurt her in any way, I swear—"

"Then join me and command my demon army!" interjected Khapre-Tum. "Together we will level Kalkas to the ground. Then your fame and wealth will be too intoxicating for her little Athenian mind to handle. I will also strike out all the draconian rules Garud set for Athenian marriage. You will also receive the highest honor of leader of my new Khapre-Tum Command Center. Then you will oversee every star system in my new intergalactic kingdom. All you have to do is forget about Garud. Forget the Supreme Being and its old-timey rubbish. Wisdom and glory are only due to those who gain more and more power, and can skillfully wield it for conquest. Your enemies will all try and do the same to you, Jonas. The Dark Ones and I have survived throughout the Ages with such skill and cunning. You must learn to do the same."

But he couldn't help imagining Isas as his bride (in his imagination she would wear a particularly beautiful yellow dress at their wedding). This gave him the most wonderful warmth of love blossoming upwards and enveloping his whole heart. The sensation was so lovely that he felt like he could pass out right then and there. The idea of ruling over entire star systems also had a thrilling ring to it. No Senior Agent had ever achieved that.

But then he beheld a poisoned pill behind all these promises, and its realization made him recoil with disgust. Should he take this path, he would become a cursed warrior of darkness. There would be no rest for him, no peace or deep friendship, or real love of any kind. True happiness would elude him forever, even if the entire universe bowed at his sandaled feet.

He remembered this from the spiritual laws of living that had been given to the Shastra races by Garud a long time ago. These stated that only selfless love, honor, devotion, simplicity, and depth-of-meaning gave one real, lasting peace and fulfillment in life. And he knew this creed well. Ever since growing up a young Shastra nomad on Monubia, he'd never doubted such wisdom, not even for a nanobleeb.

A feeling of shame and agony accompanied just the thought of abandoning Siegfried, Garud, and the Supreme Being. He'd rather die than live like a traitorous wretch, no matter what levels of fame or power he attained.

He'd had enough of this conversation and didn't want to hear any more. "Never! I'll never join you!" He yelled this so loudly the skeleton holding the tray of wine and cakes fell backward, spilling the wine and the snack cakes all over the floor. Then Jonas jumped up from his seat, manifested a new sword, and lunged at Khapre-Tum.

"You have chosen poorly. Now the Underworld will be your resting place," said Khapre-Tum somberly, before he suddenly vanished. Jonas followed through with his sword and when the skeleton god vanished he plunged his blade through the now empty chair.

Jonas cursed and looked around to find he was all alone. The next thing knew, a second whirlwind appeared, flew towards him, and swept him up as the palatial chamber vanished from sight. The whirling black cloud dropped him, all dizzy and disoriented, within a forest of twisted trees, their low-hanging limbs dangling long, fingerlike branches that brushed his pointed jackal ears.

Well, Khapre-Tum was definitely gone now. Jonas had just gone from one predicament to an even stranger one. Where in the Underworld was he exactly? He felt cold and started shivering. His breath began misting up in front of his jackal face.

Through the pale trees he could just see the stone towers and battlements of a castle rising from a volcano's flank in the distance. If he squinted just right he could see magma running down channels carved into the mountainside. As he looked closer he saw that the entire hill was carved into the shape of a giant skull. From hologram images he knew that this was Skull Castle, and where he would probably find Talley and Khapre-Tum.

As he began walking he kept shivering for the winds had whipped up into a blistering gale and he had no cloak with him. His sandals crunched the gray dirt path beneath him while the trees seemed to be growing thicker and closer together as he went along.

He heard the screech of dragons high above him and looked up. Meanwhile, a large group of horribly ugly and lanky, ghostlike apparitions floated past him and he froze. But thankfully, they just gazed right through him and flew on as if they hadn't seen him at all.

"Jonas, the physical rules of Earth you are used to don't apply here in the Underworld," spoke a voice from somewhere nearby. He could tell it was Garud's voice. So Jonas looked around trying to find him, but the Guardian was nowhere to be seen.

"Okay.... Is there anything else you can tell me, sir?" he asked hopefully. But when Garud didn't reply he knew this meant there was no use trying to call the Ashtar Command with his comm. link device, and that the Lone Ranger probably wasn't going to show up and help him anytime soon.

As he stood there, shivering and vigorously rubbing his arms to warm up, he realized that his only option was to continue along the ashen path. As he did, each white and twisted bough turned and followed his lonely steps.

This strange realm made Jonas think back on his agent studies. He remembered the minor dark realms from Dimensional Studies Class. But as he walked on he realized that he knew almost nothing about the deepest realms like this one.

He continued walking towards Skull Castle when soon the stench of rotten eggs made him stop and carefully sniff around for its source. Distant growling made his jackal hair stand on end, and he detected the distinct odor of wet dog fur. However, glancing between the trees revealed nothing and the stench quickly vanished. But before he continued on he searched the ground at his feet and found a nice stick that was just about the right size. He chewed on this and it helped him to relax a little.

So, chewing on this stick vigorously now, he reached a small clearing where he stopped again. A much stronger stench made his sensitive jackal snout recoil painfully. He snarled angrily, but almost immediately, five giant wolves crept out from the thick wooded area up ahead.

These yellow colored wolves were all huge and covered in dark black stripes. Each one had two growling heads that snarled at him while they pawed the dirt and paced back and forth across his path. They watched him with their crazed-looking wolf eyeballs and with rows of the sharpest fangs imaginable all drooling with greedy anticipation. He estimated that from snout-to-tail each one was about four times longer than he was tall, which was to say, absolutely humongous. There was no telling how many Nooblars each of them weighed. He'd never fought an animal so big. He did feel lucky that they weren't Mega Honey Badgers, though.

Jonas tracked them, also snarling and glaring, until one of them charged. With snapping jaws, it leapt high into the air while Jonas instinctively materialized a bronze shield. The wolf's claws drew sparks as it mauled his shield and nearly crushed him under its weight.

As they went tumbling through the dirt its powerful jaws bit through his shield and clamped hard around his forearm guard like a vice, almost crushing his arm. Jonas screamed and punched the beast as it tried to wrench his arm out of its socket with powerful jaws. Jonas just managed to gather his blade and plunge it into the wolf's hairy yellow chest. The beast howled and rolled over, pinning him under its body with its snapping fangs mere micro cubits away from his jackal face.

Streams of blood and drool sprayed everywhere, completely covering him as he pushed the blade in deeper. The wolf let out a loud yelp, but continued to wildly claw at his shield. When his shield had become just a twisted pretzel of metal Jonas covered his face with his forearm guards and held on for dear life. But only a moment later, the heaving, snarling beast stopped its flailing and lay still. Jonas could barely move it was so heavy. He finally pushed hard enough until the wolf rolled off him and flopped to the side where it rested, limp yet panting quietly.

Within a micro bleeb a second wolf pounced, clamping its cold, dagger-sharp fangs right through his bronze armor and piercing his shoulder. Jonas yelled out and could barely see as they rolled together through the dirt. The beast was right on top of him now, with blood and drool soaking his tunic and flying all in his jackal eyes. Chinks of his bronze armor went flying as the wolf's long fangs wrenched it apart and dug deeper into his shoulder.

The wolf's second set of jaws snapped and drooled, but Jonas pummeled the wolf with a mailed fist just enough so that it unclamped its jaws at last. The pain was overwhelming him now. But before the second set of jaws bit his face right off, Jonas kicked the wolf as hard as he could in the stomach. The beast yelped and scampered out of range.

Now the third beast charged him, and with a quick swipe of his sword Jonas gashed it across the neck before its claws could touch him. The wolf yelped and fell, clawing helplessly at the dirt. Dark blood oozed from the wound and soon its primal wailing died away.

Before the second wolf charged again, Jonas manifested the Golden Bow and strung an energy arrow, burying its blazing tip right in the beast's hairy yellow chest. The wolf instantly collapsed, forming a charred heap of hair and flesh and smelling absolutely dreadful.

Shaking all over with adrenaline now, Jonas leaned on the Golden Bow to rest and catch his breath. Meanwhile, the three wolves lay there, all whining and whimpering sadly. But he wiped his jackal eyes in disbelief at what transpired next.

Each slain wolf transformed, crumbling into dust and then blowing off with on a strong gust of wind. Jonas just stood there, watching all this with amazement. Two wolves still remained, however. But after seeing what happened to the others, they both tucked their tails between their legs and sprinted away through the trees.

When they were finally gone, Jonas lowered his head and slumped against his bow. Both his forearm and his shoulder were on fire with pain and half his chest plate was eaten away.

Being part jackal, Jonas hated seeing any wolf or canine-being harmed. He whimpered sadly while sniffing around right where the three wolves had collapsed and then turned to ash. Convinced now that no traces of them remained, he decided to stumble on, albeit very slowly and gingerly, while dabbing at his bleeding shoulder with a strip torn from his tunic.

He placed his chew-stick back in his mouth and began to follow what appeared to be the quickest path to Skull Castle when he heard a loud shriek come from above. Thinking it was a dragon, he ducked just as a dark shadow sailed overhead. The shadow barely missed him before alighting on a thick and withered branch just up ahead. But it wasn't a dragon or a ghost, or any other type of flying monster for that matter.

Instead, a beautiful eagle-being with large eyes was gazing back at him and ruffling its red and gold plumage. He didn't know much about eagle-beings, save for Pramohana, but this one appeared far smaller than the Danaan Eagle queen. In a funny way it reminded him of Siegfried. It had to be because of the lone, stringy, white beard dangling from its beak.

"Jonas, it is I, Siegfried," said the eagle, reading his mind.

He raised his jackal eyebrows and dropped the chew stick from his jaws. "Really? How do I know you're not a shape-shifting demon in disguise?"

Right then the eagle transformed before him. When it had finished the Guardian, Garud, stood there, twelve cubits tall and all glowing and golden. The Guardian's bright aura seemed to instantly banish all the dreariness from the dead forest around them. A surge of peace and strength filled Jonas and he fell to his knees, bowing over and over again as he touched the Guardian's golden sandals. There wasn't anyone else in the entire cosmos that he'd rather meet at that moment.

"The Supreme Being has sent me to guide you to Skull Castle, my boy. If I didn't then you would be trapped here forever," Garud said. Then he transformed back into the eagle-being with the large, piercing eyes and beautiful red and gold feathers. Jonas looked closer. The third eye in its eagle forehead was twirling brightly, with countless ancient symbols all swirling around.

"I'm glad to see you, sir," he said. He then knelt and retrieved his chew-stick. "I have no idea how to get to Skull Castle from here except to follow this path here. Actually, I have no idea where I am at all to tell you the truth."

"Why, my boy, you are currently in the deepest level of the Underworld. It is also the most dangerous, but you are fortunate that Khapre-Tum has no further depths to which he may retreat and hide. That over there, as you have correctly guessed already, is his infamous fortress of Skull Castle."

"But, how will we get back to Kalkas from here?" he asked while he gnawed and slobbered all over his chew-stick.

"There is a portal within Skull Castle that will return you to Kalkas. But you must face the worst terrors of this realm, first, if you would reach it."

"I think I've already met a few of those," said Jonas, indicating his bandaged shoulder and forearm. The bleeding had stopped, thankfully, but if he moved wrong the pain was sharp enough that it made him wince and clench his jackal fangs.

"Oh, yes, the Mega Wolves of this realm are quite vicious. But you won't face them again, I promise."

"Good. That's great to hear. Let's get going then," he said, and he threw down his chew-stick, having chewed it down to almost nothing.

Siegfried raised an eagle wing and studied his two-thousand-year-old pocket watch. As always, Jonas craned his jackal head over to get a good, long look at that watch's intricate face. Its dials all whirred, ticked, blinked, and flashed as usual with bright lights and sacred symbols, none of which Jonas understood no matter how long he stared.

"We must hurry, my boy. Only a few cosmic micro-cycles remain for you to save Kalkas. If you don't find Khapre-Tum soon, the city will be a fiery mess upon our return," Siegfried said as he shoved his two-thousand-year-old pocket watch back between his breast feathers.

Jonas agreed, being thoroughly uplifted in Siegfried's presence. So, Jonas followed as the eagle-being flew on up ahead. In this fashion they maneuvered the dead forest, soon arriving at a bubbling swamp. The swamp's boiling gases smelled so bad that Jonas plugged his nose to prevent himself from passing out as he leapt across the gulf on a path made of large stones.

Next, they arrived at a valley filled with ancient stone pillars once belonging to a temple that was now abandoned. They then came across a pit of what Siegfried said was quicksand, before they finally arrived at the foot of Skull Mountain.

Breathing in deeply, Jonas made up his mind and decided to gingerly test his arm and shoulder by grabbing some hand and footholds and starting to climb the hillside. It really did hurt to reach up and climb, but he knew he had no other choice. So he carefully scrambled up the mountain's flank while Siegfried flapped away and alighted on boulders while he waited for Jonas to catch up.

As they climbed Jonas passed small caves, nooks, and recesses, some of which contained frisky, winged snakes and large armor-covered rats with two heads. But none of these critters bothered him for he just glanced inside before continuing on, making sure not to linger at their front door for too long.

They both paused upon seeing a skeleton mountain lion prowling among the rocks up ahead. It stopped and studied him and Siegfried the eagle, before it decided not to try and eat them and just bounded back up the mountainside.

Jonas climbed on the best that he could despite the pain, until they finally reached a plateau with a statue of Khapre-Tum carved into the vertical rock off to their left. "It is a warning not to proceed," said Siegfried, studying it closely.

"How interesting…. I'll take your word for it, sir," said Jonas. He couldn't read any of the demon language printed on the statue's base. And at the sculpture's feet lay offerings of blood and bone. Upon seeing these Jonas sniffed them thoroughly, before turning away with disgust. But he turned away and approached

Siegfried, knowing that they had to continue. "But we're still going upward, right, sir?"

"Of course."

"Good. I'm ready then."

However, he soon found that the only available path was basically up a vertical rock cliff. In order to move on, Siegfried grasped Jonas by the arms with his large talons and ascended into the air.

They flew upward, past small trees, caves, and ledges, and Siegfried didn't stop until they reached a second plateau where they rested. They sat on rocks while Jonas mentally directed healing energy into his arm and shoulder. Both of these wounds closed up but nasty scars were left behind as a reminder.

When Jonas was finished, he found that Siegfried had transformed himself into a bleating, bouncing goat. But still, a spindly white beard was hanging from beneath his goat chin.

"Jonas, you must climb one of those towers," bleated Siegfried, pointing with one of his goat hooves. "You will get the clearest shot at Khapre-Tum from that tallest one, right there. But you must hurry. Our current micro-cycle only has twelve nano-cycles left."

Jonas glanced up at those mammoth stone towers and gulped hard. He'd been pleased with their progress up until then, but now looking at the castle's main tower, it appeared much taller than just a short time ago. "Ummm, what are the lengths of micro and nano-cycles, exactly?" he asked, trying not to think about climbing one of those towers by hand.

"Cosmic time cycles are extremely complicated. You probably wouldn't understand them."

"Alright, fair enough, sir," he said. He knew it would be pointless to ask any further questions so he began to scramble up the slope, being far more manageable than the vertical wall of rock.

Siegfried still outpaced him, though, always bleating happily along and urging him onward.

Finally, the slope leveled out again when they reached the castle's main outer wall. Jonas quietly crept along its massive stones and came to a large gate patrolled by three skeleton guards.

He snuck right up behind the first two and snapped their skulls right off their long boney necks. Then he decapitated a third with one quick swipe of his bronze sword.

Jonas watched its skull and helm bounce together crazily and all the way down the hill and then launch off the cliff. He imagined the skull landing next to some demonic creature and scaring the pants off of it as he grabbed the skeleton's keys from off its belt, unlocked the gate, and finally slipped through and into Skull Castle.

One Shot

SIEGFRIED TURNED INTO A BAT and followed Jonas by flying in through the creaky wooden door behind him. They crept through an empty portion of the square and quickly entered the nearest tower through a door at its base. To Jonas's eternal thanks they ascended a set of corkscrew stairs instead of climbing the tower's outer face like he'd anticipated doing.

They reached the top and opened a door which led out onto the tower's upper battlements. Jonas was grateful to find them empty. So he knelt and leaned against the stone wall while wiping the sweat from his jackal forehead. Siegfried fluttered his bat wings, and being small and light enough, he alighted on Jonas's good shoulder (his pointy white beard was still present even in bat form).

From behind the battlements Jonas peered down into the square far below. Demons marched about, looking like black bugs all in formation, and carrying deadly swords, spears, and axes. He scanned the additional towers in the castle complex. Menacing skeleton titans on lookout guarded all the rest. They bristled with heavy armor, their red auras glowing bright.

Dragons and floating phantoms clogged the dark and fiery sky just above them. Then Jonas finally glimpsed a grand, palatial stone building just across the square from his current tower. But even among all this, there was still no sign of Khapre-Tum. He dreaded having to search every building to find him and Talley. That would prove impossible.

Jonas soon grew antsy, so he manifested the Golden Bow and scanned the grounds more carefully. The bow glowed brightly and hummed vibrantly in his hand. After a while his jackal eyes finally fell on a tall window in the central stone building in the complex. He could just make out a giant white shape within. Tall and spindly, it paced back and forth and was covered with spiked black armor. It was Khapre-Tum. Clad in full armor and helm, the skeleton god was giving orders to the glowing holograms of the Hiixian bounty hunters, Necrat and Tarsus Riggs.

Flushed with excitement, Jonas raised the Golden Bow and carefully threaded an energy arrow. He then exhaled deeply and pulled the silver bowstring back to his jackal ear.

"Be careful, Jonas. You only get this one shot," Siegfried whispered from his shoulder.

So it all boiled down to this, he thought. Jonas exhaled and tried relaxing more, but his heart wouldn't stop pounding loudly in his pointed jackal ears. Jonas listened closely and his powerful hearing picked up everything they said.

"Nuke the royal place, Necrat," Khapre-Tum yelled. "Jonas will never return from the Underworld. Let Kalkas and the entire planet see the strength of my demon army."

"Affirmative, ion nuke torpedoes are set to launch," beeped Tarsus.

"Siegfried is nowhere to be found, sir," added Necrat. "The entire Kalkan army is shut inside the city. They're completely helpless, like monkeys in a cage."

"Yes, yes, Siegfried has abandoned the city and left it defenseless. I say that we finally burn that Navan-infested slum to the ground!" growled Khapre-Tum.

"Yes, sir!" said Necrat. "It's about danged time! Tarsus, let's go!" he said to his half robotic, half lizard-being partner. And they both marched right out of the chamber.

Jonas gasped and his jackal ears shot up straighter. He knew that those two would do it. He had to act fast, so he closed one eye and breathed deeply. The energy arrow was now glowing warm almost right against his hairy jackal cheek.

"Aim for the neck, that's his weakness," Siegfried whispered into his pointed jackal ear. "Fire, Jonas. Now!"

Jonas's ear twitched and he let the bowstring go. The arrow flew across the square like a blazing streak of light. He breathlessly watched as it sailed through the open window and headed straight for Khapre-Tum's exposed neck.

But at the last moment, Khapre-Tum turned. With a giant mailed fist he knocked the arrow right out of the air. Not finished, however, the arrow bravely regrouped. Jonas concentrated and mentally steered it while Khapre-Tum ducked and dodged to avoid its blazing point. But finally the skeleton god caught the arrow with both hands and snapped its bright shaft in two.

"No way! Come on!" Jonas yelled in frustration. He had no time to waste so he threaded a second arrow. But Khapre-Tum turned and spotted Jonas and Siegfried through the open window. He immediately vanished.

"He's gone…" said Jonas. He glanced up at Siegfried, who was flapping in the air just above him.

But Siegfried didn't answer.

A sudden movement off to Jonas's left gave him a surge of dread. He ducked instinctively, just as a flash of silver shone brightly above him. He rolled and came to a stop right as a giant axe cleaved off a section of the stone battlements. Something struck him in the back and Jonas went flying forward into the stone barrier. Now lying against the stone wall, he unraveled himself, shaken, his shoulder throbbing with pain. He managed to glance up at a horrible sight.

Khapre-Tum, all thirty cubits of him stood above Jonas, pulsating with a bright aura of terrible, crackling flames. The skeleton god roared and swung his axe again. Jonas dodged it, throwing himself against the tower's ledge. He looked down at a moat of lava flowing past the tower's base where a company of demons marched by far below.

Khapre-Tum continued to stomp about, slashing his giant axe, and easily breaking the stone tower apart as he did. Chunks of stone went flying everywhere, even in Jonas's face, blinding him as he ran, dodged, and jumped out of the path of Khapre-Tum's axe as it just grazed his bronze shield.

Khapre-Tum kicked out and struck him several times, while each of his stomping skeleton feet caused the entire structure to shake, sway, and threaten to topple right over.

Siegfried turned back into an eagle-being and began diving and thrashing wildly at Khapre-Tum's face with his very large and very sharp talons. This bought Jonas some time. So he manifested an energy arrow and raised the Golden Bow again. But just as he did, Khapre-Tum's axe swung down right on his jackal head.

He raised the Golden Bow above him just in time to block the axe's blow. But the force shook Jonas's arms so hard that the bow shot from his hands. Jonas's hopes dissolved as he wildly grasped outward and watched the bow slowly disappear into the river of lava below.

Jonas shook off his panic just in time to raise his bronze shield and block Khapre-Tum's eye-lasers that grazed its glowing surface. The beams were deflected and exploded against the stone tower, showering them with rock and dust as Jonas turned and covered his jackal face. He smelled jackal hair burning, but knew that he had to move quickly before Khapre-Tum shot his eye beams again.

He raised his shield and dashed between the skeleton god's long and boney legs. But Khapre-Tum swung around and his massive axe cleaved the top half of Jonas's shield right off, barely missing his arm in the process. Jonas looked down in disbelief. Only the lower half of his shield remained. The upper half was now completely gone.

A sudden and terrible shriek pierced the air and Jonas quickly turned. A group of skeleton soldiers came flooding out through the tower's door, shaking axes, swords, maces, and lances. Their desperate charge pushed Khapre-Tum back and out of range.

With his bronze sword, Jonas immediately sent four of skeletons flying from the tower. With his now half-shield, he blocked three lances and two maces, and then jumped aside before a giant hammer struck him right in the chest. He stumbled backward while he blocked five more furious attacks, one right after the other, and then separated three soldiers' skulls completely from their spines.

The skeletons were closing around him now. Faster sword thrusts sent three skeletons clattering to the floor, all three perfectly severed in half. But soon he was pinned against the stone battlements, the soldiers banging on his bronze shield, threatening to shove him over the ledge.

He grasped at the cold, stone abutments and dug his fingers in, holding on with one hand. He couldn't stop sweating and shaking, his fingers ached, and his hand felt like its tendons were tearing themselves in half. He was just about to let go when suddenly the skeletons all stopped pushing and shoving.

Instead, they all turned and lowered their weapons. Strange, thought Jonas, a few skeletons were even rattling in fear. But why? Jonas's pointed jackal ears pricked up with curiosity as he looked around and listened. Then suddenly all his jackal hair stood on end. A loud ringing noise finally reached his jackal ears, and it was growing louder by the second.

That was when he looked and caught Khapre-Tum staring right at him, with red eyes glowing bright and hot. Jonas finally realized what was happening and ran as fast as he could. He sprinted and leapt headfirst, sailing through the air right as Khapre-Tum released his eye-lasers again, blasting away nearly a quarter of the tower.

The tower now rocked back and forth, and the explosion of heat, force, and all that flying rock flung Jonas across the hard stone floor. When he stopped it felt like those fires had seared his arms and legs. His head throbbed with pain now and he heard skeleton soldiers running from the tower. Some were even flung off its ledge, towards the lava below.

Before Khapre-Tum could fire again, Siegfried dove and clawed violently at his giant skull. The skeleton god swatted back, forcing Siegfried to ascend out of reach. But Siegfried kept diving and swiping, again and again.

Jonas's head hurt so much that he could barely see let alone stand. But he forced himself up off the stone floor and stumbled about, finally leaning against the tower wall. He ached and had lost his sword and shield somewhere in the rubble. Incredibly weak, his vision kept fading in and out, although according to his quick assessment his hearing and acute sense of smell worked fine.

He had almost no strength left and was just regaining his vision again. He could see Siegfried still harassing Khapre-Tum, repeatedly diving and scratching his white skull.

It hurt Jonas to even move, but he knew that if he didn't act fast, those deadly eye-lasers would turn him into a Shastra shish kebab before too long.

So he dashed around Khapre-Tum's long legs and looked backward and up. Dark armor covered the skeleton god's back and sprouted huge spikes with a crackling field of energy lighting its black surface. Jonas had no other option, so he leapt up, grasped Khapre-Tum's glowing armor, and started to climb. His hands and feet grew hot but he just continued on, using spikes for hand and footholds.

He reached the top and grasped Khapre-Tum's massive collar. Trying to grab him and throw him off Khapre-Tum twisted violently about, but Jonas hung on. He quickly materialized an energy arrow in his free hand and with one motion he plunged the arrow's glowing tip right into the base of Khapre-Tum's neck.

A terrible scream pierced the air and Jonas struggled just to hang on. Khapre-Tum began to shake uncontrollably and when the arrow grew too hot to handle, Jonas let go. Then the whole thing suddenly exploded.

Blinding sparks shot in his jackal face and Jonas turned away. The explosion expanded, launching him off Khapre-Tum's back and out over the edge of the tower. He had to think fast as he plummeted towards the bubbling lava below, so he tried jamming his shield and then his knife into the tower. But nothing he tried could stop his fall.

He grew hotter as the lava drew closer. He covered his face and soon his arms were being burned by the fast increasing heat. He prayed for help as he plunged headfirst towards the bubbling pool. His arms and face, his whole body felt the searing heat now.

But then two hard objects clenched tightly around his arms and a refreshing jet of cool air fanned his jackal face. He was still too scared to look and see what was happening, knowing he would be swimming in lava any second now.

When he finally opened his eyes, for some strange reason the fiery river was receding away from him. He looked up to see Siegfried, in the form of a large eagle-being, lifting him through the air by his talons. Siegfried set him back atop the tower where Jonas fell to his knees, happy to be touching cold stone once again. He couldn't believe that he'd almost gone swimming in fire only a moment ago.

Standing now, he noticed that nearly half the tower had been blown away. "Where's Khapre-Tum?" Jonas asked. Was he dead? Had he flown away or maybe back into castle? He searched the smoky black sky and found nothing. Then he glanced down at the lava below, still nothing. However, he didn't trust that it was over.

Siegfried waddled over, ruffling his large wings and chest feathers. "Yes, Khapre-Tum is dead; banished to a dark place which none may reach," he said, reading Jonas's mind. "He will not return for a very long time. You and I will be long gone by then, my boy."

"Is that so?" asked Jonas. He was tired but also felt amazed to hear this. "So, it's over then....?" he asked. Waves of peace flowed over him upon realizing that his struggle was finished at last.

He felt a surge of pride and looked out over the rest of the towers and battlements of the complex. The hardest portion of his mission was now over. But there was still much work to be done. He had to find Talley and return to Kalkas, and then he could finally relax.

Siegfried spoke again. "All of Khapre-Tum's remains must be gathered and disposed of. Look around for his skull, my boy. That is the most important part. As much as we can find, we should bury."

"Why bury it?" Jonas asked. "You said he's dead, right?"

"Even though his spirit has fled them Khapre-Tum's bones still consist of pure, concentrated energy. Should any demons or dark gods recover those objects, they would reap powerful magic from the currents animating their boney fibers."

So, Jonas and Siegfried carefully searched through the piles of bricks, bones, shields, helmets, maces, lances, and axes spread out over the tower. Every last skeleton soldier had fled or been killed by Khapre-Tum's eye-lasers. As Jonas searched about, he was secretly glad that he couldn't find any bones big enough to belong to Khapre-Tum.

They'd searched through most of the rubble, finding nothing, when Siegfried finally yelled out. "Jonas, come here!"

Jonas sprinted over to where Siegfried stood, looking down at a monstrously large white skull lying on its side. Siegfried ruffled his feathers while he pecked at its eye sockets. It was Khapre-Tum's skull alright. The black helm with its curved horns was still attached. Jonas's hair pricked up and he shivered violently. He then shook with fear as he crept closer.

Siegfried transformed back into the tall and glowing form of the Guardian, Garud. His stern golden jackal face squinted down at his two-thousand-year-old pocket watch. "Ah, just enough time is left, my boy!" Then he shoved the watch into his golden tunic. "We must bring the head of Khapre-Tum back to Kalkas for proof. But be careful, you mustn't touch it."

"So then how do we transport it?"

"We will carry it in this magical sack."

Garud then manifested a glowing brown sack which he carefully kicked the skull into before cinching up. The sack was extremely heavy and it hummed with power as he handed it to Jonas, who struggled to hold it away from himself the best that he could. He keenly sensed the need to get rid of this cursed thing as soon as possible. But where should they bury it?

"Sir, we still have to rescue Talley. He's inside the castle, isn't he?" Jonas asked, straining to keep the magical sack from bumping him in the shins.

"Yes, we will find him within the castle's largest dungeon," said Garud. "Follow me, please."

So they descended the tower's twisting stairs until they reached the main square. Incredibly, not a single demon could be found as they easily entered the central structure. All skeletons and demons seemed to have fled the fortress altogether.

After a lengthy search they finally located Talley. The frail Shastra hung limply from the cold dungeon wall of a dark cell, chained up and clothed in rags. The cell was littered with dirt and straw, while a single refuse bucket, plus a bowl for food, rested in the corner. Giant rats scampered about, screeching, and the whole cell smelled terrible.

Jonas tried waking Talley, but he didn't answer or even move. His heart ached to see his agent friend like this. He raised Talley's head carefully and pried open a blank and sunken jackal eye. But his eyeball just stared back lifelessly. Talley's Shastra frame was thin to the point of starvation, but Jonas could still hear weak and shallow breathing.

Appalled, Jonas was speechless as he unchained Talley and lifted him onto his shoulder with ease. Talley had once been a much fuller and beefier Shastra than Jonas, but now he weighed next to nothing. He also smelled absolutely dreadful.

"You said there was a portal inside the castle, right?" Jonas asked as he repositioned Talley on his shoulder.

"With Khapre-Tum now gone, the Rulebook allows me to transport you back to Kalkas myself," Garud said, taking the sack holding Khapre-Tum's skull from Jonas.

"So, does that mean that—" said Jonas.

"Yes, let's blow this popsicle stand."

"Wait, what? Isn't that an old timey—"

But Garud quickly reached down and touched Jonas right over his third eye. There was a bright flash, and only an instant later, Jonas and Garud both stood beside the entrance of Kalkas. The city's massive iron gate had been flung aside and now lay in a twisted, mangled wreck.

"Look, Jonas," said Garud as he pointed out over the dusty Kalkan plain.

The entire demon army was assembled there, resembling a wall of dark fur and white bone, stretching from the frothy sea to a mountainous horizon. Then suddenly the demon and skeleton soldiers all yelled out as one voice and rattled their weapons, shaking the whole plain beneath them.

Jonas's heart skipped several beats. Would they all attack at once in an endless wave of swords, spears, and drooling fangs? Or would Garud maybe destroy them all with one single, powerful glance?

Thinking of what they should do, Jonas carefully set Talley in the dirt and manifested his Golden Bow. It felt good to cradle it in his arms again and its bowstring sang a twangy note when he plucked it. Meanwhile, Garud's third eye flashed bright with symbols, and immediately, twenty Navans rushed out from within Kalkas, picked Talley up, and then carried him back behind what was left of its once cyclopean walls. Jonas silently prayed that he could recover, and soon.

Jonas wasn't sure just what made him do it. He didn't think, he just acted, as reaching into the magical sack, he removed Khapre-Tum's skull by one of the curved horns on its helm (holding it so as not to touch any white bone), and then set it in the dirt, facing the demon army.

Wave upon wave of shock rippled through the demon and skeleton ranks. Then almost every demon, skeleton, lizard-being, bounty hunter, and hairy beast groaned in unison and dropped their shields, swords, spears, and laser rifles in the dirt. Some yelled in anguish while others wept.

Jonas's jackal ears listened, perking up when he heard a loud horn. It came from behind the Kalkan wall and immediately silenced the enemy's wailing. Then, one by one, and then in growing numbers, the exhausted, bandaged, and beaten soldiers of Kalkas slowly emerged from within the battered city. These soldiers all gasped in shock, jumped for joy, and shook their heads when they beheld both Jonas and Garud, shining golden and bright, and with Khapre-Tum's skull lying at their feet.

Garud spoke. "The war for Kalkas is over," he said. "The great enemy of the earth is dead. Its head here is proof of Jonas's victory! From now until the sun sets, the demon army will receive safe passage back to the Underworld. But in return, all Kalkan prisoners must be set free. This is the Law. I promise it be followed, as a Guardian of Earth-1."

Garud then lifted Khapre-Tum's gigantic skull from the dirt, better for the demon army to see it more clearly, especially those way in the back. After an animated discussion amongst themselves, all demons, skeletons, and every other evil being present, bowed their heads, and dragging their swords and spears through the dirt, retreated from the field.

As he watched the demons return to camp, Jonas felt that the battle for Kalkas, and his mission as a whole, could finally be considered done and over with. A sudden chill ran all up and down his spine. His pointed jackal ears perked up proudly and he stood taller, realizing that he'd achieved something great.

He could return to the Ashtar Command Center with the promise of receiving the rank of Intermediate Agent. Afterward, he might take a nice vacation before preparing for atomic chariot fighter weapons school. Then when Ashtar called on him again, when a new threat arose somewhere in the cosmos, he would take his next mission, going wherever the Command Center chose to send him.

Hearing loud voices, Jonas turned to see Bheem, Isas, Mamaji, and Pramohana all running towards him. They bounded over and crashed right into him, forming one yelling, shrieking, crying blob of excitement and joy. They refused his protests to not squeeze so tight, and he just bore it until they let him go. Finally they let go and then just gazed upon both him and Garud with their misty and quivering eyeballs all wide with happiness and wonder.

Bheem and Mamaji violently shook his hand in greeting, while Pramohana simply nodded respectfully. Isas kissed his jackal cheek while holding him tightly once again. He sniffed her scents of jasmine, bananas, and salty tears as he stroked her soft, black hair. They separated and he playfully licked the wet tears from her dark cheeks. She giggled and scratched him behind his pointed jackal ears, which he absolutely loved.

"Jonas, we thought you were dead..." she cried, wiping away the tears he hadn't licked yet.

"Aye, lad. Ya gave us more than a wee scare for a moment there," added Bheem, his jackal eyes shining with joy.

"I thought it was over more than a few times, myself," said Jonas, absolutely thrilled to see them all still alive. "I'll tell you the whole story about it later. Garud and I still have one task left."

Garud set Khapre-Tum's giant skull back in the dirt where it hummed and glowed, which Jonas compared to the ruins of Telos after being enveloped in green flame. His jackal instincts wanted to sniff and chew the jawbone and lick the empty eye sockets, just for a minute, just for a little taste. But wisely, he resisted, for Garud's warning not to touch it was fresh in his mind.

"Sir, I can tell that this is a major object of power," he said, pointing at the skull.

"Oh, my..." commented Isas. "Is that thing still alive? Why did you bring it back?"

"No, Khapre-Tum is officially dead, for now," Jonas said, looking up at Garud.

"Yes, but it is still very dangerous. That is why we must dispose of it," said Garud.

"But where? And how, sir?" asked Jonas.

"Pramohana, come here for a moment, please," said Garud.

The giant Danaan eagle waddled forward through the crowd now surrounding them. Jonas was saddened to see how her proud breast, once covered in beautiful rows of blue and green feathers, was now all wrapped in bandages. She stopped before Garud and bowed low, although in obvious pain.

"Yes, sir, Pramohana is here. How might she serve the Guardians?" she asked.

"Please, Pramohana, take this special sack and drop it in the deepest, coldest, and highest glacier on the tallest mountain you can find. Through the churning of land and ice, the passing ages will slowly grind the skull into a faint memory."

"Pramohana will gladly perform this task," she said. "Serving Garud is the highest honor."

Replacing the skull inside the magical sack, Garud cinched it tight and then handed it to Pramohana. With the bag tightly grasped in her large talons, and clearly in pain, Pramohana flapped her large wings and soon had lifted herself into the sky. They watched her soar over the plain, heading towards a range of mountains in the distance that were all clad in a thick veil of mist.

She finally disappeared over the horizon. Jonas imagined her reaching a jagged, ice-clad mountain peak, and swooping low and dropping the sack into a deep crevasse to be lost forever.

When the demon army had all returned to the Underworld through the portal and every prisoner from the demon camp had been freed, Siegfried and Mamaji, along with a group of Navan engineers, closely surveyed the city's walls and gates, making detailed notes of what needed to be repaired and how it should be done. But only a few hours later, the fun-loving sentiments of the Navan culture had prevailed. That meant the three days that followed contained the most righteous party ever recorded.

Jonas tried taking in the entire spectacle, but it was just too crazy, going on all day and all night, and in the end he was just too overwhelmed to continue. The party was just that huge. After a full day he had to bow out for some much needed rest.

According to the final reported tally, the party's aftermath included; no one sleeping at all (except for Jonas), emptying whole cellars of whale jerky and banana mead, and consuming the city's entire supply of barbequed beetles on just the first day.

As Jonas had anticipated, every town and village within twenty leagues filed noise complaints with their local shaman, who then visited Kalkas to officially inform Siegfried and king Masha, and which they all graciously addressed in turn.

After the festivities had fully wound to a close, the Navan Guardian, Mobius, appeared and helped them rebuild the Kalkan wall. With the king's blessing, Mobius, along with Garud's help, mentally levitated freshly-cut stones into place, one massive block at a time. A large crowd gathered around them, eager to watch this engineering spectacle unfold.

When the towers, the main gate, and the worst damaged sections of wall were satisfactorily repaired, Siegfried next gathered Jonas, Isas, Bheem, Pramohana, and Argos all together in one of the largest conference rooms in the palace.

Siegfried excitedly explained to them how just the night before, while out on a nighttime stroll along the seashore, he'd encountered Necrat and Tarsus Riggs busily fitting an earth-digger machine with invisibility in an attempt to tunnel back into Kalkas and kidnap Jonas. Siegfried had easily destroyed their digging machine, but the bounty hunters escaped, and Siegfried believed them to already have returned to Hiix.

But that wasn't all, as Siegfried revealed that Minerva had been hacked by The Brain, the massive bio-computer within the Machine City of Hiix. This is what caused the critical malfunction, leading to the failure of her circuits controlling the Kalkan energy shield.

By then Kalkan life had returned to normal, with both Minerva and the energy shield running like new again. Jonas spent most of these days relaxing in Kassam's vacation tent, busy constructing his final mission report for Ashtar. He anticipated that after this report Ashtar would offer him a portal time to return to the Command Center for a full debriefing session. He hoped this would be followed by a super big and extremely fancy awards ceremony.

Finished with his report, filled with pride and excitement, and eager to speak to Ashtar, Jonas set his comm. link on a table and dialed the Command Center. His anticipation had been building for days now and he couldn't wait to see Ashtar and the Command Center again. He'd felt like he'd been away on Earth-1 for far too long. Plus, he could really use a vacation to some exotic and distant world.

But then he was assailed by sharp pangs of separation when he thought of leaving Isas, Bheem, Khafre, and Siegfried. He was clearly visualizing their looming faces just as the hologram of Ashtar's blue human face popped into view.

"Greetings, sir!" he said, saluting stiffly.

"Hello, my boy! I've already heard the wonderful news of your great victory! Minerva told Hermes, who then alerted the entire Command Center. You're quite a celebrity back here, son. I'm very proud of you," said Ashtar.

"Thank you, sir!" he said.

Ashtar was sitting in his office chair, beaming back at Jonas. "What a wonderful achievement! It's beyond any expectation I've ever had for a Junior Agent, I must tell you. This one should go in a playbook some day. It might even form a course for Intergalactic special agents. I must admit that this turned into a much tougher match than I had anticipated. I regret not fully preparing you for it. That one's on me, son."

"Yes, sir! I understand, sir," he said, saluting again. He couldn't help smiling as wide as was possible for his jackal face, knowing that it actually was Garud who had inspired Ashtar to send him to Earth-1 instead of an experienced senior agent. "Siegfried helped and guided me the whole time, sir. He even led me through the Underworld, to Skull Castle where I faced Khapre-Tum, and then transported me back to Kalkas. He's actually Garud, the Guardian, in disguise, you see. Did you know that, sir?"

"Ah, yes, yes. I did know that. He has appeared to me as Garud many times now," said Ashtar. "That old rascal has a book of trick plays over three fields long. He still has a few game-changers on his clipboard that he won't reveal even to me. But please, Jonas, I want to hear a complete retelling of your victory. Tell me everything that happened in the Underworld, son," he said.

Jonas told Ashtar everything; about the energy shield's malfunction, about his capture and the chair and the torture droids, of being freed by Bheem and the Lone Ranger, finding Khapre-Tum alone in his tent and then winding up in the Underworld, alone and powerless, before Siegfried unexpectedly showed up to guide him to Skull Castle. As he described his fight with Khapre-Tum and plunging towards the river of lava, Ashtar yelped and nearly fell out of his hovering office chair.

"Amazing! I'm so happy for you, son, and for Earth-1," Ashtar said after he'd pulled himself back up. "You are well on your way to becoming a Senior Agent. And that Khapre-Tum! He is a true war daddy, that one. Just incredible work, son! Incredible!"

"Thank you, sir! Also, sir, our scout teams have rounded up many groups of demons that were attacking or had already occupied cities like Heliopolis and others in nearby kingdoms. Most of them have been captured and returned to the Underworld. Some were put on secluded islands where they've promised to remain and behave properly. Siegfried says they can stay there if they keep to their promise. And, lastly, Pramohana's spies report that both bounty hunters are holing up in the Machine City of Hiix and are too afraid to leave."

"Wonderful! Jonas, I'll make sure that you receive a long vacation as soon as you return to the Command Center."

"Thank you, sir." He let out a big sigh of relief, for that was exactly what he wanted. He'd never felt so happy to speak to Ashtar, and now he couldn't wait to return and pack his things. There was a whole catalog of beach and recreational planets available for him to visit.

"You'll be given Intermediate Agent status as soon as possible, and start chariot fighter weapons school soon after that. I promise you, son," Ashtar said proudly.

Jonas couldn't stop smiling even if he tried.

"When will that be, sir?" he asked, eager to see Zarry, Digger, and his other agent friends, as well as his training partners, once again. Of course, he'd definitely miss Siegfried, Bheem, Pramohana, Tanis, Khafre, and especially Isas. But he could always plan a holiday to Earth-1 to see them anytime.

"Ah, well, there's the rub, son. If I had my wish, you would return to the Command Center today. However, I'm afraid your mission is not considered over just yet."

"What do you mean, sir?" he asked. "Khapre-Tum is dead and Talley is back safe on the Command Center."

"I know, I know, son...but I need you to stay on Earth-1 and serve as the king of Heliopolis for a few more periods. That planet is fast becoming a prime outpost for our Command Center as well as the Galactic Federation. And we need you to act as an ambassador to strengthen our presence there. And truthfully, son, your experience makes you the most qualified agent for the job."

Shocked, Jonas struggled for words, not knowing what to say. He paused for a moment and contemplated this strange news. "Well, sir.... I was really looking forward to returning. But, if the Command Center requires it, then of course I'll do whatever is needed," he said. He saluted again, but this time much more seriously. The thought nagged him that it might actually be a long time before he could return.

"Good, good. That's the right mindset, son. You've made me very proud. You gave it one hundred and ten percent one day at a time. When this mission is finally done, you will return, I promise."

"Thank you, sir," he said as he saluted. "But, sir, how much longer should I remain on Earth-1?"

"We don't know that quite yet, son. There's still some analysis we need to do on our end. It won't be for too much longer, though. I promise you that."

"Yes, sir." Jonas wondered just how much time celestials like Ashtar considered to be 'long periods of time.' "Do you have anything else for me, sir?"

"Nope, that's it for now. But please keep me updated on anything that happens down there. We will make sure to send you updates of any moves we need to make on our end," said Ashtar. "And don't worry about the job of serving as king of Heliopolis. Siegfried will fill you in on everything. I've already talked with him at length about it and he's promised to look out for you."

"Thank you, sir."

"Well, that's everything then. Over and out, you powder monkey," said Ashtar, quoting ancient pirate.

"Over and out, you buccaneer, sir!" said Jonas. He saluted back just as Ashtar's hologram vanished.

Well, it was settled then. He would remain and act as the king of Heliopolis. He hoped that it wasn't for too long, though. He was disappointed but also excited, ready to sink his jackal teeth into whatever new challenge he faced. Plus, it meant more time spent with everyone, especially Isas.

Afterward, while soaking in a plasma-spin-whirly tank and sipping mango beer, he tried imagining what it would be like being a king. It really wasn't something that he'd ever considered. How could he possibly do it justice? For one, he knew absolutely nothing about it. There were no kings on Monubia, only warlords, saints, and prophets that led their different Shastra tribe.

If his memory proved to be correct, the Intergalactic Agent manual did contain one small section regarding pretending to be a king, but that was for emergencies only. Or was it a high priest? He couldn't remember, only that it was meant to only be for a very short period of time. He decided to review that section later on for any tips and pointers.

Pramohana, Siegfried, Bheem, Isas, and a now fully-recovered Khafre all jumped for joy upon hearing the news that he was now staying on Earth-1. They all hugged him tightly and then badgered him with questions. When asked how he felt about it, Jonas admitted that the prospect still contained too many unknowns to judge, but it did have obvious pros and cons. However, he didn't reveal that he actually feared being stuck in endless meetings, listening to agonizingly long interpretations of boring rules and regulations that he didn't care about, or having to solve problems which he considered to not be within the scope of an agent's responsibilities. He secretly hoped being a king meant more than that.

But then again, anything was possible. Earth-1 was a wild and crazy outpost, and pretty far from the galactic center. What if an erratic Mega Honey badger migration leveled Heliopolis to the ground or the demon army invaded again? He dreaded such future possibilities, but then used solid reasoning to calm himself down. Chewing on his rubber squeaky toy also helped.

In only two weeks Tanis recovered to the point of being healthy enough to leave the healing chamber under his own power and walk around a bit. Although he walked gingerly, the moment he saw Jonas and the others he beat his chest and pledged retaliation against Khapre-Tum.

Tanis refused to believe that Jonas had defeated Khapre-Tum, and even after engaging Siegfried in two full hours of argument, detailed recounting, respectful rebuttals, and then additional counter rebuttals. Unfortunately, their only true physical evidence, that being Khapre-Tum's skull and helmet, were now long gone, dropped into a deep crevasse by Pramohana.

Siegfried made Tanis swear to never go searching for Khapre-Tum, which thankfully Tanis agreed to. However, in typical Tanis fashion, he promised that he would wait until word of Khapre-Tum's reappearance, at which point he would then hunt down the skeleton god and kill him. Satisfied with this agreement, Siegfried immediately dismissed Tanis before calmly assuring everyone that such a scenario was impossible.

Now fully healed, Tanis began his archery training again in earnest. By the time the next major archery tournament rolled around, Tanis had left Kalkas, at which point Siegfried decided to fly Bheem, Khafre, Pramohana, Argos, Isas, and Jonas on his energy chariot to Heliopolis.

Upon reaching Heliopolis, all of them were shocked by the city's sad and dilapidated appearance. The golden streets had almost all been dug up, many of its towers and statues of the Guardians had fallen over, and its once bustling intergalactic space port was shut down completely. All its many registered star chariots had either been stripped for parts or gone missing.

Amidst the sad ruins of the Heliopolan royal palace, Jonas was crowned king by Siegfried, before moving in and while the structure was still undergoing extensive repairs. These repairs included several collapsed walls and caved-in sections of roof, replacing priceless stolen vases and free-energy glow-globes that lit the rooms and hallways, and most importantly, cleaning up countless piles of shed demon hair found throughout the entire complex.

The rebuilding of Heliopolis took almost a full year to finally finish. Thankfully, they accomplished it just in time to host the next Garud Harvest Festival. During that year Siegfried taught Jonas about Heliopolan royal protocol (thankfully, it required less meetings and hearings than he'd anticipated). Tanis also managed to pop in a few times and talk about the archery circuit. He revealed to them that he hadn't yet uncovered news of Khapre-Tum's return, to which everyone just politely smiled and nodded.

Jonas and Isas's friendship grew much deeper while they all busily worked together to manage and run the kingdom as a team. However, with all the duties required of him as king, Jonas had zero time to even think of traveling to Mt. Nabi for an Athenian marriage form, and didn't manage to mention it to Isas again, although, it was always on his jackal mind.

Their time in Heliopolis went by peacefully and without major incident. Then on one fateful Moonsday, exactly one year since Jonas, Bheem, and Khafre had left Heliopolis to search for Siegfried, the start to the first Garud Harvest Festival following Jonas's victory arrived at last. Pilgrims traveled from all over the kingdom in anticipation of meeting Jonas and Siegfried, who were now both famous household names.

Pilgrim chariots formed a long caravan leading into Heliopolis, running beside the ancient ruins of a city named Nataal. But strangely, almost immediately after the last chariot passed these ruins, a lonely, unassuming bush beside an oasis moved slightly and quite unnaturally. Unnatural, because presently there were no animals living there. It happened once again, and then slowly its branches parted.

Two cloaked hermits, both carrying wooden canes, poked their heads out from behind the bush and peered anxiously around. The coast was clear so they emerged from the bushes and removed their patched garments, dropping these into the sand along with their canes.

"It's clear," said the first hermit as he scratched behind his scruffy wolfman ear. "Those fools are finally done traveling for the day. I can't believe how many are showing up to Heliopolis for this dumb festival thing."

He spoke again into a comm. link device, giving out their coordinates. And within bleebs, the desert sands were blasted everywhere as two space chariots zipped over the land and then stopped, hovering silently overhead.

Now these two star ships weren't the type one usually saw near Nataal. No, these were rare and very much feared. For each one was plastered with a very specific set of markings.

And if Jonas, Isas, or Siegfried had been present, these markings would be instantly recognizable and cause them all intense anxiety. For in fact each star ship belonged to the most infamous bounty hunters on all of Earth-1, throughout the solar system even. For those two weren't really traveling hermits. They were none other than Necrat and Tarsus Riggs.

Necrat boarded his sleek space jet, put on his pilot helmet, and fastened himself into the cockpit while the ship's computer loudly beeped and hummed. Tarsus boarded his cross-shaped space chariot and checked its gaping gun ports, where in turn there loomed an evil looking serpent-being or a growling demon bandit, always ready to fire at anything.

Chapter Sixteen

Then, wasting no time, and with both ships equipped to the teeth, they lifted off the sand and shot three thousand cubits straight in the air in under a second.

Necrat laughed to himself, reveling in what he considered their assured victory. He wouldn't fail this time, no way. "Tarsus, the Master's plan is foolproof, perfect. Jonas and Siegfried don't suspect a thing," he growled as he punched his ship's controls. He then lit a long cigar, clenching the end in his sharp wolfman fangs. "That mendicant, Siegfried, won't escape us again. He won't have that brat, Jonas, around to bail him out. The Draco King will help us make sure of that."

"Affirmative. Deducing factors and calculating possible outcomes..." Tarsus beeped through his black helmet. "The Master: a Draco serpent, highly intelligent and deadly. Calculating odds of success to be one hundred percent." Tarsus's life-support hummed and chirped as he spoke through his comm. link from within his star ship. "The plan is guaranteed to work."

"Of course it's guaranteed," Necrat snorted, puffing his cigar into his comm. link. "It was my idea...and I'm the most brilliant bounty hunter in all of Hiix. Now, let's get the heck out of here and let the Master know what we've seen. This desert is just sweltering...."

Necrat checked his ship's thermometer. It said that the temperature outside was over one hundred and twenty degreedoes. "Danged air-conditioning..." he cursed, panting and sweating profusely as he banged on the vents and twisted its dials, but with no result.

"Affirmative, Necrat. Setting return course for the Master's hideout, Earth's first moon," Tarsus beeped. "Cloaking devices, engaged. ETA is under ten micro-cycles."

One Shot

Necrat took a large puff of his cigar and punched his space jet's controls. And now with both ships cloaked and invisible, they ignited their plasma drives, locked onto the moon's coordinates, and shot off towards the border of space and sky.

About the Author

 Jacob graduated from the University of Washington and lives in Seattle. Check out his website, jakehansennovels.com, where you can read about his upcoming novels, his thoughts on writing, and his varied blog posts and musings on different books and movies.

CPSIA information can be obtained
at www.ICGtesting.com
Printed in the USA
BVHW042149270521
608360BV00018B/216